Juliette Hyland began crafting heroes and heroines in high school. She lives in Ohio, USA, with her Prince Charming, who has patiently listened to many rants regarding characters failing to follow their outline. When not working on fun and flirty happily-ever-afters, Juliette can be found spending time with her beautiful daughters and giant dogs, or sewing uneven stitches with her sewing machine.

Born and raised just outside Toronto, Ontario, **Amy Ruttan** fled the big city to settle down with the country boy of her dreams. After the birth of her second child Amy was lucky enough to realise her lifelong dream of becoming a romance author. When she's not furiously typing away at her computer, she's mum to three wonder[illegible]n, who use her as a person[illegible]

Also by Juliette Hyland

Mills & Boon Medical

Fake Dating the Vet

Alaska Emergency Docs miniseries

One-Night Baby with Her Best Friend

Mills & Boon True Love

Falling for His Fake Date

If the Fairy Tale Fits… miniseries

Beauty and the Brooding CEO

Also by Amy Ruttan

Nurse's Pregnancy Surprise
Reunited with Her Off-Limits Surgeon
Tempted by the Single Dad Next Door
Rebel Doctor's Boston Reunion

Discover more at millsandboon.co.uk.

ER DOC'S SOUTH POLE REUNION

JULIETTE HYLAND

THEIR ACCIDENTAL VEGAS VOWS

AMY RUTTAN

MILLS & BOON

First published in Great Britain 2025
by Mills & Boon, an imprint of HarperCollins*Publishers* Ltd,
1 London Bridge Street, London, SE1 9GF

www.harpercollins.co.uk

HarperCollins*Publishers* Macken House, 39/40 Mayor Street Upper,
Dublin 1, D01 C9W8, Ireland

ISBN: 978-0-263-32510-2

06/25

FSC
www.fsc.org
MIX
Paper | Supporting responsible forestry
FSC™ C007454

This book contains FSC™ certified paper
and other controlled sources to ensure responsible forest management.

For more information visit www.harpercollins.co.uk/green.

Printed and Bound in the UK using 100% Renewable Electricity
at CPI Group (UK) Ltd, Croydon, CR0 4YY

ER DOC'S SOUTH POLE REUNION

JULIETTE HYLAND

MILLS & BOON

For reformed perfectionists
and those still finding their way.

You are enough, just the way you are.

PROLOGUE

THE SHIP WASN'T going to sink. It wasn't going to sink. It wasn't.

The mental ramblings sloshed against Dr. Sam Miller's brain as he made his way toward the onboard clinic. The Drake Passage was a notoriously difficult stretch of sea. He'd known that when he'd signed up to work at the McMurdo Station at the South Pole.

Hell, his mother had sent him every social media video she could find about the trip. Her algorithm must have been hyperfocused on the Drake Passage, given the volume of related content that had landed in his text messages.

It had been sweet, and he'd reassured her each time that he knew what he was doing. He'd worked in remote locations for the last five years as a traveling doctor assigned to emergency clinics in the wilderness. He *hadn't* told her about the time he'd been on a prop plane headed to a remote Alaskan village, and he'd been certain he was going to die in a fiery crash.

That hadn't happened.

And this ship wasn't sinking, either.

Didn't mean his brain wasn't pushing doubts through his nervous system. But he'd ignored the heightened awareness for years. His parents claimed he was an adrenaline junkie, constantly seeking out locations with at least some sense of danger. He disagreed, but he knew one of the most important jobs a parent had was to keep their child safe.

So he'd answered every worried text. And had no intention of letting his mother know exactly how unsteady the trip through the passage really was.

"Doctor Miller, so glad to see you." Dr. Nicole Sapson gripped the edge of the table like a pro as the ship rolled again.

Sam didn't have the same dexterity and, before he knew what was happening, he was pressed up against the wall.

"Still getting your sea legs, I see." She let out a low chuckle.

"How does anyone get used to this?" He braced himself against the wall and took a deep breath.

"It's the Drake Passage." She rolled her head from one side to the other. Apparently, no other answer was needed. "I've seen most of the ship's residents today. All needing medication for sea sickness. I appreciate you stepping in for me while my nurse practitioner is under the weather."

"Of course." After working in remote locations, Sam understood the need for relief. He'd worked in two locations where he was the only physician for a hundred miles. He'd delivered babies, provided trauma care and stitched up little ones from falls. All while chronically exhausted. So he was more than willing to provide support when others needed it.

"Like I said, I've seen most everyone headed for McMurdo, it seems like. Ordered them to stay in their rooms while we finish riding out the rolling. They will be most comfortable there." As soon as the words were out of her mouth, the ship rolled again.

Luckily, this time Sam was more prepared. Barely.

"If you need me—" Dr Sapson started. Her worried gaze was focused on his less than steady legs.

"I will be fine, Doctor Sapson. Get rest—now. I won't be on the boat headed back."

"But the doctors you are replacing at McMurdo will be." She winked as she headed for the door.

"Touché."

Sam looked around the little clinic. He'd helped out once before and knew his way about, but the ship hadn't been tilting in all directions then. So he headed to the small closet where the meds and supplies were located. Always a good idea to start by making sure he was well acquainted with what he had to work with.

"Anyone here? Please?"

The low call sent a buzz through Sam's already overloaded nervous system.

It wasn't Forrest Wilson on the other side of the supply door. Couldn't be.

His former best friend, turned lover, had ended things years ago, just as Sam had been headed for residency in emergency medicine in New York. Ended things and taken a residency in internal medicine in Seattle, as far across the country as he could get.

I love you, but you deserve more.

The words were seared into Sam's heart. Nothing he had said in response had mattered. The man had disappeared from his life after years of being Sam's anchor. Left him reeling.

Forrest was not here now. He wasn't.

"Anyone? I have a migraine." There was a long sigh at the end of the word of *migraine.*

Forrest had suffered from migraines. Just a coincidence. Sam grabbed the medication he needed, no matter who was on the other side of the door, and headed out into the clinic to meet his patient.

"Sam?" Forrest pinched his eyes closed and reopened them.

"Not a migraine hallucination, Forrest." Sam forced the words out despite his tongue's near refusal to move. Forrest was here. On the ship to McMurdo. Outside of the crew, everyone would be getting off and heading to the station for the winter.

For eight months.

The man looked good. Even breathing through his teeth and holding his hand over his eyes to cap the light. His dark hair was mussed. The three-day-old growth on his chin showed how bad he felt.

Forrest always kept his face free of hair. Something his grandmother had drilled into him as a young man.

There was a woman Sam had not mourned. He'd attended the ceremony to support Forrest only. She'd made the man he loved feel worthless no matter what he achieved. If there was an afterlife, Sam hoped she was answering for every bitter tirade she'd leveled at Forrest.

Sam moved and dimmed the lights. "Better? Or do you need them all the way off?"

"Better." Forrest rubbed his chin and Sam turned them all the way off.

"You still rub your chin when you're lying."

They'd roomed together in college, a random piece of luck of the draw that had worked out better than either could have expected. Been best friends until med school when one night, a silly game of spin the bottle with their group of overtired friends had finally lit the fuse of something Sam had wanted for so long.

Their love had burned bright and Sam had started to think about weddings and forever. Until Forrest had just walked away, two days before Sam had planned to ask him to marry him.

For nearly their entire twenties he'd lived with this man, loved him. And apparently, he still knew his tells.

"I didn't know you were working as a ship's doctor. I thought emergency medicine was the aim." Forrest took the small plastic cup of migraine pills Sam passed him.

Did he make sure our fingers didn't touch? And why am I noticing?

Sam bit the inside of his cheek hoping that would stop the racing thoughts.

"I'm not. I'm just helping Dr. Sapson while her NP is under the weather. She needed a break and I figured since I am not seasick…" He shrugged as the ramblings echoed in the quiet.

"I'm headed to McMurdo. I'm the primary facility doctor for the winter rotation."

Forrest blinked and looked like he was at a loss for words. Sam didn't blame him for needing a minute to adjust to the idea of eight months being co-located with Sam, not to cope with the migraine ripping through his head.

Then he nodded and crossed his arms. "I work for a research company—I'm working on a project studying human immune responses in isolated conditions. I'll be in the McMurdo lab every day trying to see…well, lots of things. Probably won't be out of the lab much."

"Lab?" That didn't make sense. Forrest hadn't been headed for research. Sure, he hadn't liked the fast pace of the ER or surgery, but that hadn't been an issue because he had planned, had *wanted* to branch into internal medicine. The pace was slower there, mostly because they were constantly waiting on lab results.

"Yeah. It's a government research grant. Immune response in isolated conditions." He pinched his eyes closed. "I already said that. Migraine makes it hard to think. I'm the internal medicine doc guiding the study. So I will be in the lab constantly."

Don't expect to see me.

Message received loud and clear.

He'd known doctors that took a year's sabbatical to get away from patients. Sam couldn't imagine that of Forrest, but if he had needed a break, then retreating to the lab made sense for an internal medicine specialist.

Not that Sam planned to ask.

The ship rolled and Sam caught the back of the counter just like Nicole. Forrest didn't have the same luck.

He knocked into Sam, his scent racing through Sam's body. One arm wrapped around Forrest's waist, catching at least some of the blow against Forrest's hips.

"Oof." Forrest moved as soon as the ship was steady. "Thanks for the catch. I should get going. Um." He looked around and was out the door before any other words could be said.

Eight months. They had eight months in one of the most desolate places on earth.

And he told me not to expect to see him.

Maybe that was for the best. Forrest had closed that door almost eight years ago. No sense reopening a scar Sam had worked so hard to heal.

CHAPTER ONE

THE LAST FLIGHT into McMurdo for the winter season had nearly finished unloading the final supplies it was dropping off. And when it left, so did every excuse Dr. Forrest Wilson had for avoiding Sam. The first three weeks he'd managed. Barely.

The urge to stop by the clinic, to knock on his quarters, had pushed against his chest from the moment he'd seen Sam on the ship. Sam Wilson.

Best friend. Boyfriend. The one he'd let go.

There were many tags Forrest could assign to the man. Sam wasn't supposed to be here. The man wanted marriage, a settled life. Not months in the wilderness.

Why is he here?

That was something he was probably going to find out now that Dr. Anderson, the other physician assigned to the McMurdo clinic, was headed back to the States for cancer treatment. He'd be on that final flight when it left. Forrest wasn't sure what the first indicators were, but a routine blood test a week ago had uncovered the markers for blood cancer.

One that must be fast-moving since everyone on station had been required to have a full medical workup before arriving. If the markers had been there when those tests were done, no one would have cleared Dr. Anderson for eight months at McMurdo.

There wasn't time to get another doctor here. When the flight left today, Forrest would become Sam's official backup. But there were two nurse practitioners working in the clinic full-time—so his and Sam's interactions would be limited.

Sure. Lying to myself is always a good idea.

Forrest closed his eyes in what he knew would be a failed attempt to ignore his inner voice. His grandmother had complained constantly that he was too lost in his head. That he was lazy, no matter how many chores he completed. He was never enough for her, no matter how much he seemed to work.

"Why don't you stop by the clinic today? I can walk you through what's there." Sam's voice was barely audible above the wind on the loading dock. He was standing less than a foot from him. Closer than he'd been in years.

If I don't count the ship's clinic.

Forrest had made sure he hadn't touched Sam when he'd passed him the pills for his migraine. He'd monitored his fingers to ensure no accidental brush.

Getting over Sam had been the hardest thing he had ever done.

He'd wanted the best for Sam. And the best wasn't Forrest. He'd grown up knowing that. And residency had reinforced it. Sam was nearly perfect and Forrest… Forrest was very much not. He wasn't strong enough to walk back through that door.

"Do you think you will need me often? I have my research." Research that was not all-consuming. Yes, there were labs to run. But tests took time to complete their cycles. Only then could he analyze the results.

He'd hidden in the lab so much that the other partner on the study, Dr. Charlee Lons, constantly gave him a hard time.

She insisted they were allowed free time. That it was even encouraged, as studies showed the human brain operated better when it had regular creative breaks.

There is a reason we call it STEAM now, instead of just STEM. You need the arts.

The proof that Charlee truly lived by her favorite line hung in frames near the door of the lab—beautiful watercolors she'd done herself. She'd already done four in the time they'd been there, one a week.

Everyone was encouraged to bring something fun to the station. Something to occupy the time. Forrest had brought a guitar and picked out a song or two when he was in his room. But he'd learned to play with Sam. *That* guitar was at home. A prize he'd never risk. And every time he picked up the substitute instrument he'd brought, happy memories rotated through his mind. It only made the urge to seek out Sam grow, so he'd put the guitar away.

He pushed himself in the gym, but his mind still found it far too easy to walk the paths back to Sam.

Why is he here?

Sam was meant to be in New York. Meant to be happy and settled—with the perfect partner he'd always wanted. The life he'd had all planned out. He'd always wanted the perfect life his parents had. Soulmates, Sam called them.

Forrest no longer believed he'd never marry anyone. Or rather, after therapy, he wasn't afraid of the idea of commitment anymore. But he also wasn't looking for a soulmate. He had no reason to believe they existed, at least not for him. His own family was far from perfect, and they'd reminded him every chance they got that he was a mistake.

He was barely looking for a partner. He'd been on three dates in the last five years. All of them busts. Now he huddled in the lab: at least specimen slides never judged you.

"Earth to Forrest." Sam's fingers snapped in his line of sight. "Did you hear any of that?"

"No." Forrest shook his head, like that could force the attention he sometimes had trouble finding to the forefront. "Sorry, Sam. I wasn't expecting this and I haven't worked with patients in years outside of a lab setting."

On paper he was an internist, a doctor of internal medicine, but he was also an immunologist who kept to the labs these days. Patients in studies were screened. In fact, most of the time, Forrest only had to work with blind data.

No telling anyone bad news. No bacterial infection overwhelming antibiotics. No family to deliver the ultimate devastation to, then returning to the grind like nothing had happened.

"The good news is I work with patients every day. And this is my fifth remote location in five years. In fact, at the last place I was the only attending. I pretty much slept at that hospital." Sam rolled his head, loosening his shoulder muscles.

He's tired.

Time and distance hadn't stopped Sam from knowing when Forrest was lying back in the ship's clinic. And it wasn't stopping Forrest from seeing the exhaustion coating Sam. The man was a perfectionist. And he nearly always achieved his goals. That didn't mean he could do everything himself. Sam needed help.

And now Forrest was looking for ways to dodge the extra assignment.

This was why he'd let Sam go. Why he'd made sure Sam knew he was too good for Forrest. That he deserved more.

"I assumed you'd be working in New York City. Working your way up to head of the emergency department in record time. That was your goal. The ten-year plan you talked about before heading off to residency. Why are you moving so much?"

The question struck a sore spot.

Someone who hadn't lived with Sam for most of his twenties might miss the subtle shift of his gray-blue eyes. Forrest wasn't sure why, but the question had hurt.

"Forget I asked." Forrest started to reach out, but Sam stepped back. Forrest swallowed the pain as he tried to cover the embarrassment by crossing his arms.

"Life's paths are weird." Sam shrugged as the plane carrying Dr. Anderson took off. "I wouldn't have expected to find you in the South Pole, either."

"No. I was more a North Pole guy." The joke flew from Forrest's mouth. Sam had affectionately complained every November that Christmas decor wasn't supposed to go up until after Thanksgiving.

It was the fight they had most often and, given that Sam helped him decorate for six Novembers in a row, one could hardly call it a fight. Forrest still had each of the clay Christmas ornaments they'd bought at the mall stall when they were together. Little men in snow hats with their names underneath. Snowmen holding hands. A new clay scene each year.

His grandmother had hated anything to do with the season. Hated those stalls with the cheesy ornaments. Forrest didn't put them on his tree anymore, but they were lovingly wrapped in bubble wrap at the bottom of his ornament bin. Precious, hidden cargo.

"I am pretty sure Santa isn't there. And definitely sure that he'd agree Christmas decor shouldn't be up until December first." Sam cleared his throat as he looked around the loading bay.

The now largely empty loading bay.

This was the way they'd been for so long. Easy conversations. Jokes. Serious talks that lasted for hours without either noticing the passage of time. It had been easy then to believe Forrest could fit in Sam's life. But unlike Sam, for him something had always felt off in med school. He had been good at it, but the passion Sam had clearly felt had just never materialized.

He was a puzzle piece that didn't fit in Sam's perfect picture no matter how hard he tried to jam himself into position.

That had been true eight years ago when they were in their late twenties. It was true today at thirty-six. Which meant sliding back into old patterns would be a mistake.

Still, he couldn't stop the words rising in his throat, clamoring to answer Sam's jest. "I think the South Pole probably has a direct line to the North Pole. Maybe while I am here, I can contact the station up there and have them radio the old man.

Settle this argument once and for all." He raised his chin waiting for the next playful dig.

But Sam waved the comment away. "It hardly matters now. We can both decorate whenever we want." He turned to go. "Please stop by the clinic as soon as you get a chance. If I am out of the clinic, I want to make sure you know where everything is and are up to speed. Patients are the most important thing."

Then he was gone. The wind bit through the thermal jacket and Forrest knew he needed to head in, too. But he couldn't force his feet to move.

Sam had stopped the banter. And reminded him that the argument hardly mattered anymore.

He was right. But that didn't fix the hole ripping open through Forrest's soul.

Sam ran his hand through his hair as he stepped into the quiet clinic. With any luck, he'd skirted the worst-case scenario for Dr. Anderson. The man was on the plane and already scheduled with an oncologist.

Running the blood test on the physician had been a stroke of luck. One that might have saved the man's life. His cancer was moving fast, and being trapped in the Antarctic was the worst-case scenario.

I should be happy. I should celebrate the success.

This was about as perfect as possible. Less than a week from initial complaint to the call to Houston requesting Dr. Anderson get on the last flight out when the final supply run came in. Sam prided himself on running as close to perfect in every setting. He should be happy.

He'd done the complete blood count, commonly called a CBC, to rule out mono and iron deficiencies when the doctor's exhaustion had continued despite several days of ordered rest. The white cell count was off the charts and his red blood cells dangerously low. It was a shocking differential from the tests they'd all had run before agreeing to this gig. A bad sign.

He'd ordered the evac before even waking Dr. Anderson from yet another much-needed nap. The head of the Center for Polar Medical Operations, based in Texas, had agreed with Sam's assessment and pointed out there was no one they could send to replace Anderson.

And Sam had mentioned Forrest. A mistake he'd regretted every moment since. Yes, the Center for Polar Medical Operations would have identified him. After all, he was on the reserve list. Everyone at the station with additional skills understood they might be called to use them when needed. It was in their contract for the pole that their mission could change if necessary.

His boss thought it was great that he already knew Forrest and had asked him to get in touch. Sam had lied; said he didn't know Dr. Wilson. Said he only checked the list because he recognized a replacement was needed.

It was sort of the truth. Sort of. He didn't know *this* Forrest. He knew the man he'd lived with for years. Or maybe he hadn't known him either, since Forrest had walked away with such ease.

Sam had believed they were soulmates. Meant for each other. And then Forrest had simply left. No fanfare. No discussion. Just that one sentence and he'd vanished from their shared life.

I love you, but you deserve more.

And now Sam was going to have to work with him again.

Luckily, his boss had agreed to get in touch with the group in charge of Forrest's research and let them know he'd need to sub in from time to time.

He'd promised to let Sam know if there were any issues. None had arisen. Forrest had agreed to the arrangement, or maybe he'd been told there was no other choice. That instead of spending all his time in the lab he'd have to serve in the hospital, too. With Sam.

But Dr. Anderson was safe. That was what mattered.

I am a selfish ass.

Because instead of celebrating the success, Sam was moping. All because Forrest had been forced to work in the clinic on rotation.

He'd looked for the man every chance he was out of the clinic. Every meal. Every social function—not that Sam had stayed at any of them. Or talked to many people. But he noticed all of them had the same thing in common. Forrest's absence.

Today when Forrest had pointed out the need to be in his lab, Sam had nearly snapped that the doctor he'd known had loved clinical work. Thrived at the bedside.

But that Forrest was gone. He'd chased a different dream. A dream he hadn't wanted to share with Sam eight years ago.

"Damn." Sam clenched his fists. He'd cried over his fiancé—*ex*-fiancé, Oliver's betrayal five years ago. Screamed at the universe's ability to gift him two loves and let him lose both. But the mourning he'd done over his failed engagement had been nothing like the dark period he'd dwelled in after Forrest left his life.

Maybe it had been made easier by finding Oliver in bed with another man.

His parents had the perfect marriage. Fifty-two years and counting. The pair of academics were tied at the hip, even working projects together. When anyone asked if they ever got sick of each other, they'd laugh and say *not yet*.

Sam craved that love. The idea of working with someone and loving them so much, it never got old. He yearned for the perfect person. The one who completed him.

Or he had, once upon a time. Not anymore. Now he was a confirmed bachelor. Planning one failed proposal and then losing a few thousand dollars on wedding deposits was clearly the universe's way of saying *No soulmate for you*. He was fine with it.

It was easier to believe that when the object of that failed proposal wasn't trapped in the same place with him for the next seven months.

"Sam?" Forrest's voice was even, no hint that this was bothering him like it was Sam. "This a good time?"

He was the one that walked away. Of course he's fine.

Sam took a deep breath before looking up from the tablet that he'd been paying exactly zero attention to in the last few minutes. "I told you to stop by."

"Ordered it, really." Forrest held up his hand. "That sounded bad and is not what I meant at all. You pointed out the necessity for me to get to know the place for when I'm needed here. A more than fair request."

"Always the diplomat." The man avoided conflict like the plague. Sam hadn't dictated his attendance, but he'd not been welcoming, either. "I wasn't exactly friendly on the tarmac."

"You were seeing off a colleague with a fast-moving cancer. I think you're allowed to have feelings about that." Forrest took a deep breath, damn near mimicking the motion Sam had made when he'd walked into the clinic. "Let's start over. As colleagues. If we hadn't spent our twenties together, we'd be acting completely normal. What if we come at this as if there is no history between us? A get-to-know-the-clinic-and-colleagues session." Forrest smiled.

Is it that easy for him?

"Fine." It wasn't that simple for Sam, but he'd handle whatever emotions this brought privately. "I'm Sam. An emergency and trauma doctor. Over the last five years, I've worked in the Arctic Circle in Alaska, rural Wisconsin and Alabama, as well as mass trauma centers in New York City and Los Angeles."

"Damn." Forrest grinned. "That is impressive. I've been hiding in an Illinois research center for the last five years. No remote locations—unless you count the lab that I probably spend too much time in."

"Hiding in the lab? But you were great at bedside." That broke the rule. They were supposed to be starting fresh.

"Why aren't you climbing the rungs at a trauma center in a fast-moving city? That was your dream. One you'd talked about nearly every night. Why are you at the South Pole?"

He'd avoided the question by pointing out that Sam wasn't exactly chasing the dream he'd wanted, either.

He'd nearly had that dream. The hospital staff he'd worked with during the two years he'd dated Oliver had all joked they'd call him chief one day. More than one had tried to talk him out of turning in his notice.

Well, Sam could avoid questions, too.

"Most of the staff here have no chronic issues. Not surprising, given the medical tests required to winter over. So hopefully the workload for you should be light, Forrest." There was more leeway with the summer staff, but if you were locked in, the station had to ensure the staff had their best chance.

"For now. Humans are social animals and we didn't evolve to live here for a reason. Anxiety and depression will set in for at least a third of the staff. Studies show lack of sun and natural vitamin D creation can induce symptoms of both, or exacerbate underlying conditions. Everyone here is an overachiever, so they may not realize or admit to the issue on medical forms."

Brilliant. Forrest was brilliant. Outlining issues impacting patients without coming off as a know-it-all. It was a skill many in their med school class had admired.

"There are a handful already diagnosed—"

"Myself included," Forrest interrupted. "I fought against the diagnosis when we—" He cleared his throat. At least Sam wasn't the only one having issues falling back on the body of knowledge they had on each other. "The point is that if anyone is struggling to admit it, I am more than willing to discuss my diagnosis and why it does not mean they are 'less than' in any way." Forrest nodded to the closet. "Medicine storage?"

"Yes. We're stocked well. Which is good, given that no help is coming for the next seven months." Sam walked over to the door and pressed his combination into the keypad. "I talked to IT. They're going to get you a code by the end of the day."

Forrest followed him in. "This looks like a closet, but wow, it's a small pharmacy."

"No." Sam shook his head. "I've worked in three hospitals that would have killed for this kind of setup. This is a small- to medium-sized pharmacy. Maybe even a true medium. Not that anyone actually has metrics for what counts for what." He was rambling. Words not fully making sense.

"Uh-huh." Forrest nodded, too polite to ask what the hell Sam was talking about.

"Everyday meds. Noncontrolled substances are here." Sam pointed to an area clearly marked. "The controlled substances are in back with another entry code. Most of them we shouldn't need. Unless we're performing surgery."

"Surgery? I am an internist who spends all his time in the lab." Forrest held up his hands, his eyes wide. "I haven't held a scalpel since residency."

Color was racing up his neck. He had always hated cutting into anyone. Which was a shame, because he'd have made an excellent surgeon. He was already a more than capable physician, but that didn't mean he enjoyed it. That was why Sam had known he'd never head into emergency medicine or surgery. Not that Forrest had ever questioned where he'd land, either. Internal medicine was all he'd wanted from day one of med school.

So why was he in a lab? At the South Pole!

"I hope it doesn't come to that, but I've done a handful of minor surgeries when no specialist was available. There was an elbow surgery overseen by video teleconference in a northern Alaskan outpost that was nerve-racking, but the patient is still going strong." His palms still sweated with the memory but Sam had managed and he could do it again, if absolutely necessary.

Forrest looked around the pharmacy then back at the door.

"How is charting done here?" He opened the door and walked back out to the clinic area.

"It's standard charting. Like many facilities in the US, we use EPIC." Sam skirted around Forrest, who'd paused a little too close to the door when they'd exited. "But sometimes we have to use paper when the satellites are acting up."

"This is weird." Forrest shook his head and rocked back on his heels. "I know I'm the one who said we should act like colleagues just getting to know each other, but it's *weird*."

Sam shrugged, "It is. But we'll get through it. We are professionals."

"Professionals." Forrest didn't quite hide the scoff. "I mean, yes, of course we are."

"And you're my replacement, technically, not a teammate. I mean, you're likely going to have to work with me now and then, if the nurse practitioners need the night or day off, but really, we probably won't work together more than a handful of times."

A handful.

Probably fewer than a dozen. There wouldn't be a need.

Sam's soul sank. He needed to make up his mind. Either he was frustrated because he'd have to work with Forrest at all, or saddened by the fact that those occasions would be few and far between.

Can't have it both ways.

Forrest looked at him—really looked. "Are you all right?"

"Of course." It was mostly true. His life hadn't turned out like he thought it would but whose did? He'd done things he'd never dreamed of.

"Sam—"

"Any chance I can get an antibiotic cream? I scraped my hand on a machine and—" The young researcher stopped in the center of the room, and looked at the pair of them.

Sam had been so wrapped up in Forrest that he hadn't even heard her come in. "Sorry for your wait."

“I just got here.” Her dark gaze rotated between him and Forrest. “If I’m interrupting, I can come back, it’s just a scrape but—”

“No. We were done.” Sam nodded to Forrest. “I’ll let you know when we need you.” Though he was going to do his absolute best to never need him.

“I guess we’re done.” Forrest swallowed and stepped past him and the researcher. Then he was gone.

It was fine. Fine. Everything was fine.

“You all right?” the researcher asked.

“Fine.” The word bouncing around Sam’s brain responded. “Let’s get you some antibiotic cream.” He had seven months left on the station. He’d done seven months or more in worse environments.

Not with Forrest.

CHAPTER TWO

FIVE DAYS OF silence from the clinic. Not that Forrest was tracking. He stared at the image on his electron microscope and tried to focus on the virus flourishing on the slide. This was why he was here. To study the effects of viruses in enclosed environments for space travel.

The idea was simple enough. If you brought in people, supplies and sealed off their location, no matter how cautious you were, millions of germs were going to hook a ride. But how fast did those germs mutate? How did they adapt? That was one of the millions of questions needing answers for long-term space travel.

That kind of space travel still lived in the realm of science fiction and Forrest doubted it would be achieved in his lifetime, but that didn't mean the research wasn't ongoing. And it benefited more than just space travel.

Bacterial and viral mutations were things that kept immunologists, epidemiologists and other doctors up at night. It was the basis for more than one of Forrest's own nightmares.

The phone rang and Forrest blinked as he looked at the contraption on the wall. It had rung exactly one other time while he'd been here. The only people who came to this lab were him and Charlee. Most contact was received via email—though the satellite-assisted internet connection meant it was hard to download attachments.

He picked up the phone, “Doctor Wilson. How can I help you?”

A cough echoed on the line, followed by the unpleasant sound of someone using a tissue. “I guess you holing up in the lab has one benefit.” Charlee’s voice was ragged. “You don’t have the flu like half the post. Don’t worry—”

Another coughing fit interrupted whatever Charlee was going to say.

“Half the post?”

“Yes. Good grief—get out of the lab. I guess that loader from the last supply flight wasn’t right when he said it was ‘just a cough.’ Obviously not.” Charlee started coughing again before taking what sounded like a sip of water. “And I’ve swabbed myself to preserve the specimen of whatever is making me feel like death.” Another round of coughing.

“I’m not concerned about the swabs.”

“Yes. You are.” Charlee sighed. “It’s what makes you so good at this. I’m taking at least today and tomorrow.”

“Do *not* come back in here until you are completely better. And I do want the swabs. But it’s more important that you get some rest. I will talk to you later.”

Charlee hung up without saying anything else.

Yes, their research was important. Yes, they were on a limited schedule. But that did not mean Charlee needed to compromise her health.

And he *had* been in the lab basically nonstop since he’d visited the clinic.

Hiding.

He didn’t enjoy admitting it, but if influenza was going around and Forrest hadn’t even realized it, that meant he’d spent far too long in the lab. Sam and his team must be exhausted. But if they’d needed him, Sam would have rung.

No. He wouldn’t.

Forrest had made it clear more than once that he was just the backup. That his research and lab came first. Those were the reasons he was here…but he was also a physician. One specializing in immunology and, to some extent, epidemiology. He might not have treated a patient in five years, but if there was an outbreak, he was still well suited to take care of the sick and then help ensure it didn't happen again.

And Sam didn't ring me.

That stung. But if the shoe had been on his foot, Forrest wasn't sure he'd have reached out, either. That wasn't a pleasant thought. He put the slides he was working on away and shut down the equipment. He was needed in the clinic. Whether Sam called or not.

It was a short walk. His quick pace was not the reason his heartbeat was echoing in his ears. He and Sam had worked side by side on so many shifts as med students. Sam excelling and Forrest doing his best to make sure no one saw how out of place he felt.

Then Sam had taken a residency in New York City and Forrest had gone to Seattle. As far away from the love of his life as possible. Hoping he'd feel like he belonged there.

There were coughs coming from the clinic and two patients were sitting on the bench outside the door. Forrest slid the mask he'd grabbed from his lab on. If influenza was making its way around the base, that meant it was a variant not receptive to the flu shot, because everyone on post had this season's vaccine before arriving. Enough people were sick; he didn't need to add himself to the ill population.

He stopped and did a quick triage. Each patient had a low-grade fever and dry cough.

"You're both sick, but not ill enough to be admitted to the clinic," he told them. "Go back to your rooms, take tea with honey for the cough and get as much sleep as you can manage." Like all medical doctors he'd done stints in the emergency room. When people felt terrible, they'd come in for reassurance that they'd be fine. At least it was a less expensive trip here than it would be in the States.

The virus needed to run its course. Unless someone's immune system was compromised, there was nothing but comfort care that the clinic could provide.

The two on the bench nodded, stood and slowly moved off.

"Come back if your fever is sustained at one hundred and three or higher."

They each raised a hand as he called out the final order.

The door of the clinic opened behind him and Forrest knew it was Sam. Just a few feet away. His heart rate picked up even more. His skin heated. The blood rushed to his face.

He turned. He was there to help. Whether Sam had called or not.

"Are you sending patients away?" Sam closed his eyes and opened them. Not a sign of frustration. Exhaustion clung to the physician. His eyes were hooded, his skin paler than normal and his lips were cracked. He was pushing himself to the edge.

"Are you the only one here?" Forrest pushed past Sam and shook his head. Two beds had occupants with IV drips. And no nurse practitioners visible.

Sam moved so he was on the other side of Forrest. Of course exhaustion wasn't slowing the former state champion rower down. "I asked a question first. Why are you sending patients away?" His arms were crossed and his eyes were fiery despite the exhaustion leaking from his pores. "Forrest—"

"They were running low-grade fevers and coughing. Classic influenza symptoms. I told them to drink tea with honey and get as much rest as possible. And to report back if their temperatures spike. This is a virus. There's nothing else we can do for them. Now—" he crossed his arms mimicking the man in front of him "—are you the only one here?"

Forrest knew the answer, but he needed the confirmation.

"Yes." Sam slid over to the desk and pulled up the tablet he used for charting.

To give himself something to do?

"Who were the two you sent back to their dorms?" Sam was typing with one hand, no glint in his gray-blue gaze.

"I don't know. Two sick people who weren't sick enough to need more than rest and recovery time." Forrest shrugged. The offhanded movement was the wrong one.

Now Sam's gaze was full on boring into him. "What?" He held up a hand while shaking his head. "I know what you said. How could you not ask their names?"

"Again, what they needed was rest and maybe some cough drops, if we have them." Forrest's chest was hollow as he said the words. They were probably fine. That didn't change the fact that there were reasons you kept track.

Reasons he knew. Damn. He was rusty. And had made a mistake less than a minute in. Not a good start.

"And what if they get to their rooms and get too sick to call or come back? They need to be added to the infirmary's list." Sam ran a hand over his tired face.

It was a rookie mistake; one Forrest wouldn't have made if he'd worked with patients in the last five years.

"Sorry." He'd failed the first assignment. "I'll figure out who they were." Sam raised a brow but didn't point out that finding two patients when he didn't have more than a few seconds with each was a long shot.

Still. He'd find them. Records were important.

So much of the post was down with the flu that accurate records might provide valuable information on who patient zero might be or how the virus was traveling so efficiently. And for that they needed to know everyone affected, time of sickness, severity.

"They'll probably be fine. Rest and fluids is all most need. But getting you out of your lab might have some benefits." Sam rolled his eyes then sat on the edge of the desk.

"How do you know I haven't been out? Keeping a check on me?" Those were questions he'd not needed to ask. Questions he didn't need answered.

Sam pinched the bridge of nose, then looked at the clock. "McMurdo Station is the largest research station in Antarctica but even at the height of its population there are a little over one thousand people here, and that's in the summer. Right now, there are two hundred and forty-seven. So a lone researcher who takes all his meals in his lab and sleeps there—"

"One time. And it wasn't sleeping, it was a nap."

Sam raised a brow, "You stand out, Forrest. Your absence stands out." He pushed himself off the desk, "Since you're here, I'm going to catch a quick nap. Natasha and Chris are both down with the flu, so it's just you and me."

"I'd have come sooner, if you'd called." Forrest said the words to Sam's retreating form. If the man heard them, he didn't react. If only Forrest could do the same.

Sam stared at the ceiling. Sleep had come—one did not work a decade plus in emergency medicine without learning to nap when and wherever you could. But that didn't mean his mind had settled.

The half-finished dreams had all revolved around Forrest. Replays of their life together. The horrid goodbye. The rudeness he'd projected earlier when Forrest had stopped in to help.

Rude was easy. It created a barrier. A wall. A case of ice around the heart he'd been forced to heal.

That didn't mean it was right.

And Forrest had had a point. Sam should have called. Should have notified his lab the second Chris went down. And certainly when Natasha developed a fever.

It was stubbornness that had kept him from reaching out.

And it was fear keeping him from swinging his legs over the bed and heading back to the clinic. It was late; Forrest needed a break. But now that Forrest knew Sam was working by himself, the man would insist on staying.

Forrest might have traded his clinician shoes for a lab coat but that didn't mean he'd sacrifice patient care. Sam had watched the color drain from his face when he'd asked for the names of the patients Forrest had sent away. Seen the realization that he'd failed to record the basics, and the shame. Known his former lover would beat himself up.

"No use holing up in here." Sam uttered the words to the empty room as he forced himself to get up and head to the clinic.

He slowly opened the door, slipping in before the creak he'd noticed last week could echo in the quiet. The lights were turned down, probably to help the two individuals he'd admitted for IV fluids sleep.

Forrest looked up from the desk. Notes were strewn all over. The flashback to university, when Sam had labeled all his notes in a computer app and Forrest had piled notecards, sticky notes and sheets of paper everywhere, cut through Sam's heart.

This was why he'd avoided picking up the phone. Because every stupid little thing made him remember a life he'd spent years forgetting.

Apparently I didn't bury the memories far enough.

"Is there a reason you have papers everywhere?" Sam slid into the chair across from Forrest, waving off his unspoken offer of the primary desk chair.

Forrest held up a note and passed it to Sam. Two names.

Dr. Felix Lorraine, biologist.

Max Center, mechanic.

"How did you find them?" No explanation needed. These were the two Forrest had met in the hall. The two Sam had shamed him for.

Forrest turned the laptop around. Dr. Lorraine's and Max's badges were on the screen. Sam couldn't stop the smile on his lips. Searching the badge records was a unique way to find them. A very Forrest activity.

"I already reached out. They gave me the pertinent details. Both are still only running low-grade fevers and exhausted. Dr.

Lorraine will stop by for cough drops later. I found the stash." Forrest rubbed his tense neck. "The two here are stable. I think they can be released to quarters tomorrow."

"Thank you." Sam sucked in a breath. "I should have called."

"You should have. But I understand why you didn't." Forrest turned the laptop back around. "However, I'm not leaving until one of the NPs is well enough to work with you."

Part of Sam rejoiced at the words. Not because he'd have qualified support but because Forrest was going to be here. With him. He needed to shut that feeling down. He could handle this himself. He'd worked by himself for years.

"I appreciate it, but—"

"Nope." Forrest's voice was low so as not to disturb the sleeping patients, "You're about to say that you've handled isolated conditions for years so you don't mind. *I* mind."

That was exactly what Sam had been about to say. Damn it. How were they both still so capable of reading the other?

"Why the remote locations?" Forrest crossed his arms. "Why are you here?"

They were repeats of the questions he'd asked five days ago. So Sam deflected with the same question he'd asked and gotten no answer to then. "Why are *you* hiding in a lab at the South Pole and not at the bedside? I seem to remember you loved figuring out what made people ill. And you were a master at it. The way you could read reports and see tiny differentials that stacked up to mean something all of us had seen one time on a med school test was one of the most impressive things I've ever seen. And now you're in a lab. Studying slides instead of healing the sick."

Forrest shifted, then met his gaze, "I had a patient—a little girl. Five. Sandy. She presented with a fever and UTI-like symptoms. And she worsened over the next few days, necrotizing enterocolitis. Every lab I saw, nothing made sense. It was cronobacter. The bacteria had gotten into her system from an herbal tea. It typically only affects newborns and the elderly. I never thought to check for it. By the time we figured it out—" Forrest shrugged.

How many times had Sam done that shrug after a hard shift in the ER? So many emotions carried on the up and down of shoulders. Only a medical professional who'd given the same shrug hundreds of times really understood the devastation hiding in such a little movement.

"The bacteria is rare. Only a handful of cases a year." Sam bit his lip to stop the words he knew wouldn't help. Statistics were comforting—when you or your loved one weren't creating the unlucky stat.

"At five, she should have had a better chance and if…" Forrest shook his head. "No use playing the if game."

That was something every doctor learned in med school. You could second-guess everything and the end result was still the same. It was a lovely platitude, but Sam had yet to meet a physician capable of truly abiding by it.

"Telling her parents broke me." Forrest spun the pen on the desk as his chest rose and fell with each word. "I failed at bedside. I wasn't able to do it."

He was in a prestigious lab in the South Pole working on foundational research. That was hardly what most people would label as failure. But it did sound like hiding.

Forrest didn't look up from the spinning pen. "The good thing about the lab is that the specimens are silent. Anonymous. Even when you look in the scope and see the worst-case scenario. It isn't my job to tell people that the person they love has less time than they thought. Or isn't coming home at all. Or that they are going to live, but won't ever be the same. I never start a sentence with *We did everything we could*."

The pen kept up its twirl, as Forrest's dark gaze hit Sam. "*That* is why I'm hiding in a lab. A failure to maintain my sanity at the bedside. Now, why are *you* here? Why are you traveling to remote locations and working alone?"

There was so much that Sam wanted to say. Rail against the

idea that somehow Forrest was a failure. Tell him that if he was hiding then he wasn't where he was meant to be.

But fair was fair. Forrest had earned an answer of his own. However, admitting that he'd chosen constant traveling because both the men he'd planned to put down roots with hadn't wanted him would be less painful if one of those men wasn't sitting on the other side of the desk right now.

"I was engaged. Five years ago."

A twitch in Forrest's cheek was the only reaction to that statement.

What more was I hoping for?

Sam shrugged. Now he was the one hiding emotion in the simple action. "It's a freaking cliché story. Engaged, wedding less than a month away. I came home early from a shift because I was running a fever. Oliver was in bed with another man."

"Sam—"

"I don't want sympathy. I don't need it. My parents got the perfect union and I am never going to have it. No soulmate here. That's fine." There were days he almost believed the BS he was feeding himself.

Forrest cocked his head, "I wasn't planning on sympathy. I was going to say he sucked and didn't know what he had."

Sam waited for Forrest to look away. After all, the insinuation was Forrest hadn't known what he had, either. But Forrest didn't flinch. Sam rested his head in his hands.

"But how does a jackass ex-fiancé make you travel the…" His former best friend stopped and now it was pity coating his eyes. "You don't want to put down roots."

Not a question. Just a statement of fact. That damn long-term connection, still unbroken despite everything.

"Two men sitting at the ends of the earth who know they will never meet someone at the altar." If only Sam had a coffee cup to raise a mock toast with, preferably one that had a bit of an alcoholic kick to it.

Forrest looked at him. His hand was moving but before it reached Sam's he pulled back.

Sam didn't want his touch. Didn't need his comfort.

"I'm no longer sure I won't meet someone there." Forrest cleared his throat, "I think, well, older wiser and all that."

The irony.

"I feel like older, wiser me knows there is no point in exchanging vows. Weird how we flip-flopped." Where had this man been all those years ago? If Forrest had felt that way then, would they be celebrating their tenth wedding anniversary this year?

Yes.

Forrest wasn't the same man. But neither was he.

A moan from the door interrupted what was feeling a little too close to a pity party for Sam's liking.

Forrest was out his chair before Sam had turned around.

"Charlee? Charlee! I need you to keep your eyes open."

Forrest had barely left the lab. He knew Sam, the nurse practitioners and the people in his lab. Since Charlee wasn't a clinician, he suspected she had to be a member of Forrest's team.

"She's burning up." Forrest put one arm under her shoulder; Sam mimicked the action on the other side.

"Charlee, how much water have you had to drink? Do you know what your temperature is?" The woman didn't answer Forrest's frantic questions.

"Forrest, get her to the bed." Charlee was dehydrated. The sunken eyes were a clear sign. A fact Forrest knew.

But when you were treating a colleague and a friend you could miss subtleties.

"Dizzy. Can't keep fluids." Charlee's breathless words echoed out as they laid her on the bed.

Sam pulled out his stethoscope. "Get the fluids while I listen to her lungs and heart."

Forrest moved immediately.

Unfortunately for Charlee, the nurses who could put in IV

drips without even thinking were both down with the same virus taking its wrath out on her immune system.

"I haven't put an IV in since fourth year med school." Forrest set the bag of fluids on the stand.

"The good news is her lungs and heart sound good. I think the dizziness is dehydration. And I've done IVs when the ER was overloaded. I'm not as fast as the nursing staff, but we got this." Sam went to the sink, washed his hands and put on a pair of gloves. Then he started the IV.

With any luck, once Charlee was hydrated the worst of her symptoms would dissipate.

"Her temperature is one hundred and four." Forrest set the thermometer back on the counter by the bed. "Do we have liquid acetaminophen to push through her IV?"

"Yes." Charlee's fever was burning through the fluids she had been able to take. They needed to get that temperature down otherwise the fever would consume the liquid from the IV, too.

Forrest headed for the med storage unit, reemerging a moment later with the tiny vial. The good news was that the IV push would get the fever suppressant directly into Charlee's bloodstream. Sam did the quick calculations, drew the syringe of meds and pushed it into the IV.

Forrest held up his hand, pressing a button on his brown watch. "It should start to work in five to ten minutes, if not then we need to push more."

"Let's focus on seeing if it comes down in five to ten." Sam swallowed as he stared at the watch—or where the watch was hidden under Forrest's long-sleeved scrubs. That was the watch Sam had given him on their third anniversary.

It was a simple piece. One bought when their funds were so tight they'd counted every penny. He'd saved for months.

It was a starter watch. One he'd planned to replace when they were settled. That day had never come.

But Forrest was more than capable of acquiring a better

watch now. A fancier piece. A piece that screamed doctor, instead of drowning-under-med-school-debt student.

"Her fever's coming down." Forrest let out a sigh. "Thank goodness. Though she's still in for a long night."

Sam nodded, not trusting any words that might slip from his lips. He was in for a long night, too.

CHAPTER THREE

"YOU DON'T NEED to be here." Chris, one of the nurse practitioners on the station was looking much better today. He hadn't run a fever for three days, but yesterday he'd still looked rundown. "Nat and I can handle it. Get out of the clinic. Rest. Have fun. Do something."

He made a little shooing motion at Sam with his hands. It was juvenile but it made the point.

"Fine. I will go. But if either of you get too tired or need anything—"

"We won't." Natasha winked as she restocked the supplies next to the bed where Charlee had slept until this morning. The researcher wouldn't be joining Forrest in the lab for at least another few days, but Sam had released her to her quarters this morning. "Go."

Sam raised a hand and headed out of the clinic…to do what? The cafeteria didn't start serving lunch until eleven. He could head to his quarters, but there wasn't much to entertain him there. He was tired, but if he napped he ran the risk of messing up his sleep schedule.

What is Forrest doing?

This was the part of life he hated, the reason he did his best to keep moving. Because if he slowed down, his brain traveled places he didn't want to go.

His feet moved and before he knew it, Sam was standing

outside Forrest and Charlee's lab. This wasn't where he'd meant to come. He wasn't really sure why he was here.

Still time to walk away. He probably should walk away. They'd spent most of the last three days working together in the clinic. There was no reason for Sam to just stop by.

But rather than retreat, Sam raised his hand and knocked.

"Come in, Sam." Forrest's voice was husky behind the door.

No turning back now. He turned the handle and stepped into the shockingly dark lab. "Is your head all right?" The man had been in the clinic for several days. Even if he was suffering a migraine, he'd show up just to ensure work got done. The man feared messing up more than anything. Or he had. It was why even though Forrest had been nearly perfect at bedside the last three days, he said more than once that wasn't accomplishing anything.

"My head is fine. You and I both seemed to avoid the Novel A Influenza strain circulating." Forrest turned the screen of the electron microscope around, showing off a beautiful image. "Weird how even viruses look pretty with enough magnification."

"You identified which flu strain took the base to nearly half capacity? How long have you been in here?" Forrest had signed off yesterday when Natasha had returned to the clinic full-time. Even if he'd showed up this morning, that didn't seem like enough time to fully work something like this out.

"I said it was *a* Novel A strain, not which one. Those tests are still running, but I'll have an answer by the end of the day. It actually doesn't take as long to type them out as you think. The most important thing is to have enough samples to see any mutations." Forrest turned the electron scope back toward him.

"I have Charlee's samples and a few from the clinic. Charlee's is a mutated variant. Could explain why the virus hit her harder than others. I didn't get samples from the two others that had to have fluids, but there's a decent chance they had the same strain. The good news is that the mutated variant didn't seem as effective at spreading."

Sam crossed his arms, not frustrated, simply fascinated watching the man at work. "How do you know it wasn't as effective?"

"You and I are standing here." Forrest looked up from the screen and smiled. "We both moved Charlee from the door to the bed. Neither of us was masked. If it *was* as effective as the other strain, there's a good chance at least one of us would have the sniffles right now. If not the full-blown virus."

That smile was always what had fascinated Sam. Forrest could look at something most would ignore or push off as stuff other scientists or doctors did, and just dive right in. It was why no one had been surprised when he announced early in med school that he planning to go into internal medicine. And why no one was surprised he had never changed his mind.

He'd enjoyed the other specialties. Excelled at several of them. One of the neurosurgeons had practically begged him to consider brain surgery. Forrest had never budged. He'd known where he belonged.

Except he did change his mind.

He was locked away in a lab. Doing important research, but not serving patients directly. Patients he could truly help by being at bedside.

Forrest was amazing. He just never seemed to quite understand that fact.

"This whole situation made me realize I need to evaluate more samples," Forrest said. "People brought germs with them. They might not get ill from them, but others could be more susceptible. It's our own microcosm. So I've set up drop sites around the post with everything people need to give me daily samples. Voluntary, of course."

"Not sure you'll get daily samples." But he would get more than he had.

"Not planning on it. But I'll take what I can get. You aren't here to discuss that, though. What brings you to my lab?" Forrest tilted his head, "I doubt it was the flu strain. It doesn't much matter for the clinic what strain it is. Procedure is the same."

"I don't know." Such an honest answer. That was one the reasons he'd fallen for him. Seen forever with him. Forrest was easy to talk to. Easy to tell secrets to. Easy to love.

But he wasn't Sam's boyfriend any longer. Not the keeper of his secrets or his heart.

Forrest shut the electron microscope's screen off, pitching the already dark room into almost complete darkness. Then a light popped on. Sam squinted as his eyes adjusted.

"Sorry. I should have given some warning."

"It would have been nice." Sam blinked a few more times as his eyes screamed at the intrusion.

Forrest was by his side, not touching him, but so much closer than they'd been in the clinic. His scent, the soft pepper and cedarwood of the aftershave he'd used the entire time Sam knew him, wafted straight to his core.

A whole host of memories banged on the barricade Sam had erected around them. A not so solid wall these days.

The moment he'd given Forrest the watch slipped through. The expression on his face. The kiss they'd shared. The happiness that had felt like it would last forever.

"Why don't you have a new watch?" The question was pointless. Its answer mattered little in life's grand scheme.

"Watch?" Forrest's Adam's apple bobbed as he swallowed whatever he was going to say first. His right hand shifted, running over the piece still hiding on his left arm. "It's a good watch."

"No. It isn't." Sam chuckled as he slid back on his heels, putting a little more space between them. Millimeters, but millimeters that hopefully would keep him from acting any more rashly than he already was. "It was the best I could afford but it wasn't a good watch. It was—"

He wasn't sure where he was going or what the pointless

words could possibly lead to, so shut his mouth to trap any more inside.

His heartbeat pounded in his ears as the lab's silence radiated around them.

Say something.

Say something.

Say something.

He wasn't sure if his brain was chanting the words in hopes that Forrest's tongue would loosen or as an order to himself to add something to the quiet.

"Did you come because of the watch?"

There was a look in Forrest's eye. A hesitation? A question? A sorrow? Sam wasn't sure.

"Maybe. I saw it the other night. Seriously, why do you still have it? And don't say, it's a good watch. I got rid of everything." He cleared his throat. That was not what he'd meant to say. It wasn't even true.

His box of mementos was stuffed in the back of his closet at his parents' house. It had been carted from closet to closet at each of the locations he'd traveled to but when he'd signed up for this trip, he'd put everything back in his old room. And he'd taken the chance to rummage through the box again. Reliving the happiness, and the pain.

Movie tickets from their first date. The key from their first apartment. A Christmas ornament with them dressed as doctors he'd gotten for the holiday they'd never spent together. All things he should throw away.

There was no Oliver box. Sam really had thrown those memories away. Rid his apartment, and his life, of the man.

But anytime he considered getting rid of the Forrest box, lifting the tiny thing felt like trying to carry the world. So it traveled with him. A piece of Forrest he couldn't cut away.

"I don't want to fight. We weren't very good at it anyway." Forrest wrapped his arms around himself, but he didn't step back.

"What does that mean? We weren't very good at it? Sure we were. We were civil and—" Sam closed his eyes. They had never really fought. They had spirited discussions. But never true arguments.

He'd always thought they were so in tune with each other there was no need to argue. Until Forrest walked away. Then he'd wondered if they'd avoided arguing because they were hiding things from each other. Except Sam hadn't hidden anything. He'd made sure Forrest knew the future he saw for them. Forrest had hidden the fact that he didn't see that future.

"Part of me hates that you're here." Sam bit his lip. "Sorry. That was mean and cruel."

"But honest." Forrest let out a sigh. "So you came to say your piece. It wasn't possible in the clinic. Even with the patients sleeping, we weren't alone."

He gestured with a hand then wrapped his arm back around himself. "Say what you need to say, Sam."

"Why are you still wearing a watch that a lover *you* walked away from gave you?" That was the part that tore at Sam. He had seen no cracks in their love. No pain. He'd believed Forrest was his person. The other half of his soul. He planned their future while Forrest was planning to walk away, shattering his soul and cratering the life he'd planned.

Yet, the man had kept the love token.

He looked at Forrest's wrist. "Why?"

Emotions clogged his throat. Damn him. Sam had done a half-decent job of keeping his feelings in check, at least around Forrest. He made sure the dirt he laid over the grave in his heart never shifted. And then a stupid watch had undone everything.

And Forrest had just gone to his lab. Restarted his day. Followed his routine. Picked up and restarted without any issues. Like he had all those years ago.

He was the one that walked away. What did you expect?

"I didn't want to get rid of it." Forrest's thumb ran along his wrist, feeling the face of the watch under his sweater. "I didn't throw everything away."

"Just the most important part, right? Me." Shit. That wasn't helpful. To him or Forrest.

"Are you mad at me and a watch or your ex-fiancé? The one that made you run from the life you planned? I can handle anger, Sam, I just need to know who you are really cursing." Forrest tilted his head, such a methodical reaction.

The man had always kept his cool in frustrating times. Never raised his voice. Never thrown hands. Never called someone a name. It was a trait Sam had admired until Forrest had used it to walk away from him.

Until Forrest had told them they were done in the same cool tone. No emotion. No fire. No tears. Just a cold hard truth.

Coming here was a mistake. One he needed to rectify. "I am fine with my life."

"You wouldn't be pissed at the watch I'm wearing if that was true."

Forrest and his damn insights.

"I apologize for coming." This wasn't the way to spend his time off. He'd barged in and made an ass of himself. Not the standard he held himself to. "I hope you get whatever answers you're looking for in there." Sam gestured to the electron microscope then turned on his heel.

He needed to be anywhere else.

Now.

It took longer to shut down the lab equipment when Forrest was the only one there. Plus there had been tests he needed to complete before cleaning everything up for the day. But he'd managed it as quickly as possible.

Sam was struggling. It was terrifying.

The man had always been in control. Perfect. A former state champion rower who had turned down a chance at the Olympics because it would impact his start date at university. His nearly perfect scores on tests had infuriated and impressed their friends.

He was always collected. Hell, even with the influenza outbreak he'd held it all together. If Charlee hadn't called in sick, alerting Forrest to the outbreak, Sam would have handled it all on his own.

But years of therapy had unlocked the knowledge that just because you were functioning on the outside, didn't mean the internal wasn't twisted unrecognizably.

Forrest closed and locked the lab then headed to Sam's quarters. He ran his hand along the watch that had inflamed the interaction. He'd kept it for a simple reason.

It reminded him of a time in his life that was nearly perfect. The one time in his life he'd known love.

He'd grown up under the ever-watchful eye of his grandmother. Her cutting remarks had been a constant reminder that he was a mistake. His mother had never shared his father's identity, if she'd even known who he was.

She'd dropped Forrest at his grandmother's door when he was less than a week old. The only thing he could credit his grandmother with was that she hadn't turned him over to the system.

He'd met Sam as an undergrad. Loved him as a med student. Walked away right before residency so the man had the chance at something better than the broken man he slept beside every evening. The man who might be top of his class but felt completely out of place. The man who internally cringed whenever marriage was brought up because he was certain he'd make a terrible spouse. Forrest had grown up in a home without that kind of love and was terrified he'd mess everything up eventually.

And instead of finding what he had wanted, Sam was hiding in rural locations, moving from place to place, not staying long enough to form real connections. It was clear he needed a friend, whether he was willing to admit it or not.

And Forrest was going to oblige. Or force his way in. Somewhere, Sam had lost sight of how wonderful he was. Put away the dreams he'd always wanted. Forrest hadn't been lying when he'd said the ex-fiancé hadn't known what he had.

His fists were clenched, and Forrest took a breath as he unclenched them. He was furious at a man he'd never met.

And jealous as hell.

Burning poured across his chest. The man, Oliver, could have had the world. And he'd thrown it away.

And destroyed a man Forrest would always care about.

Forrest reached the door of Sam's quarters and knocked on it. He waited a minute, but there was no response. So he knocked again.

"Go away, Forrest. I am fine."

So Forrest wasn't the only one who knew when the other one was standing on the wrong side of a door.

He grabbed the handle and walked in. The good news was that, in the winter, with so few people at the pole, most people didn't have a roommate. Forrest himself was currently using the extra bed in his room to store the clean clothes he kept meaning to put away.

"Hey!" Sam's mouth was hanging open as he stared at Forrest.

Forrest closed the door behind him and moved to sit on the extra chair in the little seating area Sam had set up. Like him, Sam was living in a double room with no additional partner.

He took the watch off and tossed it on the table between them. "Do you want it back?"

"Don't be ridiculous." Sam leaned back, trying to put as much distance between them in the small room as possible.

It stung. But Forrest wasn't going to give in to that feeling now. There'd be plenty of time to wallow when he was in his own room.

He gathered the watch and slid it back onto his wrist. Then he crossed a leg over his knee and put his arms on the back of the chair. He'd stay until Sam physically removed him or started talking.

Sam's gaze held his. His chin raised. Challenge set. "It's not fair."

"Little in life is. But what exactly do you mean this time?" Forrest's stomach twisted and he prayed the uncertainty raging through him wasn't clear on his face. He was here for Sam right now. Not himself.

Sam took a deep breath and rolled his head from one side to the other. "I said we should be colleagues. Act like none of the history is there. I'm the one who suggested it. And yet—" he flung his hand out at Forrest "—you are the one unconcerned by it and I'm pissed at a watch."

Forrest wasn't unaffected. His stomach tumbled right now, just to prove that point. "I think you're pissed because I'm a reminder that you didn't get the life you planned. You're in one of the most interesting places in the world. A place you could convince yourself was the plan...if I wasn't here."

Sam cleared his throat. "I always hated how you could look at something and just get right to the point."

Forrest had never felt like he had that skill. He was just quiet. Saw more than most because he wasn't attempting to control conversations. Most physicians he knew were extroverts. There was nothing wrong with that, but it meant that in many conversations they were waiting to say something, rather than fully listening.

It occasionally caused a problem when doctors figured they knew what was going on without really listening to their patients' concerns.

"We were friends for a long time. I think enough time has passed that we could be again. I know you're stinging from the end of your engagement..."

"My engagement ended five years ago." Sam bit his lip like that was the last thing he'd wanted to say. "You're right. You are a reminder of a different life plan. One I thought I had buried when I found Oliver. But none of that's your fault."

"You need a friend." Forrest knew Sam was about to kick him out. About to tell him to get lost. And that was fair. After all, he'd ended things between them. But the man was an extrovert by nature. And just like Forrest had holed up in the lab, Sam was doing the exact same thing.

Except he was holing up in locations he knew he wasn't staying in. Everyone was transient in his life. So no real connection. No heartfelt goodbyes. No life plan to mess up.

"A friend who cares and will listen to whatever. And who actually knows you."

"Volunteering?" Sam laughed but there was no humor in the sound.

"Yes." Forrest forced the emotions clawing their way up his throat down. Sam was important and the man was doubting himself, whether he wanted to admit that or not.

He deserved a happy home. He could have that as a traveling physician, with the right partner. Or he could chase the dream that Forrest suspected was still in his heart.

A stable home. A long career at a top trauma unit. A family to come home to every evening. He was getting a later start on it than planned, but it could still be his. If he opened himself up.

"We are good friends. Or we were." Forrest held up his hand. "We were always able to have conversations and laugh before—" he hesitated for only a moment before continuing "—before we took it to a different place. We have this Antarctic winter for you to come back out of the shell you've retreated into since you started traveling. Think of me as practice for when you get back to the real world, if you need to."

"And if I don't want a friend?" Sam raised his chin, but Forrest could see the indecision in his eyes.

"You do. And I need to get out of the lab. We can do this." Forrest was nearly sure of it. "We'll both be better for it."

"Fine."

Not a ringing endorsement, but a start.

CHAPTER FOUR

SAM CONSIDERED CALLING things off and hiding in his suite all day. He looked at the phone and shook his head. What was the point? Forrest had already barged in once.

Friends.

He'd agreed to be friends—with Forrest. Maybe he needed his head examined, because this had disaster written all over it.

But hiding away wasn't fixing anything, either. And there was part of him that missed his friendship with Forrest. Before they'd been lovers, he'd been the one Sam turned to with everything.

This era of their friendship would not be like that one. Forrest was right about one thing. Sam was lonely.

Had been lonely for so long.

He'd swoop into a place, serve the three or six or even nine months that was on his contract. He'd be friendly with the locals but did not make friends. Did not plan out his life or try to find forever.

Grabbing the light jacket off the hook, Sam opened his door—and paused.

Forrest raised a hand. "Morning."

"Wha—" Sam couldn't even finish the word.

Forrest shrugged and put his hands in his pockets. "I thought you might be second-guessing this and trying to avoid breakfast."

"I considered it." Sam matched Forrest's shrug as he closed

the door to his room and pulled on his coat. Their dorms weren't located in Building 155, the main facility at McMurdo Station. There were lines between the buildings you could hold on to to make sure you got where you needed to go. Today it was still bright enough that they didn't need them.

They marched across the way and walked into the canteen. Grabbed their trays and breakfast. All without saying a word.

A group of mechanics stood up and cleared out a table. Forrest slid into the recently vacated chairs and Sam followed.

"Did you sleep all right?" Forrest grabbed a banana from his tray and tore open the peel. The bananas grown in the hydroponic farm on the station were a dwarf variety and tasted slightly different from the ones you got at home. But on the days when you got "freshies," the nickname people gave fresh fruit and veggies grown or flown into the station, you enjoyed the prized commodities.

"I slept fine." Sam did not hide the yawn the question seemed to call from his soul.

Forrest raised a brow but didn't push. "I have a colleague studying sleep patterns in a confined environment. He put in for a stint down here but wasn't approved."

"There's always next year." Sam wasn't a scientist, but he knew getting lab or research space in Antarctica was a prize most never achieved. It was impressive that Forrest was "hiding" here.

Forrest nodded as he dumped more than a healthy amount of brown sugar in his oatmeal.

"You know they serve this buffet style. There are a ton of options. You aren't required to eat oatmeal." A smile pulled at the corner of Sam's lips.

An old running joke.

To cover a painful childhood when all Forrest was permitted for breakfast was bland oatmeal.

"I like oatmeal."

“You like—” Sam held up two of the four empty packets of sugar “—brown sugar.”

Forrest smiled and looked at the overly sweetened breakfast. “I like oatmeal. *With* brown sugar.”

He took a big bite of the meal and put a ridiculous smile on his face. The over-the-top dramatics were funny and Sam couldn’t contain the chuckle that slipped out.

It felt weird and somehow not, to be joking and laughing. This was Forrest. His soul knew this man. Recognized him. Enjoyed spending time with him.

“So where are you based at these days?” Forrest took another bite of oatmeal. Maybe determined to finish the meal to prove a point.

“You picked me up from my room.” Sam cleared his throat. That sounded a little too much like this was a date. “You know where I’m based.”

“Very funny.” Forrest pointed the spoon at him. “You move all the time, but where are you based? Where are you heading back to after this?”

Sam shrugged. It was a question his mother asked him far too often.

Where to next, Sam? Is there a plan? A point to the journey?

The worry in her eyes always made him fidget. And he fought the urge to do the same now.

“That is a problem for future Sam. I’ve put feelers out to places, but no final destination in mind.” He winked and managed not to look away when Forrest raised his eyebrow. “And you? Where is home now?”

“Indiana.”

“Indianapolis?” There was a huge pharmaceutical company there. One known for their research throughout the world. But that didn’t tally with Forrest’s posting in Antarctica, examining remote locations and viral modifications in small populations. That wasn’t something the company studied.

Or maybe it was.

Sam had never investigated the company himself. His interactions had been limited to the sales reps that showed up at clinics far too often.

"Yeah. Indianapolis." Forrest nodded, "But the research here is government based. A contract." He set his spoon down, all the oatmeal gone. "Been there for about five years. It's a nice enough place."

Such a glowing recommendation.

That meant Forrest had completed his residency and spent less than two full years at bedside. Those early years on the wards could be tough. It would be easy for the Forrest Sam had known to see any mess up as a reason to run. Perhaps this friendship could remind Forrest why he'd gone to med school in the first place—to work with patients.

"Anyone waiting for you at home?" Jobs, weather, family. Such bland topics. Except this question cut to Sam's core. He wanted Forrest happy.

He'd mentioned he was open to the idea of marriage now. Was it because he'd met someone that had made him realize it was for him?

Someone better than me.

"No." Forrest laughed but there was discomfort layered under it. "I am perpetually single." He pursed his lips before looking at the door. "What do you do for entertainment these days? Do you still go to opening nights for huge movies, even if you don't know much about the fandom?" Forrest's dark gaze hit him.

"Nope." Sam had stopped that not long after residency started. Used residency as an excuse. After all, he'd always gone by himself most of the time. Forrest hadn't had the money for many extras. Even when they'd started dating, it had been rare they were both free on a Thursday or Friday night.

But with no one to come home and tell about the experience, what was the point?

"Ah," Forrest said. "I went to the last major superhero opening. Got to see everyone in costumes. I hadn't seen all the movies though, so I missed some of the subplots. But the special effects were unbelievable. As was the storyline about a virus turning someone into a supervillain."

"I didn't see any of those." Sam had meant to. And he'd bluffed his way through a conversation about them more than once with a young patient who came into the ER needing distraction from a broken bone, or other ailment. But Oliver had scoffed at seeing the first one with him and Sam hadn't argued because he wanted the man happy. He'd always wondered if he could have found ways to make Forrest happy if he'd stayed. Except Forrest had never *seemed* unhappy with their relationship until it ended, while Oliver had never been silent regarding any slight, perceived or real.

When the engagement ended the series had been several movies in and Sam had never gotten around to seeing them alone.

"Wow." Forrest took a deep breath. "Do you still cook?" He waited a minute and shook his head. "No, because for one person what is the point? That used to be my line."

"Doesn't make it untrue." Once upon a time Sam had taken pride in the meals he created. Most of them had worked, but the terrible mistakes had been highlights, too. "I'm pretty rusty on friend talk."

Forrest grabbed his juice and drank it down. "Guess it's a good thing we still have most of the winter to unlock you then." He gave Sam a wink but red was creeping up his neck.

At least Sam wasn't the only one struggling with this.

"I was planning to stop by the clinic today. Just to check in on stuff. Stay up-to-date in case you need anything from me."

Work talk. That was something Sam was good at. In fact it was pretty much the only type of conversation he'd had since his engagement ended.

Now, that was a sad thought.

"Good idea." His throat was tight, but he managed to push

out a question—after all, why should Forrest ask nearly all of them? "You still play the guitar?"

He'd gotten him one for Christmas when they were college roommates, after Forrest discussed how much he'd always wanted to learn. Had he thrown it away after they'd broken up?

"Yes. I brought one. It's in my room. Luckily there's no way I will annoy a roommate with my skills."

"Annoy? You were good at it. Do you not practice at all? Or are you just denigrating your talents?" It was the second one. Forrest never gave himself enough credit.

He stuck his tongue out at Sam. "I still prefer pop songs and they're not everyone's favorite. That's what I meant by annoy my roommate."

"Uh-huh." Now it was Sam's turn to raise his eyebrow. His chest loosened as Forrest playfully shook his head at him.

"The *point…*" Forrest pointed the spoon at him "…is yes. I still have the guitar. I even have an electric one, a bass guitar, and a drum set. The drums get no use. I bought them on a whim. Probably because my grandmother would have hated the bright red noisy thing. I keep thinking I will sell the set, but then I keep it—despite the fact that I can't keep time on it at all!"

"You can't keep time? Of course you can. You play guitar. You have great hands. I mean Dr. Poled wanted you to be a neurosurgeon so bad." Sam raised his hand. "Come on, Forrest."

"Keeping time for my guitar or the bass is *not* the same. I mean, you're supposed to hit multiple different drums or cymbals with different timing. I was steady in the surgical suite. That's not the same thing as keeping time. And Dr. Poled wanted me to go neuro because I was one of the only ones who excelled in it who wasn't an asshole. She hated the others, and I can't say that I blamed her."

"That field does have more than its fair share of people with God complexes. I think it's a necessity given that they are cutting into people's brains—literally."

"God complex or not, there's no reason to act like a jerk." Forrest grabbed his plate. "We need to get going."

Sam picked his tray up, too. It was time to go, but somehow in the space of half an hour they'd gone from awkward as hell to pseudo-normal.

And he'd enjoyed it.

Forrest looked over the selection of DVDs in the community room. He hadn't watched a DVD in forever, but the station's internet was reserved for research and contact with home. So people brought DVDs and left them here for others to enjoy when they had downtime.

He'd brought a handful of movies himself, but with the exception of a foreign film he loved, they were all repeats of the ones already here.

"Find anything good?"

Forrest didn't jump at Sam's voice. That was positive. Over the last week they'd eaten nearly every meal together. He'd stopped by the clinic a handful of times.

They were acting closer to friends. Sure, the ease they'd had once upon a time was gone. But then they weren't those people anymore. Too much had happened to the men they'd been to go on the same way.

Plus, the mild awkwardness that remained was a good reminder that the time on the ice was temporary.

"Find anything?" Sam repeated the question and slid up next to him to look at the stack. He smelled like fresh-cut grass.

So he still used the same soap. Forrest could practically see the green bar. A horrid color that stained the shower wall. But the smell was so perfect, Sam said it was worth it.

It is.

"Do I have to ask a third time? If you don't want to do movie night—"

"I want to do movie night," Forrest interrupted. "I just don't know what to select. I mean, 'anything good' means so many different things to different people."

And there would be others here tonight. Sam had said he was bringing the popcorn. Charlee was planning to hang out and Chris, one of the NPs for the clinic, had said he'd stop by. What movie should he select for a group like that? A rom-com? A comedy? Horror?

Not horror. There was a reason that stack was collecting dust on the side.

And not a superhero flick. That might alert Sam to the fact that Forrest was spending far too much of his time remembering every word he had said over the last few days.

"It's just a movie, Forrest." Sam squatted down next to him. His body so close. If either of them turned their head, their lips would—

Shut it down, Forrest.

During the week they'd spent eating breakfast and dinner together, his brain had brought forth all the old feelings. The ones that had never gone anywhere. He'd still loved Sam when he'd ended things, just wanted more for him.

Sam deserved the world. And he hadn't taken it.

"I know. But Charlee likes documentaries, Chris mentioned comedies, you like superheroes—or you did."

Sam laid his hand against Forrest's shoulder. "You're in charge of movie night tonight. That means you get to choose what you like."

Forrest rolled his eyes. If he wanted a crowd-pleaser, following his own taste was the worst way to find one. He'd only watched the one superhero movie he had seen because so many lab techs had been talking about it. Not because he'd really wanted to see it. "What *I* like is documentaries that the person standing next to me has repeatedly remarked are depressing." He focused on the collection. What was the right answer?

"You liking depressing documentaries was surprising. Given how you grew up, I was always stunned you didn't stick to happy films. Fluff." Sam squeezed Forrest's shoulder then moved his hand.

The ghost of the touch lay heavy on Forrest's heart.

Sam pulled back, a little. "There isn't a wrong answer."

"I know." Forrest let out a sigh as his gaze hovered on the selection.

"Do you?" Sam's hand started back toward him.

Forrest couldn't let him touch him again. The touches were comfort. Meaningless moments that his heart saw as anchors. He grabbed a movie and pulled out of Sam's reach.

"This one." He handed it to Sam hoping Sam wouldn't ask what movie he'd chosen because he didn't know.

Sam looked at the movie, pursed his lips and headed over to the player.

"What are we watching?" Charlee rounded the corner.

"Ever After." Sam held up the DVD of the Cinderella retelling.

Forrest knew the movie. Their suite mate in sophomore year had had a girlfriend that had watched it over and over again during finals week. She had sworn the Drew Barrymore movie was the best Cinderella story ever.

And I just grabbed it from the stack.

"Fun choice." Charlee grinned. "A fish may love a bird but where would they live."

Sam clapped. "She can quote the movie just like..." He put his hand on his chin and scrunched up his nose. "What was Dan's girlfriend's name? The one that had this on replay?"

"Rebecca." They'd married right after graduation. Forrest and Sam had danced together all night at their reception. Another good memory. His brain seemed incapable of keeping them buried.

"Oh. You guys went to college together?" Charlee grabbed one of the bags of popcorn and dumped some into the bowl she'd brought, then took a seat in one of the only single chairs.

"We lived together all through med school." Sam poured

popcorn into his own bowl and took the other chair. At least they wouldn't be crammed together on the couch all night.

"Who lived together? Oh, popcorn!" Chris had entered. He grabbed a bowl too and put a healthy amount of popcorn in it. "Now, who lived together? I love gossip."

"It's not gossip." Forrest shook his head. "Sam and I were freshman roommates, then we lived together through med school. He got an ER residency at the top trauma unit in New York City and I was sent to Seattle to work in immunology."

"You chose Seattle." Sam threw a piece of popcorn into his mouth. "It was a choice. Not a *sent.* You were their top pick and they were yours."

Forrest saw Charlee turn her gaze toward him but he wasn't going to say anything. After all, Sam was right. He'd listed Seattle first on his match list. The way the US medical system worked, the match was binding. But the truth was that every hospital program he'd listed was on the West Coast.

And he'd known that Sam had been planning to put several New York–based hospitals on his list. Given Sam's expertise, Forrest had known he'd end up at the other end of the country. And hopefully find someone there that had a plan. Someone who felt like they belonged in their chosen world, rather than someone like Forrest. An imposter. A person wearing a mask, acting like they'd found their place.

At the time stepping out of the way had seemed like a worthwhile sacrifice. Now he wasn't so sure.

"You two knew each other in college, stayed in touch and both ended up on the winter rotation here. That is so cool." Chris grabbed a fistful of popcorn and started munching.

They hadn't stayed in touch, but neither man spoke up. Thank goodness. Because if Chris really loved gossip, then that fact was bound to prick his interest.

"Movie time." Forrest grabbed the remote and pushed Play.

The title screen appeared along with music his brain could replay from memory.

Sam's hip buzzed.

"What's up?" Forrest pushed the pause button. "Does Nat need help?" The nurse practitioner was the only one on duty at the clinic tonight. Technically, the station called it a hospital, but the building was too small for Forrest to think of it that way.

"There was an accident in the motor pool. Several mechanics need stitching up." Sam frowned as he put his popcorn on the table. "There are at least four coming in."

"What the hell were they doing?" Chris groaned as he set his popcorn bowl down. "I was looking forward to movie night."

"Stay." Forrest hadn't even gotten popcorn for himself yet. "I'll help patch them up. Enjoy your evening."

Chris wasn't interested in arguing. "Thanks."

Forrest waited until he and Sam were out of hearing range. "I wanted you to have the life you wanted. The perfect family you dreamed of. That was why I went to Seattle."

"And yet we're both here. At the end of the world. Alone." Sam pulled on his coat and stepped out into the cold.

CHAPTER FIVE

THE LAB WAS quiet this morning. That was the way Forrest liked it. No questions. No judgment. His own little hidey-hole.

The lab he worked in back home had ten stations and unless he came in around five the noise level was always pretty high. Not because people weren't working but because the everyday movements of twelve or so people added up.

Today he'd walked to the lab around four. When it had become apparent that he wasn't going to sleep. Charlee was a late arrival person. That meant he had until at least nine on his own.

Coward.

He'd skipped breakfast. Or rather he was currently skipping breakfast. He and Sam had met in the canteen every day for the last week at six thirty. Usually they were the first and second people to grab food.

It had become a routine he enjoyed. Maybe too much.

Last night he and Sam had patched up the mechanics—who'd bet each other they could slide farther on the patch of ice out their door. All four of them had made it around the same distance and ended up with stitches in their legs, hands or both from the sharp ice.

A lesson learned. Maybe.

Antarctica was amazing. But the winter was also long and dark, and boredom set in easily.

Forrest would have liked to pretend boredom was why he wanted to march out of the lab right now and see if Sam was still eating breakfast. He might be hiding in the lab but he wasn't lying to himself. He liked hanging out with Sam. Loved it. It made him feel whole for the first time in a long time.

The lab door opened and Sam walked in. "I figured you might be hungry." He set the to-go box on the desk by the front door. "I even put a container of oatmeal in there and five packets of brown sugar."

"I don't need five packets." Forrest stuck his tongue out and walked over to the food. "Four is plenty."

Sam grinned and put his hands in his pockets. "Sorry about what I said last night."

Forrest just nodded. He hadn't been wrong. They were both at the end of the world—alone.

"I feel like one of us is always apologizing and I feel like it's usually me." He let out a breath. "I missed you and there's still part of me that's pushing you away."

Forrest opened the box. Four packets of brown sugar sat next to the oatmeal. The exact right amount.

"The extra one is in my pocket." Sam pulled the little packet out. "Just in case."

"Thanks." Forrest got the oatmeal ready. "I was actually just thinking about stopping down there for food."

Sam nodded. "I figured you were working. Now that I'm here, I'm realizing I never asked." He coughed and looked down before meeting Forrest's gaze, "What *are* you working on in here while you're hiding? I mean, you said immunology in isolation, but I honestly have no idea what that means. I thought your company worked on new prescription drugs."

Forrest understood why he hadn't asked. Other than his admission of why he'd swapped the bedside for lab work and Sam's acknowledgment of his failed engagement, they'd kept the conversation topics light.

He took a bite of the sausage Sam had added to his breakfast. Swallowing, he pointed to the electron microscope. "They do work on drugs, but also on other government and private projects. Plus the information gleaned from this could benefit new drug development. But the focus here is viral load changes in small populations. It's a major concern for space travel. And things like long submarine stints, even research stations like this. In theory, fewer people equals fewer germs and fewer chances for a virus to mutate. However, no matter how careful you are, germs are coming into your environment. So, what if one mutates and is able to run through the whole population, or close to it?"

Sam crossed his arms, tilting his head, but he didn't say anything.

So Forrest continued, "On a submarine, you could surface and get aid. At the station, we have meds and can self-isolate. But what about on a space station? Or on a rocket to Mars? On a Martian outpost? For humans to have successful space flight, we have to understand the immunology changes that happen. How do our immune systems change in isolation?"

"You think we will have an outpost on Mars?"

Forrest chuckled. Sam wasn't the first person to ask that question about his research. "I doubt it. At least not in our lifetimes. But eventually? Maybe. Humans are curious creatures. We want to explore. The earth is known. At least that's what people will tell you. I think there are still so many mysteries to discover and solve."

"Research with an outcome you won't see." Sam shook his head. "I don't think I could do it. I want answers. Now."

"That isn't true. You live in a world of uncertainty in the emergency room." Forrest finished off the oatmeal and put the trash in the special container every room had. Everything that entered the station was taken off. Nothing was left. It was an interesting program designed to protect the South Pole as much as possible.

"No. That isn't true. I know what the outcomes are."

"But you don't." Forrest had seen it so many times during the med school emergency room rotation. During every rotation. “Everyone thinks doctors have all the answers. Hell, even some doctors think we have all the answers. That with enough tests, enough scans, enough something, we will unlock whatever the mystery is.”

“I am not talking about internal medicine or neuro or some other unique specialty, Forrest. I know there aren’t enough tests sometimes.” Sam’s fingers were clenched on his arms. His shoulders tight.

Forrest reached over, pulled a hand loose. The connection burned as he forced Sam to relax. “What happens to the patient when they leave your emergency room? When the car crash victim gets home, when the drunk who dented their head detoxes and heads out, when the teen boy who broke his arm jumping from the roof into the pool gets another wild idea?”

“That’s different.” Sam flexed the hand Forrest had touched, then released it.

“How?” Forrest looked at the lab he enjoyed so much. “I know that I’m making a difference. But exactly what that difference is? No human can truly know that. Your job is to stabilize people. Then they move on. Hopefully, you provide something that will stick with them.”

He shrugged as Sam looked toward the lab. He’d done a rotation in the ER. Patients cycled in and out. Some came in so often the staff knew more about them than their friends or family. Others came once and you never saw them again.

“What’s the coolest thing you’ve seen in that microscope?” Sam’s words were barely audible.

Whether he meant to ask the question or not, Forrest knew the answer. “Yersinia pestis.”

Sam’s head swung back toward him. The man’s perfect mouth was hanging open. “Black death. Your answer is the black death?”

“It’s the bacteria responsible for the plague. I studied under the scientist that basically confirmed the bacteria was responsible for wiping out more than half of the European population."

Forrest stood and grabbed Sam's hand as he pulled him toward the lab.

"If you have that bacteria here, I do not want to see it." Sam chuckled but he didn't let go.

"I don't." He turned the microscope on, and pulled a slide onto the deck, a little awkwardly since his hand was still holding Sam's.

"This is the virus that took out the station." He pointed to the edge of the virus. At magnification of one hundred thousand, the virus was well defined.

Sam dropped his hand but he didn't step away.

"Charlee's virus looks different in the edges from the other samples. That is where the mutation happened." He pulled the slide out and slid the one with Charlee's sample on it. He gestured to the same edge. "See the difference here?"

"No." Sam tilted his head. "But I don't need to." He took a step closer.

He's just getting a better look at the microscope.

His scent filled Forrest's lungs. Sam. His heartbeat pounded in his ears as he stared at the only man he'd ever loved. The only person who'd loved his flawed self.

"Never forget—" Sam didn't look at the microscope; his gaze was rooted on Forrest "—just how smart you are. A genius."

"Hardly," Forrest scoffed, "I left the bedside and had to do something to pay the bills. These are influenza samples, if you looked, you'd see—"

Sam's finger was laid over his lips.

Whatever he'd been about to say evaporated from Forrest's tongue. All he could focus on was the gray-blue tones in the eyes holding him.

"You are brilliant." Sam took a deep breath and pulled his hand away.

There were no words coming to mind. Nothing but the two of them. The tiny space between them burned.

Sam's lips were so close, the moment frozen. Sam leaned closer.

The door to the lab opened and Charlee entered, letting out a sigh.

Sam jumped back, whatever the moment was about to be gone in an instant.

"I swear Mondays are terrible no matter where you are in the world. Even at the end of it." Charlee hung her coat on the hook by the door before finally recognizing that Sam was in the lab standing next to Forrest.

"Doctor Miller? Is Forrest boring you with the tiny hook difference on my sample? It *is* there. But you have to look really close. Really, really close." She laughed and winked at Forrest. "Only he would spot it. Though he won't take credit."

"It's not boring. I am not surprised by the credit thing, though." Sam cut Forrest a look before taking another step back. " I should head to the clinic."

"Thanks for bringing breakfast. I appreciate it." Forrest swallowed his desire and the dozens of questions pooling in his brain.

"You're welcome but it was a one-time thing. Tomorrow, eat in the canteen. Time away from here is good, too."

"Hear, hear." Charlee offered Sam a high five which he took as he headed out the door. "I like him."

"Yeah." Forrest nodded and turned his focus back to the microscope. They'd nearly kissed. That was where the moment was leading. Wasn't it?

Forrest ran a finger over his lips then shook his head. As if that would force the thoughts of Sam loose, thoughts that had lodged there since he'd seen him on the ship.

"Maybe you should ask him out? You guys seem to get on well."

He was not discussing Sam. Not with Charlee or anyone else. Forrest pointed to the edge of the virus. "It's a tiny adjustment, but it is important. This was likely what made you so ill, and the hook may be why it wasn't as capable of spreading. Hardly boring."

Charlee tilted her head. "Okay, I get the point. No personal talk."

He'd nearly kissed Forrest. That was where the moment was leading yesterday. Sam had stood in the lab fascinated by the impressive work his former love was doing.

How Forrest could consider his life path a failure was beyond him. Maybe he thought that because he missed bedside. He'd been great at it. If Sam got him to see that he needed to give it another chance, maybe Forrest would realize where he really belonged.

Sam raised a finger to his lips. If Charlee hadn't walked in, he'd have leaned all the way in.

The skin on Sam's finger still burned from touching Forrest's lips. It had been an automatic reaction; the deep-seated need to silence Forrest's self-deprecations.

But once he'd touched him… Sam swallowed as he looked at the lab work in front of him. A patient had an infection in a tooth.

The station's dentist, Dr. Abrams, had pulled the aching tooth, but that hadn't fixed the infection. And neither had the antibiotics Dr. Abrams had ordered.

Maybe Forrest has an idea?

Sam shook his head. There was no reason to ask Forrest. Not yet. Sam was in control of the clinic. This was why he'd been hired. He'd worked alone in so many places. He could figure it out, if his brain would focus on the numbers.

Or I could stop being ridiculous and ask the internal medicine doctor.

Sam's hand went for the phone on the desk. The headset was heavy in his hand. It might be nice to pretend that was because, before coming to the South Pole, he hadn't used a landline telephone for years. It wasn't like there was cell service here.

Now I'm thinking about a phone rather than calling the man who can take a look at this and figure it out.

"Any chance you have something for me to do?" Forrest asked the question as he was pushing the door of the clinic open. His lips were pursed. "I have three lab tests running. There's nothing to do for the next twelve hours. Staring at tubes is not very exciting."

Sam opened his mouth but didn't know what to say. It was like he'd conjured the man of his dreams.

At exactly the right time.

"Were you calling someone?" Forrest pointed to the phone in Sam's hand.

Sam finally registered the sound of the busy tone that meant the phone had been off the hook for too long.

"You. I was calling you." He set the phone back on the receiver. "Dr. Abrams pulled a tooth from one of the scientists two days ago. Raging infection in the jaw."

Forrest made a face. "I am glad dentists exist—I can't stand teeth. Something about them." He shuddered and rocked back on his heels, then raised his hands. "So no help with mouths."

"Actually, it's the bacteria I need help with. It's resistant to the antibiotic Dr. Abrams prescribed." Sam passed the tablet chart to Forrest. His arm vibrated as Forrest's thumb brushed his finger taking the chart.

Damn.

A simple touch was enough to light his entire body up.

"Bacteria?" Forrest looked over the notes on the chart.

"Yeah. And given our location and the limits of our stocks, Dr. Abrams wants to make sure the next one we give the patient isn't ignored by the bacteria, too. If this was a summer stint, the scientist would have been on a flight out to have oral surgery. But." Sam shrugged.

Everyone here knew the risks. If you came in the winter and had an emergency, there were no guarantees the weather would hold for you to be evacced. In fact, the odds were good no plane would arrive.

That did nothing to alleviate the pit in Sam's stomach. Every time you used an antibiotic against a resistant bacterium, there was a chance it created a superbug that was even more resistant.

"You have carbapenems?"

"Yeah. And tigecycline, doxycycline and a few doses of zosurabalpin." Sam had gone over their inventory of antibiotics used to treat resistant bacteria this morning. There were several, but it was still early in the season. If there were multiple patient needs—

He shut that thought down. No need to borrow worry.

Forrest looked at the tablet and closed his eyes, probably running through the mental storage cabinets in his brain. He didn't open his eyes as he started, "There is a good chance this a streptococcus oralis bacteria, given that it's the most prevalent cause of periodontal infections. According to a British study, twenty-seven percent of those are resistant to penicillin and amoxicillin. However, that study also found that only seven percent of the strains were resistant to clindamycin."

"I've got that. And the dental office has it, too." Sam picked up the phone, this time dialing the number with no hesitation. He relayed the information Forrest had given to Dr. Abrams and set the phone down. "For someone who doesn't care about mouths and teeth, you pulled out a pretty specific statistic."

Color rushed to Forrest's cheeks as he passed the tablet back. Once again, their fingers brushed and the fire that hadn't died from last time exploded.

Sam's chest tightened, his heart cried out and his brain couldn't find any of the reasons he'd kept as a mantra for why he needed to keep his distance.

"I'm an internal medicine specialist who works in immunology. My reading list on antibiotics is deep. Not exactly light bedtime reading, but it comes in handy." Forrest pulled his lip between his teeth for a moment.

"No fiction? Sci-fi? Fantasy? I seem to remember you reading fantasy novels with witches, vampires, feys, back when we lived together." A smile touched Sam's lips as he said the last words.

Forrest looked toward the clinic door, but instead of heading for it, he took a step closer to the desk. "When I shifted out of the bedside to the lab, I put the fiction away."

He punished himself for making a change.

It was something his grandmother would have done. If you fail, then you lose something. The man needed to be back at bedside, needed to realize he *wasn't* a failure.

And there was no reason Sam couldn't find an excuse to have Forrest here in the clinic. He was good at planning. Good at sculpting life…as long as it wasn't his love life.

Sam stepped around the desk. "Forrest." He reached for his hands. There was no word to describe the rush of joy that poured through him when Forrest didn't pull away.

"You—"

The alarm on the wall echoed. Both men jumped back.

"What the hell is that?" Forrest looked at the red light as Sam picked up the phone on the first ring.

"Where?" Sam took the emergency information and set the phone back on the receiver.

Forrest was behind him as Sam took off running. "What are we running for?"

"We need bandages, wound care and anything else we have to treat burns. Fire suppression failed in the maintenance room. Two patients. One burned badly, the other unknown. I don't know what badly means." That would be Forrest's next question, so Sam was just going to answer it now.

It was a fair question, but one he hadn't had time to ask.

"We prepped for burn care?"

That answer to that was *It depends.* The station called the clinic the general hospital, but it wasn't a hospital by most people's definitions. "For second-degree superficial, yes. Full second-degree and third..." Sam swallowed the worry. There were a lot of *ifs* right now, but this was what he'd trained for. Emergency critical care. "We are a critical care unit, but I have no surgeons, no MRI or CT scanner. If infection sets in or there is nerve damage... Well, we will cross that bridge if we get to it."

They gathered the materials, laid them out and then started for the front door. He'd waited for patients in the receiving bay a handful of times before, when he worked in trauma care in New York City. But it was an activity more reserved for television dramas than real life.

"If, Sam? Infection comes with burns. That's what burns do." Forrest spoke the truth as they headed for the front door.

With burns, crossing the bridge to infection was a near certainty. Second- and third-degree burns ripped away the protective layer of epidermis. And if they needed to do skin grafts, there were no supplies here.

The wind whipped Sam's face as he stared into the darkness. He'd wanted a reason for Forrest to be in the clinic. Now he had one. Sometimes it was best not to wish for anything.

"You can smell the smoke." Forrest stood next to him. "The ambulance isn't here yet. That isn't a good sign."

"I know." Sam bit out the words. His fingers tapped against the scrubs he was wearing. Neither of them had thrown on their coats. He'd expected to have sight of at least one of the two ambulances on their way to the clinic. Expected to stand outside for no more than a few moments.

"We have to go inside." Forrest grabbed Sam's arm, squeezing it. "Now."

Sam let Forrest pull him back in. He wanted to get to the patients as soon as possible. With burn care, or any emergency care, time was of the essence. But if he and Forrest stood outside too long, frost bite was certain, and that wouldn't do their patients any good.

"Sam!" Natasha pushed through the front door. "You can smell the smoke, and I heard the alarm in my dorm room."

"Thanks for coming. Head into the clinic—get prepped for

burn patients. We've already pulled supplies. I've got Forrest with me to meet the patients. When the critical patients get here, we need to be as ready as possible."

"Critical." Natasha's voice was low, but she rushed past them. "I'll call Chris."

"This is going to be a long night," Sam breathed out.

"It isn't just tonight. What are the odds of an evac?" Forrest's voice was low, too.

He knew the answer. Or at least had to suspect it. It was one thing to sign papers saying you understood the risk you were taking. Another to be face-to-face with the consequences.

"Almost zero. At least historically. I got Anderson out on the last flight for a reason. In previous winters, there have been exactly two evacs from McMurdo. The good news is that we aren't at Amundsen-Scott. The answer there is zero."

"Not zero is something we can work with," Forrest stated as they heard the ambulance pull up and stepped back outside.

"Doc!" Frank Opalin, the station's head paramedic, was speaking as soon as he opened the door of the ambulance. "Mark's arm is bad. We loaded him first. But I got another on the way. That one isn't as bad but..." Frank pulled the stretcher out.

Mark's arm was elevated; his shirt had been cut away and wet bandages covered the arm. Tears were running down his face.

"I gave him pain meds." Frank held up the clipboard so Sam could see the exact amount. "Not that it's helping much."

That was actually a good sign. Not that Sam was going to waste time voicing it right now. If there was pain, it meant the nerves were still active. In the long run Mark would be happy about that. But it was little comfort now.

"I've got the next one." Forrest raised his chin. "See you in there."

Sam nodded and followed the gurney carrying Mark into the clinic.

CHAPTER SIX

"I KNOW IT hurts but we have to keep the arm elevated." Forrest made sure he kept his face devoid of emotion as he started redressing Mark's wound. Sam was on the other side of their patient, evaluating the burns Mark had sustained while pulling away from the fire.

The last four hours had been about stabilizing. But in order to keep the arm clean they were going to have change the dressings regularly, particularly because the wound was already seeping fluid through the bandages. Not the best sign, but not unexpected.

"I am going to up your morphine drip and give you a sedative." Sam said the words but Forrest wasn't sure Mark truly registered what he was saying. He'd told them not to sedate him when he came in. That he needed answers.

Informed consent was important, but with Mark in so much pain, Forrest knew the man wasn't able to focus on his care. The request to stay awake was just a sign of shock, of the fear that if you went to sleep something bad would happen.

It took a few minutes, but the sedative Sam placed in the IV took hold.

"The burns on his feet are superficial, thanks to his shoes, but the one on his side… It's deepening." Sam crossed his arms as he looked at Forrest.

"Deepening to superficial second-degree or into full partial thickness?" Most people didn't realize that burns could get worse over the course of hours or even days after the initial intake. Particularly when they were more than superficial.

"I am hoping we can keep it at superficial." Sam took a deep breath.

"*We* can't do anything but wait." Forrest waited for Sam to meet his gaze. It took a minute, but Sam finally met his eyes. "The burns will be what they will be. We can keep him comfortable and do our best to prevent infection. The rest is out of our hands right now."

There was nothing to do but wait and worry. This scenario. This dread and uncertainty. This was the reason Forrest had failed at bedside.

Sam nodded, but the twitch in his cheek meant the message hadn't been well received. Sam was a doctor dedicated to getting his patients the best care. It was admirable, but there were some things no doctor could fix. Sam needed to focus on what they could control, not what he wanted to control.

"His arm…" Sam didn't finish the sentence. But there wasn't any need.

Forrest understood. The side was bad, and maybe getting worse. With the arm, they already knew the worst was here.

Mark needed at least one skin graft by the elbow. It was possible his forearm was going to need one, too. Luckily his fingers were surface burns, sustained when he'd pushed the blazing equipment off his arm. A small miracle that was hard to focus on when there was no way they could offer the necessary procedures here. And the storm that had set in just after they'd gotten Mark and his fellow mechanic Adina into the clinic meant the odds of an evac in the next forty-eight hours was zero. And probably not much better than that for at least the next week.

"Right now we focus on pain reduction and infection control." Forrest kept his repeated words quiet. Sam falling into what-ifs and worries wasn't going to help the patient.

Plus, Adina was in the other bay. She would be listening in, hoping to hear what was happening with her friend. The pair had partnered at the south pole for two summer seasons. This was their first winter over.

"Is he going to be okay?" The call came over the curtain.

Sam looked at the curtain and frowned. "I can't tell you anything, Adina. It's protocol."

"Protocol my ass!" Adina was shifting in her bed.

Forrest started toward the other bay and knew Sam was following him. He rounded the corner and hoped his smile looked comforting and not panicked.

She wasn't going to like the words Sam was delivering. "Adina, we can't give patient care out to nonfamily members."

"We are family." The woman crossed her arms and let out a hiss as she rubbed the burns on her fingers. Luckily, her wounds were mostly superficial. There was one they were watching, a burn on her shin from an ember catching on her pants while she pulled Mark to safety. Though it wasn't second-degree, it was close. But she didn't need a skin graft. Her recovery was going to be rough, but a hell of a lot easier than Mark's.

She pointed to the bay where Mark was in the medicinally induced nap. "Family does not mean dating. It does not mean married or screwing." She sucked in a deep breath. "We are friends. Best friends. His wife divorced him a year ago and I have no interest in a relationship. We're neighbors back home, run a mechanics training business when we aren't here."

"I understand, Adina." Forrest said the words before Sam could. Because from him, they were the truth.

Sam had a family that loved him. Something Forrest was so grateful for.

But Forrest had no family. His grandmother was meeting whatever fate waited in the afterlife. He had no idea who his father was and no interest in taking any commercial DNA tests to possibly find out. His mother had bounced in and out of jail for most of his life for petty and not so petty financial crimes. Last he'd heard she was serving twenty for the latest insurance fraud she'd run.

Sam had been his family long before they were dating. And rekindling their friendship had wiped away so much of the loneliness that had been his only companion for years.

A tear slipped down Adina's cheek. "I am his family. So tell me, please."

Forrest's heart squeezed as Sam swallowed.

"I am bound by HIPAA here. I can't give you details." Sam's jeweled gaze met his.

Forrest weighed the risk and stepped around Sam. If it cost him, it cost him. "He needs a procedure we can't do here."

He felt Sam tense beside him, but he didn't say anything.

"A skin graft." Adina nodded. "I know burns, man. You don't work in heavy machinery and mechanics without seeing injuries." She closed her eyes and shook as tears streamed down her cheeks. "The weather means evac is impossible for at least a week."

"It might not be a week," Sam interrupted and was rewarded with a glare when Adina opened her eyes.

"You're right. It's probably a lot longer than that."

Sam lowered his head. There were no comforting words rushing into Forrest's mind to help the situation. Sam couldn't control the weather. No amount of planning would magically make an evac appear when the visibility and wind made any flight so dangerous.

"Do you want a sedative? With the burns and the worry I doubt you'll get much sleep, and your body needs it for healing." Sam took a step toward the medicine cabinet as the silence stretched between them all.

Forrest wanted to push. Wanted to urge Adina to accept the sedation. Sam was right; it would help her recover. Her burns were not as substantial as Mark's, but her body still had a lot of repair to accomplish. But in his experience combative patients did not appreciate the push.

"Why, so you can discuss his procedures and needs without me hearing?" And Adina was hostile. Hostile on behalf of her friend, but still hostile.

"I know you're mad about the requirements that are legally in place. When Mark wakes, we can ask him to sign documentation agreeing to have you as a care partner. That's all I can offer right now, but I understand your reaction." Sam moved next to the bed, medication in his hand.

"Do you? Do you have a friend that, if they were hurt, you'd want to know everything? *Need* to do everything to make sure that they were okay. That you would run through fire for… literally." Adina glared at the medication then back at Sam.

"Yes." Sam answered with no hesitation. "I have someone who is incredibly special to me. Who would make me feel exactly the way you do. I understand the anger and frustration." Sam took a deep breath as he kept his gaze on Adina.

"Take the medication, Adina. Get the rest. Fight for Mark tomorrow." Forrest heard himself say the words, but it was like he was watching a movie, not participating in the event. He was outside looking in.

He tried to stop the buzzing in his ears. Tried to shut off the feeling ripping through him. Sam had said he'd kept to himself since his engagement ended. That he had no friends. That he was a lone wolf now. Forrest had had to force him into this friendship.

But there was someone. Someone special to him. Someone he hadn't told Forrest about. Someone he'd kept hidden.

They were exes. He could hardly demand full entry into Sam's life. The jealousy in the pit of his stomach was unfair. He should be happy. Joyful even. Sam hadn't cut himself completely out of people's lives.

But all he wanted to do was scream. Demand to know why he'd said there was no one.

Instead, Forrest looked at Adina, holding her gaze. "Take it."

Her glare didn't let up, but she did nod and look at Sam.

"Fine. But I will make sure that Mark tells you both that we are family and signs whatever you need, because he is going to need an advocate here."

"I know you will." Sam pushed the meds into her system and after a few minutes she was yawning and slipping into slumber.

Forrest moved toward the door. "I think my skills aren't needed right now. We should save our strength for the rotation we're going to need to maintain for Mark and Adina's care. Give me a ring if anything changes." He needed to leave. Needed to gather himself. A few minutes to handle the passion he'd heard in Sam's voice as he spoke about this unknown friend.

A few minutes to push past the wish that it was him.

"Wait!" Sam held up his hand as Forrest was heading for the door. The outburst was unplanned, but he also didn't want him to leave.

He'd meant what he said to Adina. If something happened to Forrest, despite the distance, the time, all of life between them, he'd need to know.

"What?" Forrest tilted his head as he leaned against the door.

The man had no right to look so enticing after such a long shift. His dark hair was rumpled and there were shadows under his eyes, but he was still so lovely to gaze at.

"I meant it, you know." Sam bit his lip to stop everything else from bursting forth.

"Meant what?" Forrest never moved from the doorway. Never adjusted his position.

"Come on, Forrest." Sam blew out a breath. "I said it once and I said it with passion and honestly, I don't remember all the words at the moment. But come *on*."

Forrest's face shifted, those dark eyes capturing Sam's own. The uncertainty Sam saw there nearly destroyed him. How could Forrest never think he was enough? Never consider that good words were about him?

"I really don't know what you mean, Sam. It's been a long day."

"If it was me in that bed and you in Adina's position, would you need to know?" Sam took a deep breath then kept going, "Would you fight to get an answer? Even if it wasn't a full one. Enough to know what was happening?"

"Yes." Now Forrest shifted, but didn't close any distance. "If it was you, I would need to know. I probably wouldn't have sat in the bed. I would have been in the way, being the reason every physician hates having family members with medical backgrounds in the room. Why?"

"You are so dense. So damn dense." Sam moved. If Forrest wouldn't leave the doorway, then Sam would go to him. "*You* are the person I was telling Adina about. You are the one that I need to know is safe." He balled his fists wanting to beat them against Forrest's chest—to punch each line into his heart.

"I… I figured it was someone you met after we parted."

"We didn't part." Sam shook his head. "*You* broke my heart and walked away." He sucked air into his lungs. This wasn't the place. Wasn't the time. Wasn't anything. But damn, getting the words out released a bubble of tension he hadn't known his soul had kept a hold of so long.

"Sam—"

"No. I don't need words from you, right now. I just need you to finally understand why being your friend is so damn hard. But also impossible to give up." He stepped back, "Also you were great at bedside today. I know you feel like you failed there before, but the doctor you were tonight was perfection. *You* were perfect."

Work. An easy topic. A necessary one. And one that could put distance between them. That was safe-ish. That might keep all the emotions he'd trapped so long ago from spilling out of his chest.

"Tonight was awful," he went on, "but there is no one I would rather have stood with tonight. Even if you did kinda give out information about a patient you shouldn't have." He winked, hoping this would diffuse the rumbling feelings still trying to burst their way through.

Forrest pursed his lips and looked toward the bays where Mark and Adina slept. "Technically, all I said was he needed a procedure we couldn't do here. She guessed. And we didn't give details. It's not technically a HIPAA violation."

"It skirts the rules." Sam looked to the bays. "I seem to remember that was something you did more than once at bedside. Found ways to make sure people got care even after insurance or a hospital administrator said no."

Most of the interns had followed every protocol human resources demanded. Not wanting to step out of place, even a hair. Even Sam.

Sam was willing to go out on a limb, occasionally. When he knew winning was a certainty. But Forrest had taken risks. Even knowing it might cost him residency recommendations.

"I was always able to rise to an emergency situation. Doesn't mean I can do it full-time." Forrest made to cross his arms but didn't. He rolled on his heels but didn't head out of the door.

Now Sam did put his fist to Forrest's chest, ignoring the lightning bolts traipsing up his arm with each touch as he punctuated his thoughts. "Stop selling yourself short, Forrest. Just stop."

Forrest's hand was warm as he gripped Sam's fist. "Take a breath."

"Not until you admit that you are damn good at this." Sam didn't pull away from Forrest's touch. And he didn't drop his hand.

"Planning to hold your breath to make your point?" Forrest raised an eyebrow. If they weren't in the clinic and reacting to a night full of emotions, Sam might just lean in and kiss the handsome man standing opposite him.

"Maybe that's exactly what I will do." Sam inhaled but

couldn't stop the chuckles as Forrest bent over and let out a belly laugh, too.

The laughter carried. It was a good thing both their patients were on sedatives.

"You two losing it?" Chris stomped in, hanging his coat on the hanger and stripping off his heavy snow boots and sliding on the tennis shoes he kept at the clinic.

"Maybe." Forrest stepped away from Sam's touch.

Sam watched him flex his hand. Watched him put it in his pocket and turn to Chris. Had the connection felt as fiery to him?

"It was a long night. The first of many, I suspect." Forrest looked over his shoulder at the bay. "I'll be part of the rotation for as long as they're here."

"Starting to feel like you're a real part of the team." Chris hit Forrest on the shoulder.

Sam looked at Forrest and nodded. He was part of the team. An important part of it. He was grateful someone else was pointing it out.

"Fill me on the patients then you head out too, Doc. 'Cause I expect to have you and Natasha here relieving me first thing tomorrow." Chris pointed toward Forrest. "Of course if you're on the rotation, then we can run two shifts of full staff. Actually, that's a good idea, I'm calling Nat. I know she works night shift at home anyway. You two pop in here tomorrow on time."

"Did we just get orders from the NP?" Forrest raised a brow.

"Yep. And if you know many NPs, then you know not to argue." Chris crossed his arms.

Forrest held up his hands. "No plan to argue. And I meant what I said. I'll see you tomorrow." He looked to Sam. "Good night, Sam."

The cool burst of air the snow doors didn't capture hit Sam, and the ember of hope that Forrest might hang out long enough for him to debrief Chris flamed out.

CHAPTER SEVEN

MARK'S ARM LOOKED bad the next morning. That wasn't a surprise. But at least it didn't look as bad as Sam had feared it might. The skin sloughing was expected.

"You gonna tell me how bad it is?" Mark crossed his good hand over his stomach. "I mean the drugs are keeping the edge off, but I know I need a skin graft."

"Adina tell you?" Sam had wanted to broach that topic himself. Let Mark ask any questions he might have and hopefully control any worry the man would understandably have about the situation. But Mark had signed the paperwork granting his friend access as soon he'd woken and she'd already known.

"No. She is lying to me. Says I'm fine."

"I heard that," Adina called over the curtain.

"I meant you to," Mark yelled back, though his voice wasn't as solid as Adina's.

Sam looked to the door. Forrest had grabbed a few samples from Mark's arm first thing to look for infection. Normally they'd wait until they got the first signs of it but given the need for an evac that wasn't coming, they were going to be checking several times a day.

Evac wasn't coming this week and probably not next week, either. If they pretreated with antibiotics, there was a worry that the bacteria would adjust and they'd run out of treatment options before an evac was possible. So they were doing everything they could to stay ahead of it. With any luck they could prevent it or catch it in its infancy.

"Come on, Doc. Tell the truth." Mark's eyes filled with tears but they didn't fall as he lifted his chin.

This was what Forrest struggled with. This was the part of bedside work that everyone hated. But it was necessary.

"You need at least two skin grafts on your arm. And maybe one on your thigh from where you were dragged across the room."

"You hear that, Adina? You did such a piss-poor job of dragging me that I need a patch on my thigh. You're going to owe me beers for life." Mark chuckled but he brushed the lone tear sliding down his cheek away.

"Nah," Adina called out. "You panicked when you caught fire. If you hadn't wussed out then maybe it wouldn't be so bad. I owe you beer for a year. Tops."

"Two years."

At least Adina's jabs were keeping Mark's mood up. Or as up as it could be in the circumstances.

Forrest walked in and marched over to the bay. Then he pushed the curtain back so the two patients had a full view of each other. "I can hear you two yelling before I even get close to the building."

There was no way that was true with the wind. But Sam suspected you could hear them as soon as the outer door opened.

"Just trying to be normal since someone got themself burned to a crisp." Adina glared at her friend. Sam wasn't sure if it was meant to be playful or not.

"Took them long enough to open the curtain." Mark rolled his eyes before looking at Forrest. "What's the outcome, Doc Two?"

"Doc Two?" Forrest looked up from the clipboard he was carrying with the results. It was old-school but with the weather right now the internet was even worse than usual.

Sam let out a relieved sigh and saw Mark's eyes flick to him.

"You annoyed that Doc Two is avoiding my answer?"

"Nope. If Doc Two, as you call him, is asking a question not related to care, then that workup came back as clean as possible." Sam grinned. It was one of Forrest's tells when they were in med school. If the prognosis was good, he was willing to entertain a little diversion. If not…

Well, if not, the man was all business.

Forrest blew out a breath. "Your labs—"

"I called you Doc Two because this guy—" Mark pointed at Sam as he interrupted Forrest "—is Doc. I can't say Doc to you as well, so you are Doc Two."

"All right." Forrest's brows knitted together. "Your labs."

"I think my jokes are fab."

"They aren't." Adina laughed.

Mark shifted in the bed and winced. He was on enough pain medication to be as comfortable as possible. But there was no way for them to keep him lucid without some residual pain. "I know the results are good. Because Doc seems to know you well. And I'm only going to get good news on rare occasions. I need to savor the moment." Mark pinched his eyes shut. "Damn it, there's no reason for tears."

"Tears provide a release to your parasympathetic nervous system. Your body uses it to self-soothe and regulate your emotions." Forrest stepped closer to the bed. "You're correct. This lab is good. It shows the wet bandages are keeping the infection at bay. I may not be able to say the same thing tomorrow, or even this afternoon. But, putting off good news to savor it is normal. And crying is normal."

"Has the home base started recommending removing the arm, since evac may be weeks away?" Mark sucked in a breath as he looked at Forrest, dread clear in his eyes.

Forrest looked to Sam. This was an answer he couldn't give. Technically Forrest was on staff here, but this was not his full-time position.

"We are way off from that discussion." They weren't. And

Mark was right. His bosses back in Houston had given the advice that they may need to amputate. Their email indicated they were already thinking of it as an inevitability.

Amputation was risky, too. If it came to it, Sam would be able to follow his field training but he was not a general surgeon. Years ago, an orthopedic surgeon had used the remote telemedicine connection to coach a doctor at Amundsen-Scott through repairing a knee. The Center for Polar Medical Operations was already looking for a specialist to do the same for Sam. But it wasn't going to come to that.

It wasn't. He wouldn't allow it. He and Forrest could keep the arm infection-free and the weather would break. It had to.

He saw Forrest's head shift toward him out of the corner of his eye but didn't look in his direction.

Mark took a deep breath and closed his eyes. "That's good to hear. Two pieces of good news. Good day." He closed his eyes. "I'm going to try to take a nap. Okay?"

"Sure," Sam stated.

"Absolutely," Forrest answered at the same time.

"I was talking to the mouthy woman in the bay next to me, Doc and Doc Two. Appreciate the support, though." Mark gave a thumbs up with his good hand and closed his eyes.

"If you can't sleep, I can provide another sedative." The best thing for Mark was for his body to rest. However, that was easier said than done when the body could only focus on pain—even pain curbed by the drugs in his system.

Mark didn't open his eyes, but he shook his head. "I'm gonna try and do this without those, at least for a nap."

Sam nodded even though Mark couldn't see him. Then he stepped around the bed, stepped into the bay next to Mark and closed the curtain.

"You don't have to worry. I won't try to keep him awake." Adina blew out a breath as she looked at the curtain separating them.

Forrest stepped in and offered a smile. “We know that, Adina. But we need to discuss your care.”

Sam saw Forrest look over the tablet chart. He’d taken responsibility for her care, so it was his job to do the discharge.

“You’re going to be sore for a few days. But the good news is the burn we were worried about didn’t deepen.”

“So I don’t need an evac?” Adina looked at the closed curtain.

Forrest shook his head, “No. I’m going to give you antibiotics. It’s very important that you take them. Your recovery should be fairly easy, at least compared to Mark’s.”

“Which is your way of saying get out.” Adina sat up and looked over to where Mark was trying to sleep.

“You can come back anytime.” Forrest didn’t look at Sam as he bluntly spoke against the actual clinic policy. “I know we have visiting hours and everything, but we will make an exception for you to check on Mark.”

No hesitation. No worry that Sam might balk. Of course he wouldn’t. Mark needed to know that he could have company anytime. It was good for his soul.

But even if Sam hadn’t been willing to break the rules, Forrest would have found a way.

“Doc all right with that?” Adina focused her gaze on Sam as she waited for confirmation.

“I am.”

She pushed a tear from her cheek. “It isn’t that I don’t trust you.”

Forrest nodded. “Of course. You just need to see for yourself.”

“My brother…” She hiccupped, “My parents accepted everything the doctor said. Didn’t question the discharge. Didn’t point out that he was so good at hiding pain because of his chronic issues. And…” Adina stopped and looked back at Forrest, “I will be Mark’s advocate. You will be so sick of seeing me.”

“I look forward to you keeping us on our toes. An extra set

of eyes that knows him better than we ever will is appreciated." Sam understood what had happened with her brother without her completing the sentence.

He also understood how it could happen. Hospitals were busy places. In the US, many hospitals were run by private equity firms that prioritized profits over patients. When you combined that with insurance companies demanding tons of paperwork to justify every extra night in a hospital, it was far too easy for a patient who was good at masking symptoms to slip through the cracks.

Hell, it was easy for a patient who was manifesting their symptoms as loudly as possible to slip through the cracks.

"I think you actually mean that." She took the tablet from Forrest, and signed the electronic forms then slid off the bed and grabbed her things.

"You will be on quarters for at least the rest of the week. No working until those fingers are fully healed. And you *need* to take your antibiotics. That burn on your leg is deep enough that if it gets infected there could be problems." Forrest passed Sam the tablet.

"Right, Doc Two. Take meds. Don't get infection." She rolled her eyes.

"I don't need two evac patients." Sam winked at Adina as she and Forrest walked past him to head out.

Forrest was back in moments, standing opposite the desk where Sam had retreated to put the notes about Mark into the clinical record. Forrest put both hands on the desk and leaned over it.

It would have been sexy as hell, if his eyes weren't smoldering in a furious, not fun, way.

"We need to talk."

"We *are* at the point of discussing amputation." Forrest made sure he kept his voice very low. Mark was snoring, but there was no guarantee the man wouldn't wake at any instant. And he wanted to make sure that when this conversation came up—and it was going to come up—that Mark heard it in a kind and gentle way, not from overhearing his doctors arguing.

"It's not." Sam leaned back in his chair. Was he pulling away from him, or uncomfortable with the confrontation over patient care?

Probably both.

Forrest stood and drew a hand over his face. "I know that Houston has already told you they're examining all the options, Sam."

Sam flinched at the soft way he said his name. Forrest didn't want to argue. Didn't want any distance between them. But this was important.

"They are. But the weather is going to break and we are going to make sure he stays infection-free." Sam's clipped words struck against Forrest's soul.

There was no way for them to promise any of those things. So much of this was out of their control. This was why he'd failed at bedside, because reality was a hard master.

"You can't plan your way through this, Sam."

"Don't *Sam* me. Don't." Sam leaned forward, dark circles under his eyes highlighted against his sunken skin.

Forrest started again, "The road we are on is treacherous. There are no guarantees."

"I know that." Sam pushed out of the chair and put his hands on the desk like Forrest had done a few minutes ago. "I know there are no guarantees. But this is something we can and will control."

Forrest looked at his feet, took a deep breath and carefully chose his words. "How are you planning to control the weather?" When he looked up, he wasn't surprised by the steel in Sam's gaze.

Sam always had a plan. A goal. A place he was moving toward. But he needed to understand the control he'd always tried to maintain over his life wasn't possible. At least not here. They needed to be ready for an evac…and a worst-case scenario.

Sam opened his mouth then snapped it shut.

"And infection? Have you found a way to ensure no germs get into the wound? Because if so, you will win the Nobel in medicine. There won't even be a competition for it."

"Stop making fun of me." Sam pinched his eyes close.

"I'm not. But I apologize if my words could be misinterpreted. That means I was far from clear." Forrest waited a moment but Sam didn't say anything so he continued, "Perfection isn't possible here."

"I left my perfectionism gene behind long ago." Now his stormy gaze met Forrest's. "I know life isn't fair. I know what Houston is saying. I know what the damn weather forecast looks like. But I am going to find a way to control this outcome."

Forrest reached his hand across the desk, gently laying his hand on Sam's. He didn't pull away and Forrest's soul sighed at the connection. But it was comfort he was offering, not anything else.

"You are a perfectionist—it's part of you. One doesn't just lose the thing that pushed them to be their best. It's what led to your high grades in med school."

"Not as high as yours." Sam stuck out his tongue but still didn't pull away.

"It's what led you to push yourself so hard on crew. You rowed at four a.m. while listening to lectures on headphones while others were listening to rock music to keep their speed up." It was one of the grumbles Forrest had voiced more than once. They never got to sleep in because Sam was out the door long before the sun rose.

"There wasn't anyone else there, Forrest. It was just me, my study guide and the ergometer." Sam's thumb ran along Forrest's thumb.

Forrest didn't look down at the connection. If he did, he'd lose his train of thought and this was important.

"This conversation is not about the rowing machine. You can't follow a carefully laid plan to get the exact result you want here. You can't promise things." Forrest expected his own words to bring up a need to return to the lab. To seal himself away with his microscopes and slides that couldn't feel hurt. But the feeling didn't come.

It was a weird sensation. He was facing up to the possibility of delivering bad news, and yet he wasn't aching to get out. Wasn't wondering whether it was clear to everybody that he felt like a fake. For the first time in forever, he felt at home in a clinic.

"I know I can't," Sam said. "And I know that we might have to do something I have never done and have no desire to do." He swallowed and still didn't pull his hand from Forrest's.

Forrest should retreat. Pull back. Put the distance they'd sworn to keep back in place.

Who was he kidding? They'd broken that rule nearly as soon as they'd announced it.

"But Mark can have another day of good news," Sam went on. "Another moment to keep hope. And so can I. Because I know Amundsen-Scott did the knee surgery via telemedicine, but this is not knee surgery. This is…"

Forrest squeezed Sam's hand. "If it comes to it, I'll be by your side."

"I don't want it to come to that."

"Neither do I." Forrest squeezed his fingers one more time, then he lifted his hand, ignoring the soft cry from his heart that it wasn't ready to let go. It would never be ready.

Sam picked his hand up, rubbing his palms together. The two stared at each other for a moment. What were they supposed to say now?

"I heard from my parents yesterday. I meant to tell you they say hi." Sam smiled.

Words said so loosely. So easily.

"I assumed they hated me." Forrest hadn't meant to speak those words. Ed and Georgina, who everyone called Georgie, were the sweetest people. They'd welcomed him into their home. Sent a birthday gift and made sure he had presents under the tree from someone besides their son.

When he'd had a win at school or as an intern, he could call them and tell them like they were his parents, too. The day he'd walked away from bedside he nearly dialed their number. He'd even pulled it up in his phone, aching for someone to hear his worry. To tell him the path he was choosing was the right one.

"I don't think they know how to hate," Sam said. "I mean, they were shocked and hurt for me, but they missed you, too." He stretched his arms over his head and his shoulder popped.

"You're getting creaky." Forrest chuckled as the smile spread across Sam's face.

"I am. I think it was all that time spent on the erg." He looked at the door then back at Forrest. "I need to put notes in. Mark is sleeping. You can go back to your lab for a while. If I need you, I'll call."

Forrest wrapped his arms around himself and tried to find any reason he might need to hang around. But nothing came. Sam had dismissed him. And there was no point in staying.

CHAPTER EIGHT

SAM PULLED AT the erg handle, relishing the burn the rowing machine gave his muscles. He'd been up since three and given up on the idea of finding sleep again sometime after four.

It would be nice to blame the South Pole for the insomnia. After all, it was a common complaint at the pole's research centers. But it wasn't a messed-up circadian rhythm keeping Sam from rest.

Forrest.

The man's face danced across Sam's tired mind and he pulled harder on the bar. His split time was going to be amazing but the workout wasn't accomplishing the goal of driving Forrest from his mind.

Forrest.

He'd dreamed of him for the last three nights. Each night the dream lasting a little longer. Last night Sam had kissed him. Held him. Clung to him.

After they'd separated, Sam had dreamed of Forrest every night for a year, his subconscious torturing him with good memories. With feelings he was never going to get again.

He'd woken this morning with the feel of Forrest's lips still on his. The scent of him whispering through the dream. If Sam put his fingers to his lips, he might feel the ghost of him even now.

He yanked harder on the erg to keep his fingers from following through on the thought.

"You're up early. No one's ever in here when I come this early." Forrest's chin was covered with stubble and he looked so damn good in that tight gray T-shirt and loose black shorts.

It was almost as if Sam's thoughts had conjured him. Like he was still dreaming.

"Couldn't sleep." He pulled on the handle and flinched at the burn running down his shoulders. *Relax.*

He'd rowed for years. He knew the form he needed and knew the risk of injury if he didn't follow it. Didn't mean it was easy for his body to slide back into it as Forrest stretched beside the treadmill.

"Thinking about Mark?" Forrest pulled an arm across his center then bent over to stretch his hips and legs.

Sam made sure to keep his eyes focused on the wall in front of him. The last thing his subconscious needed was updates added to the memory jar for his dreams.

"No. I wasn't thinking of Mark." The words slipped out and he wanted to slap himself. That was the easy answer. The right answer. The answer that would drive the line of questions away.

Thinking about a burn patient was a good reason to be awake at this hour. Dreaming, fantasizing really, about your ex was very much not. Particularly when that ex was the one asking the question.

"Why can't you sleep then?" Forrest stepped onto the treadmill and pushed the button to start a slow jog.

Sam had cheered him on through six marathons and more half marathons than he could count. He'd always made sure he was at the finish line with a sign and kiss. "You still run marathons?"

It wasn't an answer to Forrest's question but Forrest didn't say anything about that as he shook his head no.

"I stick to halves and 10Ks these days. Less training time." He wasn't even breathing hard as he pushed the treadmill speed up.

"Oh, yeah." Sam kept his tone light. "Thirteen miles and six miles are no distance at all."

"A little over six point two miles technically." Forrest stuck out his tongue as he upped the speed on the treadmill again.

"A little over six point two." Sam rolled his eyes and pulled on the handle of the erg as he repeated Forrest's words.

"No need to pick on me." Forrest chuckled and he pushed the speed up more. "How long have you been on that machine?" He adjusted the elevation and finally started breaking a sweat.

His gaze met Sam's as his feet pounded on the tread. If Sam was running and looked around like that, he'd trip over his feet and face plant.

"Don't avoid *this* question. How long, Sam?"

"I don't know. Over an hour." Sam stuck his tongue out, mirroring Forrest's earlier move.

"An hour on an erg? You do realize you aren't training for the Olympics anymore, right?" Forrest blew out a heavy breath as his feet continued to pound the treadmill. "Or are you training again?"

"No, I'm not training again. Those days are behind me." A ridiculous question added to point out the obvious. He'd worked out for far longer while aiming to make the Olympic team. But it wasn't necessary anymore. That didn't mean he was going to stop rowing. He usually stuck to forty-five minutes. But he was not stopping now, at least not until Forrest stopped running. Purely on principle.

"How long are you running?"

"How long are you rowing?" Forrest raised a brow before turning his attention to the stats on his machine.

"Not stopping until you do." It was silly. Playful, even though Sam's muscles were burning and his split pace had slowed considerably. A rowing machine was a full-body exercise and he'd not done more than an hour in years. He'd feel it tomorrow. But hopefully he'd get a night of dreamless rest.

Forrest chuckled and pressed the button to speed up the machine again.

He ran and Sam rowed in silence for the next several minutes. He could almost pretend they were just two men who happened to be in the gym at the same time rather than former lovers thrust back into each other's lives.

"Five miles. Done." Forrest panted as he hit the stop button and kept time as the treadmill slowed down.

"How the hell did you get five miles? You basically just started." Sam let go of the handle grateful to see it pop back into the rowing machine. Then he stood, ignoring the burn in his back and legs.

Forrest blew out a breath as he stretched by the machine. "It's a light day so I only do five. I run a little over a five-minute mile so done in thirty."

"Well, nice workout." Sam nodded and started for the door.

"Wait."

His stomach tightened and lightning shot through his body. Sam turned, focusing on keeping all of his emotions in check. "What?"

Color was cresting along Forrest's cheeks but he didn't break Sam's gaze. "You were on that machine for well over an hour and a half. If you don't stretch your body is going to tense up and you'll be sore for days."

He was going to be sore anyway. "I'll stretch in my room."

"No." Forrest shook his head. "To get to your room you have to go outside. The cold will tighten you up. Stretch here. I will stay quiet, but you are not hurting yourself just because you don't want to be around me."

"Don't want to be around you?" Sam took a step forward. "Hell, I am here *because* of you. I can't sleep because of you. I dream of you. My thoughts wander to you in every single free moment of the day and even some of the times when I'm supposed to be accomplishing something. *You*—" Sam pushed his finger into Forrest's chest "—are the only person I want to be around."

Suddenly, Forrest's lips were on his. His strong arms wrapped around him and the world tilted back into the right position for the first time in years. Sam leaned into him. Grasping Forrest's body as their tongues entwined and years of separation vanished.

Forrest was home and peace. The past and the present.

His fingers splayed across Sam's back, and Sam ran his hands through Forrest's dark hair, craving the feel of him after so many dreams.

Sam's hand moved from Forrest's hair to his face, running a thumb over the stubble on his cheeks before finally pulling back.

Both men stared at each other and the silence seemed to drag on infinitely longer than the kiss.

"That was not stretching—technically." Forrest bit his lip as he let out a soft chuckle. "Bad joke. Sorry."

"Don't apologize." Sam could stand a lot of things in this life but not Forrest apologizing for kissing him.

"I was saying sorry for the bad joke. The awkwardness I created after." Forrest pulled one arm behind his back. "Not the kiss. I…"

Whatever he'd planned to say after that fell away.

"It was quite the kiss." Sam barely caught his hand from lifting to run his fingers over his lips. His mind was going to have a field day filling in his dreams from now on.

"It was." Forrest pursed his lips and looked at the door. "If you don't want to stretch, I won't make you. But don't come crying to me when your body is so sore you can barely move."

Sam shrugged. He needed to get going and he'd stretch in his room quickly before he hopped in the shower. "I have to get to the clinic. I'll have the samples ready for you to test as soon as you get there."

He turned toward the door, then turned back. "I'm glad you interrupted my workout."

Forrest shook his head. "I'm in here every day at the same time." He pointed a finger toward Sam but didn't step closer. "*You* interrupted my workout. And I am glad you did."

The hot shower had done nothing to drive his thoughts away from Sam. Forrest put on his coat, pulled the beanie over his still damp hair and looked at the door. He needed to head to the clinic and pick up the samples.

But that meant facing the aftermath of the kiss. It had happened without him thinking. A reaction based entirely on emotion, something Forrest tried very hard to avoid. After all, he'd spent his entire childhood paying for the sins of his mother's inability to control herself.

Forrest prided himself on his control. His ability to step back when the emotions got heated. But when Sam's fingertip dug into his chest all rational thought had vanished.

Running a finger over his lip, Forrest closed his eyes recreating the moment in his mind. Sam was perfection. His kisses still curled Forrest's toes and sent his soul to the moon.

For a moment, a not so brief moment, everything seemed right in the universe. Like nature was sighing in relief that the two of them were connected.

"Stop being ridiculous." Forrest shook his head. The universe did not care about him. And if it was really watching, it wanted something more for Sam.

He's not taking more.

Forrest pinched his eyes closed. He'd worked with his therapist; he knew that wasn't a safe thought. Wasn't an accurate thought.

Still feels that way, though.

Nope. He was shutting this down. They'd kissed. Then Sam had said he had to go to the clinic and Forrest had let him go.

It was a good memory to add to his bank but didn't have to mean anything else.

Who am I trying to fool?

His mind wasn't going to accept any answer there so Forrest pulled the door open and marched his way through the cold and snow to the clinic building. At least the chill finally cooled the blood the kiss had ignited.

"I have the samples." Sam was at his side before he even had a chance to take off his coat. "There's infection developing. The arm is warm to the touch and he has a low-grade fever. I need these typed as soon as possible. I am doing everything I can today to get an evac out. It has to be now." The container holding the sample slides was pushed into Forrest's hands. "Please hurry."

Forrest nodded and headed back out into the snow. This wasn't the worst-case scenario. Low grade fever and warm were simply the start of an infection. But it wasn't good, either.

The fact that they'd kept infection at bay for almost two weeks was no small accomplishment. But that accomplishment meant nothing if they ended up having to perform the amputation. A risk that rose with every passing hour, let alone day.

Forrest forced his way back through the wind and ice toward his lab. The odds of an evac were still close to zero. The storm had broken last night and the wind was less intense, but that didn't mean help was coming.

If we don't get the infection under control...

Forrest shut that thought off, too. No use catastrophizing. A term his therapist had had him use to identify the thoughts that did not help him.

He got the samples under the microscope and saw what looked like bacterial growth. He'd start the bacterial enzyme test, leave a note for Charlee to call as soon as the test was done. With any luck it would take closer to four hours to have an answer, rather than twenty-four. But until the test completed there was no way to be sure.

The wind felt like it had died down as he headed back to the clinic. Or maybe that was just him wishing for a change so an evac might happen.

He pushed open the door and wasn't surprised when Sam strode through the inner door.

"I don't have news other than it looks bacterial, which isn't surprising." Forrest took his coat off and hung it on the peg. "I left a note for Charlee to call when the enzyme test completes. Is Mark resting?"

"Yes." Sam blew out a breath. "I talked to Houston and they say they might have an evac option open late tonight. The weather looks like it might hold. It's a strong might."

Sam had said the word *might* three times. Trying to remind himself, or to force it into being by pure force of will?

So the wind really had died down then. Now they just needed it to hold.

Adina burst through the door and Forrest let out a yelp as the blast of cold air hit his now–coat-free body.

"Don't stand in here, if you don't want to get cold." Adina barked as she took off her coat and walked past them. "Weather is breaking."

"How do you know?" Sam asked as he followed her.

Forrest took up the rear.

"I've done multiple stints here. Snowstorms happen in the summer too. You get a feel for it. The money is good and you get a feel for things. You need to call whoever it is and get a plane here. Now." She pointed her finger at Sam.

Adina's face was stern, but the wobble in her lip gave away the fear. "And you need to tell them the evac is for two." She lifted her pants, showing off the burn she'd received. It was swollen and angry.

Dark red lines grew from it. It looked like the infection was traveling. Lymphangitis or cellulitis symptoms. Both critical.

They'd spent so much time worrying over Mark they'd never even considered this. Adina had been here every day. And always said she was fine. Never let Forrest see it, though. And he hadn't pushed. She should have healed as long as she took the antibiotics.

The truth hit him as he looked at the red streaks and drainage.

"You aren't taking the antibiotics we gave you." Forrest kept his tone level, not accusing just observing.

Sam's eyes widened but when Forrest just barely shook his head, he didn't say anything. Adina was Forrest's patient. His responsibility. And he'd failed to see the choice she had clearly been going to make.

Adina swallowed but didn't confirm or deny what he was saying. "Mark doesn't have anyone. His ex-wife got all the friends in the divorce, not that he minds. He's a loner."

"He has you."

Sam's interruption was rewarded with a swift glare.

"Yes. And when he has surgery, he is going to need someone there." She flinched as she moved her leg.

The infection they'd been so worried about in Mark was now second to the one crawling through Adina's system.

"I'm admitting you." Forrest's tone was harsh this time. He was not going to accept any argument. If he let her go and this worsened, and it would, her life was in danger.

"I'm fine." Adina raised her chin, but the wobbling lips were still there.

"You are not." Forrest shook his head. "I failed to realize you were a danger to yourself last time. But you are, which means we are allowed to hold you here against your will. Don't make me file that paperwork."

He looked at Sam. The frustration was clear in his eyes, but his face was serene. Good. He could play the role of good doctor, a sympathetic ear to listen to Adina, while Forrest took on the role of ass to make sure she got the care she needed.

She looked at the door, clearly questioning how serious the threat Forrest had issued was.

"If you are admitted, it will be easier for me to get you on the evac plane." Sam's calm words made Adina let out a breath.

"It hurts." She bit her lip. "I didn't think it would get this bad. Two days ago it was just really warm and sore, but now…"

Forrest put one arm under her left shoulder and Sam followed on the right side. "We need to take a look and get an intravenous antibiotic started immediately."

Sam looked over her head. "I will call Houston as soon as we get you to the bed. Forrest can evaluate."

"So you'll tell them it's for two?" She hiccupped the words out as tears started down her cheeks.

"Forrest is right. You are a danger to yourself, if you stay." He helped Forrest get her into the bed and then walked off.

"I didn't mean to put myself in danger." Adina pushed away a tear. "Not really. It happened so fast. I just need to be on that plane with him. He needs someone to look after him at home. He has no one else."

Forrest nodded as he looked at the burn. The red streaks were light but clearly headed toward lymph nodes. He took her temperature, not surprised to find it elevated.

Lymphangitis. Dangerous and fast moving, but treatable.

"It's painful to the touch and there is discharge. I'm starting an antibiotic, now." Forrest went to grab the IV bag and the needle he needed.

It would be nice if one of the NPs was here. People complained sometimes that they wanted their doctor to place the IV. Forrest was capable, but it was routine for nurses. They were the experts.

But all Adina had was him. So, he found the vein and got the bag hung. Set her leg up in elevation and took a deep breath. "I am going to give you a sedative because I'm guessing you didn't sleep last night."

"No." She pursed her lips. "Thank you, Doc Two."

Forrest administered the sedative then walked over to where Sam was on the Wi-Fi phone.

"Seven hours? I'll have both of them prepped. I know I said one this morning, but you are sending the plane anyway. If she stays here without him, she's a danger to herself."

Forrest wrote on a note and passed it over.

It's lymphangitis.

Sam raised a brow and passed the information on to the person on the other end. "There were streaks headed toward the lymph nodes this morning. There is drainage and clear infection." He pinched his eyes closed as he listened to whatever the person was saying on the end of the phone.

"I know this is unorthodox, but so is having a patient evacced. This is not a normal situation and he needs surgery as soon as possible." He tapped his free hand against the desk, eyes still closed.

Forrest reached out, putting his hand over his. Sam let out a breath and looked at him. He mouthed *Thank you* as he listened to whatever was being said on the other side of the world.

This was frustrating. But it was far from the first frustration Sam had handled in his career. Growing up, Forrest had watched television shows about doctors and the nurses working beside them. The dramas were always nerve-rattling. The diagnoses rare and terrifying.

It made for good television but did not give an accurate representation of life in a medical setting. You fought with insurance companies who thought they knew more about what was happening than the physician with the patient in front of them. Fought with administration about resources. Stuff that did not make for good television but was the everyday reality.

It added more stress to an already stressful job.

"Thank you. We'll get *them* prepped." Sam's blue eyes met Forrest's as he said *them* and held his gaze. "Separating them is not a good idea. They aren't lovers, but they love each other."

The words spun around them. They were about Adina and Mark. But maybe...just maybe there was another message there, too.

CHAPTER NINE

THE WIND WHIPPED around them as they watched the operators of the C-130 wave as the door to the plane on skis closed. The US Air Force 109th Airlift Wing operated the plane that could land in the most inhospitable place on the planet. There were a doctor and nurse on the plane who were now in charge of Mark and Adina's care.

Sam and Forrest's jobs were done. They'd given Mark his best-case scenario. With any luck he'd be in surgery a few hours after he landed.

And Adina. Forrest pursed his lips as the plane engines revved in preparation for takeoff.

She was going to be okay. Though it was possible she'd need a skin graft too, if the infection spread any more. He should have seen the possibility. Should have suspected.

There were signs. And he'd missed them. Chalked her statements up to jokes. To banter. And now she was on the plane, with her best friend, as a patient herself.

If she'd talked to him, to Sam, maybe they could have figured something else out. Mentally harping on it wasn't doing him any good.

"This is the second evac we've stood next to each other at. Hopefully they get the same good news Dr. Anderson got." Forrest shouted the words as the plane headed down the ice runway and took off. At least this was a topic to clear his mind. Dr. Anderson had a long road to recovery, but he'd emailed and said his oncologist expected him to make a full recovery. With any luck, in a couple of weeks they'd get similar updates on Mark and Adina.

"Yeah, but this one is very different," Sam shouted back as he motioned for them to head back.

Very different? Hardly.

"Not really. Double the patients, sure, and more dangerous for the ones on the plane but otherwise same deal. Patients need evacuation and we are out in the cold." Forrest lowered his voice as the plane's roar disappeared into the dark sky.

"Yeah, but we're talking now." Sam rolled his shoulders, cringing as they got up by his ears.

Good point. "I told you you'd be sore if you didn't stop rowing this morning." Flutters danced through Forrest's stomach as he tried to keep his focus on something other than the hot man next to him.

You wanted to think of something other than your patients. Mission accomplished.

"You did. You were right. I am tight as a spring." They walked into the dorm area. Sam's room was down the left hall, and Forrest's was down the right.

"Want to hang out for a little while? I'm exhausted, but my brain's not going to shut down after the day we've had. You can come to my room. I have a little couch area. I've got some beers in the fridge." Forrest wasn't sure where the offer came from.

Except he was. His heart wanted Sam. Wanted time with him.

They'd kissed this morning. How could one twenty-four-hour period be so long and so short? The smart move might be to put a bit of distance between them. But distance was the thing Forrest wanted least in this world.

"Sure." Sam grinned. "But let me go to my room and get into comfier clothes."

"Good plan." Forrest nodded and walked down to his room. There was no sense trying to ignore the butterflies dancing around his stomach.

He got to his place, stripped and put on some comfortable pajama pants and a soft blue T-shirt. He grabbed the beers from his fridge. McMurdo allowed the station residents to purchase an alcohol ration each week. Forrest made little use of his allotted amount. But that meant he had a decent stash for hosting.

Not that he'd ever hosted anyone in his room.

The clock ticked past ten minutes and Forrest tried not to ignore the tiny voice whispering that Sam had changed his mind. It wasn't a huge deal if that was the case.

Except it was.

Forrest closed his eyes and took a deep breath.

"What will be will be." The mantra was one his therapist had recommended, but it didn't bring any relief as the door to his room stayed un-knocked-on.

Another deep breath, another quiet moment.

Then a swift knock.

Forrest let out the breath he very much knew he'd been holding. He strode to the door, opened it and his heart sang as Sam stood on the other side.

His hair was damp and he smelled like the shampoo that had been in their shower for so long.

"Sorry." Sam shrugged and winced. "The shower took longer than planned because raising my hands over my head was painful." He took the beer Forrest offered and took a deep sip. "Guess I was running on adrenaline to get Mark on the plane, because I didn't feel it as we were loading him."

Forrest wasn't surprised by the admission. The body could ignore a lot when it was running on stress. And injured muscles liked heat, but only after the initial inflammation died down. "You overextended yourself this morning. Heat was the worst thing for the muscles. You need to ice them."

"Forgive me for not wanting to ice anything when we are surrounded by the ice all the time." Sam took another drink. "Guess I'm not great company."

"You are fine company." Forrest set his beer down and stood.

"And I seem to remember the best cure for this anyway." He stepped behind Sam and put his hands on his shoulders.

Pressing his thumb into the pressure points, he wasn't surprised when Sam let out a grunt. "You're stiffer than I imagined."

"That was something you used to joke with me about." Sam chuckled at the old innuendo.

"That wasn't exactly how I put it." Forrest dug into Sam's shoulders with his thumb. Yes, the massage would break up the knots he'd created with the oversized workout, but it would also teach him a good lesson about such jokes.

"Ouch." Sam looked back over the chair, his jeweled gaze gripping Forrest. "I earned that."

"Do you want the massage or do you want to go to bed sore?"

"I think we are both going to bed sore, but yes. Thank you." Sam leaned back up and sighed as Forrest worked through the knots on his shoulders.

"You should make sure you take some pain reliever tonight. Anti-inflammatories." It was advice Sam didn't need.

"Yes, Doc Two." Sam chuckled and drained the last of his beer. "I should get going." He stood and moved around the couch.

Forrest didn't argue. The room was hot. Crispy with tension. And if Sam stayed any longer, he'd act. Just like he had this morning.

Sam hadn't brought up the kiss. The innuendo-laden jokes were little pitfalls on the way to the giant landmine they seemed to be dancing around.

"I hope you sleep well." Forrest took a deep breath as Sam stepped a little closer. The scent of him was going to stain the room for the next several hours.

Thank God.

Sam leaned toward him and Forrest waited for the connection he saw in his eyes. Instead, Sam dropped his beer in the waste bin behind him.

"What are we doing?" Forrest wasn't sure the question had actually made it out of his mouth until Sam paused.

Their lips were inches from each other.

"You were the one that kissed me this morning. You tell me." Sam's body heat pressed against Forrest.

"I don't know." That was the truth. He wasn't sure what this was. What it wasn't. They were at the end of the earth, literally. Trapped together. There was no plan here.

"Me, either." Sam whispered, then closed the distance between them.

This kiss was slow. Not the passionate rampage of this morning. Sam's mouth pressed against his as he ran one hand up Forrest's back and stroked his cheek with the other.

A worshipful remembrance.

"Sam." He breathed out the name. Locked in the sanctity of the moment.

"Forrest."

His name on Sam's lips. His body tightened and his soul ignited. Damn he'd missed him. Missed the jokes. The talks. The passionate kisses and these moments.

Him. He'd just missed Sam.

The kiss continued, or maybe time stopped to allow them everything they needed.

When Sam finally broke the moment and stepped back, Forrest put his hands to his lips, staring at the man. No words breaking forth.

"Good night, Forrest." Sam smiled and headed for the door. "And thanks for the massage."

The door was closed before Forrest could say good night.

Or beg him to stay.

"Earth to Sam." Nat waved a hand in front of his face, as she stood in front of him.

Sam blinked. The nurse worked night shift back in the States, but he hadn't been aware she moved like shadows. "Sorry, my brain slipped out a moment when I didn't see you here."

Slipped out was not even a lie. With no one around, Sam's mind had hopped to the kiss he'd planted on Forrest three days ago.

A lifetime ago.

She raised a brow and pointed to the currently empty bays. "I figured that you'd enjoy a restocked unit to start the shift with."

"Not an incorrect assumption." Sam grinned, grateful she hadn't asked for details about his wandering thoughts.

"Given the week we've had, you're entitled to more than a moment of daydreaming." She let out a breath.

"Was last night rough then?" Since they'd deposited Adina and Mark on the C-130, the clinic had had a steady stream of patients. All minor things, thankfully. But no restful periods. Which for a station holding only a few hundred people was surprising.

"Not rough, just continuous." She pulled up the tablet. "All of it was standard. Stitches for a scientist who slipped on the ice. Two with headaches so bad they were having trouble sleeping and a case of insomnia."

"Insomnia is something we are likely going see an uptick in. It's a common complaint here." And something people had a tendency not to report. But it could cause a multitude of health conditions.

Natasha sighed as she looked out the small window near the front door. "I love working the night shift at home. My friends joke that I live for the night. But twenty-four-hour darkness messes with you."

She pushed her finger along the tablet. "The good news is no new admissions. Chris and I were able to patch everyone up or administer medication and release them. So."

Sam chucked as she ended the sentences on a word others might expect to have follow-on commentary attached to. Natasha was an ER nurse. He was an ER doctor. Both of them were superstitious enough not to mention a quiet morning.

No need to tempt fates already seemingly hell bent on overworking the limited medical staff in residence.

"Forrest coming in today?"

Natasha didn't look up from her scrolling as she said it. Still, he thought he heard the hint of another question there. He knew there were questions about the pair of them. How could there not be? When they were not in the clinic, they could usually be found together.

McMurdo Station was basically a small town and rumors kept the boredom at bay. Or at least lightened the doldrums.

"He'll stop by, but he needs to get some stuff done in the lab." Sam hadn't broached the topic of their kiss in Forrest's room. The soft, exploratory connection that seemed fierier than the one in the gym. His brain kept replaying the moment.

He hadn't brought it up. And neither had Forrest. It was a weird limbo hovering over their morning workouts and mealtimes. An undiscussed boulder that Sam kept waffling between bringing up and burying deep inside.

The only thing he couldn't do was forget it.

"He's working two jobs. He needs to be careful." Nat yawned as she passed the tablet to Sam. "All yours."

Sam took the tablet and asked, "Careful, how?" Had she seen something he hadn't? A problem he'd missed because he was focusing on Forrest's lips and perfectly sculpted body?

"I worked here three winters ago. It can be easy to work constantly. To lose track of how much stress you are putting on your body. The constant darkness and limited activities do something to your brain. Make it forget, or depress, the stress its dealing with. I've seen more than one scientist crack." She yawned, again. "He's probably fine, but you should just keep an eye on him. Not that that will be hard, right?"

She winked and walked toward the door before Sam could mutter any kind of response. He looked around the room, the quiet room… At least he could use this time to catch up on a doctor's worst nightmare—paperwork.

"Sorry I took so long." Forrest shook the snowflakes from his head as he stepped into the clinic. "The lab results all seemed to come together at once."

"We aren't anticipating another outbreak, are we?" Sam's day had included two individuals with colds that had created serious sinus infections. Both were incredibly uncomfortable, but he didn't think they were super contagious.

"No. At least not one that the results are predicting. I mean it could happen—we have a lot of people living in close proximity. And even when you don't the odds are always greater than zero with germs."

"Geez, Forrest." Sam shook his head, "Doom and gloom much?"

"What?" Forrest's dark eyes were sparkling as the tips of his lips tried to keep from forming a full smile.

Sam tilted his head, "You know what. I get that you look at germs all day. That you test individuals at random around the base. And of course you have those boxes all around this place. I know you are excited by those results, but the ER physician—" Sam pointed to himself and ignored the chuckle coming from Forrest "—hears germs, population density discussion and odds not zero and his nervous system starts to race."

"That is why you never showed any interest in internal medicine or epidemiology." Forrest stepped a little closer.

Heat erupted across Sam's skin. The temperature rising had nothing to do with the "scary" topic Forrest was discussing and everything to do with the six-foot Adonis that haunted every single dream these days.

Forrest stopped at the edge of the desk and looked toward the empty bays. "Looks like you didn't really need me today."

Sam let out a breath, as he looked at the empty beds too, grateful Forrest hadn't used the dreaded word *quiet*.

Forrest must have noticed. "I chose internal medicine and then the lab, but I rotated through the ER. I know better than to mention certain things." He leaned against the desk, looking hotter than any man had a right to.

"It was steady but no one needed admitting. Natasha said she and Chris had the same last night. That is the pattern I was told to expect."

The front door of the clinic opened and both men turned as a petite redhead walked in. Tears were frozen on her cheeks.

Forrest was closer than Sam was and reached her first. "What's wrong? What hurts?"

"My heart, and no, I am not having a heart attack." The young woman wiped away fresh tears as she looked between the men. "I need medication for depression. There I said it." She blew out a breath then pinched her eyes closed.

"All right." Forrest gestured to an empty bed. "Come tell us what's going on."

"I *told* you. I need de… de… Damn it! I just said the words."

"Depression meds?" Sam helped out and was stunned to see Forrest's gaze cut to him. The man gave him a subtle shake of the head.

"What do you need?" Forrest took the woman's coat from her and hung it across a chair. She hadn't bothered to hang it on the hooks by the door, probably because she was too focused on getting in and getting out the words that she considered so hard.

One of the toughest issues for Sam in the ER was explaining to family members, first responders and others that mental health care was needed as much as trauma surgery or oncologists. The stigma behind it was why the woman on the bed was struggling so much.

"He said the words." She pointed at Sam.

"I know." Forrest offered a gentle smile. "But I need you to talk about what you need and why. I've taken medication for anxiety and depression. I have a therapist that I still meet with over email while I'm here. There is nothing wrong with asking for help. But being able to ask is the first step."

Damn, he was good at this.

"I need medication for—" she cut her eyes to Sam in mute appeal, but he shook his head.

Forrest was right. She needed to ask. Needed to accept that this was what she was struggling with and that there was nothing wrong with that.

"Depression." She bent her head and let out a sob.

"All right." Forrest grabbed a chart from the wall. "Let's start with the basics, your name?"

"Megan Pauli." She hiccupped. "If life was fair, it would be Megan Smith. How silly is that? I wanted, craved, such a bland last name. But it was..." Her words died away in a sob.

Sam understood the heartache happening here. "What is today the anniversary of?" The day he'd had marked on his calendar to wed Oliver he'd packed his bags and moved across the country, determined not to look more than a few months into his future. And he still made sure to work overtime on the anniversary of the day he and Forrest first kissed. A date that was coming up.

"My fiancé's birthday. He died a year ago. I came here because..." She shrugged.

"Because it was easier than staying home." Sam finished what she couldn't say.

She nodded.

He understood. He'd taken to the road for the same reasons.

Forrest looked at him, just a quick glance, then back at Megan. "Have you ever taken medication for depression?"

"No. My mother, well, she told me to just get over it. Work and not think. And it was working."

"No." Sam shook his head. "It wasn't. You were just putting off the support your body needs. And no one should tell you how to handle your grief."

Megan bit her lip so hard Sam worried she might be tasting

blood. "I loved Dillon so much. I thought I knew how lucky I was, but now, now I wish I could go back in time and tell that version of me to soak up every moment. Because I had no idea what I had when I had it."

Forrest's gaze met Sam's again, for just a moment. "All right, since you've never used depression medication, we are going to start on the lowest dose. These medications take time to work as they build up in your system. I want to check back in two weeks on how they are working, but it will be a full thirty days before you enjoy all the effects."

"In the meantime, we are going to set you up with weekly therapy appointments." Sam would email Houston and make sure they found someone who could use the telehealth system so Megan could talk to someone who wouldn't tell her to bury her emotions. Who would just let her be.

Forrest got the meds and went over the requirements, possible side effects. Sam stood to the side. Unneeded in this moment. Lost in Megan's simple words.

I had no idea what I had when I had it.

Sam's eyes fell on Forrest. His heart, his mind, everything had made sense when they were together. And nothing had truly fit since they separated.

"Eh! Megan. Glad you made it in." Chris raised a hand as Sam turned. "I recommended she visit, glad you did. Want to go over notes so you can head out of here, Doc?"

"Yes." Sam wanted out of there. But for the first time in forever he also knew where he wanted to go.

CHAPTER TEN

FORREST DIDN'T TRY to stop his feet from moving down the hall. He wasn't giving himself time to think this through. Megan's words had haunted him as he'd showered. Echoed through him as he threw on his clothes. Followed him with every step he took.

He needed Sam. It was as simple, and as complicated, as that.

Reaching the door, Forrest didn't hesitate to raise his hand, but before he could knock, Sam opened the door.

"Oh, good."

Forrest wasn't sure what he'd expected Sam to say, but that wasn't it.

Sam reached for his shirt and pulled him in. "I was just on my way to you." He closed the door and took a deep breath. "Forrest."

His hands cupped Forrest's cheek. His thumb running across his cheek. "You're a little scruffy."

His smile sent lightning bolts through Forrest. "You said you liked it." He'd picked up the razor in the shower, then set it aside. Years of being instructed to keep a shaven face. Decades of shaving in the morning and at night. But Sam's words had echoed in his head.

"I do like it." Sam's free hand ran along Forrest's stomach.

His groin hardened and need pushed against every nerve. His body was a lightning rod, specifically designed for the man in front of him. "Sam."

"I love how you say my name. I always did."

Before Forrest could react to that statement, Sam's mouth was on his. The kiss jolted him. His hands were on Sam's body, tracing paths his mind knew by memory.

He broke the kiss and bent his head to the crook of Sam's neck. He swept his tongue across the skin and was rewarded with Sam gripping his ass.

"Tease." Sam's husky voice whispered into his ear.

"There is no tease here." Forrest put his hands on either side of Sam's face. "I want you. I need you."

"You have no idea how many dreams I've woken from just after you've said those words." Sam dragged a finger along Forrest's stomach.

Forrest hated that admission. "I'm here now."

"You're here now." Sam repeated the words before grazing Forrest's mouth with his lips.

"Who's the tease, now?" Forrest pulled Sam against him, very aware of how turned on they each were. Their hips pressed together, their bodies reacquainting with each other.

Forrest craved this man and was fighting every urge to devour him. He was not rushing a single moment of this.

Sam's hands gripped Forrest's and pushed them over his head as he captured Forrest's mouth with his own. Being pressed up against a door, with his lover worshiping his lips was certainly a match for any fantasy Forrest's mind had managed to conjure up. Each stroke of Sam's tongue stirred the flame the first sight of him on the ship had ignited. The ember that had refused to die. "Sam."

Sam released his hands and he took the opportunity to lift Sam's shirt over his head. As if in answer, Sam's fingers gripped his shirt and ripped it from his body.

Forrest took a deep breath as his former lover stared at his body.

The man in front of him could have been an Olympian, but he'd put that goal aside to focus on med school. But while his six-pack wasn't as defined as it had been in college, it was still there.

Forrest still worked out, but he was not as toned as he'd been. And then there were the tattoos. The last time they lain together his skin had contained no ink.

Now his stomach and his back were etched with pictures. Memories. Things he'd never be able to let go. Images carefully picked but placed where no one ever saw them. Only the tattoo artists had ever glimpsed them.

Sam's finger ran over the Christmas tree over his right bicep. "This one makes sense." He looked at the phoenix stretched across his abdomen. "This one, too." He kissed the words on his collarbone. "I hate that I understand why you have this one, too." His tongue flicked along the phrase.

"It was the first one I got." Two weeks after he'd walked away from Sam. The words *We're All Mad Here* were meant to make him feel like he'd made the right choice. It hadn't worked. But it had created a need to continue to modify his body.

Sam's touch feathered along the waistband of his pants and Forrest's groin tightened. "Any others?"

"Not there." Forrest winked as he reached for Sam. He was too turned on to let the ink he'd placed on his body distract him from the Adonis before him.

Sam's hand slid along Forrest's length. There were two layers of fabric between his palm and Forrest's skin, but still need nearly drove him to his knees.

"Turn." The order echoed in the room. "I want to see the others. I find that ink turns me on."

Forrest lightly traced a finger along Sam's erection, enjoying the groan echoing from his lips. He let his touch linger for just a moment before turning.

His back piece was a road. With a man walking a broken path between woods and ocean. It was the signature piece in the artist's portfolio.

Sam's body pressed against his. "Any on your tight ass?"

"One way to find out."

His pants and boxers disappeared with record speed. Sam gripped his very tattoo-less butt.

"No tats, but still hot as hell." Sam massaged his butt before slipping between his legs and cupping his balls. He stroked Forrest's length but their position against the door kept Forrest from moving with the touch.

It was torture and explicit pleasure all wrapped in one.

Every nerve ending was pulsing and Forrest had had enough. "Sam…" Before he could finish the plea, Sam gripped his shoulders and spun him around.

Then he slid to the ground and took Forrest in his mouth. The heat, the longing, the need, all of it hit him as Sam gripped his ass, pulling him closer.

Forrest closed his eyes and let Sam take him fully over the edge.

Sam stood, grinning as Forrest's eyes darkened in the aftermath of his orgasm. "Forrest."

"My turn."

Forrest had captured Sam's mouth and was guiding them toward the bed before Sam could utter another word. Not that he had much interest in saying anything else when Forrest was taking charge.

Forrest wasn't soft. Wasn't hesitant. His hands were cascading over Sam's body, touching all the places guaranteed to make him come undone.

When Sam's knees hit the edge of his bed, Forrest reached his arm around his back to stop him from falling backward. "I am completely naked," Forrest purred.

"Trust me, I know." Sam's gaze slid over the phoenix on Forrest's belly. He hadn't been kidding. The tattoos were a huge turn-on. He'd never cared about tattoos. He'd been with men who were covered in them and those who had none. They'd never registered as anything significant.

But on Forrest… The hidden gems were catnip to an already greedy need.

Forrest's hand slipped into his loose sweats and Sam sighed as it slid around his length.

"You still don't wear boxers to bed." Forrest pressed kisses along his neck, pausing at the exact spot that never failed to elicit a moan from Sam.

This was new. *And* familiar.

Forrest yanked on the drawstring of Sam's sweats, grinning as the pants hit the floor. His palm splayed across Sam's chest as he pressed him back on the bed.

Forrest's lips drifted along his inner thighs as his fingers teased ever closer to the aching length. Sam gripped the sheets as Forrest's tongue trailed along his thigh, over his balls and finally to where he craved him most.

Sam woke to Forrest shifting in the bed next to him. There wasn't much room and it reminded him of the first night they'd fallen asleep together in a college dorm.

"We haven't slept in such a confined space since college." Forrest sighed but made no move to exit the bed.

Dropping a hand around Forrest's waist, Sam kissed his shoulder, where a bird in flight was imprinted. "I was just thinking the same thing." He ran a hand over Forrest's stomach.

There was nothing sexual about the motion. It was a simple touch. One he'd missed so much. Oliver hadn't liked to snuggle. In fact, the man had insisted on a king-size bed so there was no chance of rolling into each other at night.

One of many red flags Sam had ignored in his pursuit of perfect love. This wasn't perfect, though. It was—well—they'd never discussed what it was. In fact when asked directly, Forrest had said he didn't know.

Sam wasn't going to press. Once upon a time he would have. Would have spent hours, days running through his life plan. Plotted the next year, five, forever.

That man was gone. This Sam spent his life moving from

one thing to the next. This was an adventure and when the winter was over, the next adventure would begin.

That didn't mean he wasn't going to soak up every moment he had now.

"Why the tattoos?" He ran a hand over where he knew the phoenix was. "You never mentioned anything about wanting ink. And you have a lot. All carefully hidden."

Forrest's body lifted as he chuckled. "The first was a fluke. I got it to feel something. Which sounds ridiculous, but I was so lost and unsure what my next steps should be." He let out a sigh.

Was he waiting for Sam to ask when that was? To press? Dozens of questions pummeled his brain but he didn't ask a single one.

"I saw a flash sale at a place I was walking by. Fifty bucks as long as it was something from the sheet they had. The *We're All Mad Here* line stuck out. I was never much for classic literature. Guess my grandmother refusing to read to me as a kid left some holes in my book knowledge. It wasn't until I saw a video on a social media site years later that I realized it was a quote from *Alice in Wonderland*."

"It's the Cheshire cat's line. At least in the book." Sam pressed a kiss to Forrest's shoulder.

Forrest shifted; his ass running along Sam's length. "Show-off."

Sam hardened, but he was not going to give in to that. Not yet. "Forrest doing something on a whim. Wow."

"Yeah. Well, that was the only one I did on a whim. But you'll hear people say that once they have one, they must have more. I got the phoenix on the anniversary of my grandmother's death."

Sam chuckled, "She would not have liked that."

Forrest rolled over; his face so close to Sam's own. "She would not. But that was the point."

"And the Christmas tree?" Sam ran a hand over the tree, then felt his mouth fall open as he took a full look at it. "The topper."

Forrest pursed his lips, as his hands stroked Sam's side. "Yeah."

It was their tree topper. A chintzy angel missing one wing. They'd found it at a holiday bazaar as freshman in college. The friendship days.

It had come with them to every room, then apartment. Sitting on top of their tree and starting conversations with anyone that saw it. It was buried in the back of the closet at Sam's parents' place with all the other things from that life that he couldn't seem to toss out.

"Another whim?" Maybe it was an unfair question. But Forrest had been the one to walk out. The one who said he didn't know what this was when Sam had asked the other night.

He was the one that showed up here last night.

But I was going to him, too.

Sam forced the argument from his brain. He wanted this answer. Needed Forrest's response to this.

"No." Forrest placed a hand on his cheek. "I showed the artists the picture. Told him the story about how we found it and had to haggle with the woman over the price."

Sam couldn't stop the grin that reminder brought. "I can't believe she wanted to charge us full price for a broken tree topper."

That tree topper meant something. A memory Forrest had permanently cemented on his body. He'd kept the memory, but not the man tied to it.

"She drove a hard bargain." Forrest's lips traced his. A soft touch, barely there.

But enough to force the hurt back into the recesses of Sam's mind.

"She did." Sam slipped a hand up Forrest's thigh, skimming close to his growing erection but not touching it. "Not as hard as you."

Forrest's fingers wrapped around his length. "You're one to talk."

Sam captured Forrest's mouth. This was what he wanted to focus on. The present. The man in his bed right now.

CHAPTER ELEVEN

"IT'S WEIRD WORKING with you." Chris pushed the cart of supplies over to the bay where he and Sam were finishing up inventory while they had a lull in patients. "Not that I mind. Just weird."

"Missing Natasha?" Sam shrugged. "Is she a better colleague than me?"

"She is." Chris winked. "But only because the woman never stops moving."

"What I hear is that you can sit back while she does all the work." Sam raised a brow, mostly joking but also wanting to make sure that Nat wasn't getting stuck with more than her share of the workload. He and Forrest had worked the same shift for the entire time Mark had needed care.

And if he was being honest, he'd prefer working with Forrest over Chris and Nat, too.

"No. I just mean there is no sitting back with her." Chris put the bandages in the cabinet. "I've spent my career in big-city trauma units. There is no down time. I mean none. I actually came here because I needed a chance to relax, but here…"

Chris looked at the door, holding his breath for a second.

"I don't think you can just wish for a patient and have them magically walk through the door." Sam understood Chris's trouble. The first time he'd landed at a rural hospital he'd gone two nights with barely any patients. After years of spending every moment of a shift running from emergency to emergency, the quiet had nearly driven him mad.

"I'm not wishing for one." Chris blew out a breath. "Not really."

"Uh-huh. Careful what you wish for." Sam's third night at that first hospital had gone to hell almost as soon as he'd walked in the door. A capsized fishing boat with two families with small children. Nightmare fuel. He'd never resented a slow night again.

"I know. I know. I just never thought I'd miss it. The chaos. The adrenaline. The pain. The excitement. That probably sounds terrible." Chris cleared his throat and started toward the desk, "What's next on the agenda?"

"Chris…" Sam pushed the now-empty cart of supplies to the side. "There is nothing wrong with realizing that you aren't cut out for certain kinds of work. It isn't a failure to find you don't like something."

"Yeah. Natasha said the same thing." He looked at the computer and sat down. "I might as well catch up on my charting." He let out a chuckle that wasn't quite happy. "Words I never thought I'd say. Right now, I think of charting as a way to pass the time. Weird."

"I get it." Sam looked at the currently empty clinic, "I'm going to run a quick errand. I have the walkie-talkie if you need me."

"I'm going to do my best not to want to need you." Chris started typing, his eyes glued to the screen.

There were still nearly four months to go on this winter rotation. With any luck there were more long, boring days in front of them. And that meant Chris was going to struggle. Sam made a mental note to keep an eye on him in case the stress needed to be addressed.

After pushing through the snow, Sam arrived at the building housing Forrest's lab. They'd spent the last three nights together. He hadn't been this happy in years. They hadn't talked about the future, though. No discussion on what was next. No planning. Despite that, Sam was determined to soak it in. Enjoy all the moments before they headed in different directions again.

He knocked on Forrest's lab door and entered when he heard Charlee call out.

"You don't have to knock. This isn't a secure lab." The woman grinned before turning back to her microscope. "He's in the back with the graphs and charts." She made a noise at the end of the sentence that made Sam pretty sure Charlee felt the same way about statistics as he did.

He'd met a surprising number of scientists and doctors alike, that loved the science but hated the metrics. Forrest had always enjoyed both. It was why he was so good at internal medicine. And yet, according to Forrest himself, he was hiding that skill away in a lab.

He was standing looking at a giant white board crammed into the side of the lab. There were notes, formulas and a Venn diagram in the corner.

Forrest was so intent on the science on the board that Sam didn't want to interrupt. So he took advantage and let his eyes roam.

Forrest had his hand on his chin. His unshaved chin. Sam's belly tightened at that small detail. It would be so easy to pretend that it meant something deep. Meant he could start thinking of the future, after they got off this ice rock.

He just isn't shaving that often. Don't run away with ideas. Don't start planning forever with a man who's never mentioned it.

"You going to say anything or are you just here to stare at my ass?" Forrest didn't turn or shift his position at the board, but Sam could hear the smile on his lips.

"I wasn't staring at your ass." It was an incredible butt. Majestic even. But Sam hadn't even darted an eye toward it.

Forrest turned his head, his eyes wide, "Should I be concerned then? Three nights together and you're already uninterested in my backside?"

Sam looked toward the section where Charlee was working. Forrest was always serious at work. Focused. It was what made him such a good internist.

"She wears headphones. With music turned up so loud I have to nearly scream, or step on the light sensor she keeps on the floor next to her station so she doesn't get a jump scare when I'm getting her attention."

"She heard me knock." Sam looked back towards Charlee clearly bopping along to the beat of whatever was in the headset.

"No she didn't. Charlee installed a sensor on the floor by the lab's door, too. It sets off a green light so she knows someone is there. Pretty brilliant." Forrest winked, then turned back to the board. "But it means she really can't hear you; so feel free to compliment my butt to your heart's content."

"I really wasn't looking at your butt, though it is a very nice ass and I am far from tired of it, Forrest." Sam walked over to the board, not exactly sure what he was looking at. "What is all this?"

"The viral load of most of the base. The changes over the last two months. The shifts. Though it's too early to really see major differences. You can see the shift when the stomach virus went through the post." Forrest pointed to a graph he'd taped to the board. "And this week's shift." He pointed to another graph.

"Anything we should be concerned about?" Sam hadn't expected to have in-depth access to advance information on what was plaguing the residents, but he'd take it.

"No. And all of it's randomized anyway. Except for that." He pointed to the graph from the virus load. "Which is Charlee and me. The base knows about the collection points Charlee and I set up around the area. They swab their mouth and their nose, put the date on the sample and place it in the collection site."

"Even randomized, it still shows spikes."

"It does." Forrest turned completely around. "Not that I don't love talking about the study I'm doing, but that is not why you are here."

There was no point in denying it. "No. I came to talk clinic schedules."

"Oh." Forrest shook his head, "Right. I should have stopped by this morning to see where you wanted me in the rotation. With Mark and Adina being gone, I assume it will be more of an 'as needed' schedule versus standard rotation."

That made the most sense. Forrest had work to do. The reason he was at the pole. The study he and Charlee were contracted to deliver.

"I mean, we won't need you as often, but I would still like to have you there at least three shifts a week. That way the NPs can get a break." Maybe Forrest would remember why he was such a good fit for bedside if he worked a few extra shifts. Stop hiding.

"What about you? When do you get a break?"

He didn't. But that was something Sam was used to. He took breaks when the clinic was slow. It was a trick he'd learned since taking on rotations in rural places where he was often the lone doc on duty. "I was hired as the primary doc. I'll rest when this is over. For now, my nurses need, and deserve, to spend time elsewhere. On the plus side, they both prefer to work night shift."

Selfishly, he wanted Forrest in the clinic full-time. What a change from the start of the winter session. And it wasn't only because Sam loved his company and was sleeping with him. Though those two things didn't hurt.

Forrest was great at the clinic. At bedside. He'd left the bedside because of some bad experiences. But bad experiences were part of medicine.

He was an excellent doctor. And honestly, there were far too few of those in the world. He should be seeing patients. Not stuffed away in a lab answering to white boards and statistics.

"I can do that. Or four shifts. Though not sure I am the best help. I missed Adina's—"

"Nope." Sam held up a hand, stopping that statement. It had been a patient going south that had pushed Forrest into the lab in the first place. Sam was not letting him focus on Adina in the same way. "*We* missed Adina."

"I was her doctor." Forrest started to turn back to his board.

Sam closed the distance between them and spun the other man around. "*We* were her doctors. I missed it, too. I was so focused on Mark that I didn't see the concern. It is my clinic—"

"Nope." Now it was Forrest interrupting him. "No. It is not your clinic. You're stationed here. It's the Center for Polar Medical Operations' clinic. You are their employee. And you need to be getting rest, too."

"Geez." Charlee rounded the corner. "Even with my headphones on I can hear you two arguing. And the answer is so freaking easy."

Forrest tilted his head. "And what is the easy answer, Charlee?"

"Just kiss already. I mean, seriously." She rolled her eyes to the ceiling.

"Yeah. That's already been taken care of, Charlee. But I appreciate the input." Forrest crossed his arms but color was stealing up his cheeks.

"Oh. Then why the hell is there still so much sexual tension between the two of you? Maybe you need to do more than kiss." She put her headphones back on and made a show of turning the volume up before stamping away.

"I don't think we need to tell her that that has already been taken care of. Do you?" Sam couldn't stop his grin as he felt his own cheeks heat.

Forrest looked around him, making certain Charlee was gone, before pressing a quick kiss to Sam's lips. His fingers grazed Sam's cheek before he shook his head. "No. I don't think we need to give her all that detail. Put me on the schedule, let me know who I am working with and when I need to show up."

Sam leaned in, enjoying the soft scent of Forrest's shampoo. "You're working with me." Then he kissed his cheek and turned on his heel before he could run the risk of fully kissing Forrest, even with Charlee on the other side of the lab.

Forrest smiled at a passing couple on their way to movie night. He was headed in the other direction; he and Sam had agreed to join Charlee and her friend Tina for trivia night in the canteen.

The last week had been blissful. Even if he was starting to feel like he was burning his candle on both ends and a little down the middle. He worked in the lab for several hours early in the morning. Then a shift at the clinic. Then hung out with Sam.

"Hey." Sam caught up to him and slid his arm around Forrest's shoulders. "You snuck out again this morning."

"I needed to check on some things in the lab." Forrest caught the yawn that was pressing against the back of his throat. He'd learned to work through exhaustion in college. High school, really. He'd had a job from the moment he looked sixteen, which was a little before he turned fifteen. So he'd shown up to a job, then gone to school, done homework, then more work and a few hours of sleep. It had been great preparation for residency.

Since he'd taken his lab position, his body had gotten used to enjoying six to eight hours of uninterrupted sleep. But it would readjust. Until then, he'd just make sure the mask he'd perfected in med school was on all the time so no one knew how close to the edge he was.

"Right. The lab." Before Forrest could ask what Sam meant by the tone he used, he was already moving on, "You ready to kick some butt at trivia night?"

Forrest pressed a kiss to Sam's forehead as they walked into the canteen. "I'm here for the company and the ice cream. I don't think we need to kick butt to have a good time."

"Speak for yourself." Sam squeezed his shoulder before letting go. "Though I am looking forward to the ice cream. Is it weird that we're living in a frozen wasteland and still want to have a cold treat?"

"It's not a wasteland. It's a desert. Which has its own ecosystem." Forrest playfully poked at Sam's arm as they took their seats across from Charlee and Tina. "And no, ice cream is good all the time and anywhere."

"Hell yeah to that." Tina raised her cup of coffee. "But I feel like we should have ice cream before trivia, just saying."

"Winning team gets first choice." Charlee looked across the room. "And from what I hear there are limited chocolate options, so we are in this to win it."

"Absolutely!" Sam high-fived Charlee.

"So." Charlee pointed her finger at Forrest. "I know you said vanilla is your favorite, but focus. You are my ringer."

Forrest shook his head, "I'm genuinely just here for the company. And ice cream."

"Your favorite ice cream flavor is mint chip." Sam's gaze was hovering on him. "We used to go get it at Joe's Creamery every Friday."

"Not every Friday." Forrest pointed to the front of the canteen. "I think they're getting ready to start."

"Forrest?"

"Is everyone ready to party?" The announcer at the front was one of the kitchen staff. And clearly enjoying the attention turning toward him as everyone in the room shouted "Yes!" in unison.

Sam squeezed his knee. "It's not vanilla."

"Trivia time." Forrest pointed to the announcer, again. He hadn't had ice cream since he walked away from Sam. No trips for cones. No pints at the grocery.

The idea of ice cream had no longer had any appeal after he'd left. So many of the things they'd done together had been off-limits. Packed away memories he never let himself remember.

"What's our team name?" Charlee leaned across the table. "It needs to be good."

"How about Scrub Club?" Sam offered.

"You're the only one that wears scrubs, Doc." Charlee rolled her eyes.

"Not true. Forrest does." Sam nudged him in the ribs with his elbow.

"Only when I'm in the clinic." Forrest ribbed him back. "We are a group of nerds, what about Fellowship of the Quiz."

Charlee made a face.

"I guess not." Forrest laughed. "Any ideas?"

"Dreamhouse Dwellers." Tina giggled. "You know—" she gestured to the bland room "—because this is definitely a dream house and we are all dwelling here for months."

"I think someone is a fan of a certain doll who famously has a dream house." Charlee raised a brow.

Tina shrugged off the comment. "I am. I started collecting them when I was a little girl. We all have our things." She pointed at Charlee. "Your room is covered in troll dolls."

"I have four. That hardly counts as covered." Charlee stuck her tongue out.

"It's a good name." Forrest looked at the announcer who was waiting, not so patiently for the groups to come up with a name. They were hardly the only ones having a hard time with the choice.

"It is." Sam leaned on his hands. "I vote for Dreamhouse Dwellers."

Forrest raised his hand at the same time as Tina and Charlee. "Unanimous."

"I'll go let them know and get our buzzer." Charlee scooted away from the table.

"So we know Charlee likes trolls and I'm into dolls. What hobbies do the two of you have hiding away?"

"I learned to knit and crochet," Sam said. "I have a wild

stack of yarn, even used most of my personal allowance of extras bringing yarn with me."

Forrest knew his mouth was hanging open. The fact that Sam was knitting. And crocheting. The man could have said just about anything else and he'd have been less surprised. "Where did you learn to do that?"

"On my rotation in Alaska three years ago. The nights are long and when it was a good night, the hospital was pretty quiet. One of the nurses taught me. It is a great way to keep your mind occupied. Most of my projects go to local shelters. They can always use the hats and socks, whereas I can only have so many pairs before it becomes too much." Sam lifted his pant leg showing of a pair of gray wool socks. "All of the socks I brought were made with my needles."

"That is so cool. My hobby is reading and that seems so unexciting compared to this reveal." Forrest devoured books. Mostly nonfiction and medical journals. As a kid he'd done nothing but borrow mysteries and horror books from the library. Those books were his only escape from the family that on his best days ignored him.

"Not boring." Sam leaned a hand on Forrest's knee as Charlee sat back down.

"Our name is registered and we are going to take this." She set the buzzer in the middle of the table and clapped her hands. "Let's go!"

CHAPTER TWELVE

"I THINK YOUR reading hobby is the only thing that saved us tonight." Sam hit Forrest's hip with his as they started back toward the dorms.

"Who would have guessed that trivia could get so cutthroat?" Forrest raised his hand to a few people walking toward the bar.

Many of the trivia crew had headed that direction when the canteen closed, but Forrest had said he was tired. And Sam had no desire to head to the bar without him.

"Everyone, Forrest." Sam reached for his hand; his body relaxed a little as Forrest's fingers tightened around his. "And then there's the fact that when first chance at a limited selection of ice cream is involved, you apparently *don't* get in Charlee's way."

"That *is* a lesson none of us knew we needed to learn." Forrest chuckled and pulled the door to the dorms open. They stepped inside, knocking the snow off their boots before heading to Sam's room.

It was their nightly ritual. They'd pushed the extra twin bed next to Sam's to create a bigger bed, though they'd woken entwined with each other on one side each morning. Or rather Forrest had woken, kissed Sam and headed out long before the night shifted fully into day.

"That last question, though, was all you." Forrest ran his hand along Sam's shoulder as he unlocked the door to his room.

"Knowing the highest peak in a random US state was certainly lucky. I think Charlee might have lost it if we got that close to first place and then blew it." Sam pushed the door open and pulled Forrest in.

"I've never been to Utah. I've read a few papers from there. And from the pictures I've seen it's gorgeous. Have you spent time there?"

"Not yet." Sam took his boots off and pulled the hat off his head. "But I always do research on potential follow-on locations."

"Utah was on your list before here?" Forrest yawned as he slipped the shirt over his head.

"No. Utah is on the list for after. Utah, back to Alaska again, North Dakota and a few others." Sam had a list in his journal. There was a constant rotation of out of the way places that needed a doctor. Hundreds of places he could go for a few months.

Though the idea of looking at that list didn't hold the same excitement as it had before Forrest had kissed him in the gym. He needed to start planning his next step. His after location, but he couldn't seem to get moving on that agenda item. "Want to shower?"

They were both exhausted. A warm shower would ensure they drifted to sleep faster. And showering with a naked Forrest was never going to be something Sam didn't look forward to.

"The shower is barely big enough for one." Forrest's gaze glowed as he stared at Sam. "I am not complaining but I am exhausted."

Sam stepped up and captured his lips before Forrest could make an excuse for tonight being a cuddle-and-snooze evening. They didn't have to be intimate every night. They had months left together.

"A hot shower, and sleep is the best recipe for exhaustion." Sam pressed his lips to Forrest's rough cheek. "I'll get the water started."

He moved into the bathroom and started the water. "It feels

wrong that this place is so cold and the hot water still takes a little while to get going. I feel like the reservoir should be kept nearly boiling so we don't have to shiver for the first seconds." Sam stepped into the cool water and shuddered.

Water rationing wasn't a huge deal in the winter with so few residents. But wasting resources was never recommended.

Forrest stepped in and gave a little shiver as the cool drops hit him. The water started heating and Sam moved to make sure Forrest felt the warmth.

"You ever consider coming to Indianapolis?" Forrest grabbed the soap from the wall and started soaping up the washcloth.

"No." Sam took the washcloth from Forrest and started running it over his back. The muscles were tight. "They have tons of hospitals. Not exactly a rural location."

"That's true." Forrest's head bounced but he didn't add any other comment.

Sam waited a moment, hoping Forrest might ask him to come anyway. Indicate this was more than just an ice fling. Two people drawn together but not meant for forever. But the only sound was the water hitting Forrest's tight back. "Relax." Sam kissed his shoulder. "You'll sleep better if you do."

"Right." Forrest cleared his throat and shifted his shoulders. The relaxation effort didn't seem to work.

"I went hiking in a forest fire once and I don't think my body was this tense." The chuckle that escaped didn't quite cover the fear that still raced through Sam when he remembered the heat that had seemed to radiate from the ground itself.

"What?" Forrest turned; the color drained from his face.

"I went hiking—"

Forrest's hand covered Sam's mouth. "I heard you the first time. Why would you do that?"

Sam took advantage of Forrest's changed position to run the soap over his magnificent chest. "I mean, hiking is fun."

"You know I'm not talking about the damn hike. Or rather I *am*, but seriously, Sam. In a forest fire? That is the definition of reckless." Forrest pursed his lips as he ripped the washcloth from Sam's fingers, added more soap then started running the cloth along Sam's chest.

"Why are you mad? It wasn't intentional. Or, I mean, it was, there were some injured hikers and the fire moved faster than expected. But why are you mad now?" Sam gripped Forrest's cheeks.

"I'm not mad."

"Liar." Sam shook his head but didn't let go of Forrest. "It was years ago. Three assignments ago. I'm fine." He brushed his lips across Forrest's. "See, fine."

"Have you been anywhere that wasn't dangerous?" Forrest raised a brow but didn't break the connection they had.

"Here." The South Pole was fun. An adventure. Truly unlike any other. "It's pretty safe. But how many people can say they've worked at the South Pole? Maybe I should see about spending time in the North Pole next. Round out the poles."

"There is no permanent station at the North Pole. The ice shifts too much."

"You have so much knowledge up there." Sam pressed his lips to Forrest's temple. The man was gorgeous but his brain was the real turn-on.

"The poles are dangerous." Forrest moved away from Sam's touch to let him into the water.

"Not really." It was a unique place, and there were dangers here. But there were dangers and unpredictability everywhere. Sam had carefully planned out his life twice in "safe" environments and gotten nothing to show for it. Why not explore new locations?

"Sam." Forrest put his hands on Sam's chest. "We are trapped on the pole."

"Evacuations happen. Trapped is a bit of an overstatement."

Drops spun from Forrest's head as he shook his head. "Yes, there has been *an* evacuation."

"Two. I got Dr. Anderson out, too." Sam rinsed quickly then

shut the water off. Forrest was handing him a towel before the final drips of the shower head had fallen.

"Anderson got out on the last flight of the season." Forrest wrapped the towel around his waist. "We were lucky to get the two we did. There won't be more. And you know it. So answer the question. Are all the locations you travel to dangerous?"

"Remote work is unique." Sam shrugged as he wrapped the towel around himself.

"Lots of things are unique." Forrest pushed a hand through his damp hair. "Are you seeking out danger?"

"You're here too, Forrest." Sam nodded toward him, then pointed at the phoenix. "Rising from the ashes of what?"

"My life. You said the phoenix made sense. Why are you changing the subject?"

"Because there is no answer to your question." Sam let out a groan of frustration that had nothing to do with the hot, naked man before him.

Or everything to do with him.

"I go where things are interesting. Add memories to my life bank while helping locations with few resources. I stay a couple of months and move on to the next place. I've climbed mountains, helped with fire rescue, damn near died in a plane crash." Sam held up a hand. "Don't tell my mom that. Technically, not a secret but also not something she and Dad know."

"That is the definition of a secret, Sam." Forrest stepped closer to him. "Does Utah have to be next?"

"Nope." Sam shrugged. "It's too soon to think of next. That's a problem for the future. Right now we are on an ice rock. And exhausted." He reached for Forrest's hand and pulled him toward the bed.

"Sam."

He turned, seizing Forrest's mouth. The kiss was deep but didn't linger.

"I do have something to say." Forrest raised a brow. "Not that I mind a kiss but..."

Sam caressed his cheek then laid a finger over his mouth. "Tomorrow."

Forrest let out a sigh.

There were things to talk about. Sam understood that. If they had truly been meant to be, they'd be celebrating a decade of wedded bliss right now and maybe even have a child. But they weren't soulmates.

He'd accepted that years ago. Mostly. This was a respite. This place wasn't real. Forrest had said he didn't know what this thing between them was. Sam wasn't ready to acknowledge the possibility of a future with Forrest stuck in a lab somewhere far from him.

Forrest's arms were around him. His mouth covering Sam's. His hands were stroking his body.

"I thought you were tired." Sam broke the kiss but gripped Forrest's taut ass.

Forrest placed his hands on either side of Sam's cheeks, kissed him and pushed him to the bed.

The questions. The talk. All of it vanished as their bodies tangled together.

Forrest kissed the end of Sam's nose before slipping from the bed. The alarm on his wrist started buzzing as he pulled on his pants and grabbed a shirt. He'd woken up just before it went off. So his body was already starting to adjust.

He'd gotten about three hours of sleep. Less than ideal, but he'd make it work.

He quietly opened the door and slipped out, careful not to wake Sam.

He blinked as the lights of the hallway hit his eyes. His brain rebelled and he sucked in a deep breath. He did not have time to get a migraine. There were two experiments to check on today. He had to gather the samples people had dropped off.

Swab them to see what was growing. And put together some reports for his team back stateside. Then he'd stop by the clinic.

He yawned as he made his way to his room. Not that he'd slept there in the last week.

A week.

That was all the time that had passed since they spent the first night together. So there was no reason for Sam to indicate he was thinking of uprooting the life he had for a future together.

He has no roots.

Forrest pushed past that thought as he hastily picked out clothes for the day. He grabbed some pain reliever, hoping that, if he got ahead of the headache, it might stay just a headache.

Trudging through the snow to the first pickup location, he nearly slipped on the ice. "Not dangerous, my ass."

He bit his lip. There was no need to talk to himself and Sam was clearly more of an adrenaline junkie than he'd been in school.

He wasn't one.

Except this didn't feel like he was chasing a rush. Sam was still in control. Still choosing his locations. He was in control; it was just instead of planning decades into the future he was only focused on the next twelve months or so.

Forrest wanted to look further. He'd wanted to talk about Indianapolis. Wanted to bring up the possibility of forever. Wanted to talk about this thing between them working.

Years of therapy had helped him identify the trauma of his youth. Helped him acknowledge that abuse. He wasn't petrified of the altar and letting a spouse down—though he hadn't properly dated anyone to test that theory.

Because all he'd wanted was Sam.

Something he'd wanted to say last night. But something in Sam's look had silenced him.

Had made him fear that Sam might walk away now. Might say this was simply one of the fun things he tried out when he was someplace new. After all, there wasn't a ton to do on the ice.

Forrest pressed a thumb to his temple. The pressure point sometimes relieved a bit of the force in his skull. Today it gained him nothing as he opened the door to a building where he'd set up a sample collection. He needed to move fast.

He grabbed the first samples and headed to the second location, blinking as an aura appeared in the corner of his eye.

He didn't bother to muffle the curse. He was on borrowed time. An hour. Maybe two. And he had at least six hours of solid work in front of him. Which meant working through the pain.

Picking up the pace he raced through collections and headed to the lab.

"Damn." Charlee lifted her head from the mat she'd laid on the floor. "Seriously? Seriously?" She slowly stood, groaning with each movement as she headed to the wall.

Forrest flinched as she flicked on a light. "What are you doing here?" Charlee didn't show up until nine. She worked late and slept in. If you counted sleeping until seven as sleeping in.

"What are *you* doing here?" Charlee crossed her arms. "I suspected you were here before six, but Forrest it is three thirty."

Forrest walked over and flicked the light off. His brain couldn't handle it. "Couldn't sleep."

"I don't believe that." Charlee reached for the light again.

"Don't, please."

Her hand paused as she looked him over. "I spent the night here to test my theory and I *hate* that I was right. You need to get more rest."

"I'm fine, Charlee. This isn't the first time my body has operated on little rest. Just settling it back into the rhythm it kept through my teens and twenties." Forrest couldn't manage to catch the yawn and saw Charlee's frown in the dimly lit lab.

"Go to bed, Charlee." There was no need to for her to be anything other than rested.

"Go back to bed, Forrest." Charlee imitated the frustration in his voice.

"I am already up and once that happens there is no point." Plus he needed to get this done before the migraine fully sidelined him.

"This is a bad idea. I'm telling you that right now." Charlee pointed a finger at him then yawned.

He couldn't stop the yawn that mimicked hers.

"I'm too tired to argue. But we *are* talking about this when I'm awake enough to make a solid argument." Charlee walked out, but at least she didn't slam the door.

Forrest took care of the samples, doing his best to ignore the growing aura in his left eye. There was no use ignoring the pounding in his head. That he was just going to have to deal with.

After getting the samples put away, he started toward the experiments he was monitoring. His brain screamed and he closed his eyes, sucking air through his teeth. If he gave it a moment, something would give.

It had to.

He shifted his shoulders and pushed at the darkness that seemed to pull at the edges of his senses. Then he opened his eyes, waiting for the sensation to cease. But it closed in tighter, tighter and then…

"Forrest."

Soft hands cupped his face. Sam's hands. The dream felt so real. Forrest tried to lift his arm to search out the man behind the hands, but his dream body was so heavy.

"Forrest. I need you to open your eyes."

Such a demand. Forrest tried to summon the energy but again his dream body refused.

"Now! Forrest." Charlee's voice echoed on the edge of his mind.

Weird. He never dreamed of colleagues, but the subconscious was peculiar.

"Call the clinic. Tell them to get a bed ready." Sam's voice sounded just like it had on their first rotation in med school. Sure, but a little afraid. "And a gurney. I doubt he can move on his own right now."

"Sam." His tongue was too large. And the headache he'd had was roaring back. This wasn't a dream, or it was too real. Either way it wasn't fair that his head now ached more than before. "Sam?"

"Forrest. Open your eyes."

He shook his head and flinched as the movement sent pain rushing toward him. "Lights off. Please."

"What the hell is that supposed to mean?" Charlee moved in the distance.

"It means a migraine. Move your right hand, if that is true."

Forrest did as he was told. His whole head felt like it might explode. "Aura started an hour ago."

"No. It didn't. It's eight a.m. You've been on the ground for, I don't even want to guess how long." Sam's clipped tone reached into his soul.

"You okay?" Forrest reached out a hand, trying to find Sam's by the sound of his voice.

"No. My boyfriend has been on the floor of his lab for hours. He cut the back of head when he fell and is suffering a migraine so bad, he can't even sit up. And I'm guessing there were hints of the headache when you slipped out of bed this morning."

Boyfriend.

Forrest thought he was smiling as the word punctured his skull.

"Thought I could work through it."

"Uh-huh." Sam's voice was rough with emotion, "Chris, let's get him loaded."

"I can walk." The idea of being brought into the clinic

on a gurney made his stomach turn. Or maybe that was just the migraine.

"All evidence points to that *not* being the case." Charlee's voice was level but he heard the hint of fear, too. He must look terrible.

"Thank you, Charlee." Sam put his hands on Forrest's cheeks just like they'd been when he thought he was dreaming. It settled him.

"If you can open your eyes right now, without flinching, and stand. Then I will walk you to the clinic." Sam's pulled back. The heat his touch provided evaporated and Forrest tried to ignore the chill sliding down his body.

He swallowed and opened his eyes. The dim lights turned his stomach and he rolled. There was a bucket before him to take care of the issue. Thank goodness.

"I think that covers it." Sam put his arms under Forrest's body and hefted him onto the gurney while Chris strapped him down.

Forrest couldn't even work up the energy to say something as the darkness pressed against him again. This time he didn't try to hold it off.

CHAPTER THIRTEEN

THERE WAS AN IV in his arm. That was what Forrest noticed before the fact that his headache was now a dull ache. A migraine cocktail must be pumping into his system.

He'd never gotten one before but had ordered several during his tenure in the ER during residency. It was an IV with fluids, nausea meds and pain meds. He'd seen more than one person begging for the cocktail over less effective, treatments. As a migraine sufferer, Forrest had never hesitated to start the drugs right away.

"Finally understand why these things are rated so highly on exit surveys."

"What?"

Forrest opened his eyes and smiled as Sam lifted his head off the bed. "I didn't mean to say that out loud."

"Clearly." Sam stood and rolled his shoulders. "I take it that means the cocktail worked?"

"Yeah. Once it's finished, I need—"

"No. You don't," Sam interrupted.

Forrest's head snapped, and the drugs had clearly worked because he wasn't ready to toss the very limited contents of his stomach again. "You don't even know what I was about to say."

"You're right." Sam crossed his arms. "I'm not sure if you're going to say that you need to get back to the lab or to help out here. Either way, I know for a fact that you're going to say that you need to head to work." He lifted his chin, the dare clear in his eyes.

"I was actually going to see about finding food." That was a lie and it was clear from the twitch in Sam's cheek that he knew it.

"Good. I have food here. That's easy enough to fix." Sam walked out of the bay.

Why the hell was he so upset? Forrest was the one in the bed.

Boyfriend.

The word echoed in his brain. Sam had said that when his voice was raised in the lab. Hadn't he? Forrest was more than a little foggy on the details.

Sam walked back in with a standard issue hospital tray.

Forrest shuddered. "That isn't just gelatin, is it?" The joke fell flat.

"It's dinner from the canteen. Charlee made you a to-go plate from the buffet. She even managed to squeeze in some ice cream. Not vanilla." Sam set the tray down.

"Dinner? Wait. What time is it?" How long had he been out?

"It's almost six a.m."

6:00 a.m.? Six in the morning? Forrest sat up further in the bed. He'd lost an entire day. An entire day.

No. He was already so far behind. This wasn't happening.

"Who took my shift?"

"That is your question?" Sam took the chair by the bed and laid a hand on Forrest's knee.

"Yeah. The first of a few actually. The sample collection…"

"You passed out from a migraine after sneaking from bed at three yesterday morning."

"I didn't sneak. I kissed your nose and I left, and it wasn't three." Forrest cleared his throat. There was no need to add that last part. This wasn't an interrogation.

Or rather it was, but he was not required to give the whole truth and nothing but the truth.

"So sorry, two forty-five? Is that closer?"

It was, but there was no reason to go down that route. "Sam, I'm fine."

Sam pursed his lips before letting out a breath. There were dark circles under his eyes and his lips looked chapped. When they'd dated, he had a bad habit of rubbing them until they bled.

He's worried about me.

Forrest understood. If the roles were reversed, he'd be terrified.

"I am fine." Forrest repeated the words. "I've suffered from migraines for as long as I can remember. They come when I am stressed." He was just exhausted from trying to meet all the expectations. He hadn't felt like he was covering so many spinning plates since med school. But he didn't want to let Sam down. The man would push himself to the brink in an instant.

Combine all that with the questions constantly popping off in Forrest's brain about the state of his and Sam's relationship, and it was stunning the migraine hadn't appeared days ago.

"I know." Sam stood, rubbed a finger along his bottom lip. "I know they come when you're stressed. You're doing too much. You're in the clinic, but the lab work is still there." He took a deep breath. "You aren't superman. I think we need to prioritize one of them."

Forrest's brain was still mushy. There wasn't a priority. He belonged in the lab, but he was helping in the clinic. Needed in the clinic—at least for now. "Says the man who never came to get me as backup when half the post was down with a bug." Forrest knew it was petulant to bring that up. But he was not the only overachieving burnt-out physician in this small bay.

"That was different." Sam moved to the end of the bed and leaned his hands on the rails. "You were busy."

"And you were drowning in patients. You were convinced you could handle it on your own."

"I could have." Sam bent his head. "But I'm glad that I didn't need to. And you don't need to do this, either." He waved a hand toward the bed. "I talked to Charlee."

"Charlee is not running the same experiments as I am." Not exactly a lie. Charlee and he were on the same team, but the microbiologist was looking for bacterial growth while he was focusing on shifting viral loads and when mutations occurred.

"You ran the lab when she was down with the virus that took out so many here. And you have free time. She pointed that out while you were sleeping." Sam leaned farther over the railing. "You need to rest. Doctor's orders. I will confine you to the barracks."

"No, you won't." Forrest shook his head. "No. You won't. You need me here. You need another physician of record. I can get everything done." He'd done it for most of his life. "I am not failing at this."

"Do you hear yourself? You didn't fail. You passed the eff out!" Sam leaned back and crossed his arms. "I am rotating you back to two shifts in here. And I will check in with Charlee to make sure that you are only working ten-hour days." He turned on his heel.

"Sam." At least that stopped him from walking out. "Don't leave." The plea was so quiet, Forrest wasn't completely sure he'd said it.

Sam's shoulder's tightened, but he stayed where he was, though he didn't look back. "I need to grab the tablet and update your chart. I will be right back. Eat your dinner. Please, Forrest."

Then he opened the bay curtain and stepped out.

Sam shuddered as the wave of emotions wrapped around him. The last twenty-four hours had been a roller coaster. He'd panicked when Charlee called. Felt his heart stop when he'd seen Forrest on the floor of the lab. And now he was angry the man was trying to do everything.

Because I keep putting him on the roster.

And then there was the guilt. Sam had added more shifts than he needed. It had been a selfish play to spend more time with Forrest. To re-create the magic they'd had in med school and help Forrest stop hiding away, wasting his talents.

All I did was drive him to a migraine.

"He isn't wrong." Nat held the tablet close to her chest as Sam walked up to the desk. "You're just as bad. You've been better since he's been on the rotation, but you're two peas in the same pod."

Sam didn't have a comment ready to fire off for that one, so he just held his hand out for the tablet.

Natasha shook her head. "You aren't allowed to be the medical person of record for your boyfriend. You know the rules."

"We aren't boyfriends." Sam's throat threatened to close as he whispered the words.

"Really?" She raised a brow and grabbed the walkie-talkie. "Should I check with Charlee to find out if she fully misheard you while you were trying to rouse the man that anyone can see is definitely not not your boyfriend this morning?"

Sam did not appreciate the double negative. Or the reminder that he'd called Forrest his boyfriend. Seeing him on the ground, the blood on the back of his head… It had taken all of Sam's training to keep his breath steady and focus on providing care.

Even now, his fingers were shaking at the idea that Forrest had lain on that cold floor for hours before Charlee found him. The cut on the back of his head hadn't needed stitches. A butterfly bandage was enough to close the wound that had mostly stopped bleeding by the time they got him to the hospital. But what if it hadn't been enough?

If he'd lain there, bleeding. Hurt. Alone.

He didn't.

"Fine." He wasn't going to argue semantics with Natasha, or Charlee for that matter. Forrest hadn't heard him. They weren't boyfriends. Not anymore.

But that didn't mean Sam's soul hadn't cracked for a moment when he saw him.

"You need to rest." Nat punched a few things on the tablet.

"I've slept."

"Oh. You are testy." She set the tablet down and crossed her arms. "I said *rest.* Not sleep. Sleep is important. It resets our cycles and helps our bodies regulate. But that's not what I meant. And you know it. Do you know how to rest?"

"Of course." Sam knew how to rest. He just wasn't very good at it. His body seemed to rebel at the idea of just sitting still. Of letting time pass without accomplishing anything. Every person got a finite amount of time on this planet, and he craved movement. Slowing down gave your brain time to think. Time to question.

"Really?" Natasha chuckled. "What did you bring as your personal item?"

He could tell from the look in her eyes that she didn't expect him to have anything. Sam raised his chin. "Yarn. Knitting needles and crochet hooks."

Her brows furrowed as she stepped around the desk, heading for Forrest's bay.

"No comment? I am pretty sure you expected me to say I didn't need a personal item." Natasha was a lot of things, but the woman did not let go of a point she was making.

Pushing the curtain back on, Nat smiled at the man picking through the food on the plate. "What was your personal item?"

"What?" Forrest looked from Natasha to Sam.

"I said, what was your personal item? The thing that didn't count against you on the weight allowance for personal belongings—within reason. We all got something we were allowed to bring provided it wasn't a weapon. And somehow, Forrest, you don't strike me as a big game hunter or shooter."

"I'm not. I brought my guitar." His dark gaze flitted to Sam before focusing back on his food.

He'd mentioned the guitar during one of their first conversations. But Sam had never seen it in his room. Was it the one he'd given him? The one he'd picked at on their old comfy blue couch for years. If Sam closed his eyes, he could place Forrest there now. Rerun a memory he hadn't thought of in ages.

Forrest had joked for a year that he'd love to learn play. For Christmas, Sam had put it under the tree, unsurprised when Forrest let out an excited squeal upon seeing it. Christmas—the holiday he loved most even though his family never celebrated it or gave him a gift. Sam had always tried to make it special, but he'd never topped that guitar.

Forrest had spent all his free time watching online videos and taking online music lessons since his schedule couldn't accommodate in-person lessons easily.

He had loved that instrument. And the apartment had been so silent after he'd left. The ghosts of music Sam would never hear again had echoed in his memories long after Forrest disappeared from his life.

"Great. A guitar and fiber arts." Natasha grabbed a prescription pad from her pocket.

"Are you planning on ordering me to knit?" Sam chuckled but Natasha didn't look up as she scribbled one note, ripped it off and scribbled another.

"No." She pressed one note into his chest and dropped the other on the tray next to the food Forrest was barely touching. "I'm ordering you *both* to knit and play the guitar. You are not to return to this clinic for the next three days." She held up a hand toward Forrest. "Or the lab."

"Hey." The fact that Forrest's complaint was so loud was a good thing. It meant the migraine cocktail had worked. Though Natasha was right, he still needed to take some time off.

"I have Charlee monitoring the lab." Nat interrupted Forrest before his "Hey" could become more than a single ticked-off statement. "Do not make that woman mad. And you—" she turned her full attention to Sam "—do *not* try me. I will not have you back in this clinic for three days. Attempt it, and I will talk to Houston."

There was very little Houston could do. There was no way

off the ice right now. But the look on Nat's face was enough to give Sam at least second thoughts about trying her.

"I'll take a day." That would be good because then he could make sure that Forrest relaxed.

"I am sorry, Doc, did I order a day?" She looked over at Forrest who shook his head.

"I think it was three."

Sam raised a brow as the man he'd spent every night with for a week sided with the NP.

"You're planning to make me take three days." Forrest crossed his arms.

"*You* were on the floor of your lab bleeding this morning. I have no such issue."

"Yet."

"Yet."

Natasha and Forrest's voices echoed into the clinic at the same time.

"I will be checking in." He was the resident physician. It was his job.

"So you don't think Chris and I are capable. That's a tough hit, but I'm not surprised." Natasha pulled back, her shoulders tight.

"That's not what I said." Sam pushed a hand through his hair. He could see how the words could be taken that way. But it wasn't what he'd meant.

"Take the time, Sam." Forrest's words were strong. Something Sam would be celebrating after the day's escapades. If they weren't directed at keeping him out of the clinic.

"Listen to him." Natasha walked over and started to pull the IV out of Forrest's arm. "I'm discharging you. I'm sending along some pain meds that you are to take if you start to feel any headache or see any aura."

"I don't usually see the aura, and never without the migraine." Forrest held the bandage over the small puncture wound and placed his hand over his head to help with clotting.

"There's a first time for everything." Natasha pulled the gloves off, walked out and was back in no time with the pain meds she'd promised. "Walk him back to the dorms, Doc."

Then she turned on her heel.

"That is one tough nurse." Forrest slid his feet over the edge of the bed and into the boots Sam had removed when they'd brought him in. "I don't think I'd want to go up against her."

Sam tilted his head. "Really?"

Forrest mirrored his head tilt. "Really."

"I'll take some time off." It wasn't going to be three days. But he could take two. Make sure Forrest was fully recovered. "Let's go. Slowly." He slid his arm around Forrest's waist.

Forrest leaned against him. "I'm fine."

Sam's mind knew that, but it was having a hard time convincing his heart.

CHAPTER FOURTEEN

FORREST ROLLED OVER on the bed and let out a moan. He wasn't sure what time it was. His head was delightfully pain-free, but his muscles were clearly upset by the lack of movement.

Lifting his wrist, he blinked as bare skin stared back. "What?" He lifted the other, not that he ever wore his watch on his right wrist, but it was also bare.

"If you are looking for your watch, it's sitting on the counter by the door. Damn thing went off at two forty-five this morning. I should have made sure you turned the alarm off." Sam looked up from the couch where he was knitting a sock.

"Sorry." Forrest had meant to turn it off.

"Were you planning to disregard Nat's orders?" Sam's hands kept moving as he looked directly at Forrest. There were creases around his eyes and dark circles indicating that while Forrest was well rested, Sam couldn't say the same.

"How are you doing that?" Forrest asked. Sam's hands were flying but he wasn't looking at the sock.

"Don't change the subject." The needles he was holding kept the same pace even though he never looked down.

"I'm not. Not really." Forrest slid out of bed and started to stretch. After so many hours in bed yesterday and then oversleeping, his body felt refreshed but tight. "I meant to turn it off. The headache. The day. It must have slipped my mind. It's habit that it goes off so early."

Sam let out a noise that made Forrest think there was more

than a little bit of doubt in his mind. “Habit. You mean to tell me that you’ve been getting up that early for years?”

“No. I shifted after Dr. Anderson left.” Not completely truthful. And the lie rubbed his soul. “I shifted after the virus. I was working in the lab and the clinic.”

“Then it is not habit.” Sam blew out a breath as his needles flew even faster through the stitches.

“You’re mad.”

The knitting needles clicked together and now Sam did look down.

“Because I got you banished from the hospital for three days?” Forrest pursed his lips. The man belonged in the clinic. In trauma centers. Sam was born to be a doctor. Forrest had fallen into it because he was good at school. A school counselor recommended it and he’d followed the path. But Sam—Sam was meant to heal.

But burnout didn’t care about your passions or callings. It struck everyone. And Sam was hovering on the precipice of it. Or already covering it up and trying to deny it.

The needles’ clicking stopped. “No. Yes. Not entirely.” Sam exhaled heavily. “You were passed out.”

“The migraine—”

“Forrest.” Sam pinched his eyes closed. “You were passed out on the lab floor for hours. What if you’d hit your head harder? What if the scrape on the back of your head was a gash? What if the migraine was the warning of an aneurysm?” When he opened his eyes, they were full of fire.

There was no way Forrest was going to point out that, if his headache was the rare sign of an aneurysm, there was nothing that could be done at the pole. Sam’s hands were already shaking.

Forrest moved to the couch. He reached for the knitting, but Sam pulled back.

“I am furious with you.” He swallowed. “And with myself for not catching it. I knew you were sneaking out. Knew you were putting too much pressure on yourself. Knew I wasn't helping with that."

"I was not sneaking—stop saying that. That makes it sound like I was doing something wrong." He'd been trying to keep everything going. Trying to ensure everything got done. Trying to make sure nothing failed. He didn't fail.

In the end he hadn't been able to accomplish it. And gotten Sam banished from the hospital for his efforts, too. "And you weren't making me do anything I wasn't fully on board with."

Sam shuddered. "You could have been seriously hurt, Forrest." His words echoed off the walls of the room and color shot up his cheeks as he realized how loud he was.

"But I wasn't." Forrest laid his hand on Sam's knee. "I am fine."

"How would you feel if it was me?" Sam sucked in a breath as his jeweled gaze captured Forrest's.

Forrest swallowed as he found no words on the edge of his tongue. If he'd walked in on Sam passed out, he'd have panicked. From the account Charlee had told him, Sam had flown into physician mode. Taken charge and never wavered.

"I'd have panicked."

"No." Sam shook his head. "You wouldn't have. That's a fiction that you are telling yourself because you're convinced you're not good at bedside. But I didn't ask what you would do. I asked how you'd *feel* if it was me."

"Broken." The words slipped from his lips. That was his heart answering.

"I asked you before this—" Sam gestured between the two of them "—started, what we are doing. You didn't answer. We still haven't addressed any of it. We slid right back into the day to day and nights." Color climbed Sam's throat. "I found you on the floor unconscious."

"And called me your boyfriend." Forrest was certain he'd heard that.

Nearly certain.

"Forrest—" Sam set the yarn to the side "—I said it out of habit."

Knives slicing through him. Each word a blade cutting deeper.

Habit. That wasn't what he wanted to be. Wasn't what he needed. But he also had never broached the topic of their relationship. "Habit." Forrest pursed his lips. "Is that what I am? A habit?"

Sam let out a breath, "I mean the word *boyfriend* slipped out because you were my boyfriend for so long. I've avoided asking, Forrest, because I'm terrified that you will just say you don't know what this is between us. You walked away once before. It destroyed me."

"It wasn't supposed to." He bit his tongue. "I didn't mean to say that."

Sam nodded. "Didn't mean to say it but meant it. Right?"

What was the point of denying it? "Yes. You aren't supposed to be here, Sam." Forrest laughed but there was no hint of humor in it. Sam was meant for so much more. "You're supposed to be in New York running a trauma unit. Visiting your parents upstate on the weekends with your husband."

"I don't believe in marriage." Sam cleared his throat.

"You believed once upon a time. Planned it all out." Forrest's neck twitched as he caught himself from looking at the door. Escape was cowardly. And Sam was right. He'd asked twice and Forrest had dodged the question.

Sam shrugged. "Not anymore. I deserve to know, need to know, what the hell this is. Because putting myself back together again was the hardest thing I've ever done. So one final ask, what are we doing?"

"I never stopped loving you, Sam." Forrest met the blue eyes that had haunted him for so long. "Never. And if you had been on the floor of the hospital unconscious, my soul would have torn apart. And yes, I would have slipped into doctor mode. Because a world without you is less bright. I know that. I lived it."

"Because you chose it." Sam's bottom lip trembled, but his shoulders straightened. "I thought this was just a fun ice fling. A moment suspended in time."

That stung. But Forrest had never indicated that it was anything else. He'd forced himself back into Sam's life. Literally. Sam was right. He'd asked, more than once, what they were doing.

It was Forrest holding back. Forrest terrified of giving the wrong answer. But no answer was also an answer. Sam deserved more.

"I don't want this to be an ice fling." This was a fork in the road. Once this conversation finished there was no going back.

"Then what *do* you want, Forrest?"

So few people had ever asked him that. In fact the first person to ever ask was the man sitting across from him. The man whose heart he'd crave for the rest of his days. "You. Always, you."

Sam nodded but didn't say anything. Silence stretched into the moment. Heavy with the past, present and hopefully future.

When he still didn't say anything, Forrest pulled back a little. "Do you want me to leave?" Sam had asked the question. Forrest had given the answer. If it wasn't what Sam wanted, needed, Forrest would honor that.

"I don't want you to leave." Sam closed the distance between them but didn't reach for him. Didn't touch him. "If this isn't an ice fling…"

"It isn't." Forrest should have let him finish his sentence but he needed to acknowledge that now. This was not a fling. Not for him.

"Then we are boyfriends. Lovers. Whatever label the world puts on it." Sam sighed.

"What label do you want?" Forrest was fine with anything, provided the other person in the relationship was Sam.

"Boyfriends feels like we are back in college. In that one-bedroom apartment with no insulation between our walls."

Sam chuckled, the mood lightening. "But lovers feels… I don't know not wrong but not right. Partners is too—" he paused for a second "—serious at the moment."

Forrest put his hand on Sam's chin, "If people ask, we can say boyfriends, but honestly, outside of Natasha and Charlee, who have both made their thoughts very clear, I don't think anyone else is paying attention. And I mean that in the best way. So for us, we are simply Forrest and Sam. Two men who don't want to be separated. Does that work?"

Sam nodded. "Yeah. That works."

Forrest leaned in. His lips brushed Sam's. A kiss to seal the moment. In many ways it was anticlimactic. But it was also perfection. They were Forrest and Sam again.

And this time, Forrest wasn't walking away. "Now, how about you teach me how to crochet? Not sure I can do two hooks."

"These are needles." Sam winked before standing and walking over to a bag and coming back. "This—" he held up a small blue device "—is a hook." He grabbed some yellow yarn out of the bag.

"I know that is yarn."

"Good." Sam dropped a kiss on his nose. "Let's get started."

It wasn't until they were in bed that evening that Forrest realized he'd said he loved Sam. Sam had said he didn't want him to leave. That he didn't want a fling. But he'd never said the word *love*.

"We should go get your guitar." Sam stretched and rolled his shoulders.

"Bored?"

"Yes!" He was not going to lie about that. This was day three of Natasha's mandated free time. But the problem with free time was that it made time pass so slowly.

"You've been so many places, Sam. Surely you didn't work *all* the time at them. You said you investigated locations before going, no point in that if you are only planning to be in the clinic."

"I did stuff." Touristy things mostly. Things to fill the space between shifts. But he hadn't gone more than twenty-four hours between shifts in years. It was one of Oliver's primary complaints.

Stop working so hard. Have some free time.

Cheating was never the answer, but Sam would only be lying to himself if he didn't acknowledge that he'd prioritized work over that relationship. Another piece of proof that, when the universe crafted him, he wasn't cut out for the type of soulmate love his parents had.

I told Forrest this wasn't a fling.

Sam still wasn't sure how to wrangle the mixed emotions in his soul. One part of him had wanted to explode with joy. Send a note back to his parents announcing that they were back together. That they could expect to see them when they got back.

But a thread of fear still roamed his heart. He'd been so sure once. Believed that Forrest was the "one." That he *had* a one. Then Forrest had walked away. Sam had never guessed he was even considering it. He'd spent months going over their time together, looking for the red flags people said must be there.

Only to find none.

So this wasn't a fling, but he was going to monitor the situation this time. Make sure he saw any changes. Had time to react. Protect himself.

Flee.

"So we could do stuff here. There are activities." Forrest walked over to the bulletin board right before the door and grabbed the weekly activity list that was pushed under the door each Monday. Sam always hung it up, but other than trivia night he'd never done anything on it.

"There is a lecture, but it isn't until this evening." Forrest pulled his bottom lip through his teeth.

"And nothing else for the day, right? This place isn't a tourist destination." Sam fought the urge to walk to the clinic, just to check in. If he did that, he'd never hear the end of it from Natasha.

And if he was honest, he was a little terrified of the NP. Which he knew was the image she cultivated—well.

"What was your favorite thing you've done? Ice fishing? You were up north."

Sam laughed. "Up north yes, I've been above the lower forty-eight, as the Alaskans call it. But no ice fishing. The weather was far too cold for my liking. Plus sitting on the ice for hours was not exactly enticing for me. There are other activities in Alaska besides ice-related ones. Not so much the case here."

"When we get ice storms in Indianapolis it shuts the city completely down." Forrest pulled one arm across his chest then the other. "But it doesn't happen often. Not even every year."

"Uh-huh." Forrest had brought up his hometown several times over the last two days but never asked him to come. "Shutting down for ice is the case in most places I am pretty sure." Sam winked, enjoying the face Forrest made,

"The *point*, Sam, is what did you do? You said you enjoyed being in new places. What did you enjoy?"

"Moving." Sam shrugged. "I know moving is something most people hate, but I enjoyed it. I liked throwing darts, sort of, and landing someplace I never knew existed. I have a goal to visit all fifty states and as many countries as possible."

A goal he only accomplished through work, but he was accomplishing it.

"So travel." Forrest blew out a breath. "Not really an option at the pole, or with only one more day off. But, where do you want to go next? We can plan it."

Plan it. Sam's stomach clenched. Plan. With Forrest. It was a lovely suggestion. One he wanted. So why was his voice suddenly absent?

Forrest looked down and grabbed a shirt that had escaped the laundry bag he kept at the end of the bed. Hiding the disappointment Sam's hesitation no doubt brought. "Or we could do laundry. It's time."

Saying the words in a dramatic fashion did not make that chore any more exciting.

"It is. But we should find something to entertain us while the machine runs. And I think you've knotted enough yarn for today." Sam picked up the ball of yellow that Forrest had managed to mangle. "How is this even possible?"

Forrest looked at the ball of yarn, but Sam doubted the frustration darting through his features had anything to do with the yarn. Why hadn't he said something about planning a trip?

Made a plan. That was what Sam was good at. Plan out the next six months. Do something. But the words refused to materialize.

"We can grab my guitar and spend time in the lounge while we wait for it. Weird how domestic duties are still required at the end of the earth."

"Let's grab the guitar." Sam was surprised how much he wanted to see the instrument in Forrest's large hands. It had always struck him how gently he cradled the instrument, how those fingers were so deft on the strings. Ironic considering the complete lack of dexterity with the crochet hook. "Then we can do what needs to be done with these."

Forrest grabbed the laundry bag that filled twice as fast with two men's clothes. Sam should be grateful that he wasn't pushing the conversation about planning a vacation. So why was he annoyed that Forrest had shifted to laundry—the most boring chore—so fast? If Forrest didn't force the issue, what did that mean?

They got to Forrest's room; Forrest opened the door and stepped inside. He went to the small closet and pulled out a hard case. Not the case Sam had gotten him.

"You changed cases?" Sam pointed at the plain black case. It was functional but lacked the fun vibrancy of the red Sam had purchased for it.

"No. This guitar came with this case. I thought of adding stickers to it. Or something to change it up, but I rarely use it, so no real point." Forrest put the guitar over his shoulder.

"What happened to the one I gave you?" The question was out before Sam could capture it. He'd kept the watch Sam had given him. The one that had brought so many emotions.

But the watch was functional. Something that had use. An instrument was useful, but the guitar was a deeper gift. A thing Forrest had always wanted but would never buy for himself. If he'd given it away… Sam swallowed.

Forrest's hand stopped as he reached for the laundry basket. He looked up and stepped toward Sam.

Sam's face must be showing the turmoil wrapping through his soul.

Forrest held up a hand. "It's at home. In the corner of my apartment that my friend Kelly is house sitting until I get back. There was no way I was bringing my prize possession to the end of the earth. It's the one thing I have that is irreplaceable. Well, that and the Christmas ornaments I've kept in a box in my closet."

Most of the heaviness, the worry, the fear coating Sam's heart melted on that statement. He closed the distance between the two of them. His mouth covering Forrest's as he wrapped his arms around his neck.

He loved this man. Had always loved this man. Sam broke the connection and put his hands on either side of Forrest's face. The stubble that Forrest perpetually left on his jaw now sharp under his fingers.

I love you.

The words were sharp in his mind. Crystal clear. But his mouth couldn't quite form the words. His brain was still firing off what-ifs that served no purpose.

"I missed those clay figures on the tree." Sam pressed his forehead to Forrest's. He'd always given him such a hard time when he sought out the yearly ornaments at the small stand that popped up right after Halloween and disappeared the day after Christmas. For Forrest it was a pilgrimage.

He'd missed everything about this man. If they made it to the end of the year, they were going to have to get a new ornament.

When, his heart reminded his brain, not if. When.

CHAPTER FIFTEEN

NATASHA LEANED BACK in the chair at the desk. "I got an offer to work in Florida."

Sam looked up from notes he was making. "Oh. I didn't know you were looking to go to Florida." Time on the ice was winding down.

Nat shrugged. "Gotta have a follow-on location."

Sam made a noncommittal sound. He and Forrest were doing great. The last few weeks had been nearly perfect. It was like before. Nearly.

Yet anytime Forrest brought up Indianapolis or even a vacation after this, Sam always found a way to change the subject. It wasn't that he didn't like the idea of Indianapolis. He'd never put it on his list, but that was because it wasn't on any list he'd seen.

Even if he wasn't ready to discuss moving in, a vacation after working pretty much nonstop on the ice for eight months was a great idea. And it had been a perfect month and a half. So he should help Forrest pick a place.

But something kept holding him back. His brain refused to listen to his heart. Refused to accept that this time maybe everything would be fine. If it hadn't worked last time, what was the guarantee it would work this time?

"I mean, I'm not sure that I want to go to Florida, but as a traveler it's a decent location. And after here—" she gestured to the ice-coated window "—warm sounds good."

Sam laughed. "That I understand."

"Where are you headed? Indiana?"

"Did Forrest put you up to asking that?" Sam feared the question sounded as pathetic as it felt.

"Of course not. But I know that's where the lab is based. Charlee and I are already planning to meet up for girls' night in the city when a big music tour comes through next year."

The two women had become fast friends after concocting a plan to force Forrest and Sam to take time off. It was weird that was over a month ago. He'd expected the time to drag here. Instead it was speeding by.

Sam knew that Forrest would be getting similar questions from Charlee. No secrets between the lab and the clinic.

"So where are you planning to go?"

The door to the hospital opened at the same time as that question left Natasha's lips and Forrest walked in. They'd started splitting shifts. Chris, Natasha, and Sam all working overlapping tens with Forrest subbing in six in the afternoon.

"Scrap that question." Natasha passed the tablet to Forrest.

"I didn't mean to interrupt. But I was sick of hiding in the lab. The tests are just spinning."

Hiding in the lab.

There was that language he'd used the entire time he was here. Yet, he didn't show any interest in changing it. Why?

And if he wasn't happy in the lab, would he uproot and change everything like he had in med school? And would Sam be the casualty when it happened again?

"You didn't." Natasha stretched an arm over her shoulder. "But I'm off and I'm not wasting an extra minute here. You two—" she pointed at both of them "—should do the same."

"We do." Sam shook his head as Natasha darted toward the door. "Most of the time."

"When things aren't busy." Forrest nodded along with him and let out a laugh. "We aren't working ourselves to the bone right now."

“I think Natasha would point out that the words *right now* make that comment suspicious.” Sam slapped Forrest on the back. If they weren’t at the clinic he’d kiss him, but that would have to wait until his shift ended.

“Then it’s a good thing she didn’t hear it and my boyfriend has no desire to inform her.” Forrest hit his hip as he looked at the bays. “How has today been?”

“Steady.” Sam had seen a handful of patients. Nothing requiring an overnight stay. “It’s a little weird.”

“What?” Forrest headed to the chair behind the desk to take a quick look at the day’s charts. Even with no patients at the moment, he always familiarized himself with the day’s load.

He noticed patterns before anyone else. Like the fact that there was a pinpoint carbon monoxide leak in one of the dorms. Three people on the same end of one hall had reported headaches when they were talking at dinner three nights ago. Each mentioned how they woke up with the headaches but they went away a few hours after work. The carbon monoxide detector would have caught it, after it got bigger, but Forrest had found it immediately.

“I don’t want to say the Q-word.” Sam looked at the door as if just thinking the word *quiet* was enough to bring a rush of patients.

Forrest put his hands on the desk. “It is a unique environment. Everyone is healthy. The kind of chronic diseases we see on the mainland don’t exist here.”

We. Sam’s heart thudded in his ears. Forrest had started talking about himself as one of the doctors. Not a stand-in. Not a failure. Just the subtle shift to the *we* language. No more othering himself.

Sam ached to push. To draw him into conversation about stepping out of the lab more than just here at the pole. Stop hiding. But he wanted Forrest to realize how good he was at it himself. See himself as a success rather than a failure.

“That’s true. Even in the rural locations, you see at least a handful of chronic conditions, particularly with an older demographic." Sam looked around the quiet clinic. At any other place there'd be at least one person in the bay. It wasn't that there was an age limit on people employed at the pole, but most older people were either settled in their careers or with their family, or both.

"Speaking of places—" Forrest cleared his throat "—I can reach out to the lab and request a transfer."

"Transfer?" Sam blinked. Had he heard that right?

"Yes. The company has labs around the US and even in some foreign countries. There are no guarantees, but you're clearly not interested in Indianapolis."

"I never said that." Sam had made sure that he never said anything bad about Indiana. It was fine. And there were several trauma centers in the area.

Forrest raised a brow. "You've changed the topic every time I've brought it up over the last month. It's fine, Sam."

"Are you sure you want to go back to the lab?" Damn it. He hadn't meant to bring that up. Why didn't life have a rewind button?

"Go back to the lab? I am in the lab right now. Completing a study. I am not returning to bedside, Sam."

"But you're so good at it." Sam moved toward the desk.

Forrest pointed to an empty bay. "Yeah. Here, where it is normally quiet."

Sam flinched as the Q-word echoed in the empty area.

"With healthy patients." Forrest let out a sigh and leaned back in the chair. "As we just discussed, this is not a standard rotation. The burns Mark and Adina experienced were the exception, thank God. Hiding in the lab is good for me."

"I know you enjoy lab work, but..." Sam stopped not sure what else to say.

"But?" Forrest rolled his hand, his dark eyes blazing.

"I don't know. I just started but had nowhere to go. I just... I just..."

"Lost the words again?" Forrest pushed up off the chair. "I like the lab, Sam. It's my place."

"If it's so good, why do you keep using the word *hiding*?" Sam's brain slammed out the words.

Forrest paused, surprise evident on his face. "I say hiding because—" he hesitated "—I don't know. I just say it. I…"

"Hey!" The call came from the outer wall of the clinic. "Hey!"

"I shouldn't have said the Q-word." Forrest muttered the words behind Sam as they headed toward the call. A reprieve. But not the kind Sam wanted.

"She keeps vomiting. Can't keep anything down." Henry Polson, a researcher who spent most of his time out in the field was clutching a young woman who was having trouble holding up her head. "Kerry, keep your eyes open. Please."

Sam bent down to focus on Kerry while Forrest kept his attention on Henry. "Can you tell me when everything started?"

"Vomiting started twenty-four hours ago. We were out in the field, and scheduled to be there for the next two weeks."

Forrest knew that the field tents were technically climate controlled to withstand the harsh winter conditions of the poles. Understood that people needed to research the ice sheath. But spending weeks in the tents was where he wanted to be least in the world.

"Is anyone else sick?" Sam put his hand on Kerry's forehead. "No fever."

A good sign. This was probably a norovirus—it accounted for most stomach bugs. Unfortunately it was highly contagious. If Kerry was ill, others would start to show symptoms shortly. And out in the field was the worst place for them.

"No." Henry shook his head.

"Not yet." Sam looked at Forrest. The same thought clearly running through his mind.

Sam hooked a hand under Kerry's exhausted frame and guided her to a bed.

"Did the rest of the team come back from the field with you?" Forrest knew Henry wanted to care for his sick colleague, but they potentially had several other ill individuals ready to drop.

Most didn't need inpatient treatment with the virus. It typically cleared the system within seventy-two hours. But they were seventy-two hours of absolute hell. And Kerry would have become contagious the moment she showed symptoms.

The field had limited bathroom capabilities. It was roughing it in the coldest desert on earth.

Assuming she was the first, the others had one to three days before the incubation cycle completed itself.

"No. They're running experiments. We need—"

"You *need* to have them back here." Sam nodded to Kerry's feet.

Forrest took the sign and moved quickly to pull the heavy boots from her feet.

"Doc." Henry's strained voice echoed in the small bay.

"No." Sam shook his head, cutting off the argument Forrest saw brewing. "We'll get her stabilized, but you need to get them here. Now." Sam turned his full attention to Kerry.

"Henry..." Forrest motioned for the man to follow him out of the bay. "I know there are experiments to run." His words were soft, but the clinic was quiet and Forrest knew Sam heard him. His shoulders tightened briefly before releasing.

"If we aren't out there, the grant funding might get pulled. There are ramifications to delays." Henry pushed the hat off his head. "I know getting sick on the ice is unpleasant, but we have a real chance here to get core samples and make a difference. Understanding the shift in the ice sheath is vital to tracking the ocean's health. Losing a few days sets us back weeks. I know that sounds dramatic, but I'm telling the truth."

He didn't doubt that Henry was giving it to him straight.

Forrest's experiments had a few days' incubation time to give samples time to grow, but there were still expectations of delivery that had to be met for his grants.

"I understand." Forrest rocked back on his feet. Given the conversation that had preceded this one, Sam was about to be pissed with him. "Is anyone else showing symptoms? Stomachache, vomiting, diarrhea, stomach cramps?"

"How are aches and cramps different?" Henry looked back over to where Kerry was losing the very little that was still in her stomach.

"Ache is constant. Cramps come and go. Are you asking because there are people experiencing either?"

"No. I just needed to know. Sound like the same thing."

Sam let out a noise but didn't call the man a liar.

Forrest didn't think Henry was lying. All doctors were scientists, but some were more focused on the science parts and others on the people side. It was a discipline that needed both.

"All right. How many are on your team now?" If there were too many, tracking this would be difficult.

"Six."

"Including you?"

"Yeah. Including me. It should be seven, but one guy always finds some reason to avoid field work—we made sure that our office back home is tracking that but there is nothing we can do here."

"Frustrating. But that means you're responsible for a manageable number of people." Forrest didn't react to the groan Sam let out. "You are to monitor everyone for the next seventy-two hours. Temperatures in the morning, at lunch, dinner and before bed. Everyone is to report to you if they have any of the symptoms I mentioned. If another member of the team reports the symptoms or has a fever over ninety-nine point seven degrees, you and the entire team are to report back to the station."

Henry looked at Sam then back at Forrest. "You sure?"

"Yes."

And no.

He was taking a risk. If there was norovirus running through the camp that was going to be very unpleasant. But no one came to the pole for fun. They were here for science. Important work that literally could not be done anywhere else.

And Sam is going to hate me.

He'd deal with that when this conversation was over. Add it to the list of things they needed to discuss.

"But I am serious, a single person reports a cramp and you pack it up." Forrest hoped his gaze carried how serious he was.

"Agreed." Henry swallowed then looked over Forrest's shoulder at Kerry. "You will take care of her?"

"Of course we will." Forrest patted Henry's shoulder. "Dr. Miller is the best in the business and our nurse practitioners are excellent."

"And you?" Henry's gaze caught Forrest.

His throat seized for a moment. "I'm capable of taking care of Kerry, too."

"Capable." Henry squinted at Forrest for a moment, then turned his attention to Sam. "Take care of her, Doc."

"Of course." Sam was already starting the IV with fluids and anti-nausea meds. "I'm setting a container right next to you—" Sam put her fingers on the metal bowl "—if you need it."

Kerry nodded but didn't open her eyes.

"We will be close by." Sam put the call button near her other hand. "But if you need something, press this."

Another nod from Kerry.

Forrest took a deep breath as Sam started toward him. But he didn't stop, just moved directly to the small desk the clinic maintained.

He followed, trying to let the annoyance flow out of him. "Sam."

"I don't want to hear it." Sam shook his head and started adding things to the tablet.

"There is a very good reason why I told Henry—"

"No." Sam's gaze burned as it met his. "No. There is not. You made a choice."

"I did." Forrest put his hands on the desk. "They have work that needs to be done."

"Yep. And six people with norovirus on the ice is a bad time, but the science *must* get done." Sam rolled his eyes.

"Hey." Those words felt like they were directed more at him than the team on the ice. "Sometimes it does have to get done. And we don't know that they have norovirus."

"Please. At least one of them does. The virus is contagious as hell and even a *capable* doctor is aware of that."

Forrest pursed his lips and tried to keep the angry words in check. "I am a capable doctor, but I prefer the lab. I am me, not some cookie-cutter piece than can fit into a carefully controlled perfect life."

Sam wanted him at bedside. And Forrest didn't understand why. He liked the lab. Was good at it. Better than he'd been at bedside.

"No life is perfect." Sam scoffed.

"Right." Forrest reached for Sam, but he pulled back. Forrest tried to keep the pain of watching that wrapped up tight. "And there is no way to control everything. If you can't accept—"

"Then you'll leave. Right? Just pack everything up and head to Indianapolis." Sam's words buzzed in the quiet.

"Sam."

"Forget it. Just forget I said anything. I need to take care of *my* patient." Sam grabbed the tablet and walked away.

Forrest didn't stop him. Didn't say anything as Sam walked past him.

What the hell?

CHAPTER SIXTEEN

FORREST HAD SLEPT in his own room last night. Not that Sam could blame him. He'd overreacted. But he hadn't been able to take hearing Forrest call himself "capable" while giving praise to every other member of the staff. It wasn't fair.

Forrest was wonderful. Gifted.

He was gifted before and ran when he thought he wasn't enough.

Sam sucked in air as he tried to force that brain worm out of his mind. It had wedged itself there. A reminder that Sam hadn't realized Forrest felt less than. He hadn't known that Forrest thought Sam deserved better. Forrest had just made the decision on his own and walked away.

Though if Sam thought about it, there had been signs last time. Not that their relationship was in trouble, but that Forrest was doubting himself. Little verbal cuts. Always directed at himself. Self-deprecating humor about how he wasn't enough.

Now he said he didn't know why he was using the word *hiding*. Did that mean there was part of him still unsure of his place like before?

Capable.

Was that another sign that he'd run one day?

Sam pushed his palms into his eyes, like the pressure could force the words out of his mind. The fears.

A knock on his bedroom door tore at him. It would be Forrest. Wanting to talk about yesterday. Iron things out. Sam pushed off the couch and walked to the door.

Time to fix what he'd broken yesterday.

"Forrest..." The man's name was out of his mouth before the door fully opened revealing Chris.

"Nope. Sorry. Is Forrest not with you?" Chris shrugged. "You two are always together. I just stopped by to ask if you were sure about releasing Kerry."

Sam was stunned by the question. He'd ordered her release for this morning, assuming she was hydrated. There was nothing they could do for her besides manage symptoms. And a hospital, even a tiny one, was full of germs.

She had a weakened immune system while the virus raged through her. It meant she was more prone to secondary infections.

"Is she not doing well?"

"She is." Chris let out a sigh. "Or as well as you can when you can barely hold anything down."

Sam shook his head. "So?" What was the issue?

"I don't know." Chris crossed his arms. "I just have this off feeling."

"Off?" Sam grabbed his coat and slid his feet into the boots he kept by the door. "What kind of off?"

"I can't explain it. I just... I don't know." Chris followed Sam down the hall and out into the cold toward the hospital. He did not elaborate on the way.

They walked in and Natasha stood, yawning. "I told him it was probably nothing."

"Nothing?" Sam took the tablet chart from Natasha. Kerry's temp was steady. She hadn't thrown up in more than six hours and had rested comfortably. She got dizzy when going to the bathroom. But that wasn't unexpected given the lack of sustenance in her body.

Everything looked like what he expected to see. "What am I missing?"

Natasha held up her hands. "Nothing." She pointed at Chris. "But he has a feeling."

Chris looked at the bay where Kerry was sleeping. "I don't know. I just…could it be something other than norovirus?"

"Like?" Natasha asked the question that was on the tip of Sam's tongue.

Chris looked at the bed and then back at them, "Ménière's disease? The chronic inner ear disorder. It can mimic a norovirus."

"Ménière's?" Sam looked at the chart. "There are only forty-five thousand cases of that disorder diagnosed a year worldwide. Has she complained of ear pressure or ringing?"

"No." Chris pushed a hand through his hair. "I know. I know."

"Chris, the most common answer is often the right one." Sam knew Chris was missing the pressure of a typical ER. Missing the pace and patient load.

The NP shuffled his feet and looked over at Kerry, still sleeping in the bed. "Yeah. Yeah. I told you it was nothing. I think I'm just bored." He zipped the coat he hadn't taken off back up and looked at the door. "My shift is over. You two enjoy." He waved and turned on his heel.

"You think he's okay?" Natasha didn't look at Sam as she asked the question. The closed door to the hospital was not going to provide any answers, but he understood her concern.

"I don't know. The ice affects everyone differently. He's working long shifts at night by himself, maybe we should switch it up, so that he isn't the only one pulling that overlapping shift."

"Oh, I am game to work more night hours." Natasha winked as she took the tablet chart from him. "I saw Kerry open her eyes. I'll start the discharge papers."

Sam let Natasha go as he ran through the symptoms of Ménière's in his mind. Kerry was presenting none of them except vomiting and dizziness. The dizziness was a direct result of the dehydration caused from the vomiting. Sam had no weird feeling. No concern about letting her go.

He let Natasha handle the discharge and got ready to spend the last part of his shift with Forrest. It would be fine. It would.

"Kerry gone?"

He hadn't said hello first when he stepped into the clinic. Sam shouldn't be surprised. Forrest was focusing on patients and that was the right move. But, somehow, after an evening of silence, he'd hoped for more.

"Yeah. We discharged her to her quarters this morning. She's to rest and stay away from others for several days and to wash her hands thoroughly for the next two weeks. Hopefully that will keep the virus from running around the base." Sam pulled at the back of his neck as he ran out of things to discuss regarding Kerry. It would be nice if there were patients. Anything to cut the tension radiating between them.

"Have we heard from the field?" Forrest crossed his arms and then uncrossed them. At least Sam wasn't the only one who was feeling awkward.

"No. Maybe they got extra lucky." Sam shrugged. "More likely, they are ill but pushing through."

Forrest shook his head, "No, Henry would pull them back."

"You know him well?" He hated the bitterness in his tone. He'd wanted the whole crew back. Ordered it. And Forrest had figured something else out.

"No. But he cares about his team. It's why he brought Kerry himself. A leader who cares stays with their team in crisis, no delegation." Forrest seemed so sure.

"I don't know. We've both worked through illness." Sam wasn't sure why he was pushing this point. He should drop it.

But, if he dropped it, would Indiana come up again? Maybe. Maybe not. He wasn't sure which outcome he feared most.

"We are not the benchmarks for healthy work-life balance." Forrest blew out a breath, "Sam, about yesterday."

Sam waited for Forrest to say something. But no words came. Now it was Forrest lacking for words.

"Did you mean it when you said you'd put in for a transfer?"

Forrest pursed his lips. "I meant it yesterday."

Sam heard the hint of uncertainty and his stomach tightened. So he was already ready to run? "But today?"

Forrest looked at the hospital. "Not sure this is the best place for this conversation."

Sam's heart clenched. His soul fell apart. This was not happening again. Not again.

He shook his head. "I get it. We aren't soulmates."

"Excuse me?"

"Soulmates, Forrest. The other half of a person." Sam tried to focus on his breathing. Keeping air moving in and out of his lungs. Getting to the next second. And then the next.

"Soulmates aren't real, Sam. They're fiction."

"No. They are. My parents are soulmates and I thought..." Sam pinched his lips closed. "I didn't mean..."

"You did." Forrest took a deep breath. "Maybe you didn't mean to say it out loud. But you meant that you thought we were. But I don't fit in your life, do I?"

Sam shook his head, but it did nothing to quiet the buzzing in his ears. "What does that mean?"

"It means, you're trying to make me fit. Wanting me at bedside. Not talking about going back to where my work is. In the lab. You've always had an idea of what your life was supposed to look like."

"You're the one *hiding* there. How many times have you said that word since we landed on the ice? I wanted you to love your place. To realize how wonderful life is instead of wasting it. And I accepted long ago that my life wasn't going to look ideal." Sam had traveled everywhere to force the dream away. And all it had taken was Forrest landing on the ice for his heart to override his brain.

"No. You forced it to go dormant but never gave up on the idea of the perfect partner."

"Why is that so bad?" Sam blinked back the tears coating his eyes. Why was it so bad to want the person that fully completed you?

Forrest pursed his lips as he looked away. "Because I am not perfect. I'm broken and messy and unsure of so many things."

This was the moment. The place where he said he wasn't good enough. Where Forrest walked. Sam couldn't do it again.

"This isn't going to work." Sam rushed the words out. This time he was in charge. He wasn't getting left. He was choosing the path.

"Okay." Forrest nodded. "Okay." He looked around the empty bay. "I'm going to leave now. Call me if you get patients… Um, can I have the key to your room? I'll grab my stuff." He held out his hand.

Sam looked at it. He could walk this back. Fix it.

Soulmates wouldn't need fixing.

He dropped the key in Forrest's hand and closed his eyes so he didn't have to watch him leave.

Again.

"Soulmates. Soulmates." Forrest sniffed as he looked through the scope of the microscope. He'd known Sam for years and slipped back into the warm feeling of their life together so easily. But he'd never known the man actually *believed* in soulmates. That the word he'd always used to describe his parents had been completely serious.

It was a fanciful belief. A fairy tale. Relationships were work. There was no magical perfect person that made everything fall into place.

He'd worked with Natasha two days ago and Chris yesterday. He wasn't sure who'd be at the clinic when he arrived today. But he was certain that it wouldn't be Sam.

Two days of silence. Two days to revert back to the way

they'd been the first month on the ice. He should feel something. Anger. Sadness. Relief.

But nothing came. No emotion. Just disbelief.

"You keep muttering and I'll have to call the clinic to report that you might be succumbing to ice madness." Charlee leaned against the wall.

"Ice madness is not a thing, Charlee." There was a phenomenon known as winter-over syndrome. The mental health diagnosis was not common, though not as rare as medical professionals would like, either. It came with hostility, insomnia and usually an absent stare that many called the long eye or Antarctic stare.

"I know. But you are muttering to yourself. Something about soulmates. You know, that annoying thing that Sam is for you even though the two of you are too stubborn to acknowledge it." Charlee rolled her eyes as she stepped closer to him.

That wasn't right. Couldn't be right.

"Soulmates aren't real. I wouldn't think that you would fall for such nonsense. A perfect person. Please." Forrest pulled up the screen of the electron microscope. He wasn't focusing through the lens, might as well shift machines and see if he could focus this way.

Charlee leaned against the counter opposite him. "Of course they're real."

Forrest scoffed. "You're a scientist. Please, you can't believe there is one perfect person for you. That if you can just find them, then everything is perfect."

"Two uses of the word *perfect*." Charlee looked at the image on the screen. "For someone who hates the word, and its implications, you're using it a lot this morning."

Was there a point to this conversation?

She held up a hand before Forrest could start his next argument. "I am a scientist. And no, I don't believe every soul is a puzzle piece looking for a match."

"Do you have a point?"

"Yes." Charlee crossed her arms. "You and Sam are still soulmates. Whether you or he wants to admit it. You balance each other. Or you would, if you could get over your personal issues."

Forrest huffed. "Sure. I can just magically morph into the perfect person. Throw all my flaws away and just be the right partner for Sam."

"And that right there is your problem." Charlee pushed off the counter. "Fix that and you might find life opens up a lot more."

"Fix what?"

But rather than answering him, she made a show of putting her headphones on and walking back to her station.

"Fix what?" Forrest raised his voice but Charlee didn't respond. "Fine."

He was supposed to be working. Not thinking of Sam.

Right, like I've ever gotten the man out of my dreams.

"Doctor Wilson?" Forrest turned, surprised to see Chris. Dark circles stood out under his eyes and he looked pale.

"Are you feeling all right? And why are you calling me Dr. Wilson?" He'd been Forrest to the team for weeks now.

"Part of Kerry's team came back last night. A supply run." Chris looked over his shoulder. "It's probably nothing but I have a bad feeling."

"Why? Were they sick?" If he'd misread Henry, Sam would be thrilled. No. That wasn't fair. He'd be upset that more people were sick on the ice. And he'd point out to Forrest that he'd screwed up.

Actually, he wouldn't do that, either. Forrest would know that all on his own.

"No. They're fine. Healthy." Chris rocked back on his heels. "I told Sam that I thought something else was up with her. I had no good reason. I still don't. But no one else on the ice is showing symptoms."

"All right." Forrest turned the microscope off. "Let's go check on her."

"Just like that?" Chris crossed his arms, then uncrossed them. "I might be completely missing this. I just—"

"Or you might not." Forrest grabbed his coat. He'd had worries that he hadn't followed through on before. The patient had always suffered. "Do you know her dorm room number?"

"Yeah." Chris led the way. His feet moving quickly for a man who'd clearly not slept because he was worried about a patient.

They reached her dorm room and Chris raised a fist and knocked. A solid knock. Then another.

"Give her a minute." Forrest put his hand on Chris's shoulder.

A minute went by and Chris raised his fist again. "We might need to get someone to open the door. If she's incapacitated." He knocked harder.

"Doctor Wilson? Chris?" Kerry called their names from the end of the hall. The wet hair meant she'd taken a shower and her coloring was far better than it had been. A patient on the mend. "What are you doing here?"

"Are you okay?" Chris looked her up and down.

"Yes. I mean the idea of food still makes my stomach turn a little. I think it will still be a day or two before I trust that what I eat will stay down. But overall…" She shrugged. "Are you okay?"

"Yeah." Chris nodded. "Sorry to bother you." He turned and started down the hallway. "I owe you an apology, Doc. I guess I let my mind run away with what-ifs."

Forrest understood. He'd been that doctor. The one who couldn't get past the what-ifs. The mess he'd made. "Which patient did you lose?"

Chris paused before heading to the door. "Patient? I've lost many. You don't work trauma without seeing it. Sucks, but no one is perfect. This one was just my imagination running away with me."

"Right." Forrest nodded. "I failed at bedside because I couldn't handle the what-ifs."

Chris shot him a look of confusion. "You work in a lab prepping the future of medicine. Your work may aid space travel in the future, but it will be invaluable to a lot of epidemiology studies. Hell, it might help prevent a pandemic. Hardly a failure, man. Sometimes, you realize you aren't cut out for certain kinds of work. Doesn't make it failure." He patted Forrest's shoulder. "I'm headed to my shift, but if what you do is failure, Doc, then what does that make the rest of us?"

He chuckled as he walked out. "Failure. Please."

Fix all my flaws.

Forrest's words to Charlee floated in his mind. This was what he was guilty of. He'd worked for years to see himself as enough. Gone through therapy, prided himself on believing he was open to the idea of marriage. Of spending his life with someone.

But Sam was right. He still joked about "hiding" in the lab.

Because part of me still feels like a failure.

Which was ridiculous. He loved the lab. Was so good at it. There was no need to denigrate the work he did. No need to put himself down.

But deep down, when Sam had gotten upset, he hadn't attempted to work it out. Hadn't waited to calm the conversation down. He'd let Sam walk away first. Asked for the keys to move himself out.

Believed he wasn't enough.

He'd walked away once. And Sam was looking for a reason he might walk away again. It was an easy pattern to see now. The hesitation on moving. The questions of Forrest's plans. And rather than reassure him, Forrest had walked. Just like Sam had feared.

Because deep down he worried he wasn't worthy of Sam. Wasn't enough for him, like he'd not been enough for his family. But Sam wasn't his family.

Forrest closed his eyes, if anyone walked by right now, they'd think he'd lost his mind just standing by a door doing nothing.

But his heart screamed as his brain listened, truly listened.

He and Sam belonged together. He looked at his watch, he had to finish the lab work but this evening they were having the conversation they should have had days ago. Years ago.

CHAPTER SEVENTEEN

"YOU WERE RIGHT." Chris walked into the clinic, his cheeks pink and eyes bright despite dark circles under his eyes.

"Right?" Sam didn't look up from the inventory he was taking. Again. He'd counted damn near everything in this place at least once. All to keep his mind away from the fact that Forrest had walked away from him.

Because I pushed him away.

"Yeah. Kerry had a norovirus. She is feeling a hell of a lot better." Chris waved to Natasha as she headed out the door. "See ya."

"She was in a hurry." Chris chuckled.

Probably sick of being around him. Sam was well aware that he was not good company at the moment.

"Her stomach issues were textbook, Chris." Sam put the swabs back in the drawer. There hadn't been a need for him to count each individual one, but it made the time pass.

"I know. I know. My feeling was ridiculous. But Dr. Wilson and I checked on her this morning. She looks tons better."

"It's been more than seventy-two hours. That's what should be happening." Chris had had a feeling, but Sam was positive that feeling was boredom.

In large trauma centers you typically saw two kinds of medical professionals. Those destined to burn out and move on and people that thrived on the stress. Adrenaline junkies, some might call them. Sam was never going to burn out at those facilities, but he didn't crave the never-ending patient load the way Chris clearly did.

Chris pulled up the tablet chart and let out an audible sigh at the lack of interesting news in it.

"Yeah. I know. But no one on the ice got sick and I just let my imagination run wild. I didn't want to bug you so I asked Forrest to check it out with me." Chris looked up from the chart. "Sorry, should I not speak about Dr. Wilson?"

Sam wanted to banish the man's name from the world. Or scream it into the void and beg the universe to reverse course. "It's fine."

It wasn't. Nothing felt like it was going to be right ever again.

"Well, you were right when you told me weeks ago that there is nothing wrong with realizing I wasn't cut out for certain kinds of work. I need the trauma unit. So that's where I will head back to."

Nothing wrong with choosing a new line of work. The words he'd said to Chris slapped him in the face. Had he been trying to force Forrest into the life he'd once planned? Two doctors working together. A partnership day and night. The life he'd given up.

Did I give up? Or did I start craving it as soon as we were back together?

"Am I a perfectionist?" Sam knew the answer as soon as he saw the look on Chris's face. "Don't answer that. I know the answer. Forrest accused me of trying to make him fit into my life. Of trying to force him out of the lab."

He snapped his mouth shut. He hadn't meant to say the last two sentences.

"Good grief." Chris shook his head before Sam could think of anything to say. "He mentioned failing at bedside this morning. Makes no sense. That man belongs in a lab."

So Forrest did still think of himself as a failure. Used the word *hiding* as a defense mechanism. A way to put himself down. And rather than soothe his worry, Sam had pressed him to return to something else.

"I mean you can be good at something and not want it." Chris clicked his tongue.

You could. Forrest was. Sam had been waiting for him to leave. Looking for signs. Forcing signs. So he didn't get hurt again.

I refused to talk about the future.

Refused to even plan a damn vacation. Of course Forrest would start to question his place in Sam's life. And as soon as Forrest had asked how he fit, asked about his place in Sam's world? Sam had run to avoid getting left again.

"Hey, I am…um…gonna go get a few hours of sleep. Call me if we get busy."

"We won't."

Sam lightly punched Chris's shoulder. "Probably not. But you're exhausted—don't tell me you aren't. And I've avoided working with Forrest for long enough. So I'll be back before his shift starts."

"Get some rest." Chris called as Sam headed for the door.

Sam planned to take a quick nap. As soon as he did two quick things. Two things he should have done days ago.

Forrest was going to see Sam as soon as his shift in the hospital was over. Natasha was working the night shift. Sam must have come on to the second shift since Chris had come to find him this morning.

He needed to finish this up and then find Sam. Hopefully, the shift would slip by quickly. If they weren't busy, it would at least let him plan out his apology speech. The one he'd mentally rehearsed for the last two hours still sounded cheesy.

"Doctor Wilson." Chris smiled as Forrest stepped in. "Good to see you." He turned to someone in the corner out of Forrest's eyes. "Your arrival means it is time for my nap. See ya!"

He winked at Forrest as he walked by.

"Natasha?" Forrest slid the shoes he kept at the clinic on. The quiet hospital sneakers that would weep if they saw the snow piles outside.

"No." Sam stepped around the corner.

He didn't look tired. Maybe he wasn't missing Forrest as much as Forrest was missing him.

Forrest's heart shut the worry down. He was not going to look for ways he wasn't good enough. Not with Sam. Not with anyone.

"The Virgin Islands." Sam grinned.

"Puerto Rico? Are we naming US territories?" Forrest raised a brow. What game was this?

"No." Sam stepped closer but didn't close the distance fully between them. "I want to go to the Virgin Islands for vacation before we head back to Indiana. Soak up all the sun on the beach. No winter coats! Though we should probably carve a weekend out for New York. My parents will never forgive us if we don't at least stop there."

Forrest closed the distance between them, put his hands on either side of Sam's face and brought him in for a kiss. There were still so many things to say. Apologies to be offered, but right now, here, in this moment, all he wanted was to kiss the man he planned to spend the rest of his life with.

"Wow."

Forrest would never mind Sam saying that after a kiss. "I'm sorry, Sam."

Sam put a finger over Forrest's lips. "I am the one that needs to apologize. I was stunned when you left. Hurt. And you were right—I had a plan for my life. I sought it out with Oliver and then pushed it aside for a while. But when you reentered my life—" Sam pressed his forehead to Forrest's "—it came roaring back. I don't think I even realized it, but I was so afraid you'd decided you weren't enough again."

"And I was so afraid that I had no place in your life that I walked away."

"I pushed you away. I was the one that said it wasn't going to work. I love you. All of you. And you belong in the lab, but I will forever say that you didn't fail at bedside. You aren't hiding. You just found your place. And that is beautiful."

Forrest sucked in a deep breath as those words knitted together a piece of himself. "I found my place. In the lab. But also—" Forrest knelt down "—at your side. I don't have a fancy ring. There is no place to buy one here. But I am never walking away from you, Sam Miller. Ever. Marry me."

Sam pulled him up, kissing him deeply. "Yes. Absolutely yes."

EPILOGUE

"SHAKE IT!" CHARLEE WALKED up to Sam on the dance floor. "The tux looks great on you."

"Love looks great on him." Forrest wrapped his arms around him.

"I feel like you are a little biased, as my husband and all." Sam kissed Forrest as they continued to sway to the music with all their friends.

"Husband." Forrest lifted Sam's hand and spun him around. "I may never tire of hearing you call me that."

"I plan to hold you on that 'till death do us part.'" Sam pulled Forrest in as the DJ started a slow song.

Wrapping his arms around Sam's neck, Forrest kissed his cheek. "Easiest promise I've ever made."

"You two are sickeningly cute." Dr. Nicole Sapson spun by with her partner Shane Gibson.

"We're going to be just as cute next month." Shane kissed Nicole then winked at Sam and Forrest.

"Cuter. We better be cuter." Nicole laughed as Shane dipped her.

Forrest pulled Sam in for another kiss, "I don't think it's possible to be cuter than us."

Mark and Adina danced by them. The friends kept a platonic distance between them.

"Our wedding is a mini reunion." There was no place in the

world Sam would rather be than here with Forrest, his parents and the friends they'd gathered at the pole.

"A South Pole Reunion." Forrest's lips brushed his. "Though the best South Pole reunion happened when we landed on the ice two years ago. I love you."

"That was as close to perfection as possible." Sam kissed his nose. "You're perfect."

Forrest dipped Sam as the music started fading away. "We're perfect. Together."

"Together."

* * * * *

If you enjoyed this story,
check out these other great reads
from Juliette Hyland

Falling for His Fake Date
Fake Dating the Vet
One-Night Baby with Her Best Friend
Dating His Irresistible Rival

All available now!

THEIR ACCIDENTAL VEGAS VOWS

AMY RUTTAN

MILLS & BOON

This book is for all the amazing authors
I got to hang with at the Harlequin 75th
and for my family, who were very patient with me
up north while I finished this book. Also, special
shout-out to the bear who passed by our campsite—
quite the shock to finish a book and see him walk by
on his way to eat flowers.

CHAPTER ONE

BREATHE. JUST BREATHE.

Grace was trying to take deep, even breaths to calm the rush of adrenaline coursing through her that was now mixed with a healthy dose of anxiety. That adrenaline was something she chased as a paramedic, especially in Las Vegas. She liked the high. It fueled her during the toughest times, but there were some cases that just got to her and there was no holding back the flood of emotions. No matter how hard she tried. And tonight had been one of them.

She closed her eyes and leaned back against the brick wall of the hospital in the ambulance bay and tried to remind herself that there was nothing to be upset or worried about. The child was going to be okay, but every time they pulled someone out of a pool or a hot tub from a near drowning it always got to her after.

Every. Single. Time.

What she wouldn't give to lie on the ground, her butt against the wall and her legs straight up in the air. It was a proven method to ease anxiety, and she did it often, at home. Really not something she could do here outside a hospital by the trauma room doors. It was also something she didn't want her colleagues to see. She worked hard to control her fear, her anxiety.

No one else needed to know about it.

"Hey, Landon. You okay?"

Grace groaned inwardly at being caught.

She opened her eyes and glanced up at her partner. They'd been paired up for the last six months, but every time she saw Jonah her stomach always did that nervous little flip because he was so easy on the eyes: tall, muscular, with a chiseled jaw and a small cleft in his chin, blue eyes, blond hair and the quintessential golden California tan. Fitting, since that was where he was from. He had told Grace so during their first meeting, after he'd told her to hang ten, which hadn't even made any sense at the time, and she had jokingly called him a surfer dude.

Jonah was exactly the type of guy she was attracted to, but as her partner he was off-limits. Grace was not going to make that same mistake twice. There was no way she was ever getting involved with someone she worked with or in close proximity to again.

She'd been there, done that and was still paying the price for it. It was hard to put the mistake of an ex behind you when he was one—a trauma doctor and you saw him on a regular basis because you were a paramedic, and two—the best friend of your little sister's fiancé and so was going to be at every single wedding event for the next month.

So no matter how attractive she found her partner Jonah, how tempting, he was completely off-limits. She was never going to mix business with pleasure again.

Even though sex would be a great way to relieve her current anxiety.

What is wrong with me?

Grace swallowed the lump in her throat and plastered a fake smile on her face. "Perfectly."

Jonah's eyes narrowed, and he smirked. "I don't buy it."

"What do you mean you don't buy it?"

"First, I'm older and wiser than you, and second, I served in the Marines. I know when I'm seeing a trauma response in someone."

Grace sighed and hugged her arms. "I guess you were bound to see it. It's drownings. They're difficult for me."

"But the little girl is going to be okay."

And it was this kind of response which made her reluctant to share with anyone her emotions. She'd learned to mask it well, even if it sometimes slipped, like now.

She nodded quickly, forcing a bright smile. "Oh, I know, but…it's hard."

Jonah didn't pry her with more questions. He just nodded. "Well, let's get this rig back, and then I think we need to go out and have a drink."

"What?" she asked, surprised. Since Jonah had arrived, she'd never really seen him socialize with others. He was friendly enough but kept to himself. Just like she tended to do. Socializing at work was fine, but she liked to keep people at a distance ever since that disastrous workplace relationship.

"We're both off duty, and you look like you could use a drink. We'll get a group together and hit the Strip. What do you say?"

I should say no.

Only he wasn't wrong. She could really use a night out, and it would be nice to let off steam with some coworkers. She'd used to have fun with them, before her ex. If she went out maybe then she could release this last bit of anxious energy. She couldn't remember the last time she had let loose out on the Strip. Most of her friends were married with families. She was the last single gal.

"Okay," she said, nodding. "Let's do that."

Jonah grinned. "I'll make all the arrangements, and we'll have some fun."

"Fun. Yes." Did she even remember what fun was?

What could it hurt?

That was a goofy question to ask herself. The last time she briefly pondered something like that she'd ended up being devastated and humiliated. It was simpler not to date. It was easier not to get involved with someone else. Sure, it was lonely, but it was better for her heart in the long run.

"Wow," Jonah said, rocking back on his heels.

"What?"

"You sound like I'm trying to drag you to out into the desert without water."

Oh, little did he know how much she would prefer the desert, and no bodies of water anywhere, but she wasn't going to get into that. Grace cracked a grin and relaxed. "That's a very random statement."

Jonah shrugged. "I was trying to think of the worst thing, but then I realized that's kind of subjective for everyone and I really don't know you well enough to determine what your 'worst thing' would be."

"You want to know my worst thing?"

"Sure."

She'd been teasing, so she was a bit surprised he was so interested. "That's kind of dark, dude."

"Now who sounds like a stereotypical surfer," he teased.

"You're really certain you want to know?"

He nodded. "Lay it on me. I can handle it."

"And you promise you won't use it against me in the future?"

He cocked an eyebrow. "Okay, now I'm absolutely intrigued."

"If I tell you this one thing, then you're going to have to dish out yours."

"Okay, well, how about we share that over a drink?"

She nodded. "We'll do that."

"Come on, let's get back to station and we can go from there."

Grace nodded again and followed her partner across the ambulance bay. She was already feeling so much better. All in all, it had been a good shift. They'd saved a life, and she had helped with that, even if she'd been terrified of running into her ex in the emergency department and the young girl's accident had brought up so many painful memories of her own experience. She'd usually just work this out on her own, but she was appreciative of Jonah for extending her an olive branch of camaraderie.

Friendship with her partner wouldn't be a bad thing. She'd enjoyed working with him so far.

It would be nice to form a closer, professional bond with him.

Wouldn't it?

Why did I suggest this?

Jonah really didn't understand his train of thought when he suggested it, but he also wasn't one to bail. As promised he made all the arrangements. Not many of their coworkers wanted to go out and a couple didn't have the day off tomorrow, but there were a few willing participants, which was good, because he didn't really want to be alone with Grace. Or rather, he wouldn't particularly mind being alone with Grace—quite the opposite, really. And that was the whole crux of the matter.

Grace was exactly the type of woman he was attracted to.

It was going to make being just friends with her tricky. But Jonah had come to Vegas for a fresh start. He'd been married once before, and he didn't want to go through that all again. Keeping people at a distance was easier on him and his pain. He'd already lost too many people he cared about.

His best friend had died in his arms overseas. His parents had been on the older side, never particularly demonstrative, and then they had passed away; he didn't have siblings or really any extended family. His ex-wife hadn't been able to handle his PTSD when he came home, and she had cheated on him. He had learned to rely on himself.

It was better to be alone.

Even if it was lonely.

It was completely out of the ordinary for him to even suggest going out with people from work, but when he'd seen Grace leaning against that wall in the ambulance bay, he'd known a trauma reaction from a mile away, because he'd lived through it. He'd worked through his with amazing therapists. He knew the signs, and it had looked like she needed a shoulder to lean on.

Grace was the perfect partner. She was strong, smart, independent. She could hold her own, and that really impressed him. No one pushed around Grace Landon, and that was just his initial impression after working with her for a few months.

There was a lot about Grace he admired.

So when he'd seen her withdrawn and agitated, it had tugged at his heart because he knew how that felt and how isolating it could be, and he'd had to reach out.

Now, as he rode in a cab to meet his coworkers at a casino bar on the Strip, he was second-guessing his decision to go out and socialize. He was a bit of an introvert—another problem his ex-wife had with him.

In high school, he had been more out there, but his time in service overseas had changed him. After watching so many of his friends get killed, it had been hard to be that "life of the party" type guy his ex, Mona, had expected him to be.

He couldn't do that anymore. He couldn't be that person.

He'd learned to lock away the emotions so that he could control the trauma.

He rolled his shoulders and straightened his white button-down shirt, which was suddenly a little too claustrophobic under his leather jacket. Although he loved living in Vegas, the bright flashing lights and the noise of the Strip was getting to him. Mona would get so annoyed when he'd want to leave an overwhelming social gathering early. She hadn't gotten it.

Not many did.

This night out was his idea, however, and he had to make an effort. Grace had been so keen on it, and he didn't want to let his partner down.

The taxi pulled up in front of Mythtopia Casino, and he made his way inside past all the clouds of cigarette smoke and flashing lights. His pulse raced, and he focused on breathing through the overwhelming overload of sensation. He focused on finding the bar, which was new and located on the upper level of the casino. He'd made reservations so they would have a place to sit and chat.

A quiet place.

When he entered the bar, he was led to a very large corner booth where a few coworkers were sitting. Except Grace, who he'd arranged all this for.

"Hey," Jonah greeted his colleagues. "Where's Grace? Is she running late?"

"No. She's at the bar. She'll be back in a few," John, another paramedic, said, nodding in the direction of the bar before turning back to the others.

Jonah turned and lost his breath for one moment at the sight of Grace seated on a bar stool. She wore a short silver strapless dress which not only accentuated her long shapely legs but her toned strong arms and shoulders. Her blond hair with that wild pink streak was usually tied back. Now it hung down loose in a bob with subtle waves that brushed the tops of her shoulders.

She was absolutely stunning.

It was the first time he was really seeing her outside of work. Usually, all her curves were hidden by the uniform. Not that she didn't look good that way, but he really appreciated her dressed up like this too. That fact had him slightly rattled. The uniform reminded him she was a partner, someone he worked with, and made it easy to ignore everything else about her.

She's your partner. She's off-limits.

He swallowed the lump in his throat and approached her. Slowly, trying to regain some control over his shock at seeing her looking so different. But it also gave him a chance to savor the sight of her. He wanted to remember this moment, because this was all he could let himself have.

"Hey," he said, hoping that his voice didn't crack.

Grace spun around on the stool and then smiled warmly. "I was wondering if you were going to show up."

"Of course. I was running late." Mostly because he was dragging his feet coming here, but he didn't tell her that. "Why are you sitting off to the side here?"

"John," she grunted, nodding in the direction of the booth. "His stories are the most boring ever."

He smiled. "Yeah, I'd have to agree."

"I'll go back in a few minutes. I was just enjoying my scotch in silence."

She drinks scotch?

For some reason he found that super sexy. She was so different from any other woman he'd met.

"Do you mind if I join you?" he asked.

"Go for it."

Jonah slid onto the barstool next to her. The bartender came over.

"I'll have the same." Jonah motioned to Grace's drink.

"Oh, you like scotch too?"

"It's my favorite. Surprised you do. Most women I've known weren't very fond of it."

She smirked. "Well, I'm not like other women."

He let his gaze travel over her, drinking in the sight of her. "I wouldn't say that."

They sat there in silence and listened to the soft jazz music which was being piped in through the speakers. The bar was decorated in dark colors, dim lighting, leather and wood. It looked like an old smoking room from another time. He actually found in quite calming compared to the loudness of the casino outside. It was why he'd chosen it, so he was glad the pictures online hadn't lied.

"It's like we're in another world here," he said, reaching for the glass the bartender had brought him.

"It's really nice in here," she agreed. "I did wonder about your choice when you picked this casino, but this is a nice little treasure tucked away."

"I did my research. I know tonight is about letting loose, but I also thought it might be nice to actually talk instead of shouting over thumping music."

Their gazes locked, and she smiled at him tenderly as she tucked a lock of her hair behind her ear. "I knew there was a reason I liked you."

"Oh?" he asked, curious.

"I can't stand overly loud obnoxious places either. I mean, it's one thing being in the thick of an emergency and dealing with that. I can usually tune out the sound of the siren blaring, but when I'm off duty I prefer calmness. Quiet."

"Same. After serving in the military..." He trailed off, not wanting to continue with too much information. "When I returned, my tastes had changed."

Her expression softened. "I can only imagine."

"I do like Vegas. I think better than California." Which was true, because there was nothing left for him there. Just painful memories. He closed his eyes for a second as he briefly thought of his past life, before the trauma and divorce. Even once he'd reopened them, the lonely ache in his stomach stayed. It was always present.

"Does anything..." She hesitated for a moment, worrying her bottom lip.

"What?" he asked.

"Does anything trigger you at work?" There was a hint of a flush on her creamy cheeks, almost like she was mortified to be asking him the question, and she shouldn't have been.

Yes, he didn't want to get too close to her. Or anyone, really. But he knew she was suffering today, and he didn't want her to feel the loneliness he'd first felt when he'd returned home from serving in the Marines.

"Things trigger me. I work to control it. Something I've been doing for some time. What about you?" Usually he didn't pry too much, but he had the inkling she wanted to talk about it. That was the point of tonight—giving her a place to talk to him. The others he'd invited so it didn't seem like a date, because it wasn't.

That wasn't what he wanted.

Really?

He ignored that voice in his head. "You can talk to me."

Grace sighed. "I get triggered by drownings. I almost drowned as a child, and... I don't swim or anything like that. Usually I can hold it together, but seeing that little girl in the water... I was about that age when it happened, and I can still remember it with clarity. Days like today, it just hits hard."

"I could tell you were struggling."

She gave him a half smile. "I try to keep it to myself."

"Why?" he asked.

Their gazes locked, and he could see the pain, one he knew too well, reflected back at him.

"People in my life haven't always been too kind or understanding. It's easier to deal with it alone."

Jonah got it, but he found himself wanting to help her, which shocked him. "Who wasn't understanding?"

"My ex. He tried to teach me to swim by dunking my head underwater repeatedly to desensitize me."

Jonah made a face. "What a douche."

Grace laughed. "Well, be careful about that. He's the head trauma doctor at Vegas Central Hospital."

"Did you leave him when he tried that dick move?"

"No, I left him when I found out he was cheating on me with a nurse. Everyone knew but me. Another embarrassing moment of my life that I can't believe I'm telling you." She took a swig of her drink.

Jonah shrugged. "We're partners. And we all have exes we'd rather forget. I was married."

She cocked an eyebrow. "Really?"

"I got married out of high school, and when I got back, things had changed. She wanted someone I wasn't anymore. She cheated on me, it ended and I moved out here… eventually."

He couldn't believe he'd just told her that. It was something he really didn't talk about to anyone. As much as he didn't usually like to open up, with Grace it was easy to do that. It felt as though he was that easygoing guy he'd once been, long before serving. Before Justin had died and Mona had left him. When life had been simple.

Less complicated.

Less painful.

So what was it about Grace? Whatever it was, he'd have to be careful.

"This is turning into a depressing conversation." She smiled at him again. "I'm glad you're letting me talk this all out. When I first met you, you were so closed off."

"I'm careful with who I trust."

Grace nodded. "Me too. Particularly at work."

"Hey, guys! We're going to karaoke at a bar down the street. Come on," John shouted.

Grace winced and then finished her scotch, sliding off the barstool. "We'd better go."

"Had we?" he asked, grumpily.

"This is a coworker-bonding outing, isn't it?" She held out her hand. "Come on. Don't be a curmudgeon."

"A what?"

"A stick in the mud."

Jonah took her hand and slid off the barstool, letting her drag him out of the nice quiet upscale bar.

He could manage one round of karaoke, and then he could go home where it was safe and he could let this social mask slip off and relax.

One round wouldn't hurt him.

CHAPTER TWO

"OH, GOD," GRACE GROANED, not wanting to pry her eyes open to let in more of the sunlight that was already blinding her through her bedroom window. But her phone was ringing incessantly in her dreams, and it was just adding to the pounding that was throbbing against her skull like a bad discotheque. The last time she felt like this she'd been hungover and a lot younger.

What had she been thinking? Why had she drunk so much?

She sat up slowly and realized she was completely naked. At least she was at home and in her bed. She reached for her phone and saw it was her mother calling—and she had been doing so for the last hour, Grace realized as she scrolled through all the missed calls.

Grace ignored the call again, because she was not talking to her mother. Not until she fully woke up. As she scrolled further back, she saw there were about twenty different text messages from her family's group chat.

The chat had been set up by Grace's sister, Melanie—who'd become a bit anal retentive about her upcoming wedding—for sharing details about the event at the end of the month, so that every member of her large family would know what was going on.

Grace tried to regain focus and opened the newest message, which was from her mother.

What do you mean you're MARRIED?!

Grace woke up then. She sat bolt upright in bed, staring at all the texts asking the same question until she found the one that she'd sent. The one that stated she was married. One that had a video attachment.

"Oh, God," she moaned.

There was a shift in the mattress beside her, and she realized in that moment she wasn't alone in the bed. On the pillow next to her were a set of feet and the discernible lump of a human being under her comforter. Her stomach knotted like she was going to throw up. She was pretty sure that wasn't from her hangover.

She gently peeled back the comforter at the foot of the bed to see Jonah sleeping peacefully, his big hand lying flat across his bare, muscular chest with a wedding band on his finger. Grace then noticed there was a matching band on her own hand.

Oh.

My.

God.

She hit Play on the video. It was shaky, so whoever was filming them could've been inebriated too, but there was no mistaking what it showed: her and Jonah, laughing and screaming as they stood at the altar of the Little Wedding Chapel. She only knew it was that particular venue because of the sign behind the officiant.

"John, are you getting this!" she screamed in the video. *"I'm married! Look, Mom. Married. I'm Mrs. Cute Paramedic."*

"And I'm Mr. Cute Paramedic," Jonah slurred.

Grace winced and set the phone down. It began ringing again, but now she *really* couldn't talk to her mother. She buried her face in her hands and then remembered that she was stark naked. She scrambled out of bed and grabbed her robe from where it was hanging up on her closet door, wrapping it around herself quickly. Then she made her way to the other side of the bed and shook Jonah—Mr. Cute Paramedic, apparently—awake.

"Jonah," she said, quietly giving his shoulder a shake.

Jonah answered with a groan, rubbing his face and then he sat up quickly, blinking rapidly. "Where in the hell…?"

"Good morning," she replied, sardonically.

"Grace?" He scrubbed a hand over his face. "What the heck happened last night?"

"After the karaoke? I suppose more drinking and then… a wedding."

Jonah snorted and laughed. "A what?"

She held up her phone and pressed Play. Jonah was smirking, but as he watched their drunken wedding unfold on her phone, his smirk melted away into an expression of horrified realization, and then he noticed his left hand and the new gold band on his ring finger.

Though Grace seriously doubted it was real gold. Especially if it had come from the Little Wedding Chapel at the end of the Strip.

"No," he said in a hushed undertone.

"Yes." She climbed back onto the bed and sat cross-legged across from him. "What are we going to do?"

"Get an annulment?"

"We slept together."

Jonah looked down under the comforter and then realized that he wasn't wearing any clothing. "Well. Damn."

"Damn?" she asked, chuckling slightly at this bizarre situation.

"Not because it was you, but because I can't remember it."

"Neither can I." She rubbed her temples. "My body remembers the alcohol."

"You're dehydrated. You need to drink water." He stood, taking the knotted-up sheet and wrapping it around his waist as he walked out of the bedroom. "I'll get you a remedy for that."

"Thanks," she murmured, watching him in disbelief. It was kind of a surreal situation. Two coworkers married and he was worried about her water intake? It was sweet but made her chuckle at the absurdity of it all.

Jonah came dashing back into her room and shut the door. "There's a person banging on the outside of your condo. I could see their shadow from your living room window."

"What?" She checked her phone to view the door camera she'd set up. It was her mother, and now as she listened, Grace could hear her calling for her faintly from outside to answer the door.

It was mortifying, and she wanted to curl up into a tiny ball and disappear.

Could this day get any worse?

Don't jinx it.

"Do you know who it is?" Jonah asked.

"It's my mother."

His eyes widened. "Your mother?"

She nodded. "Yep."

"Does she live nearby?"

Grace didn't really think that was an important point given the situation, but then again she really wasn't thinking straight either this morning. "She lives in St. George. I guess I texted her last night that we got married. I texted everyone."

Jonah sat back down on the edge of the bed, looking a

bit dumbfounded. There was another sharp rap at the door, and he stood quickly.

"Well," he announced. "I'm not meeting my mother-in-law like this!"

"Your what?"

"Mother-in-law. I suggest we get dressed, Mrs. Cute Paramedic."

Grace chuckled nervously as Jonah moved around the room gathering up his clothing before disappearing into the bathroom. She tried to tame her hair a bit and went to answer the door before her mother broke it down. It was bad enough she'd announced to the whole family she was married, but the fact it was a drunken mistake would disappoint her mother and annoy her already stressed-out little sister. Then would come the inevitable disappointment, which Grace always seemed to provoke when it came to her family.

She let them down. She was a burden.

Her hospital stays after her near drowning when she was a kid had been a financial burden. And her failure to marry Victor, whom her family thought was a good match, deeply disappointed them.

She wished her relationship with Victor had worked out. It had been like a dream being with him, in the beginning.

He was a surgeon, successful, and his best friend was dating her sister. She'd been in love with him.

It had been a fairy-tale romance.

Almost too good to be true.

And that was exactly what it had turned out to be. In the end, it had been more like nightmare than a dream.

Happily-ever-afters just weren't for Grace. She'd learned that lesson well. But her mother wouldn't take that for an answer. Ever since the breakup, she had always nagged Grace about settling down, finding The One.

Now a drunken marriage so close to Melanie's wedding had probably sent her into sheer panic mode.

Worse, Grace knew Melanie would be *so* angry that she was ruining something else. Stealing her sister's thunder, taking away attention and focus from her, just like Grace had done when they were kids. It was a point of contention between the two of them.

She had to make this right somehow.

Grace opened the door. Her mother's eyes were wide and she was holding her phone. Actually, it was more like she was clenching it. "Finally."

"Morning, Mom." Grace stepped aside to let her mom come in out of the heat.

"Morning? It's almost noon."

"It's my day off."

"From what? A honeymoon?" her mother asked.

Grace worried her bottom lip. "Look…"

"No. I'm happy, Grace. After your breakup with Victor, you were so upset and I never imagined you'd ever find love again. You didn't seem interested."

Grace blinked a couple of times in disbelief. Her mother was…happy? "So, you're okay with this?"

"Why wouldn't I be?"

"So you drove from St. George to Summerlin for that?"

"Well, I'm shocked too. Obviously." Her mother sat down on the couch. "Your sister was beside herself when the news came out. She was at dinner with her fiancé and… his best man."

Grace's stomach sunk. "Melanie and Travis were out with Victor?"

Her mother nodded slowly. "Yep."

Grace groaned. Her mother had never known the full reason why things had ended with Victor. Melanie had already been dating Victor's best friend, the man who'd since become her fiancé, so Grace had kept it all to herself to make peace and never told anyone what happened or how embarrassed she was to be cheated on. At least when she was just running into Victor at the hospital, it had been all business and she could ignore him. Then they'd been put in the wedding party together, and things had stopped being so simple.

And now everyone, including Victor, knew Grace was married. How could she tell her family it was a drunken mistake? Just another humiliating moment to live down.

Maybe it doesn't have to be?

And a wild idea occurred to her. Perhaps Jonah would stay married to her for the month. Just until this big wedding was over, and then they could get a divorce. It would take that long to end it all anyway.

"So?" her mother, asked breaking her erratic chain of thoughts. "Where is my new son-in-law?"

"I'll go get him." Grace dashed from her living room back into the bedroom, causing Jonah to jump slightly. He was doing up his belt. It gave Grace a pause as she got to really appreciate the sight of his tanned, muscle-honed body.

A flash of a hazy memory hit her: her hands running over his chest as he kissed her neck. Heat rushed through her, and all she could do was stare at him.

Jonah paused and cocked an eyebrow. "Grace?"

"Sorry." She pinched the bridge of her nose and shook her head. "My mother is here."

"So you said. Is she angry?"

"No."

"Well, that's good. You're an adult, and mistakes happen."

"About that…"

He crossed his arms. "You say that with hesitation. What's going on?"

Grace wrung her hands together. "We need to pretend to be married. Not a mistake, but for real."

Jonah was shocked, and not for the first time this morning. Waking up married was pretty mind-boggling. He'd vowed to himself, after the divorce from his first wife, that he was never going to let this happen again. Yet here he was.

At least this time it wasn't a rebellion against parents and they weren't straight out of high school. Of course, a drunken elopement with a coworker wasn't exactly any better.

And now here was Grace coming in and asking him to pretend to *stay* married. He had heard her say time and time again at work she wasn't interested in a relationship. So what had changed?

He took a step back and just stared at her, her back against the closed bedroom door, her eyes wide and her hair untamed. She was adorable and disheveled. Bits and pieces of last night were coming back to him, and he was only disappointed that he didn't recall the time they'd spent together with stunning clarity. He had an inkling that was something he'd want to remember.

"What?" he asked, still trying to process it all.

She gulped. "We're married."

"I know."

"And we have to convince my mother that we really are and that it's a good thing and not at all a mistake." She was saying all of this at a mile a minute.

"Why?"

Grace exhaled. "My little sister is getting married."

"Okay, but I don't understand what that has to do with us."

"Her fiancé's best man is my ex, and he knows we're married too. Everyone. Knows." Her cheeks flushed crimson, and she dropped her head into her hands. "This is a disaster."

Jonah moved toward her and put his arm around her, trying to comfort her. She was so soft in his arms, and he remembered this feeling from the night before—wanting to hold her. Part of him wanted to tell her no, because this would muddy the waters at work, and he wasn't here to form any personal attachment. Just work and live out his life…which, when put that way, sounded ridiculously boring. He really did like Grace as a partner—maybe even, one day, a friend—and there was nothing wrong with supporting her. Perhaps he could do this for her, temporarily, even if it went against everything he'd vowed to himself before he moved to Nevada.

So much for keeping your distance.

"So you want to pretend to be married? For how long?"

She grimaced. "A month."

"A month?" he asked, hoping it didn't sound too high pitched as he stepped back.

"I know," she grumbled. "It's a lot."

"It is." He ran his hand through his hair. They'd be together on paper for a month, maybe more anyway, depending on how long it took to fix this situation. There were drive-through wedding booths but no drive-through divorce places he was aware of. He could use one of those right about now.

"What're you thinking?" she asked.

"Okay. As long as it won't affect our work, I can pretend to be your husband to navigate this whole family-wedding thing to help you save face."

Her face relaxed and then lit up, and she threw her arms around him. "Oh, my God. Thank you!"

He held her awkwardly at first, and then he melted into

her arms. She felt so good. He had to remember she was not really his.

They were partners.

Partners who were married and about to lie to her family. She stopped clinging to him.

"We can't let this affect our work though." Jonah needed to make that clear. "I want things to stay the same. Professional. I don't want to have to leave Vegas."

"Why would you leave?"

"If it got weird. I don't need that complication in my life."

"Well, I don't want to make it awkward either. So yeah, completely agree—this won't affect our professional relationship."

Even though it seemed unlikely, he kind of believed her. "So I guess I should meet your mother and try to convince her that we're not messing with her?"

"I appreciate you so much." She opened the door.

"Wait! One thing."

She turned around. "What?"

"Your mother's name? I mean, we have to present to her the illusion that we're married and we know each other."

"Good point. Her name is Leslie." Grace opened the door.

Jonah nodded, sucked in a deep, calming breath and walked out of Grace's bedroom to meet her mother.

He still wasn't sure why he'd promised to do this, but he never went back on his word. Especially to a partner.

Except one time…

"I'm not going to make it," Justin grunted.

"Of course you are," Jonah insisted, pulling him tighter, trying to ignore the mortar shell sounds from above.

He was trying so hard to hold on to his wounded best friend, as if that could save him, but that hope was fleeting.

"I'm not. We're pegged down. Medics are far away," Justin murmured.

"You need to stay awake."

"Don't leave me here, Jonah. Take me home. Promise me. I want to go home."

Jonah swallowed back the tears. "Of course."

He shook that painful reminder away, because it haunted him even after all this time. Jonah hadn't been able to bring Justin home. He'd broken that promise because bombing had started and his best friend's body had been buried under a collapsed tunnel overseas. It ate away at him. It was why he'd left the military; it was another reason why he'd moved to Nevada after his marriage ended, because with his marriage over and Justin dead, there were no ties in California. He had nothing. Nevada was a fresh start.

It was because of Justin, and because of the way Mona had broken her oaths about being faithful to him, that he took promises seriously. And he'd do this for Grace because he liked her and she'd been so kind to him when he'd first arrived. If her family lived in Utah, then he wouldn't see them too much. He'd only have to keep up the act when they were around.

And it was just an act. Grace really wasn't his. She wouldn't be. Yet he wouldn't do this for just anyone, so why was he doing this for her?

You're hungover and vulnerable. That's why.

"Mom, this is Jonah Crandall. My husband." Grace had plastered a big wide grin on her face and seemed to be talking through her clenched teeth.

Jonah extended his hand out to take the dark-haired,

shorter, older version of Grace by the hand. "Pleasure to meet you, Mrs. Landon."

"You can call me Leslie. We're family," Leslie gushed. "It's nice to meet you, although we were all shocked by the surprise. We couldn't quite believe it."

"As were we," Jonah replied, slipping his arm around Grace's shoulders and pulling her rigid body closer.

"Well, why don't we go out and have a nice lunch somewhere?" Leslie offered.

"Don't you have to shop for dinner tonight?" Grace asked.

Leslie waved her hand dismissively. "I can shop and get home in time."

"Well, actually Jonah has to go back to his place," Grace explained quickly.

Leslie looked confused. "His place? Doesn't he live here?"

Jonah glanced down at Grace, who seemed to be doing a good job of digging a hole with her perceptive mother. "I will be. Soon. Moving in tomorrow. Everything about us is a bit…muddled. Besides that. We've been planning my moving in for a couple of months."

His insides clenched at the lie. Maybe Grace wasn't the only one digging a big old hole for themselves. He seemed to be doing a good job too.

Leslie smiled. "Well, that makes sense. Maybe I will get the shopping done early, in that case. There's a big family dinner tonight in St. George. We have a lot to discuss about Melanie's wedding, and Grace, you are a bridesmaid—you should be there. Now you can bring Jonah, because I'm sure everyone wants to meet this mystery man you raced to the altar with."

"We'll be there," Jonah answered while Grace gave him a slightly crazed look. And he didn't blame her. He was surprised at himself for suggesting it as well, because it was the last thing he wanted to do.

"Good." Leslie headed toward the door. "I'll finish my errands and head back to Utah. I'll see you both tonight at six."

Grace let her mother out of her condo and then spun around to face him. "Why did you agree to that?"

"The family dinner? I assumed you were going."

"No." Grace sat down on the couch. "My family can be a little over the top."

"Are they super religious or something?"

"Several of them are LDS—Mormon. But we're married, so they won't blink an eye about living together," Grace replied. "I'm not religious."

"Well, you wanted to pretend we're married, so let's go and convince them of that fact."

Grace chewed on the bottom of her lip and didn't look convinced at first. Her whole body was tense, like she was on edge. "I don't know."

"Come on—you know if you want them to believe you, you'll have to go to dinner."

Her shoulders dropped, and she let out a sigh. "You're right. You know my mom will be popping in after this… to check on us."

"I'll move in." And he couldn't believe he said that out loud, that it was his idea.

What is happening to me?

Grace's eyes widened. "What about your place?"

"I've been living at vacation and short-term rentals since I got here."

"For six months?"

Jonah shrugged. "I was waiting to find the perfect place and save money. I can sleep on your couch."

Grace wrung her hands together for a moment, glancing at her couch. "If you're okay with this, then of course. I did put you on the spot."

"You're not totally to blame for this marriage. We both had too much to drink when we said our *I do*s."

Grace chuckled softly. "I suppose."

"I'll go pack up my stuff, get cleaned up, and I'll be back in time for us to head to St. George and face your family."

"You're being super supportive. I can't thank you enough."

"Of course. It's what good partners do. They back each other up."

Something Justin and he had always said when they went through basic training together. It was something he continued to live by.

"That's a good practice. I like that," she agreed.

"Try not to worry." Which he knew was easier said than done. He opened the door and stepped outside to call a cab as the reality of what was happening sunk in.

His marriage to Grace wasn't a forever situation, but right now they were legally tied together while they got their paperwork done, so why not have some fun and show her ex she'd moved on? He'd worked with Grace long enough to know she was professional and wouldn't let this affect their partnership. He'd believed her when she reassured him of that.

He could keep this whole marriage platonic, even if it had been kind of nice to wake up next to her this morning. Scary, but nice all the same. Jonah touched his lips as he remembered the softness of her kisses, her sweet taste and thought of how he wouldn't mind experiencing it all again without the haziness of alcohol. Only he couldn't give in. He had to remind himself of the fact that he'd tried marriage once before with someone he thought he knew, and it had ended so badly.

He was never going to put his heart on the line again.

No matter how much Grace tempted him.

CHAPTER THREE

GRACE CHECKED HER watch nervously, which was just a fidgety nervous reaction. She was freaking out about going to this dinner and facing her family. The last thing she wanted to do was be late, but she was being silly. They had plenty of time to make the almost two-hour trip to St. George. Jonah had texted her that he would be back to her place by three thirty so they could get on the road and head to her family's home.

Her phone had been pinging all morning with messages from various family members, some who were going to be at dinner tonight and some who weren't, all questioning her and wondering about Jonah.

Her mother had hopped on the group chat and let all those curious family members know that she had met Jonah, thought he was really nice and good looking and that he was coming to dinner that night.

Melanie hadn't said much. Well, except for insinuating that Grace had rushed to beat her to the altar, hinting that her big sister was once again deliberately stealing the spotlight. Their mother had jumped in and shut it down, but as with all their childhood fights since the near drowning, Melanie would just see that as their parents protecting Grace once again. It made Grace feel so guilty. She really didn't mean to infringe on Melanie's big day.

She'd never even planned on getting married. After what happened with Victor, Grace had a hard time believing in happily-ever-afters. He had said he loved her but cheated on her. How was that love? She wouldn't let herself ever go through that kind of hurt again.

At least Victor wouldn't be at the family dinner tonight, but she'd see him soon enough as the wedding crept closer.

Please be short-staffed and call Jonah and me in to work.

It was the mantra that she was repeating over and over in her head, but it wasn't working.

Usually, she loved her days off, especially after a long rotation on shift, but right now she wouldn't mind being called into the station and avoiding the awkwardness that awaited her in St. George.

A cab rolled up, and Jonah got out. He pulled out a large suitcase and a duffel bag before waving the cab driver off. She was shocked that Jonah had his whole life in two bags. Apparently, he was very minimalistic, whereas she was bit of a hoarder when it came to nice clothes, work-out clothes—really any kind of clothes—and shoes. Plus bags… It was a good thing he hadn't looked into her large walk-in closet.

Why are you thinking about that now? Focus.

"You don't have a car?" she asked as she flung open the door to greet him as he climbed the steps to her condo.

"I have a motorcycle, but since you don't have a garage at your complex I decided to put it into a little storage unit I have. To keep it safe."

The idea of Jonah on a motorcycle sent of ripple of thrill down her spine. She could imagine him sitting astride it, dressed in leather and traveling across the desert.

With me on the back?

The suggestion from her brain surprised her. She'd never

even ruminated on the idea of going on a motorcycle before. Yet picturing Jonah and wrapping her arms around him kind of titillated her.

"I've never seen you ride to work on your bike," she mused, trying to clear the image of him and her riding off into the Nevada sunset together.

"No, I don't usually ride it to the station. I've always had rentals that were close by. I can still walk from here," he said, glancing around. "Summerlin isn't far."

"It's far enough. I'll drive you in. We work the same shifts anyway."

He nodded curtly. "Deal."

"So that's all you have? Just a couple of bags?"

"Well, a few boxes in storage, but yeah, I travel light. I learned that in the military. When I got divorced my ex kept everything, and I had no problem with that. I wanted to leave California."

"Do your parents know about our little mishap?" she asked, taking the suitcase from him to walk it into her condo.

"No." He slung his duffel bag over his shoulder.

"Should you tell them?" she queried, alarmed by his nonchalant answer.

"Nope."

"Are you sure you didn't drunkenly text them too?"

"No, because…" He hesitated and sighed. "My parents are long gone. They were older when I was born. And no, I don't have siblings. I was their only child."

"I didn't mean to pry. You seem bugged by telling me that."

"No. I just… I like to keep things to myself. I'm kind of private."

"I've noticed," she mused.

"It's fine," he said tightly. Somehow she didn't think it was, and she felt guilty for questioning him.

"I'm sorry." She moved to the side so he could drop his bag in her living room.

"It's okay. I guess you should know in case it all comes up. Dad died while I was overseas and I lived with my mom for a bit after my marriage ended, but she died within a year of my returning. She was eighty. I was a surprise baby." She spotted a twinkle in his eyes. "I miss them."

"No other family?" she asked, thinking about her own large family and how involved they were in her life.

"Nope. They were only children too. I never knew my grandparents. There were no cousins. It was the three of us for a long time."

She couldn't even begin to contemplate the idea of such a small family.

Of being alone.

Aren't you alone now, Grace?

Suddenly she felt really guilty for wanting to get out of this dinner with her family. Jonah's story made her appreciate them. They were numerous and got in her business, but she was glad she had them. "Well, are you ready for this? I mean, you're not used to a large, in-your-face family. Some of them, the Mormon ones, are quiet, but for the most part they really like to be in each other's business."

Jonah laughed, but there was a nervous edge to it. "I think so. It'll be fine."

"You say that with such confidence."

"They'll ask the conventional questions about how we met… Well, that's easy—we met at work. I think we can handle mostly everything. We've both seen the unfortunate video, and they've seen it too. We'll stick with what I told your mother—we've been thinking about it for some time, and it just happened."

"You're so calm about this," Grace teased.

"Believe me, I'm not that calm. I prefer solitude."

"I do too."

"Is that why you moved away from Utah?"

"Bingo."

He smiled slightly and looked away. "We'll get through this."

"I'm a nervous wreck."

He cocked his head to one side. "I've never seen this side of you. When you're at work or in the station house you're, like, no-nonsense."

She smiled. "Lives are on the line at work. I take it seriously. Whereas with my family, sometimes I get close to losing my cool and then I might actually have to call in a paramedic to help."

Jonah laughed quietly to himself. "I'll forget you said that."

"Just you wait. Do you need anything before we leave?" she asked.

"Nope. I'm ready." He opened her door, and she locked it behind them. They headed back down to the parking lot and to her car.

"Is that pool for everyone?" he asked offhandedly.

Grace's body stiffened. "Yep. You can use it whenever you want. I have a key card."

"Great."

What she didn't tell him was she had never used the condo's community pool. Not once since she moved in. She'd tried to find a place without a pool, but it was difficult to find in this area.

Mostly, she just ignored its existence when she walked by it.

She relaxed once it was behind them and they got to her car.

Jonah climbed in and buckled up. Grace thought again about how much she would have loved to show up on the back of his motorcycle, clad in leather, to a family dinner. It would definitely turn some heads. But she really didn't mind driving. As the senior partner, she was often the one who sat in the driver's seat of the rig at work, and it felt right to have Jonah seated next to her. Except now there was an awkward tension that settled between them. The silence had never bothered her before. Now it felt different, probably because of the lie and the sex.

Memories of that were coming back to her, and it was hard not to think on it when it had felt so good.

"Is that a pie?" he asked, peering in through the rearview mirror.

"It is."

"I didn't know you baked."

"I don't, but there's a bakery down the street that does."

Jonah leered. "That's disappointing."

"That's a bit chauvinistic…expecting a woman to bake!" she goaded good-naturedly.

He laughed, his eyes glinting. "That's not what I mean. I was excited to learn a hidden talent about you, wife."

"It's not 'wife.' It's Mrs. Cute Paramedic, I believe."

"Oh, Lord," he groaned. "I'm sorry about that."

"It wasn't you. I think it was me."

"It's a terrible name."

She rolled her eyes but couldn't help smirking. That awkward tension she'd been feeling a moment ago melted away with some easy banter. They drove away from Summerlin and headed out onto the Bruce Woodbury Beltway, which connected to the interstate leading them through Arizona and then into Utah.

Grace was dreading what lay in store for them there.

Her family.

And a whole lot of questions.

At least it was a nice day for a drive, and riding with Jonah was a breeze. They were conversing freely, a bit more freely now, even than when they were at work. It never really bothered Grace that Jonah kept to himself a lot of the time at work; he was a good partner. But she also kind of liked this chattier side of him. Hopefully he wouldn't be too annoyed with her for forcing the conversation by asking way too many questions.

It surprised her how nice it felt having someone to talk to. She hadn't realized how solitary her life had become. There was no time for friends when she worked so much. Work was her life.

"You look distressed," Jonah remarked.

"Do I?" she asked, gripping the steering wheel a bit tighter.

"Your knuckles are going white."

Grace relaxed a bit. "Just mentally bracing for what's to come."

"Don't fret about it. Believe it or not, I'm quite charming."

She glanced over him and laughed. "What?"

"I can be social when I want to. I did arrange that work get-together."

"True. I suppose you're responsible for this whole mess."

Jonah frowned. "What do you mean?"

"It was your idea to get married."

"Pardon?" he asked.

"I distinctly remember you asking me to marry you after our duet at karaoke."

"I think you asked me. After you grabbed my butt," Jonah countered.

Grace's mouth dropped open. "I would never do such a thing."

"You did. Several times."

Heat flushed into her cheeks, and little bits of last night came back to her. She had been a bit handsy with him. "I will concede I was the one who initiated the kiss."

That she definitely remembered.

And her stomach fluttered in excited remembrance of how she had pulled his hard body against her. How good it had been to melt right into that kiss. She couldn't remember ever feeling that way with Victor. It had been hot, but with Jonah it had been something she'd never experienced before. She wanted more.

You're partners, remember?

And she had to keep that thought in her head. Jonah agreed to this whole arrangement on the condition that it didn't affect their working relationship, and she'd promised him it wouldn't. So she couldn't let herself even entertain the idea of touching him or kissing him.

She had to put that all out of her mind.

The drive to St. George was good. Jonah didn't mind long rides. The best thing in the world to help him relax was to get onto his motorcycle and ride across the desert. It was a way to connect himself to the elements, so it wasn't exactly the same in a car, but it was still nice to enjoy the scenery and engage in pleasant conversation with Grace.

And that shocked him. The last time he'd been this at ease was when he'd originally been dating his ex. Before his time in the service had changed him. Before Mona had changed.

It was hard not to talk to Grace.

And talking about nothing kept his thoughts off the fact that she was wearing a very cute and flattering sun dress. It went past her knees, but he knew very well all the curves that were hidden underneath the flowery, breezy fabric and how they had felt under his hand as he'd traced the lines of her body when they were naked together in her bed.

Get a grip.

It was hitting him how fast he'd agreed to this fake marriage. Why? Why hadn't he just walked away? It would have made it so much easier to keep his desire for Grace at bay.

Maybe because he was lonely.

Really, he had no one left. His parents were gone, his first marriage had been over for years, Justin was dead.

In California he'd spent years healing and closing himself off. Grace was like a breath of fresh air. It was scary, this lying and pretending, but maybe it would be fun to be included in some family normality.

Or maybe a bit of abnormality if what Grace was saying about her family was true.

"We're almost there," Grace said, breaking in on his reflections. There was a nervous edge to her voice, and she was gripping the steering wheel again.

"It'll be okay," he reassured, but truth be told he was starting to feel a bit nervous too. Never mind the lie they were telling, socializing with crowds of people bothered him enough. Did he even really know how to be that same person he used to be? The last thing he wanted to do was snap or have a moment where he lost control in front of complete strangers.

It won't be like that.

He only hoped his inner voice was right.

Leslie Landon had been really nice and pleasant, even in spite of the fact he'd drunkenly married her daughter, but he couldn't help but think about the rest of the family. What would they think of him?

Mona's family had never been keen on him. Even when he and Mona had been dating in high school. Probably because they'd eloped right after they graduated and Jonah had enlisted the day after their wedding. Now he knew that leaving her alone so soon hadn't been the best move as a supportive husband. He'd thought their love would be enough to sustain them, but it hadn't been.

Marriage was a two-way street, a partnership. It took work. He'd realized that too late. When he'd gotten back from deployment, he'd tried to heal the rift that had grown between them. Instead of working on it with him, Mona had cheated, then demanded the divorce.

The day of the divorce he'd lost what little family he had.

Thankfully, his mother had been around. She hadn't been crazy about Mona either, but she was the support he'd needed then. He missed her.

Mom would've liked Grace.

Warmth spread from the center of his chest as he pictured his mom meeting Grace. Just thinking about it made him happy. His mom definitely would've liked her. Even in the few months that he'd known Grace, he could see similar personality traits in her, and that softened him.

You have to be careful, his inner voice warned.

Thinking like that made him vulnerable.

"Right. It'll be okay," Grace responded nervously. "However, I do have a strong sensation like there's a flock of birds taking up resident in the pit of my stomach."

"Tell me about your family. I know your mom, Leslie, but tell me about the others. Who else will I be meeting?" Maybe if he focused on names and details, he wouldn't worry so much.

Grace took a deep breath. "Well, there's my dad, Rick. He might be a little hard on you. He's protective of his daughters. Then again, he calls me tough cookie. I was a bit of a tomboy."

Jonah smiled. "I can believe that. Who else?"

"The bride-to-be is my younger sister, Melanie. She's two years younger than me, and honestly, we're polar opposites. She's a bit of a princess, and I'm pretty sure she's angry with me for getting married. Her fiancé is Travis."

"And his best man is your ex?"

"Yes," Grace said, stiffly. "Victor."

"The surgeon, right?"

"Yes. At least he won't be there tonight," she groused.

"Anyone else?"

"My little brother, Aidan. He's sixteen. He was a surprise to my parents."

"Oh, so we have that in common." They shared a smile, and he tore his gaze away. "So, Leslie, Rick, Aidan, Melanie and Travis?"

"And our elderly, neurotic dog, Pepper. She's a golden doodle."

"A what?" he asked.

"Golden retriever and standard poodle. A golden doodle."

"Okay. Sounds good."

"There might be extended family there, but I don't know." Grace gripped the wheel again as she flicked her blinker on and turned off the interstate. "Welcome to St. George."

Southern Utah was different from all the pictures he'd seen of Utah, which usually involved the Salt Lake area farther north. St. George resembled Nevada and Arizona but with beautiful red rock vistas. There were gorgeous palm trees, and it looked to be a happening city. Not as big as Vegas, but a nice place to live.

Grace didn't say much as she navigated the streets. They made their way to an affluent middle-class neighborhood, and she parked in front of a modern brick bungalow home in the subdivision of Bloomington, on a corner lot that overlooked the red rock hills. It had a beautifully manicured desert garden and stonework out front and a triple garage. The wide boulevards were lined with lush green trees.

It was serene. Like something out of a magazine. Maybe it was almost too picture perfect.

There was a young man outside on the driveway shooting hoops, and Jonah had a suspicion this was Grace's younger brother, Aidan.

Grace took a deep breath. "Here we go."

"I'll grab the pie." Maybe if he was holding on to that, he wouldn't want to bolt.

She nodded, and they climbed out of her car.

"Grace!" Aidan called, his basketball under one arm as he came running over to give her a side hug.

"Hey, Aidan. How's the mood inside?" Grace asked.

Aidan shrugged. "As expected. Melanie is freaked out!"

Grace inhaled another deep breath. "Jonah, this is my little brother, Aidan. Aidan, this is Jonah, my..."

"Your husband," Aidan grinned, his eyes twinkling. "Oh, I know!"

Grace groaned.

"It's nice to meet you," Jonah said.

"It's nice to meet you too. Prepare to be grilled. Grandma and Grandpa are in there, as well as Auntie Gert. Plus some of the wedding party."

Grace's expression dropped. "Some of the...what?"

Aidan was indifferent to his sister's change in tone, but Jonah was aware.

"You know, Melanie's maid of honor and the best man with his wife. Mom wants to talk about the wedding. I'm escaping all that boring talk until dinner." Aidan jogged back to his basketball hoop.

Grace nodded, and Jonah could sense the anxiety melting off her. Without even thinking about it, he reached down and took her hand, squeezing it.

"It'll be okay," he reassured gently.

"Will it?" she asked, her voice breaking slightly.

"If not, I can always pie him." He was surprised at the suggestion—and the way he found himself waggling his eyebrows—but it made Grace laugh, and that was all that mattered. This wasn't going to be easy for either of them, but it would be best to get it all over and done with. "Come on. Let's get this over, then."

She nodded, and they walked up the driveway to her front door. She was still trembling, but she didn't let go of her death grip on him. Jonah remembered clearly having to deal with Mona and the man she cheated on him with. Mona hadn't ended up marrying the other man, but Jonah knew exactly how Grace was feeling. It had been humiliating.

And he was dead serious about shoving a pie into her ex's face if he got out of hand.

He had a wife to protect, even if she was fake.

For the next month, she was his—something he'd never thought he'd say to himself ever again.

CHAPTER FOUR

KNOWING VICTOR WAS HERE, all Grace wanted to do was run. When she opened up the front door of her parents' home and stepped in, it felt like she was walking the plank to her own demise.

Instantly, she felt bad for Jonah—really bad, because she was putting him in a precarious situation. Well, maybe *precarious* was putting it too strongly, but if the situations had been reversed, she'd be nervous as heck. Jonah had plastered on a million-dollar reality-television kind of smile—fake and really, really big. It was almost comical. She was kind of glad that he was too pretty for his own good, something she always thought when she looked at him and his classic California good looks. Right now, it worked to her advantage; as far as she was concerned, Jonah was definitely more attractive than Victor. And that gave her a small amount of petty, devious pleasure.

"Mom?" she called out, hoping that her voice didn't shake. "We're here."

Her mother came rushing out of the back, where the sunroom was. It was where they entertained guests. She looked flustered, but then again she'd always been something of a whirlwind.

"You both made it," her mother said, quickly letting out a big breath of air.

"Did you have doubts?" Grace asked.

"I did."

"I said I would be here," Grace replied.

"I wasn't sure," her mother said in a hushed undertone. "Melanie is having a slight meltdown."

Grace knew exactly how that felt in a way, because she was on the verge of having one herself. "Why?" she asked.

Her mother made a face, as if to say *You should know*, and Grace's stomach knotted up into a tight little ball. Her sister was upset by her drunken elopement with Jonah. Coming here tonight had been a bad idea.

"I brought pie. Or rather, we brought pie," Jonah piped up, breaking the tension which had descended.

"How thoughtful of you." Her mother took the pie from Jonah. "I'll take care of this, and Grace can introduce you to the rest of the family."

"Family. Right," Grace muttered as she took Jonah's leather jacket to hang up in the closet by the front door. Her mother scurried off to the kitchen.

"How are you so calm with this?" Grace hissed under her breath.

"I'm not," Jonah whispered back. "Fake it till you make it."

"I'll run if you want to," Grace suggested.

"Don't act so eager," Jonah teased as she put his jacket on a hanger. "We can do this."

"What?"

"You act like you're going to your own funeral."

"Aren't we?"

"Maybe."

She chuckled and shut the door, leaning against it. "I feel like I might be."

"It went fine with your brother, and I'm sure this will

be okay too." There was an edge to his voice like he was trying to give himself a pep talk.

"Aidan's a sixteen-year-old boy. My sister is a bride, and she might even be that more mythical creature."

Jonah cocked an eyebrow. "And what's that?"

"Bridezilla," Grace whispered, though she couldn't help but grin as she said it.

Jonah snickered and playfully rolled his eyes. "Great," he snorted. "I can handle that."

"You say that with sincerity."

"Come on—we'd better go in there holding hands. Show our solidarity against all those monsters," he joshed.

Grace glanced down at his outstretched palm. She was not a touchy-feely type of person, but seeing him offering unanimity made her calm, and she gladly took his warm, strong hand in her own. It was support, an anchor she hadn't known she needed until that moment. She was sure she was shaking, but having him here was grounding. Especially when she knew she was perpetuating a lie of her own doing. Even if he was just as nervous as her, it felt like they were together as a team. In this moment Jonah was her rock to stand on, and she really appreciated him.

As she approached the sunroom, she could hear the voices of her family: the high-pitched excited sound of her sister, followed by Travis, her future brother-in-law, trying to calm her. Yeah, it was clear to Grace that her nuptials weren't being very well received.

And she felt bad about that.

It was never her intention to encroach on her sister's wedding, let alone marry her partner after a drunken night of karaoke. Her situation was like something out of a sitcom from the eighties or nineties.

Surreal. That was the word.

"Hi, everyone." Grace knew her voice broke as she said

those words. Jonah gave her hand a reassuring squeeze, and she returned it.

Everyone in that room turned their heads slowly and stared at her. Melanie, who had been perched on the arm of her fiancé's chair, stood up and crossed her arms.

"Hi yourself," she stated through pursed lips.

Yep. Definitely mad.

Jonah squeezed her hand again in reassurance. As if he could sense it too.

"This is my…my husband, Jonah." It was hard to get those words out.

"Hi," Jonah greeted brightly. It was completely unlike the real him that Grace knew, but then again when he was on the job he could be very personable with patients and their families.

She held her breath, waiting for someone to say something.

Anything.

No one said a word. She could have heard a pin drop in that room.

"Jonah, is it?" Victor asked, breaking the silence finally. "Aren't you a paramedic?"

It was an innocent-enough question, but it made Grace clench her free hand into a fist, because she knew Victor's view on paramedics. It was nothing short of egotistical for him to think that way. Paramedics might not have gone to school as long as trauma doctors like him, but what they did was vital. It was something she and Victor had argued about often enough.

She knew Victor's wife agreed with him on the superiority of doctors. He'd always needed constant praise. Honestly, years later, Grace realized she should've seen that as the red flag it really was.

"I am. Grace and I are partners. That's how we met. So

glad I work with her. She's the best partner." Jonah brought Grace's hand up to his mouth and kissed it. The moment his lips touched her skin, need raced through her, settling deep in her belly as some fragments of memories from the drunken wedding night ran through her brain.

His lips on more than her hand.

The pleasure she'd experienced with him.

She knew her cheeks were red because she could feel the heat, the desire burning through her blood. In that moment, it was just the two of them in that room and she forgot about everyone else.

Victor didn't say anything else. No one did. They all stood there, staring.

"I'm glad I work with you too," Grace said softly, meeting his gaze.

Victor snorted. Just slightly, but Grace heard it.

Apparently, Jonah did too. His eyes narrowed in on Victor. "She's one of the best paramedics in Vegas. I'm proud to work with her and I'm proud to be married to her."

He was standing up for her. Despite the fact that he didn't even know her family. She appreciated it. No one really did that for her—not that she would have let them—and the fact Jonah had was making her heart beat just a bit faster. She had been dreading all these get-togethers, and there was a small fraction of her that was uneasy about forcing Jonah to go ahead with this charade, but right now, she wasn't regretting anything. In this moment she felt strong with him by her side.

"Well, I guess congratulations are in order," Travis said, standing up and extending his hand to shake Jonah's.

"Thanks, Travis." Grace gave her future brother-in-law a quick hug.

Melanie was frowning, but she hugged Grace. "I'm happy for you."

"I'm happy for you too," Grace responded.

"I'm glad you came tonight. I was worried you wouldn't," Melanie admitted, her eyes darting quickly over to Victor.

"I'm here. You have to be excited about wedding planning. Right?"

Melanie nodded. "I am."

Grace pulled her sister aside. "I didn't mean to steal your thunder."

She wanted to make things right for Melanie. She really hadn't done this on purpose.

Melanie relaxed. "I know. And I know it's hard for you with Victor. I was…shocked when I saw that video sent to the wedding chat."

"So was I," Grace said, chuckling. "I won't let this ruin your day. Okay?"

Melanie nodded.

There was a loud bang from the hall that made them all jump. The front door, slamming.

"Aidan?" her mom called out. "Do you have to slam every door in the house?"

"Help!" Aidan shouted as he came busting in the room. "Mr. Petersen next door collapsed walking his dog."

Grace didn't even hesitate. She ran after her brother with Jonah close behind her and Victor following even closer. She told her mother to call emergency services. When she got outside there was a crowd gathered at the end of the driveway.

"Did someone call the paramedics?" Jonah shouted over his shoulder as they dropped down next to the unconscious man lying on the ground. She wasn't even sure if she heard anyone reply, because calling for backup wasn't her focus. Someone in her family would definitely take care of it. Instead, all her attention went to the patient. She'd learned in situations like this how to block out everyone else and focus completely on her work.

Even when in situations that got to her, like drownings, it was never until her adrenaline had dipped that she crashed and was laid flat on her ass.

“I told my mother to call,” Grace answered.

“His pupils are reacting. That’s good. How is his airway?” Victor asked as he flashed a small penlight he carried everywhere into Mr. Petersen’s eyes. He was checking the man’s pupils, and she was glad he carried that little light around, because the sun was setting and it was very dark at the end of the driveway.

“Clear,” Jonah said, checking the man’s throat. They got him onto his back.

“His pulse is thready,” Grace remarked. “Shine that light on his hands, Victor.”

Victor did, and she immediately assessed that there was a bluish tinge to the nail beds, which definitely meant there was a lack of oxygen. It could’ve been a coronary, it could’ve been a stroke, but she wasn’t a doctor and couldn’t speculate.

Mr. Petersen was breathing, and that was the main thing.

“Mr. Petersen?” Jonah called out loudly. “Can you hear us?”

There was no response, but Grace could hear the distant wail of the St. George paramedics on their way. This was their jurisdiction, their hospitals, and she didn’t have the equipment. At least he would get help.

The paramedics arrived, and they helped get Mr. Petersen loaded up into the ambulance. Jonah stood back with her as Victor, the physician, spoke with the local emergency medical workers. Jonah was frowning as he watched the whole thing.

“What’s wrong?” she asked.

"I hate stepping away from a job," he murmured, and then a half smile tugged on his lips. "I like to see a job through and make sure the person is okay. I guess it stems back from my military training."

"Then how would that explain me?"

Jonah cocked an eyebrow. "What?"

"I feel the same, and I wasn't in the military."

He smiled down at her tenderly. "I knew there was a reason I liked you."

"Well, that's something at least."

The doors of the ambulance slammed shut, and the crowd was dispersing. The siren let out a wail and then drove away.

"Well, that was a bit unexpected," Grace's mother said. "Hopefully Mr. Petersen will be okay. Good thing you were on the scene, Victor."

Grace tried not to roll her eyes, but then her mother turned to them.

"And both of you…as well," her mother explained.

"I'm glad we were here too, Mrs. Landon," Jonah responded. "All of us."

Her mother smiled at Jonah. "Well, dinner is ready, and there's nothing more we can do here."

Jonah reached down and took Grace's hand again, squeezing it reassuringly, and Grace returned the gesture. This whole thing might've been a ruse, but with Jonah, the right partner, she could overcome this.

Jonah had sensed that awkward tension the moment they walked into that sunroom. It had grated on him. It was the absolute worst, and he tried so hard to take it just so everyone would buy into their act. Especially seeing how Grace's ex was there. And he'd recognized Victor right away. He was a good trauma doctor but kind of a snobby jerk. There was another word that Jonah could use, but he wouldn't let himself actually think it because even thinking it would be pushing the line just a bit.

He really didn't see what Grace had seen in Victor, but then again he'd asked himself the same questions time and time again about Mona. He had been a different person then, and he was pretty sure the same would be true of Grace.

He didn't know that version of her. He barely knew the current version of Grace beyond work, because he hadn't intended to get to know *anyone*. So much for that plan.

Honestly, he was still trying to wrap his brain around the fact that he'd agreed to this whole marriage-of-convenience thing, something that he assumed was only done in romance novels. But here he was, living the dream.

And that was how he had to keep his focus—thinking of it as a fun dream, not a nightmare. If he didn't try to put a positive spin on it all, he wouldn't be able to keep up their charade of being husband and wife. In fact, he'd probably run for the hills, because marrying for real and trying to make a life with someone else relying on him was not in his cards.

There was no way he was ever going to put any piece of himself out on the line for someone and get hurt again.

Reminding himself that this was all a fake while they waited for the divorce had helped him play along, because he truly did like Grace and he wanted to be friends with her. He wanted to be able rely on her as a partner.

Surprisingly, it had been easy to turn on that Californian charm when he'd walked into her family house and met everyone. And the fact that a neighbor had had a medical emergency hadn't even fazed him.

That he could deal with, but now sitting around a large dining room table with a bunch of people he didn't know, people who had multiple questions for him, was a bit nerve wracking. That urge to bolt came over him again. It was crowded, claustrophobic, and he was stuck right in the middle of a bunch of strangers.

Case in point: meeting Aunt Gert, who wore her black mascara *really* thick. He was trying hard not to stare at the clumps collecting in the corners of her eyes as she ogled him. Grace had noticed and was endeavoring not laugh.

Traitor.

He tried to focus in on the wedding chatter, but it was difficult because he was not interested in it.

“We’re getting married at the country club,” Melanie piped up. “I have a wedding coordinator, and it’s going to be outdoor and elegant.”

Grace’s nose wrinkled at the mention of the country club, and Jonah wondered why.

“Do you golf a lot, Travis?” he asked, trying to make conversation because he hated the awkwardness of being seated at this table. Grace’s father, Rick, still wouldn’t even look him in the eye. He was the one person who Jonah really hadn’t met because when they’d briefly been introduced, Rick just nodded stiffly at him. Jonah remembered what Grace had told him—that her father could be overprotective.

If Jonah had daughters he might be too.

He shook that thought away. He was never going to have a family—ever. Why dwell on it?

“I do,” Travis said. “Right, Rick?”

“We do,” Rick answered. “In fact, we’re coming down to Vegas in a week to do a bachelor thing for Travis. We’re going golfing and having a steak dinner. Jonah, you should join us.”

Jonah was shocked by the invite. And he couldn’t really tell if it was genuine or not. It sounded almost as if it was perfunctory.

Grace's eyes flew open. "Dad, you don't..."

"No, it's no trouble. He's your husband," Rick stated firmly. "I need to get to know him."

Jonah's stomach knotted.

"I would love to. Just let me know where and when." He actually despised golfing, had never played it and found it boring to watch, but it would seem kind of rude and suspicious not to accept the invitation, since he'd been the one to bring up the sport. And he'd brought it up because he associated golf with country clubs.

"Great," Rick said. "We'd love to have you since you're a member of the family now."

But Jonah wasn't sure how much *love* was really in that statement. It was a nice sentiment, but it seemed kind of forced.

"Right." He swallowed the hard lump in his throat. Part of the family? No, he really wasn't, but there was an appeal to being included in a family again.

It had been so long.

Even though his parents had been a bit distant with him because they'd been older, he'd never been lacking in love while they'd lived. But they'd been gone for a few years now. It had been some time since he'd had a chance to bask in a family environment. He kind of liked it.

He missed it.

Don't let yourself think like that.

Since he planned to live alone the rest of his life, he couldn't let himself get attached to anything. Last time he'd done that had been with Mona's family. They might not have really warmed up to him or liked him, but they'd been there and supportive. Until the marriage had ended—then they had completely shut him out.

He lost his best friend, his wife and his parents all in a short amount of time. Those were dark years, and he was never going back to that.

He had to keep his distance from Grace and her folks so when this pretense was over and they went back to being nothing more than partners, it wouldn't hurt so much.

The rest of the dinner passed in a blur, and everyone ate the pie that Grace had brought. Once the meal was over, he found himself sitting outside alone and staring up at the clear night sky. You couldn't see many stars, because St. George was a city just like Vegas, but it was a bit darker here and they were higher in elevation, so there were a couple popping out.

The quiet and the stars helped him refocus and not let those past hurts take over. Even if he was concerned about the upheaval of his emotions, he'd made a promise to Grace and he wouldn't back out now, especially after meeting her family.

"There you are," Grace said, quietly slipping through the sliding glass door.

"Yeah, I wanted a few moments of peace before we hit the road."

She nodded. "Contemplating your choice about golfing with my dad, maybe?"

Jonah slightly lifted his shoulders. "Maybe."

"Do you even know how to golf?"

"No. Do you?"

"I do."

He was taken aback. "You do?"

"Why are you so shocked by that? A lot of women play golf. I actually enjoy it."

"You like golf?" He made a face and shook his head. "Seems kind of boring."

"It's not, and it's clear I'm going to have to give you

some golf lessons before you get out on the green with my dad, Travis and Victor."

He groaned. "Victor too?"

"It's a bachelor-night thing. Remember?"

He scrubbed a hand over his face. "Why did I agree to all this?"

Grace sat down in the chair next to him. "I know. It's a big ask, but you don't know how much I appreciate it."

"I'm glad. I mean, you're not the only one at fault here. We both got incredibly drunk that night."

"Still, it meant a lot to have you there supporting me," she whispered.

He glanced over her at her sitting next to him, in that beautiful flowing summery dress, her silken blond hair blowing in the evening breeze, and all he wanted to do was pull her into his lap and hold her. Only he couldn't. No one would think anything of it here and it would just all be part of the act to her, but for him there was suddenly a very real yearning to hold her close. A yearning for intimacy which he hadn't felt in a long time.

It overwhelmed him. He wanted to tell her strong she was, stronger than she thought, and that he'd meant all of what he told Victor, but that would only lead somewhere he'd sworn never to go again. So he said nothing.

"Do want to head back to Vegas?" she asked.

"Yes." And instantly he felt relieved.

They both stood up and walked back into her parents' house to say good-night.

This was all a big ruse—Jonah knew that, and for better or for worse he'd promised her that he would keep it up. He just needed to learn to harden his emotions better, because if he didn't…

He couldn't bear the idea of loving and losing someone else and having to start all over in another new place.

* * *

Jonah offered to drive back to Las Vegas because when he was driving, he was able to block out all his indecisive thoughts and focus on the roads. It calmed him. The fact was he was enjoying his time with Grace more than he should've let himself. The night had been so awkward, but with her by his side, it had been easy to put on the facade—easy to pretend and play her husband. It kind of freaked him out that it had been so simple to slip into that role.

"You've gone quiet," Grace said. "You okay?"

"Just concentrating on the road. You should be used to me driving by now. I mean, I've driven before."

"I drive the rig," she teased.

Jonah heaved a big disdainful sigh. "True."

"Then what's up?"

"What do you mean?" he asked stiffly.

"You were like a totally different person with my family."

"It's all part of the act, right?"

"Right," she responded hesitantly, like she didn't believe him. "And now?"

"I'm fine. Just…worried about lying to your family. They're nice."

"I know, but trust me…this will be less stressful than telling them the truth."

"For them or you?" It was a blunt question. He knew that, but he was hoping for a truthful answer. Something he'd never gotten from Mona. He hoped Grace wouldn't lie to him.

"Both," she admitted. "Exes are complicated, as are rash decisions made when intoxicated."

He grunted. "Understatement of the year."

"You were married before, right?"

"I was. It ended badly. I was also cheated on. Trust is… It's hard to give."

Which was true.

When he'd come home after serving, he'd been so broken and had needed to heal.

"Mrs. Crandall? I'm Dr. Severn, your husband's therapist."

Jonah looked over at Mona, who only took his therapist's hand with a bit of prodding.

"Pleasure," she said through gritted teeth. "Not sure why I'm here. I don't have post-traumatic stress disorder."

Dr. Severn frowned for a moment. "I'm aware, Mrs. Crandall, but...you're Jonah's wife, and it's important that you're here. Your support is needed in this healing journey."

Mona nodded. "Okay. Medication dosing and such? Is that what you mean by support?"

"Well, yes, there are medications, but emotional support too," Dr. Severn responded.

"Okay," Mona replied quickly. "I thought he was over all of this PTSD when he took his discharge. I guess I don't understand what's happening or what more I can do. I mean, I already work two jobs since he went on disability."

"It's not about money, Mona," Jonah said quickly. "We need to repair our relationship. I need your emotional support. Can I trust you to make this work?"

Immediately he knew he'd offended her. Her body went ramrod straight, and she snapped her mouth shut. Out of the corner of his eye he saw Dr. Severn was looking back and forth at the both of them, clearly uncomfortable.

He hadn't meant to embarrass her, but her combative comments had put him on edge too.

"Of course," she replied tightly and plastered on a fake smile.

* * *

Jonah shook that painful memory away. The lie she'd told. She never had come to another therapy session. She'd never understood why the medication alone couldn't just fix it all so he could enlist again.

He'd foolishly thought Mona could help him out, but she hadn't wanted that burden. She'd always wanted the quick fix. As if medication alone was the solution to Jonah's problem. It did wonders for some and he promoted it to patients, but for him it just hadn't been enough alone.

The work he'd done in therapy to process his trauma had been long and difficult, but he'd been determined to stick to it because he'd been so invested in saving their marriage. Mona just hadn't wanted it like he had. She hadn't been willing to fight for him, for them. She didn't want to put in the effort.

He'd been a fool for wanting to save them so badly. All because he thought love was enough.

"That's it exactly," Grace said, interrupting his brooding. "Trust. I trusted Victor with my whole being, with my soul, but the fact that he cheated on me and everyone but me knew…it was humiliating."

"Did your family know? I mean, it's kind of crappy of them to be so okay with him after hurting you."

"No. I didn't tell them why it ended. I was so ashamed. They had to help me so much when I was a kid…" Grace trailed off and covered her mouth with her hand, like she was physically trying to stop herself from saying more. "They think I ended it. Maybe Travis knows, but I don't think so."

"I think you should tell them. They care about you."

"None of that matters now. I don't want to cause further rifts or friction leading up to Melanie's big day. It's going to be bad enough when this ends."

Jonah nodded. He understood that. But if Travis did know about his best friend doing that to Grace—his future sister-in-law—and saw no problem with it, well, who was to say Travis wouldn't do the same to Melanie?

Though Jonah prided himself on being a good judge of character, and Travis didn't seem like the type of person to do that. From the brief time he'd spent with them tonight, it seemed like Travis genuinely cared for Melanie. There was tenderness, respect, love. All the things Jonah wished he'd had with Mona back then but it was now clear he hadn't.

He secretly wanted all that still, but he didn't know how to reach out and take it without the fear of being hurt.

The same way Grace had been hurt by Victor. Wouldn't she *want* to talk to her family about it? One thing Jonah had learned working through his PTSD was that you had to share and be more open. Bottling things up was never good.

Of course, he was one to talk.

But then, it was about opening up to the right people. And if you couldn't speak to your family, then something was wrong.

She must have her reasons.

Only those reasons, whatever they were, were not his concern. He had a part to play, and getting involved emotionally was not part of the deal.

"You can see the Strip," Grace remarked, changing the subject.

"Yeah, you can. I've never seen it from over here. It's nice."

All the brilliant lights illuminated the night sky. The *Welcome to Nevada* sign was big and bold as they crossed over the state line and left Utah behind.

"I'm ready to be home," she murmured, resting her head against the window.

"Yeah. I'm tired too." He was looking forward to tonight

because he had a steady place to stay for a month. Not a short-term rental where he constantly had to move around. Grace's place was a nice condo, close to work, in a quiet residential neighborhood, and he was looking forward to staying put for a short time.

He just had to be careful. They might've been man and wife legally, but that was only a fragile piece of paper.

He couldn't let her in. This was all temporary. He couldn't get wrapped up in her life.

There was an expiration date on this marriage, and if he wanted to keep working with her afterward, it all had to stay professional. No matter how tempting she was.

CHAPTER FIVE

IT WAS A thousand percent awkward when they got back to Grace's place after the family dinner in St. George. Jonah might've had a great stage presence when it came to her family, but much like when they were at work, he was a bit more withdrawn and quiet in private.

Normally when he was like this they were busy and it wouldn't bother her or faze her. Now it did. Probably because, thanks to her impulsiveness, they were stuck in this lie together.

Stop taking all the blame.

And that was the crux of the matter. She was putting it all on herself, like she usually did.

Jonah followed her up the stairs, and she spun around to say good-night, like they were on a date or something. Then she remembered he'd moved in.

"What?" he asked.

"I forgot you lived here."

A smile played on his lips. "Well, you invited me to move in."

"I did not," she gasped. "I believe it was your suggestion."

He grinned. "I guess it was."

"Still, I just forgot." She unlocked the door, swearing at herself inwardly for being such a weirdo. She unlocked the door, and he followed her in, shutting the door behind him, locking it.

"I want you to have my bed."

His eyes widened. "Your…what?"

"Not sharing," she said quickly. "I want you to have my bed. I know you said…"

Jonah held up his hand. "Grace, it's fine. I'm perfectly comfortable on the couch."

"You're sure?"

"Positive. I think I'm going to make use of the pool and go for a swim first."

Her stomach churned just at that thought. "Oh?"

"You okay with that?"

"Of course. Why wouldn't I be?"

"Do you ever use the pool?"

"No," she responded quickly. "I don't swim."

"What if I teach you?"

"No." She shook her head.

"Sure, but if you ever change your mind."

"I'd rather ride the motorcycle."

He cocked an eyebrow. "Well, that can be arranged."

"No helmet." She was really getting herself into somewhat of a pickle tonight.

Jonah didn't say anything else, and they just stood there, staring at each other.

"Well, I'll leave you to your swim." Grace backed away and retreated to her room.

She didn't want this to get any weirder than it already had. Not that the weirdness was a surprise. Awkward situations seemed to be her specialty a lot of the time, and getting drunk with a coworker and marrying him was definitely the epitome of that. How could it not be?

She heard the sound of the condo door shutting and relaxed a bit, taking the opportunity to get ready for bed.

When she glanced out her bedroom window, she could see Jonah was swimming laps, and truth be told, she was a bit envious of his ability to do that so easily. Something most people could do, but not her. There was a part of her that couldn't help but admire his strong body gliding through the crystal-blue water.

He was so handsome.

He's off-limits.

She shook her head in disgust at herself for lusting after him.

Again.

She was pretty sure this was also one of the reasons they'd ended up married. Why did she have to do something so foolish? Another stupid choice, just like the one she'd made as a kid that had led to her costly hospitalization. And, as her sister always liked to remind her, had taken up so much of their parents' attention.

As she sat there mulling and stewing about it, she heard the door open. Then it closed and there was a click of the lock, followed by Jonah puttering around her condo.

She turned out the lights. Tomorrow would be a new day. They'd both vowed to try and work together. She'd promised Jonah that, and she had to make it work. When all was said and done, he was a good partner.

The one good thing about living with your partner was that you both could leave for work at the same time. At least that was the positive spin that Grace was trying to put on the entire situation as she got used to having Jonah underfoot.

Actually, it wasn't bad having him around. She felt guilty that he'd been sleeping on her couch for the last couple of days, but he said he didn't mind it at all and that her couch was comfortable.

Still, he should've been the one to take the bed.

He was doing her a huge favor.

They'd had a couple of days off before their next shift, and they'd fallen into a sort of routine, just like they did at work. She'd get up, and he would be outside swimming laps. They would often share a meal, but it was always quiet. It didn't bother her, the silence. They ate their lunch together like that, and to her it was comfortable. If anything, there was a little bit more conversation at dinner, just a touch. She kind of enjoyed it.

It was cozy, and it was freaking her out at how easy it was to be around him. She couldn't honestly recall ever being this comfortable with Victor in the beginning of their relationship.

You're not in a relationship with Jonah. Remember?

Now came the true test of this whole fandangle situation. They would have to go into work and deal with their coworkers—who, judging by a flurry of text messages both she and Jonah had received, were completely shocked that they had gotten married, because both of them had been so vocal about not wanting to get involved with anyone ever again. The only people who weren't surprised were the ones who'd been there. Like John, who had been their wedding videographer—something he was bragging about apparently.

Nothing stayed secret for long.

Grace took a deep breath and tucked her uniform shirt into her work pants and headed out into the other room. The moment she opened her bedroom door, she could smell coffee. It smiled like heaven, and her stomach rumbled in appreciation. She made her way into the kitchen.

"Good morning, partner," she greeted brightly.

"Want a cup?" Jonah asked.

"You never have to ask me." She took the mug from

him and breathed in the rich, deep scent that she loved so much. "Thanks for this."

"I figured we'd both need liquid courage heading into work today. We're going to be bombarded." He pursed his lips together. "Not looking forward to it."

"I know. Me neither."

"At least we're not going to get fired for it."

She nodded. "No, there's no policy on spouses working together. For now. As long as our personal feelings don't interfere with the job, we should be fine."

A strange expression crossed his face. "Right."

"You don't seem convinced."

"Honestly, I have a hard time working with people I'm friends with." His voice was tight and he had this far-off expression. She wondered what was wrong but knew she probably wouldn't find out. He didn't open up very often.

She cocked an eyebrow. "At least you're admitting we're friends now."

Jonah grinned, a dimple forming in his cheek. "Well, of course. We're married, and that's a good basis for marriage, right? Friendship?"

"Yes. I suppose so." She finished off her coffee. "I suppose we should arrive together. I mean, it would look weird if we traveled separately."

"Are you telling me you want to jump on the back of my bike?"

Adrenaline rushed through her as she pictured Jonah between her thighs, her arms wrapped around his waist, holding on to him, her body pressed against his and the rumble of an engine beneath her. She had been fantasizing about it since she learned he rode a motorcycle. On Sunday he'd gone to his storage unit to get it and go for a drive. She thought he'd taken it back.

Apparently not.

"Don't you usually walk? I thought you didn't ride your bike?"

"I don't, but I forgot to take it back after my ride yesterday. So what do you say?"

"I could jump on the back of your bike." And she hoped her voice didn't break as she said it. "But we had this conversation before—I don't have a helmet."

"I've got you a helmet." He nodded to the direction of the front door and she saw the pink-and-black helmet. It definitely wasn't a spare one that he'd had lying around, which meant he'd gone out and gotten it for her. A pink one at that—her favorite color. He must have been inspired by the streak in her hair.

"You bought that for me?" She sat down her mug and picked it up, absolutely stunned.

"Yeah, I was out yesterday wandering around and saw a used-motorbike store. It was on sale, and I figured we could take some rides around the desert. I've always wanted to go to the Hoover Dam and Lake Mead. You've lived here for some time. You could show me."

Her stomach clenched. The dam was so high and the water moved so fast. And while Lake Mead was gorgeous to look at from afar, she had no desire to get up close and personal with it. She avoided bodies of water, deep water, fast water at all costs.

"There's also the red rocks," she offered. "Great rock climbing."

She wasn't fond of heights either, but she could deal with that over water any day.

"That sounds like a plan. You ready to go to work and get this day over with?" he asked.

"Yes." She grabbed her bag and slung it over her shoulder, grabbing her helmet. Jonah followed her out, and she locked it behind them. She could see his motorcycle parked in her second parking spot, and her stomach did a little flip of nervousness and excitement.

She was pretty sure her aunt Gert or her mom would completely freak out knowing that she was on the back of what they liked to call a "death machine," but she was so excited to try it, and it was only a short drive to the firehouse.

Once upon a time she'd used to be a lot more adventurous and fun loving, but that was before her breakup with Victor. Then she'd sort of retreated a bit into herself, even when she was with him. She'd been so head over heels with him, and it all seemed so perfect. He had to impress the board of directors to further his career, so she'd tried to be the perfect girlfriend.

Now, looking back, that was what she regretted the most—hiding herself.

If being with someone meant she had to change to fit their ideal, she didn't want it. It just didn't appeal to her.

"You okay with this?" Jonah asked as he slung one leg over the seat and put on his helmet. He seemed a bit nervous too. Grace knew it took a great deal of trust to have someone ride on the back of a bike with you. Maybe he was relaxing around her just a bit.

She nodded confidently. "Yeah, I am."

She climbed on behind him, his body so close it made her pulse race as she gingerly wrapped her arms around his hard, muscular chest and tucked herself against him. He started the engine, the motor rumbling beneath her as he revved it.

"Hold on," he said over his shoulder as he slowly pulled out of the parking lot and onto the Summerlin streets. She closed her eyes and gripped him tight; she knew he was laughing by the way his body moved under her arms, but with her helmet on she couldn't hear a thing over the sound of the wind the motorcycle's engine.

Eventually, she opened her eyes and was able to enjoy the scenery of their suburb going by. The beauty of the ochre-colored mountains, the subtle wave of the palm trees lining the boulevard and the bright blue sunny sky.

It reminded her why she loved living in the desert. Her favorite moment was in the morning, when there was no heat to the sun and everything was bright, crisp and new. No dust devils or tumbleweed. Just peace. She wanted to savor that moment a little longer before they got to work and their shift started, because if there was one thing she had learned about being a paramedic in Las Vegas, there was never a day off.

They pulled into the parking lot of the fire station and parked around back. There were several of their coworkers milling about when Jonah parked the bike. The knot in the pit of Grace's stomach grew as she slowly slid off the bike and realized they had to face the music.

Jonah was grinning as he got off. "You okay?"

"Why are you asking me that?"

"Oh, maybe because of the death grip you had on my nipples," he whined, jokingly rubbing his shirt over his chest. "Seriously, did you have to give me a purple nurple?"

She was surprised at his joking, and she kind of liked it. When he'd been around her family, he was like that—affable, jovial, social and charming. Someone she rarely saw when they were alone.

Maybe the mask is coming back because we're at work?

But she shook that thought away.

"I didn't!" Then she giggled. "Okay, maybe I was a little nervous. You drive fast."

"I like it fast, but I can always guarantee that it's a

pleasurable ride." He winked and sauntered off, leaving her stunned.

Well, she'd walked right into that one. She stood there for a few more moments, watching him as he was surrounded by their coworkers, who were all obviously dying to know the details about their wedding.

Grace took a deep breath and walked into the fray. There was no better time than now to rip the bandage off the proverbial wound.

Grace rubbed her temple, hoping the headache would subside. She was very glad to be in the rig and out on patrol and away from all the questions. She couldn't remember the last time she had been so bombarded with so many. It was overwhelming for her, but Jonah seemed to take it all in stride. Honestly, she thought maybe their coworkers were more shocked by the fact he was being so social than the news of the wedding itself.

"Thanks for letting me take the wheel this shift," Jonah said. "I like driving."

"Thanks for offering. My head was pounding by the time they were finished grilling us."

"They were definitely curious."

"That's putting it mildly," she teased. "And thanks for answering the vast majority of questions. I was in shock. I don't usually get that much attention."

"I don't *like* that much attention," he admitted. "So much for keeping to myself."

They shared a smile. "I can see why we were paired together when you arrived," Grace said.

"Because we're antisocial?"

She laughed. "I think so."

"We're not mean per se."

"No. We just like to keep to ourselves." She enjoyed this teasing conversation. It was breezy.

"That backfired," he groused. A smile quirked on his lips.

"It was your suggestion to go out that night!"

"Sure. Blame me!"

They both laughed at the absurdity of the conversation.

"I will admit it's so easy to talk to you now. Why is that?"

His expression softened and he shrugged. "I suppose that's a good thing, seeing as we're married and all."

"Was that all it took to get you to open up?" she pondered out loud.

"I am trying to put myself out there."

"I appreciate that."

There was an awkward silence, and he sighed. "I don't want our working relationship to be ruined when this is all done."

And that was the truth to it all. There was a finality to this whole marriage, and then she'd go back to her regular life, which didn't seem that appealing at the moment.

"Right," she agreed quietly. "I filed a petition online. It's going to take a month. I'm sorry about that, but since we were..."

Grace couldn't even bring herself to say the words, which was silly because she was an adult and had done the horizontal mambo before. Although in this case, foggy memories told her they'd spent some of their time together vertical and sideways too. And thinking about those hazy flashes made her blood crackle with want. A coil of pleasure and anticipation wound tightly deep in her belly, seeking release.

Focus, Grace!

"You mean since we had sex?" Jonah said, finishing off her sentence.

Her cheeks flushed. "Right."

"You know what? It was worth it."

Her heart skipped a beat as their gazes locked across the rig. She wanted to tell him she agreed, because as the days went on from their encounter, she was remembering more and more of their night together—that amazing, magical, pleasure-filled night. But before she could reminisce with him, a call came over the radio from dispatch.

"Rig three, we have a code four, color orange. Male complaining of abdominal pains post-surgery. Sending you the address," dispatch stated.

"Roger that. En route," Jonah responded as the address popped up on the screen. Grace flicked on the lights and siren as Jonah navigated the streets to get to the location. She gripped the door and relaxed as the ambulance whizzed through Vegas streets.

It didn't take them too long to reach the address. Grace shut out everything else as Jonah and she worked seamlessly together, getting their gear and making their way to the patient's house.

Just like at her parents' place there was a crowd gathered outside, but the man they were going to assess was inside, so they wouldn't have an audience while they worked. A middle-aged woman holding a phone was waiting at the door.

"Manuel Lopez?" Grace questioned.

"I'm his wife. I called because Manuel had gallbladder surgery two days ago. He's had severe pain and hives. He can't keep anything down, and I don't drive."

"Show us," Jonah said gently.

Mrs. Lopez nodded, and they carried the stretcher up over the front steps into the house. The patient, Manuel, was lying in bed and appeared jaundiced. Grace could see the yellowing of his skin from the doorway, even in the dim lighting.

If nothing else was wrong, that right there was a reason to go to the hospital.

"Mr. Lopez? I'm a paramedic. Grace Landon. And this is my partner, Jonah. We're here to help you."

Mr. Lopez nodded. "The pain—it's not from the incisions."

"When did you have surgery?" Grace asked, pulling on her gloves.

"Three days ago," Manuel stated, wincing.

"Mind if we check the incision sites?" Jonah asked.

Manuel nodded, lifting his shirt. "Go ahead."

Jonah palpated around the incision sites as Grace assessed the jaundice in Mr. Lopez's eyes.

"No redness or swelling at the incision sites, but he does have some swelling and petechiae," Jonah remarked.

"Jaundice too." Grace took the patient's temperature. "Fever as well."

Jonah nodded. "We're going to take you to the hospital to have you checked. Where was your surgery performed?"

"Vegas Central," Mrs. Lopez answered. "I've called his surgeon's office."

"Good." Grace prepared the intravenous line to get some medication and fluid into Manuel for the transport. It also gave them easy access in case something happened on the way to the hospital.

"We'll get you there safely, Mr. Lopez," Jonah reassured as they worked side by side together.

That was the thing she liked about working with Jonah. Neither of them had to say anything. It was like they knew what each other was thinking and were on the same page. It made him a good partner, and that made her a little sad.

Had she royally messed up their good working partnership? When this all ended would she lose the best partner she'd ever had?

She wasn't sure, but she wouldn't let her mind get bogged down with that.

Not right now.

They got Manuel prepped, loaded into the ambulance and safely delivered to Vegas Central, and thankfully she didn't have any run-ins with Victor. They were able to hand off Mr. Lopez to the doctor who had done his surgery.

As she and Jonah wheeled their empty gurney out to their rig, he let out a soft grunt as they loaded up the equipment.

"You okay?" she asked.

"Yep. Just hungry. Lunch break?"

Grace checked her watch. "I suppose so."

"Great. I know an awesome food truck on our route."

"Food truck?"

"I didn't pack a lunch today, did you?"

"No, I guess I didn't."

"Food truck it is, then." He locked the back door. "I'll drive, and you can finish the report."

She laughed out loud. "So that's the real reason you're offering to take me out for lunch—to get out of paperwork."

Jonah winked. For the most part he was quiet, but she liked this other side to him, the little glimmers she was getting to see. They climbed back into the ambulance and belted up as they left the ambulance bay of Vegas Central.

"I also have an ulterior motive to this food truck lunch," he said.

"An ulterior motive?"

"Well, we have to book a tee time for ourselves."

"Oh, golf. Right."

"Travis texted me. It's on Friday, and I have no idea

what I'm doing." He frowned again, his lips a tight line. "Ugh. I hate this."

"What?"

"Golf—and with strangers particularly."

Grace shook her head. "You could back out."

"What, and let your father down?"

"Does it matter? I mean, a month from now this will be all over."

"I know, but I don't like letting people down and we'll still be married by your sister's wedding date. I guess I should try, keep up the pretense."

A pang of guilt hit her. He was doing so much for her, and he was so nice. This whole thing was absolutely her fault because she'd panicked and was embarrassed about having broadcasted her drunken wedding nuptials.

This wasn't her usual modus operandi but just further proved to her the point that there really wasn't such a thing as a happily-ever-after.

No fairy-tale love.

No romance.

She'd learned her lesson.

Jonah had been going to buy Grace lunch, but she insisted on buying as he'd driven her to work and to the food truck. That was the excuse she gave him, but he had a hunch she was feeling guilty about this whole fake-marriage thing.

She wasn't totally at fault. He'd agreed to it as well. Honestly, he was experiencing a bit of guilt too because he was enjoying spending time with her a little too much, and he knew Grace didn't want a relationship with someone she worked with. It was hard not to think about that when she'd climbed on the back of his bike this morning, clinging to him. It had made him think about her in his arms. It had felt so right.

When he'd originally bought that helmet, for one moment he'd thought he was wasting his money because he'd never believed she'd actually go for a ride with him. He was glad she'd said yes, but then he'd started to worry about keeping her safe on the back of his bike.

He'd seen enough motorcycle accidents in his years.

Yet she'd trusted him, and it felt good that she did. Mona never had. She'd hated his bike.

That trust was something else he liked about Grace. He was so attracted to her, even more so now that they'd spent more time together.

If they didn't have to work, he'd have been tempted to keep on driving, maybe head up to Lake Tahoe and woo her in a cabin. He had a friend who was a surgeon in Vegas, Dr. Nick Rousseau, who had a cabin up near Tahoe.

And he knew for a fact Nick and his wife, Dr. Jennifer Mills, weren't using it at the moment, as they were waiting on the arrival of another baby.

He could totally take Grace there. More importantly, he wanted to.

Get your head on straight. She's your partner, not your wife!

Jonah had to push all those romantic notions to the side. That wasn't in his plan. Only it was easy to forget that when he looked at her.

Especially now as they sat on picnic table, outside their rig on the side of a desert highway eating fries and gourmet hot dogs from a food truck, like any couple would. It wasn't weird or awkward; it felt natural. Like they had done this one hundred times before.

Like it was supposed to be.

But he'd been duped by these emotions before, and it was hard not to think about that.

Grace isn't Mona.

Grace was someone he felt like maybe he could open up to.

"Oh, my gosh. These fries are amazing," Grace remarked, dipping another one into a big blob of ketchup.

"Told you."

"Where did you find this food truck?"

"When I was moving to Vegas. There's a cool fifties diner between here and California too."

She smiled, her mouth full of fries. It was adorable, kind of like a pink-haired chipmunk. "That would be fun."

"I'll make you a deal."

She cocked any eyebrow. "Is that what our marriage is all about? Deals?"

He laughed at her gentle ribbing. "Do you want to hear my idea or not?"

"Fine." There was a glow in her eyes, a mischievous glint he'd seen before. It had been that look she got on her face right before she suggested they get married. "Lay it on me, daddio."

"Daddio?" he asked.

"You were talking about a fifties diner, and I was just using the lingo."

"I suppose I was…uh…mammio."

Grace choked. "What?"

"Never mind," he groused. "Clearly I don't know old-timey lingo."

"You don't. And you're older than me," she ribbed.

"By seven years."

She snickered. "Old man."

"Well, this conversation is not going as I pictured."

Grace chuckled. "Sorry, sorry. I derailed you. What were you going to ask?"

"Never mind."

She rolled her eyes. "Come on. What were you saying?"

"My suggestion, or deal, was that you teach me to golf before Friday, and Saturday we'll take a bike ride out to that fifties diner."

"Do I have to dress up?"

"No."

"That's a shame."

Now he was intrigued. "Are you telling me you want to wear a poodle skirt?"

"No," she responded emphatically. "Look, you don't have to make a deal with me for me to teach you to golf."

"So you don't want to go to the diner?" he teased.

"I didn't say that."

"Well?"

She moved to sit next to him. "Sure. It's a deal. We could go golfing tomorrow night and the night after that, and then, if we survive Friday, we'll go to a diner sometime to celebrate."

"I can't learn golf in one night?"

"Uh…no."

"Damn," he muttered but then looked at her in growing awe, imagining her kicking ass on the golf course. There was so much about her he didn't know, but he wanted to learn more. She was vivacious and interesting. "Where did you learn to play?"

She wrinkled her nose. "The country club."

"That's the second time you've barely hid your contempt for the country club. What's with that?"

She sighed. "Well, my dad had to give up memberships for a while. My hospital bills were hefty after my accident. He missed it and rejoined a few years ago. I always felt bad."

"That wasn't your fault."

She gave a half shrug like she didn't believe him. "I don't know… It's so pretentious. Victor loved it. My dad and him bonded over it. It's just a reminder to me of a lot of failings."

"Your dad puts value on that?" he asked.

"No. I don't think so." She shrugged again. "It's all so superficial."

"Agreed, but at least you learned how to play golf."

She laughed and gave him a nudge with her shoulder, leaning against him. He could smell her clean scent, only this time he could also get a whiff of the malt vinegar and ketchup on her fries.

It was weird, but it reminded him of his dad, who had been British. Not so much the ketchup, but the malt vinegar. His mother would make homemade fries—or chips, as his dad called them—and he would douse them in salt and vinegar. If his dad could've had his way, he would've had them every day.

"You went really quiet," she remarked. "What're you thinking about?"

"My dad, actually."

"Oh?" said softly. "How many years ago did he pass?"

"Years ago, when I was overseas. He was a bit aloof, but he wasn't ever mean. My parents were in their mid-forties when I was born. Actually, Dad was closer to fifty."

All of it came rolling off his tongue so easily. It felt natural to talk about them with her. He hadn't spoken about them in so long.

Grace's eyes widened. "Wow."

He nodded in the direction of her fries. "You put malt vinegar on there, and it reminded me of him. He was British. He met an American girl, moved to California."

She smiled. "Well, I'm glad the smell isn't making you want to retch and gave you a happy recollection."

"Yeah, I'm glad too." And he let that pleasant little memory percolate for a few more moments in his mind as the cars from the highway whizzed by them. It was always easier to lock them all away so he could work, but it was nice to have that reminder of his dad.

Almost like a visit from his father, letting him know he was here.

Still.

For a moment Jonah was less lonely.

Grace sighed and finished her fries. “I guess lunch break is over.”

“I suppose.” He collected up the trash from his lunch and took it over to the garbage receptacle, and Grace followed him. They sanitized their hands and headed back to the ambulance to continue their shift.

There had never really been a moment like that that he shared with Mona. Not that he could think of. When he’d come home from duty, there had been things he wanted to talk about with her so that he could move on and heal, but she’d never wanted to hear it.

Or maybe she couldn’t hear it. So he’d spent so much time keeping things to himself.

Back then it was so much simpler that way, but when he was around Grace it was different.

He could be himself and he didn’t have to lock things away.

CHAPTER SIX

A couple days later

"YOU KNOW...MAYBE I should go with you on Friday." Grace winced as Jonah took another swing once again and missed the ball. It was almost comical, and she was pretty sure she had never seen play this bad in real life. He was trying though—she had to credit him with that.

She'd decided before she booked a tee time for an actual game that maybe it was best they try the driving range first. Boy, was she glad she had. He had the swing and the power; it was just the connecting part he seemed to be struggling with.

"Seriously?" He grunted staring at the ball in frustration. "I can play hockey."

She laughed to herself. "A puck is bigger."

"I know. I was making a joke about a movie—the golfer who was a hockey player."

She was painfully aware of that movie now. Since their lunch at the food truck, their own dinners at home had gotten more chatty. And then that had morphed into watching movies at night. They took turns to choose, and so far it was working.

Even if Jonah's movie choices were terrible.

"And that's why that was a movie. A far-fetched movie. A lot of pro hockey players do play golf, but I'm not sure that should be your argument on why *you* should be able to play golf."

"So you're not going to tell me it's all in the hips?" Jonah winked and lined up again.

"Well, it is in the hips and your…" She trailed off as he swung, a whooshing sound slicing through the air, but the ball was remained on the tee. "It's your follow-through."

He grunted. "What follow-through?"

"Line it up again." She stood behind him, slipping her arms over his, her hips pressed against his backside, and she was suddenly very aware at how close she was to him.

Just like when she'd been pressed up against him on the bike. Her hands were so small over his tanned, muscular forearms, and all she could hear was the thundering of her pulse between her ears.

Galloping would be the correct word to describe it, and she fought the urge to caress his arms, because she remembered what it felt like to run her hands over his skin. The more time they spent together, the more she thought about it.

"Don't take your eyes off the target," she said, finally finding her voice. She imitated the swing behind him, guiding his hands as they grasped the club.

"Okay," he responded.

Grace stepped away quickly, hugging herself and trying to shake away the remnants of her arousal from being so close to him again, because she did want him. She wanted to be close to him, even though he was off-limits.

Jonah took a swing, and this time there was contact, a definite thwack as the driver met the golf ball, and it sailed up and over the green toward the big black net at the end of the range.

His eyes widened, and he raised up his arms, like a hockey player scoring a goal. "See that?"

Grace grinned, enjoying his enthusiasm. "Great job. Now you have to do it again. Over and over until this bucket of balls is gone."

"Are you insinuating that it was a fluke shot?"

"Maybe," she hinted with a wicked smile.

Jonah frowned. "I'll show you."

She watched as he placed a new ball on the tee and lined up his shot, hitting the ball again.

"Woo-hoo! See that? I've got this."

His confidence was absolutely adorable. As she got to know him she was beginning to see little fragments of it. Like he was feeling safe with her. And at least he could now hit the ball and wouldn't look like a train wreck out on the course with her father, Travis and Victor. However, she'd feel so much better if she went golfing with them, but usually golf was a party of four or six, not five, and how would that look to everyone? Like she was keeping tabs on him or something. So she'd just have to make sure she got Jonah up to speed on the game.

It was nice he was willing to play along with this, even when it was all fake.

"Uh-oh."

"What?" Grace asked, quickly looking over her shoulder.

"You're worrying your bottom lip and wringing your hands together. What're you thinking about?"

"Nothing."

Jonah raised an eyebrow. "Sure."

"Fine. I was thinking how you really don't have to do this."

"Do what?" He took another swing, driving the ball farther this time. "Be excellent at golf?"

She rolled her eyes. "This is one aspect of the game."

"I know. So what's eating at you?"

"You're going to a lot of trouble to help me perpetrate this…this lie."

"I don't mind, Grace. We're friends, right?"

"We're partners," she teased.

"Ouch." He winced. "Right in the feels."

"You are incorrigible. What happened to that quiet partner I used to have?"

"I've adjusted." He swung again, hitting the last ball out of the bucket they'd bought. He set his driver back in the bag, came over to her and rested his hands on her shoulders. "Look, we both made rash decisions that night. Stop shouldering the blame for it all."

"Still…"

"No. There's no *but*. Grace, you're a good partner and I like spending time with you."

Her heart fluttered, but it also terrified her that this was going so fast. From partners to friends…and then where? She didn't want to date someone from work. She couldn't have more with him.

She couldn't accept more.

"I'll concede we're friends. And as a friend, I think I need to buy you a congratulatory ice cream to celebrate your success."

"That I will accept." Jonah picked up the rented clubs, and they headed back to return them then made their way to the car. This time it was up to Grace to pick a spot for ice cream, and she knew a perfect little cafe in Summerlin which overlooked the mountains and a cute park where people walked their dogs and kids came to play. There was a pond and picnic tables, and best of all, it was quieter than trying to find a place on the Strip.

Once they got to the park and ordered their ice cream, they took a walk and found a secluded bench by the pond to watch the ducks.

"So, since we're friends you won't mind me asking you some questions," Grace said.

"Sure," he said, nodding his head.

"How can a man who served in the Marines not hit a target?"

Jonah chirped gleefully. "Well, that's different. Also, I was a medic."

"You still needed to have good aim."

"Yes, but there was no swinging involved." He frowned.

"What're you thinking about?" she asked gently.

"Nothing."

"Hey, friends, right?"

Jonah frowned and shrugged. "I thought the Marines would be good. My best friend, Justin, and I joined up and…"

Immediately she could tell he was upset, that it was hard for him to talk about. Just like she struggled to speak about her own experience almost drowning as a child and how she'd been duped by Victor. Jonah was hedging, and she wondered if it had something to do with trust.

And she understood that.

It was hard to give.

They were friends, and she wanted to give him that support. She wanted to get to know him. They were in this situation together, and she wanted to be there for him, like he was supporting her.

"And?" she asked quietly.

"He was killed." Jonah swallowed hard and then stared at the half-empty cup of ice cream in his hands. "Killed in the line of duty. He died right in my arms."

Seeing the pain etched across his face made her feel that dejection just as keenly. It was always hard losing a patient, but to have your best friend die in your arms… She couldn't imagine it.

That look on Jonah's face was the same one her mother would get face when she'd talk about Grace's drowning incident. Grace always felt bad about it, that she had caused her mother than much pain.

And it had been her own fault for not listening to her parents and being defiant and going into the pool without supervision.

"Oh, my gosh. I'm so sorry."

He nodded. "I've put a lot of effort into working through that."

"I'm sure."

"Therapy, medication. Still..." He trailed off.

"It's hard." She admired him for doing the work. She was envious. Maybe she could confront her own fears. Maybe Jonah could help. Only she didn't know how to ask. "So you became a paramedic because you were a medic?"

"It's why I love being a paramedic. Once I was discharged, I worked so hard to become a first responder, to get to this level, because I wanted to save lives. Yeah, I'd been a medic, but I wanted to do more because I really didn't want people to experience the pain that I felt. It came at a price though. My first wife didn't understand what I was going through, and honestly, the more I think about it now, she really didn't want to understand it."

Grace nodded. "I'm sorry that happened to you. And you should be proud of all you've accomplished."

"You should too," Jonah said fiercely.

"Really?" she responded gruffly. "I haven't faced my fear."

"Oh, I think you do."

"How so?"

"Well, you do save people in drowning incidents. I mean, what made you want to be a paramedic?"

No one had really asked her that before. "My near

drowning when I was a kid is why I got into this profession. It was a woman who saved my life. I've never forgotten her. She was my hero, and I wanted to be strong and badass just like her. I wanted to be first on the scene."

What she didn't say was that the more lives she saved, the fewer mothers had to be sad. Like she could somehow atone for putting her parents through that. She was sparing pain, saving somebody's loved one. Every patient belonged to someone.

Their gazes locked across the bench, and they shared a smile. Grace melted. She'd never really talked about Liz, the paramedic who saved her life before. How she idolized her and wanted to be like her, because in her mind Liz was a superhero. Grace had only met her once after the accident, when she was finally released from the hospital. And she never forgot that moment. She carried it with her.

And she hoped that she was half the kind of person that Liz was to her.

"You are badass," Jonah said, looking away and scooping up a spoonful of his ice cream.

"Oh?"

"Come on. When you're out there in an emergency situation you have this calm demeanor and nothing fazes you."

"Water does."

Jonah shrugged. "Yeah, but you continue to work hard to save lives."

"Thanks. I'm glad you're my partner. Honestly, I couldn't pick a better one. Even if you were a bit quiet in the beginning." She smiled slyly. "I sometimes miss that quieter version of you."

He laughed. "I guess there's no going back now."

"No, but I do worry about the future. Things have changed."

Jonah nodded quietly and finished the rest of his ice

cream. "I do too. I don't want things to change too much when we finally get our divorce or annulment, whatever you want to call it. We're not strangers, but what we have now is nice."

"I don't want that either. It was bad enough dating a surgeon that I have to deal with on a semi-regular basis. I really don't want it to get awkward with you."

"It won't," he responded.

"How can you be so sure?"

He held up his hand, pinky up. "Let's pinky swear. We won't let any kind of personal emotion at the end of this fake marriage stop us from being friends or partners."

Grace nodded and hooked her pinky around his. "Pinky swear."

"Good."

She nodded, because it was the truth. She wanted to stay friends with him after this was all said and done. She didn't want to ruin what they already had because of a drunken night.

She was completely ignoring the other part of her, the part she was keeping buried deep down that wanted to explore more with Jonah.

The part that wanted that happy ending.

The part that still believed in all that.

Once they got back to Grace's condo, Jonah quickly changed and went down to swim some laps in the pool. Bringing up Justin and talking a little about his PTSD had made his anxiety spike. When he'd been discharged and trying to move forward with his life, he'd worked so hard with therapists to deal with the unbelievable nightmare of having his best friend die in his arms and the rejection that came from his ex-wife.

He didn't like to talk about it much.

Grace was the first person in Vegas that he'd actually admitted it to. Grace was the first person to whom he'd actually said Justin's name out loud. It had been so long since he'd talked about his best friend with someone who hadn't known him.

It had been good to let it all out, but he was a bit nervous about sharing that moment with her. It was hard being vulnerable with her, and while he didn't regret it, he really needed to blow off some steam away from her.

Swimming was a great exercise. Even though it was blistering hot during the day, it was cold at night when the desert got dark, and he really liked swimming in the heated pool then, even with the tendrils of steam curling off the surface.

He swam a few laps to work off that energy and then got out, wrapping his towel around his waist, running barefoot up the stairs to Grace's condo. He unlocked the door and headed inside. The door to her bedroom was shut, and she had said that she was going to bed. That sounded like a good idea to him. Though a very loud, demanding piece of his mind wished he could climb into bed with her and hold her.

If he was being honest, he wanted to do more than just hold her.

Don't think like that.

He shook all those thoughts from his mind and stepped into the bathroom to have a quick shower. A cold one.

When he got out, he realized he'd forgotten his jogging pants that he usually wore when he went to sleep. He cursed under his breath at his forgetfulness, wrapped a towel round his waist and dashed out. When he went to grab the joggers from where they were folded on the end of the couch, he let the towel drop to the floor and heard a gasp from behind.

He spun around and saw Grace standing there, a glass of milk in her hand, her eyes wide and a pink tinge on her supple cheeks. Their gazes locked, and all he could do was just stand there, staring at her in her oversized T-shirt. The hem of the shirt brushed the tops of her tanned thighs, so he got a full view of those long, firm legs. He wanted to run his hands over them. Hell, he wanted to run those hands higher.

She cleared her throat and looked away quickly. He grabbed the towel off the floor to cover himself back up.

"Sorry—I thought you were in bed," he apologized.

"No need to apologize. I couldn't sleep." She held up her milk but wouldn't look him in the eye. "Were you taking a shower?"

"Done."

"I can see that," she whispered, tucking her hair behind her ear.

Make a joke. Anything to ease the tension.

"Well, we had a pretty good run. Living together for a whole week and we've just now had our first naked interlude."

It was the goofiest joke and completely cringeworthy. He regretted it instantly, and if he could hide, he would.

Grace laughed and sputtered. "A what?"

"Naked encounter, I mean." He winked, hoping it melted the tension.

She snort-laughed. "*Naked interlude* sounds like a one of those strip clubs."

"It does." He smiled. "I hope this won't make things weird between us."

"This? No, I think this is not as weird as our wedding. Awkward, yes, but not enough to scare me away."

"Good."

This time she was looking him in the eye, but there was still that twinkle, that sparkle that made his heart beat a little beat faster. He was a sucker for her soft, tender glances. He could get lost in her gaze if he wanted to, and he very much did want to.

"Well, I better get to bed" Grace said. "We have work, and I booked us a tee time for an actual game after our shift."

"A game?"

"You have to be ready for Friday, and then we're having dinner with my family in St. George on Saturday. A pre-wedding thing. My mom didn't explain it well in her text."

"It sounds good." He was lying, and he knew Grace knew that, because she was smirking.

"Oh, it'll be fun," she replied sardonically.

"Hopefully Aunt Gert has mastered the mascara this week." Just another joke to dispel the awkwardness.

Grace laughed loudly, holding her belly. He noticed the oversized shirt rode up, and he caught a sight of pink lacy underwear, making his pulse pound. He tried to look away.

"Doubtful. Aunt Gert always does lay it on thick. Thank you for not staring at it."

"It was hard not to. It was like orbs or planetoids of mascara. Things were orbiting the tips of her lashes."

"You're awful."

"Just easing the tension." He winked.

"Good night, Jonah."

"Good night, Grace."

He watched her as she walked away, back into her room. She was pulling at the back hem of her T-shirt in an attempt to cover up the delicious curve of her bottom. It was cute that she tried, though he still got a tempting eyeful. He exhaled and stared at the couch, wishing he was back in her bed.

The sleeping arrangements hadn't really been bothering him.

Until now.

Maybe he needed a glass of warm milk too. Maybe that would help him sleep, but he seriously doubted it.

CHAPTER SEVEN

THE WEEK SEEMED to drag on until the dreaded G-Day for Jonah.

Also known as Golf Day.

The game wasn't bad; he just wasn't any good at it. Grace had tried to show him several times. They'd even played a whole round of mini golf. It was just no use. He'd come to the foregone conclusion that he'd never be any good at it, and that was mostly fine by him. Did he want to impress Grace's father? Yes, but then he had to ask himself why. Grace wasn't really Jonah's, so what her dad thought of him didn't particularly matter in the long run.

Except it did.

It surprised him that he wanted to be the best fake son-in-law he could be. Which was kind of pathetic when he really thought about it.

He liked Grace, and from what he had seen of her family, he liked them too. They were loud and eager to be in her business, but they genuinely seemed to care. At first he'd really dreaded it, but he had spoken to Grace's little brother a couple of times since the family dinner, and her mother too.

It was nice to be invited to the pre-wedding stuff. It had been a long time since he felt like he belonged somewhere and with a family group. Grace was lucky that way, and he slightly envied her.

And if he admitted it to himself, he was going to miss it when this whole fake marriage was over. Part of him didn't want to let that feeling go.

Do you have to let it go? a little voice asked.

It shocked him for a moment, but he'd been mulling this over all week. It annoyed him that he was brooding on it, being vulnerable about that deep desire for more than solitude. He'd thought he'd learned his lesson, but being around Grace it was hard not to let those happy what-ifs trickle through his mind. And they were coming frequently.

Truth be told, he'd assumed the awkwardness of having slept with her would eventually catch up to them at work, but it hadn't. Grace was strong in herself and mature. It was a breath of fresh air compared to other women he knew.

"You ready?" Grace asked, interrupting his thoughts as she came out of her room. She was dressed in a white skort and a pink athletic shirt with a visor. Her hair was tied back, like she had it styled when they were at work. She was absolutely adorable, and he couldn't help but admire her muscular, shapely calves.

"You're dressed for golf," he said.

"I am. It seems Victor was called in for a patient, and Dad asked me to be the fourth. Is that okay?"

Jonah grinned. "Is my relief showing?"

He hadn't been looking forward to spending time with her ex; he saw enough of him when they took patients to the emergency department at Vegas Central. And now that Jonah was married to Grace, Victor had been weirder at work for sure. The energy was off-putting. Almost like Victor was jealous of him, which was childish seeing how Victor had chosen another over Grace. Then again, Jonah got the impression that Victor was the possessive, competitive type.

"Just a little bit," Grace chided. "It'll go great. I'm sure of it."

"You keep saying that," he teased.

"I know, but it's because I know it to be true."

"Well, do I look okay?" He held up his arms wide and slowly turned.

Grace cocked her head to one side, tapping her chin thoughtfully, studying him and making him sweat, thinking he'd got something wrong. "I think so. You're very dashing in your khakis and polo shirt."

"Dashing?"

She nodded. "Yes. You'll fit right in."

"Good. By the way, I quite like that word. *Dashing*."

"I figured you would." She grabbed some of their gear, but they'd have to rent clubs at the course, because Jonah wasn't going to invest in something he wasn't going to play again.

"Come on, then. We better not be late for tee time, or my dad will be annoyed."

He didn't say anything, but he was struck by how Grace was so eager to please her family yet groaned when she was around them. It was almost like she thought she wasn't enough and needed to make up for it, when clearly that was not the case. She was more than enough. At least he thought so, and that fleeting little thought gave him pause.

The country club was a bit north of the condo and the Red Rock Canyon. As they drove out into the desert and mountains, it seemed a bit surreal that there were greens from the course and bodies of water sprawled out under the burning heat amid the browns and ochres that usually dominated the Nevada vista. As they turned down the long drive, the clubhouse looked a little bit like a modern-day adobe mirage, rising white out of the sands. He liked it quite a bit. It was out of place and yet fit in. Maybe a bit like him.

They parked and made their way to the check-in, where Rick and Travis were waiting. Jonah stood back as Grace greeted her dad and Travis.

"Sorry," she apologized. "Work ran late."

"Oh? Was it a hard day?" Rick asked, hugging his daughter.

"No. Just long."

"Jonah, good to see you," Rick greeted gruffly, turning to him. "It should be a great evening."

"It should. Thank you for inviting me, Mr. Landon," Jonah said, hoping that he sounded somewhat enthused by this whole prospect, because he wasn't.

"You can call me Rick instead of Mr. Landon. We're family."

Family. What a nice thought. Except they weren't. Not really. And Rick said it tightly, almost protectively, like he didn't quite believe it either. Not that Jonah blamed him at all. He knew all about trust.

Jonah nodded, and Grace's eyes were a bit wide with worry. Rightfully so. Not only did she have to worry about the fake marriage lie and hurting her family, but he knew, even if she didn't admit it, that his golf game was nil. And what should've been an enjoyable evening might end up a tedious slog.

Would Grace's father still let Jonah call him Rick after he saw how he played? Time would tell.

"We have two carts booked. We could pair up. I'll take Travis in mine, and you two newlyweds can take the other," Rick suggested.

"Sounds good, Dad," Grace responded. She nodded, and Jonah trailed after her, dragging his feet a bit.

They found their assigned carts and got all their clubs

and gear loaded. Rick and Travis took the lead golf cart, and Jonah and Grace had the one behind.

"Sorry you're stuck with me," he groused half-heartedly.

"This is better than it would have been."

"Why, because I suck?"

"Well…" She grinned deviously. "But also imagine making small talk with Victor." Grace shuddered. "At least I know how bad you are at the game. If he knew he'd tease you every time he saw you again."

"Right. Good point."

"Now I can tease you."

"Hey!" Jonah nudged her as she laughed. They followed behind Rick's cart to the first flag on the course. "So, any tips?"

Grace continued to giggle. "Well, think about connecting the ball when you go to take your swing."

"Why is that so funny?"

"It's not. I laugh when I'm nervous sometimes."

"And why are you nervous? You don't suck at golf," he groused.

"Getting you involved deeper with my family."

"Yes. That thought had crossed my mind. Man, if your dad tolerates me now, he'll loathe me later."

"He doesn't just tolerate you."

"Oh, really?"

Grace worried at her bottom lip. "He's protective of us kids. He treated Victor the same. He treated Travis the same too. Would you like to leave?"

He wanted to say yes, but that wouldn't look good at all. "Well, we're here now. We've just got to play the part."

"Right. Of course."

He sensed a little disappointment in her voice. It was just for a moment though.

She rolled her shoulders and plastered on a determined

expression. "As for your game, connect and keep your eyes when you follow through."

"Yes. I know."

"You're going to be okay."

"Uh-huh. Sure."

She shook her head as they pulled their golf cart up next to her father's. Travis was going to tee off first, as he was the bachelor for whom this evening was meant. He took his shot, and they watched at the ball sailed off across the green. Jonah's stomach knotted; this was going to be really bad or really funny, and he wasn't sure which.

Grace took her turn, and he watched her form with deep appreciation, especially her posterior as she bent down to set her ball and swung with her hips. It was effortless, the way her body moved to drive the ball down the green, going farther than Travis.

"Good shot, honey," Rick said proudly, and then he turned to Jonah. "You're next. I'll shoot last."

"Right." Jonah nodded and stepped up to the tee. He put his ball down and glanced over at Grace, who was nodding encouragingly.

Stupid golf, he cursed inwardly.

He took a deep breath and visualized the ball as he swung and connected with it. It sailed up into the sky.

"Wow," Grace exclaimed. "Great shot!"

"Thanks." Jonah had no idea where his ball landed, but he'd figure that out later. At least he didn't make an ass of himself by missing.

"I'm impressed," Rick admitted. "Grace, your husband has a great long shot. He might be a keeper."

The idea of being a keeper struck a chord with Jonah. He'd never been thought of as someone to be kept, except by his parents, and even then they weren't the most affectionate and never really expressed that sentiment out loud.

Hearing Rick say it made him feel good and it shouldn't have, because it wasn't true and it wasn't going to last. But still a part of him liked it. He liked being included.

Jonah stood to the side so Rick could take his turn, and Rick patted him on the shoulder, giving him an "Atta boy."

Grace sidled up next to him. "You're smirking," she said under her breath.

"Well, I'm a keeper." He winked.

"Well, I think so," Grace stated, but then her eyes widened and a pink blush stained her cheeks. It thrilled him.

He raised his eyebrows in surprise. "You do?"

A sweet smile pressed across her lips. "I do."

Her admitting that made his heart beat a bit faster.

It means nothing. It's platonic. Don't get carried away.

He shook those emotions away as Rick took his shot.

"Good shot, Rick," Travis called out.

Grace stood on her tiptoes and made a kissy noise, to make fun of Travis slightly. *Suck-up.*

"Behave," Jonah warned teasingly.

Although he liked this side of her. Devious. A little competitive streak, but also light-hearted.

It had been a long hard day at work. They were both tired; that might've been why Grace was a bit giggly. Golf had been the last thing he wanted to do after his shift tonight, but with Grace here instead of her ex, maybe he would get through the evening after all. At least he was spending time with her. There might've been a time limit to their arrangement, but he was going to enjoy it fully.

They finished the game, and he didn't do too badly. He might have come in dead last, but it was so much fun spending the evening with Grace and joking around with her. After they'd finished, they went to the clubhouse to have dinner. The big boys' night out would be saved for later when Victor could come. That was fine by Jonah.

Even if it hadn't gone terribly, he'd still been stressed all day. When they got back to the condo, he was going to change and go for a swim. He needed that.

"That was a great evening." Grace sighed as they left the clubhouse. "I thought it was going to be so much worse."

"It was a good game. Thanks for the lesson. I think it helped."

"You did good," she agreed. "My dad seemed to like you. He was way more talkative tonight."

"I like him too. And your mom. If you don't mind me saying so, you really seem to want to please them."

Grace paused. "Do I?" she asked, startled.

"Well, I mean, this lie for starters—we're pretending to be married to keep them all happy. This whole farce is about that, pleasing them."

"I guess you're right."

"I didn't mean to upset you," he apologized. "I just honestly I don't think you have to try so hard."

"You didn't upset me. I guess it all stems back to my almost drowning."

"So you almost drown as a child, and now you have to make up for it?"

"Partly. I was in and out of hospitals right after. I was in a coma on life support for a while. There were a lot of expenses, things were sacrificed for me."

"That's not your responsibility," Jonah said gently.

"Isn't it? I disobeyed my parents and snuck into the pool."

He didn't know how to respond to that. He knew he was broaching a touchy subject with her and had to tread lightly. He didn't want to make her mad or push her away. "I think they love you and you worry too much."

She nodded. “Well, I guess it’s my turn to ask you a hard question.”

“Go for it.”

“You swim every night, even when it’s cold out. Why?”

“It’s a coping tool to ease my anxiety. It helps. My therapist suggested it.”

“Really?”

“Why so surprised?”

“You just seem so sure about yourself.”

“It’s been a lot of hard work.” He cocked his head to the side. “Is that really what you wanted to ask me?”

Her shoulders slumped. “No. There’s something else.”

“As I said before, go for it. Ask away.” Although he had a feeling he might regret this.

“Why did you agree to this charade?”

He turned to look her straight in the eye. Her arms were crossed, her mouth set in a firm line. It was a fair question and one that he’d been asking himself since he said he would do this for her.

“You never let a partner down. That much I’ve learned. Especially in my time with the Marines. I didn’t want to let you down. I wanted to be there for you.”

Her hard expression softened, and she looked away. “Well, thanks again for going along with it.”

“Especially the golf bit. That was torture.”

Her laugh rang out across the parking lot, and he liked making her laugh. All that tension and hard stuff melted away. “Well, yes, I suppose I owe you one for the golf.”

“So you taught me to golf…how about I teach you to swim?” Jonah knew it was a long shot, but he wanted to help her get over her fear, to work on her PTSD when it came to drownings and water—and he wanted to change the subject. Although logically, he knew it would take more than just swimming lessons. She needed to talk it through with someone, just like he had. But at least he could offer this and help her.

Grace froze. "What?"

"Swimming. I can teach you."

She laughed nervously as they piled their gear into her trunk. "Victor tried to teach me once. He dunked me, if you remember. I don't go in pools."

"I do remember you telling me that. I swear, no dunking. I want to show you some moves so you can feel safe. It'll help ease your anxiety on the job when we're called in for those situations."

"I don't..."

"Trust me." It was a big ask.

He could see it all there. The trauma of what had happened to her was holding her back, and he wanted to help her. She was so strong and amazing. She could conquer this. He reached out and gently stroked her face, getting lost in her big brown eyes, her pulse was racing under his fingertips.

All he wanted to do was kiss her in that moment, but he resisted. Again. He seemed to be doing a lot of that around her lately.

It was monumental, him asking her to put her precarious faith in him, especially about something she was so terrified to do. But once upon a time she'd been more adventurous.

That was before Victor. And she was learning that she didn't have to diminish herself when she was around Jonah. Maybe, just maybe she could do this thing. Maybe she could go back to being that person she had been before.

She was still a bit shocked at the way this conversation was turning. They were tackling some deep stuff.

The way he had gotten her to open up to him was surprising, and the fact was she didn't mind it at all.

"Okay," she agreed quickly. "You can show me some stuff, but the moment you dunk me—well, it won't be a purple nurple that I'll inflict on your nipples. It'll be worse."

"How?"

"I'll tear them off."

"That sounds like a promise," he stuttered nervously, rubbing his chest.

"Oh. It is."

He winced. "Ouch. Noted."

They drove back to her place, took their gear inside and changed for swimming. All she had was a two-piece, from the rare times she'd sunbathe.

At first she hesitated because she thought it was too revealing for someone she worked with, for a friend, for Jonah. But the truth was he'd seen her naked, and vice versa.

And just thinking about that made her cheeks bloom with heat.

With need.

Stop that.

By the time she'd changed Jonah was already down at the pool. She was thankful it was empty so no one else had to see her completely scared of getting in the water. She opened the gate and made her way to the pool steps. Jonah paddled over and stood up. A few lustful notions about the water trailing down over his bronzed skin flittered in her mind.

It was like part of her was craving him, like he was the only cure for her affliction of lust. Her body definitely remembered their wedding night.

Mostly it remembered the pleasure.

"You ready?" he asked.

For what? she wanted to ask him, but she assumed he meant swimming and not what she had been thinking about.

"Nope." Her voice shook, like her body. Her knees were about ready to give out.

Jonah held out his hand. "I've got you."

Such simple words, and she wanted to believe them. She wanted to trust him, but it was hard.

He hasn't let you down yet. You can do this.

She reached out and took his hand, stepping slowly into the warn water. She remembered the freeing sensation of floating, how she'd loved it as a child, but then her throat clogged and it felt like she couldn't breathe as the panic overtook her. Her body was completely rigid, and she closed her eyes.

"It's okay." He slipped his arms around her. "I'll hold you. Tonight it's just about getting your footing. Ground yourself and feel the solid bottom beneath your heels. You're safe."

She nodded. "Okay."

"Come on." Jonah guided her through the water, and soon her body relaxed. His hand was on her waist, his fingers brushing her skin, his body warm and sturdy. Like a rock, something she could lean on. She'd never had that before.

"This is…this is okay."

"Does it feel good?" he asked.

"It does." She glanced up at him. Their gazes locked, and a rush of fire flowed through her veins. When she was with him, it felt so right. She was stronger and safe. Almost powerful again. Like she could do anything.

"You can let go of me," she said.

"You're sure?"

"Positive."

Jonah stepped away so she was on her own in waist-high water, and it was so thrilling. Scary but exhilarating as she stood there on her own feet, in a pool. Before her near drowning as a child, this was where she'd been so happy. Every summer she'd been in the water like a fish. She'd missed this.

She took a deep breath and on her own terms sank down below the surface, only for a second. Jonah's arms came around her as she stood up, sputtering and wiping the water from her eyes. A few nightmarish recollections flashed before her eyes—her mother's face, the feeling of fighting against the breathing tube—but they dissipated as she drank in the night air, telling her terrified body she was okay and that she could breathe.

"Amazing," he encouraged. "You did it."

"I don't think it worked. I'm still scared."

He smoothed back her hair gently. "This wasn't a quick fix."

"So how did you work on it all?"

"Cognitive behavioral therapy. Talking it out. Medication. There's nothing to be ashamed of."

"No. You're right." And looking at him she saw such a strong, caring man. One that made her weak in the knees.

She had to get out of here, out of his arms before she did something she regretted—or something she'd like very, very much.

"Thanks, but I think I'm done now."

Jonah didn't argue and guided her to the stairs. She clambered out of the pool and grabbed her towel, wrapping it tight around her like a security blanket.

"You okay?" he asked.

"Yeah. Cold. But yeah, I'm fine."

She was more than that. It felt like she'd conquered a mountain.

"Do you mind if I keep swimming? If you need me, I can come up with you."

"I'm good. Swim. I'm going to shower and head to bed. I'm exhausted from work and golf, and tomorrow is that dinner with my family again."

"Right. I'll lock up. You did great, Grace. You should be proud."

And she was, but she was overcome with a lot of emotions in that moment, ones she couldn't quite put her finger on. Or maybe she didn't want to identify them, because she was scared what it all meant. Jonah had given her the courage she hadn't thought anyone could give her, because she'd always refused to let them. She'd only relied on herself.

"'Night."

She quickly headed back upstairs, turning once to watch him swim his laps. Jonah was so kind and caring. He completely helped her face her fear and believe in something she thought was impossible again.

And she couldn't help but wonder what else she'd been wrong about for all this time. Maybe she'd been wrong about marriage and love.

Grace didn't get much sleep that night. She tossed and turned, and when she did close her eyes all she could think about was Jonah and how he made her feel when she faced that huge fear of hers. How amazing he had been with her father, how her father had liked him and opened up. How kind and gentle he'd been with her in the pool. In that moment she had been safe with him. Even though she put on a brave face at work, that wasn't always a true reflection of the inside, and it had been a long time since she had felt that strong. It was a long time since she had truly believed in herself.

When she got up in the morning, Jonah wasn't there. He'd left a note that said he'd gone for a motorcycle ride but that he'd be back in the afternoon to go to her parents' place for dinner in St. George.

Instantly, she worried that maybe she had stepped over the line with him.

Maybe she was pushing him away. Victor used to get annoyed with her when she hid things. He'd blamed her for the failure of their relationship, and she'd shouldered that responsibility: She'd been too closed-off, he'd said. It had pushed him into the arms of his now wife.

Now she was trying to hide again, hide all the confusing feelings racing through her.

Feelings like hope.

Like love.

Stop going around in circles.

Maybe it wasn't her fault that he'd left this morning. Maybe none of this was her fault and she didn't have to shoulder this blame. They'd both agreed to this farce with her family. They were both in on this together. If Jonah needed some space, then that was fine with her.

Jonah will come back. It's your anxiety.

Disgusted with herself, she kept busy for the rest of the day. She ran errands, she took a walk, cleaned and then got ready for the trip to St. George. Jonah came back as promised. He cleaned up quickly. He didn't seem weird or aloof at all. He was totally at ease, which she slightly hated him for, because she wished she was a little bit more laid back like that right now.

When had he got so laidback?

She reminded herself it was just the mask he wore when he was around her family. It wasn't real. It was also proof that what she was feeling was one-sided and that she had to be careful with her heart. Someone who did care wouldn't be so at ease and would have spent a sleepless night brooding.

So yeah, they were completely one-sided, these emotions.

How could she be so foolish?

She didn't chat much during the car ride to St. George, but Jonah didn't seem to notice.

They made it to the family dinner. The conversation was easy and light. This time they were greeted like usual; there was no awkwardness at all. Her family seemed to have welcomed Jonah, and he got along so well with them. Even her dad was opening up. It warmed her to her core, but she dreaded to think what was going to happen when it all ended. Her mother had made Grace's favorite dinner of roast chicken and potatoes, but she had a hard time swallowing any of it. There was a time limit to this seemingly picture-perfect happiness. There was a court date in their future, and it was looming like a ticking time bomb.

"Grace swam yesterday," Jonah announced, starting a conversation and shaking Grace out of her racing thoughts.

Her mother's eyes widened. "What?"

Grace kicked Jonah under the table and then looked at her family's stunned faces. "It was nothing."

"But you don't swim," Aidan stammered. "Like…at all."

"Right. I don't," Grace corrected. "I went in the pool with Jonah."

"He's trying to teach you to swim again? That's great," Rick said. "I knew I liked you for a reason, Jonah."

Jonah beamed at her proudly. "She put her head under the water and everything."

"You did?" her mother asked, amazed. It almost looked like she was going to cry, and that was the last thing Grace wanted. Melanie's lips were a thin line, tightly pursed together, and instantly Grace felt bad for stealing the spotlight.

"It's no big deal. Can we talk about something else?" she asked, trying to change the subject.

"Sure," her father said. "So after Melanie's wedding in a couple of weeks, we're going to throw you and Jonah a wedding reception at the club."

She exchanged a concerned glance with Jonah, who was clearly trying to hide his shock.

"Dad, you don't have to do to the trouble," she said quickly, hoping it would dissuade him from the idea. That kind of event came with a price tag, and she didn't want her parents to spend it on something that wasn't real.

"Sure I do," Rick argued. "You're my daughter and it's right."

"I'm sad I didn't get to see much of Mr. and Mrs. Cute Paramedic's wedding," her mom teased.

"Yeah. It was blurry," Melanie giggled, a little unkindly. "We didn't even get to see the kiss over the altar. The one sealing the deal."

If Grace could reach out under the table and kick her little sister, she would. Jonah looked at her like he was ready to bolt out the front door, and she couldn't blame him.

"We kissed. I can't help that our video guy was also drunk that night," Grace replied through tight lips.

"Why don't you just kiss now?" Aidan suggested, shrugging. Grace shot her little brother a death glare.

"Yes. Kiss now." Melanie held up her wineglass and tapped it, like people did at weddings.

She was giving a saucy look, and Grace knew Melanie was just doing this to irritate her. She'd noogie Melanie later.

Grace glanced at Jonah, silently apologizing to him. Now she wished they were still talking about her swimming.

"It's okay, sweetie," he said stiffly. "It's not like it's the first time."

Which was true—it wasn't. She didn't really recall the first time, but she had foggy memories of the few times after and how much she had liked them. Just thinking about kissing Jonah again made her nipples harden, her body clench in anticipation.

A jittery, butterfly sensation swirled in the pit of her stomach.

She didn't want to kiss him again because she had promised him they wouldn't. But she also did want it.

Badly.

I can do this.

She closed her eyes, her body trembling in a mixture of both dread and excitement, her emotions racing as she felt the light touch of the tip of his nose brushing against hers.

"It's okay. Breathe," he whispered, his breath hot against her neck. That simple reassurance eased her, and she leaned in as his lips brushed against hers in a feather-light kiss that made her burn for more.

The kiss deepened quickly as she sank into the pleasure of giving in to what she wanted.

Him.

Her body ached for him. His hand cupped her cheek as his tongue slipped past her lips. It was like she was melting, and she wanted to stay in this moment longer.

Then someone cleared their throat and she remembered that they weren't alone. They were at a family dinner. She broke away from the kiss, her cheeks flaming with heat. Jonah didn't move, his eyes dark with need, which was what she was feeling keenly in this moment. It was a hunger, a longing they just couldn't indulge in.

"Wow," Melanie said. "That was some kiss. Almost like a first kiss."

"Well, every time I kiss her it's like the first time," Jonah murmured, his eyes locked on her, hooking her soul and making her insides melt.

"I thought it was gross," Aidan stated, breaking the sizzling tension in the air.

"You're the one who suggested it," Travis quipped.

"Yeah, but I assumed it'd be a peck or something. Bleh." Aidan shuddered.

Her mother laughed, and the conversation resumed, except Grace knew things had changed in that moment. Maybe not for Jonah, but definitely for her. And she had to figure out how she was going to protect herself from being shattered when this all ended.

CHAPTER EIGHT

To say that he slept well that night was a big fat lie. Jonah didn't actually mind the couch; the reason he didn't get a wink of sleep was the fact that he couldn't stop thinking about that kiss with Grace. The sensation was plaguing him, burning through him like a fever, and he wanted more.

They'd kissed before. That was obvious from that blurry video and all his fuzzy-edged memories, but he'd meant what he said to Melanie. That kiss in St George really had felt like the first one. It had been intoxicating.

If there hadn't been people around, he would have let it go on forever. When Grace's lips had parted and their tongues had entwined, every fiber in his being, every nerve ending had lit up like a Christmas tree.

Thankfully, someone had piped up and brought him back to reality. He had remembered she wasn't his.

It was all an act.

Even though he kept repeating that over and over in his head, it didn't do him any good in the sleep department. Eventually, he gave up, had a shower and dragged himself to work.

Grace had left earlier to attend a meeting with the chief of the station house, which wasn't strange or unusual. Senior partners were called in once a month for a state-of-the-union kind of meeting. Jonah didn't mind losing his ride. He could use the walk in.

After grabbing coffee at a local coffee shop, he got to the station just as their patrol was about to start. And just as they had promised each other, there was no time for chatting or focusing on the awkwardness that was now between them. They'd sworn that this would not affect their work and he aimed to keep that promise. Work came first.

But it was hard not to think about how soft Grace's lips had been or how she had melted against him when they kissed. How he had drunk in the taste of her, the scent of her. He wanted more.

So much more.

He wanted to run his hands over her body, touch her skin, bring her to pleasure. He wanted to care for her, cherish her. It had been long time since he'd even contemplated a relationship. Since his married had ended, he had resigned himself to the fact it was just him. It was lonely but okay. He could keep his feelings in check.

Now he was starting to think he wanted more with a woman who didn't want him. Or at the very least didn't want to be tied down.

As they finished up a call that hadn't required them to transport anyone, he could tell that she was watching him and that she wanted to say something.

"I know you're staring at me," he said offhandedly.

"Sorry. It's…about last night."

"No." He turned around quickly. "When I agreed to this whole thing the promise was that it wouldn't get weird."

"But it did. Right?"

He relaxed, not realizing how tense he was holding his body. "Yeah, I suppose it did."

"I still want to have you as my partner. I don't want that to change." She swallowed hard. "When I checked my email this morning, I got something from the courthouse. We've been given a date to end the marriage."

The moment that she uttered those words, his stomach sank to the soles of his feet. Logically, he'd known it was coming, but maybe he just wasn't as prepared for it as he thought he might be.

"Oh, when is it?" he asked, trying to be nonchalant about it.

"Three days after my sister's wedding. How is that for timing?" she joked dryly.

"Terrible."

She nodded. "Well, at least the not knowing isn't hanging over our heads any longer."

"No," he exhaled. Then he bit his tongue for a moment, because there was a part of him that wanted to blurt out that he wanted to be with her.

That kiss they'd shared had stirred up everything he'd been trying to hold back. His desire for Grace, his need for her… It burned deep within him.

For the first time in a long time, he wanted to explore something more with someone. With Grace.

Something physical.

Friends with benefits?

A preposterous thought. Even suggesting it was risky. She might not want him, and he really didn't want to face rejection. Especially not from her.

Not from Grace.

It would ruin their friendship and definitely sour their working relationship. Or…would it?

When Mona had turned against him, when he'd come home, when she hadn't wanted to help him get through the grief of Justin's death and then cheated on him, *that* had been a rejection. Thinking about Grace doing the same didn't make any sense.

She was so different from his ex. She was more like his best friend.

Like Justin.

Still, it was hard to find the words or take the chance.

She won't reject you.

Jonah ignored that little niggle itching at the back of his mind. Even after all this time it was so hard to believe that if he put himself out there that he wouldn't be setting himself up for heartbreak.

Dispatch called, snapping him out of his reverie.

"Rig three, requested presence at an accident scene. Pedestrian struck. Peakness Pass and South Grand Canyon Road South."

Grace hit the button on the radio on her sleeve. "Ten-four and copy that. En route."

There was no more talking now as they had work to do. They got everything loaded back up, and Grace climbed into the driver's seat as Jonah took down the information scrolling on the computer screen about the accident. The sirens came on, and Grace drove through the streets of Vegas until they got to the Summerlin intersection, which was a residential area and not a main thoroughfare. Still, people were known to speed through these side streets.

The police were already present. He could see the flashing lights. A car was pulled over, and the police were questioning the driver.

"At least it wasn't a hit-and-run," Grace remarked.

"That's something." Jonah scanned through the milling people, and his heart sank when he saw it was a child who was lying on the ground. "Crap."

Grace frowned. "Yeah."

She pulled the ambulance over, and they moved quickly to get their equipment out of the back. Grace went over to talk to the police officer who was waving them down. No doubt he had pertinent information for them.

Jonah made his way to the little boy, who looked broken and was being cradled by his mother. The boy's mother was calling his name over and over as she rocked slightly. What struck Jonah, like a thunderbolt from the sky, was how much the little boy looked like Justin had when they were kids. There were so many similarities—the hair color, the facial features. The sight of the blood draining from that face made Jonah sick to his stomach.

Then an image flashed through his mind. Justin, in his arms, the life light draining from his eyes as Jonah begged him to hold on.

His breathing quickened, the world spinning.

You need to focus.

Swallowing hard, he locked it all away. Just like his therapist had taught him: compartmentalize and focus on the task at hand.

"Ma'am, my name is Jonah, and I'm a paramedic. Can you tell me what happened while I take a look at your son?"

"Sure," the woman responded with a wobbly voice. "Justin and I were walking, and then we heard this screech and I looked behind to see that car over there jump the curb. Justin went flying."

Justin. Even the name triggered him, but Jonah tried to ignore the flood of emotions, the trauma from when he'd held Justin for the last time.

"Was he conscious when he hit the ground?" he asked, checking Justin's pupils. One had blown, but the other was still reacting. There was no doubt in his mind that there was a brain bleed and broken bones. It wouldn't be surprising given the impact and how small and young the boy was.

"He was," Justin's mother sobbed.

"Justin, can you hear me?" Jonah asked, checking for

the sound of breathing and assessing whether the air way was clear.

Grace knelt down on the other side. “The police filled me in on what was happening.”

“I’m worried about spinal damage from the force of the impact. We need to get him on a backboard,” Jonah stated.

Grace nodded, and they set to work stabilizing Justin so they could load him up and take him to the children’s emergency room at the nearby hospital. They used braces to stabilize the neck and strapped him down. He was easier to lift as he was just a small child. If Jonah had to guess the boy might’ve been around seven. Way too young to have such a bad accident.

“We’re going to take Justin to the children’s hospital,” Grace explained to Justin’s mother. “You can come with us. We’re going to get fluids and oxygen into him.”

Justin’s mother nodded. “Okay. What about the police?”

“They’ll know where to find you,” Jonah answered. “We have to get your boy healthy again.”

Justin’s mother nodded and followed them as they lifted Justin onto their gurney and got him in the back of the ambulance. Grace knew all the streets like the back of her hand, and Jonah wanted to stay with the boy, so he stayed put, taking care of his little patient.

Grace locked up, and Jonah worked on the IV and monitors. There was no way, if he could help it, that he was going to let this Justin die. Not on his watch.

Come on, buddy, he silently entreated.

There was a pulse, but it was rapid and thready. Justin’s blood pressure was high. Jonah drowned out the sounds of the siren as Grace called into the emergency department at the local children’s hospital.

“Talk to me, Crandall,” Grace said over her shoulder as she drove. “Need some stats for the dispatch desk.”

"BP is elevated. Using permissive hypotension en route to stabilize. Suspect fractures and blunt force trauma, possible subdural hematoma."

Grace nodded and repeated everything back the hospital emergency room dispatch. They turned the corner and headed straight into the ambulance bay. The moment they pulled up a team of trauma surgeons in gowns rushed out to meet them. Grace parked and jumped out of the rig to open the door, rattling off information to the doctors.

"Patient is a male, aged seven. Blunt force trauma after being struck by a motor vehicle. Thrown approximately two hundred yards. Was conscious after the crash, but was unconscious upon our arrival to the scene. Trituration of permission hypotension used in field. Bolus of fluid, central line started."

"Left pupil nonresponsive," Jonah stated as he helped lift the gurney down. "Right pupil normal. Breath sounds shallow."

Grace had a doctor sign the release forms, and Jonah walked in with the gurney into the trauma bay. He helped the doctors as they transferred Justin onto a hospital stretcher.

"Thank you," a doctor said. "We've got it from here."

It was Jonah's cue to leave, but he had a hard time pulling away. Logically, he knew the boy wasn't his Justin, but he still didn't want to leave him. He wanted to stay, to make sure the boy was going to make it.

Watching the doctors work over Justin, the little boy, it felt like Jonah was a million miles away, and he closed his eyes, trying to steady himself enough to move.

"Jonah?" Grace asked, coming up beside him. She laid a hand on his shoulder. "Come on."

He nodded and let Grace lead him out of the trauma

bay. There was nothing more he could. He'd done his job, so why did he still feel like he failed?

Not much was said the rest of their shift, because Jonah was still struggling with how to process it all. Constant thoughts of his best friend ran through his mind. He was quiet at dinner, and Grace didn't pry, which he appreciated. After dinner he went for his usual swim, but it was like a switch had been flicked on in his brain. One that held back his emotions about Justin, his failed marriage, Grace. And try as he might, using all his usual techniques and tactics, today he couldn't compartmentalize it all and lock it away again.

Visions of the accident kept morphing into the whole scene of Justin's death, playing over and over again behind his eyes like a bad, tormenting horror show that he couldn't escape from, and he tried to fight back, to right the wrongs, but he couldn't manage it. He couldn't save him. It was always out of his grasp, and he tried to fight back the screams.

"Jonah," Grace whispered.

He jolted away. Her hands were on him; it was dark, and he was in the living room. He hadn't thought he'd fallen asleep. It was like a waking dream.

"What time is it?" he asked, groggily.

"Two in the morning," she replied. "Are you okay?"

"It was a nightmare. Nothing to worry about." He tried to roll over on the narrow couch. He didn't want Grace to fuss. Mona would get so annoyed when he'd have these lapses.

Grace. Isn't. Mona.

Still, she didn't need to see this side of him.

"You were screaming," she said, gently rubbing his back. "I don't think it was nothing."

Her touch was soothing, and he couldn't remember the last time he'd been comforted so sweetly. He should've just pushed her away, but he couldn't. He needed her here with him. He rolled over. "I was having flashbacks. Thinking of my best friend who died in my arms overseas, how I couldn't save him. It's a symptom of my PTSD."

"Justin, right?"

He nodded. "I'm sorry for waking you up. I'll be okay."

Grace stood up, and then she took his hand. "Come."

"Where?"

"You're coming to bed with me. We can share a bed. I don't think you should be alone tonight."

Jonah had no fight left in him at that point, and she was right about one thing—he didn't want to be alone. He grabbed his pillow and followed Grace into her bedroom.

"One thing though," she said with a serious tone, spinning around.

"What's that?"

"You sleep with your head on the pillows this time. No feet up there."

He laughed, softly hoping his voice didn't shake. "Deal."

She pulled back the covers, and he got settled. The sheets smelled liked her, which was no surprise. He loved that soft, sweet smell of her. It was vanilla and something else. It should have been soothing; instead, all he could think about was her lying next to him. And he didn't want to close his eyes and have this end or have a repeat of the nightmare he'd been having.

"That case rattled you today," she said. "It's because his name was Justin, wasn't it?"

"It was."

"I called the hospital after you fell asleep."

"Oh?" he asked, his interest piqued.

"He's going to make it. He came through surgery just

fine. What you did to control his blood pressure helped save him."

Relief washed through him. "He looked a lot like Justin did when we were kids and had the same name. It was all…"

"I understand. Trust me. I still remember the moment I almost drowned. I remember when I woke up fighting the tube. Water triggers me, so I understand those dreams."

"My ex didn't."

Grace grunted. "I'm not her. You said to me that I was safe with you. Well, you're safe with me."

That meant everything to him.

He leaned on his elbow to stare down at her in the darkness, her blond hair loose over her pillow. There was a thin beam of light sneaking through her blinds from the streetlights outside. It made her skin glow, and he could see her eyes sparkling. He touched her face, gently, brushing the tips of his fingers over her silken skin, reveling in the softness. He wanted to stay here forever, in this moment.

"Grace," he whispered huskily. "I think I'm going to have to sleep on the couch."

"Why?" her voice hitched in her throat.

He wanted to stay, but there was no way he could. "Because I'm scared. I want you more than I can bear it."

She let out a gasp, just a quick one, as she processed what he said to her, because she'd thought it was all one sided, those raw emotions she'd been grappling with. It appeared, by his own admission, that Jonah was feeling the same.

She couldn't promise him forever, but she could give him tonight. Because she wanted that now more than anything.

She wanted him close to her, nothing between them. The mattress dipped as he got up to leave, and she reached out, grabbing his arm to stop him.

"Stay. Be with me." Her voice shook as she said it out loud.

"And what about beyond tonight?" he asked. "I don't know what the future holds."

"I don't need forever. Just tonight."

"I don't have protection."

"I think we're okay. We didn't have it on our wedding night, and I'm on the pill. Stay. I want this, Jonah. I want you."

And it was exactly what she wanted. She wanted to be selfish in this moment with him. She was done fighting all these feelings.

He hesitated, only for a moment, and then gathered her up into his arms. "I want you too, Grace. I've been burning for you for a long time."

Jonah kissed her again with an intensity that she felt keenly deep within her soul. All she wanted to do was touch and taste every inch of him.

Part of her wanted to savor this moment, but the other part of her, the one that had been not so patiently waiting, wanted this to be as fast and furious as the insatiable need that was burning a hole deep within her.

Being with him right now was a huge gamble because she didn't want to leave anything to chance with them. She didn't want the awkwardness if things went south; she didn't want it to affect their partnership or their friendship. She didn't want Jonah to feel like he had to stay away from her. But as he kissed her, his hands burning her skin with his fiery touch, she was willing to bet away every last inch of herself to be with him in this moment.

Her body thrummed with electric need as they made quick work of their clothes so that there was nothing between them. It was just the two of them now, naked and vulnerable to each other. Jonah ran his hands over her body, trailing over her curves slowly, making her hunger for him.

"You make me so hard, Grace."

Grace kissed him again, pulling him closer as she touched him. He leaned over her, cupping her breasts, running his thumb over her pink nipple.

"Tell me what you want," she mewled.

"I want to bury myself inside you." He stroked her between her legs, making her wet with need as she gripped his shaft, touching the hard velvety skin.

Jonah moaned and jerked against her palm as she stroked him.

"Do you like that?" she teased.

"You're killing me, Grace."

"I want you, Jonah." She wanted to tell him that she only wanted him, but she couldn't formulate the right words. She arched her back, pleasure coursing through her as his tongue circled her sensitive nipple.

She raised her hips, silently begging him to take her, possess her.

Then he was at her entrance, hot and hard as he slowly slid inside, filling every inch of her, and she succumbed to the heady sensations of letting go to Jonah, of being vulnerable to him.

His thrusts came quicker, more urgent, and she met the rhythm of his pace, clinging to every heightened sensation. Her fingers dug into his shoulders. She came hard and fast, crying out as she tightened around him.

In this moment she wanted this to last for an eternity, but she knew it couldn't. She didn't want to think about the eventual end or else she'd cry.

Jonah's thrusts became shallow, quicker, and his hands held on to her hips tight as he rode her. He cried out as he finished and rolled over onto his back, pulling her tight against his chest where she could listen to his heart racing under her ear. It was soothing.

He wrapped his arms around her, holding her, like he too knew their time together was fleeting. He ran his fingers down her back. “What’re you thinking about?”

“About us. This.”

“I know. Me too. I promise it won’t affect our work.”

“I know it won’t.” She laughed softly. “What about friends with benefits? Or partners with benefits.”

He grunted. “Wife-and-husband with benefits you mean.”

“Something like that,” she chided.

“Oh, I think I can make that work.” And he kissed her again, down her neck and over her stomach.

She giggled as his lips trailed lower. She wasn’t going to think any more about the end, the court date, the fake marriage. Tonight all she wanted was him. Everything else could wait.

CHAPTER NINE

IT WAS NICE to wake up holding her the next day. It took Jonah a moment to realize that he was not on the couch and that he was in Grace's bed. Then it all came back to him in stunning clarity, and when he cracked open his eye, he saw her there, in his arms sleeping peacefully.

No wonder he'd had a dreamless sleep.

A comfortable sleep.

Actually, he couldn't remember the last time he had slept so soundly. It had been badly needed. He shifted slightly to get up, trying not to stir her, but she opened her eyes and then smiled at him.

"Good morning," she said, her voice a bit muffled.

"Did I wake you?" he asked.

"No." She rolled onto her side, tucking her hands under her head. "We might've slept in."

He glanced at the alarm clock. "It's seven. We didn't sleep in that much, and our shift starts in, like, an hour and half."

"Yours does."

He cocked an eyebrow. "What do you mean?"

"I have to go for training at Vegas Central. Something about new protocols. All shift leaders are going at separate times. So you'll be with John today."

"Well, I'm a bit disappointed."

"Because you'll miss me?"

"Yes, but also John is boring," he groaned.

Grace laughed gently. "So? He thinks you are too. He likes to chat, and you don't."

Jonah moaned. "I'm a loner, remember?"

"Were, I believe."

"Still, disappointed."

"Same. I really don't want to spend the day with Victor. I'd rather spend it with you."

"About work..." He trailed off because he really didn't want to ruin this lovely morning by talking about what happened, but then he didn't want it to affect their work either.

"I know. We've been doing well so far. I don't think this will be a problem."

"You sound so certain," he mused.

"Of course. We're adults, and there's an end date."

Jonah sensed a bit of sadness in her voice when she mentioned the looming court date. It was bothering him too. Last night had been so wonderful, so magical. It was everything that he had wanted for the last couple of weeks. Actually, if he was honest with himself, he'd been attracted to her the first time he met her. It had just been easier to ignore that attraction when they were nothing more than partners and he didn't know anything about her.

Now he was getting to know her. She wasn't just this woman he worked with. She was turning into so much more. Even more than a friend, and it was a bit paralyzing to even think about trying to take it further. Grace had said she wasn't like his ex-wife and that was true, but it was still hard to trust himself to her, especially when it came to his heart.

He also didn't want to hurt her either. Grace had been through so much too.

He should've felt bad about making love to her last night.

He didn't regret it at all. In that moment, being vulnerable with her was exactly what he wanted.

What he needed.

"You've gone quiet again. You okay?" she asked.

"I'm fine. I think everything will be all right. Though I don't know how, given I have to listen to John's boring stories at the station all day."

Grace laughed and then kissed him on his lips. "Remember—we said friends with benefits. We can make this work."

"Are you saying you wouldn't mind a repeat of last night?" He asked, intrigued.

"Maybe." She grinned. He reached for her, and she ducked away. "Later. How about a motorcycle ride out to the Red Rock Canyon after work? We can find a place to eat."

"You want to go for a motorcycle ride?" he questioned.

"I do." She stood up, and he admired her nakedness, groaning inwardly that she was being all responsible and getting ready for work. "Don't look at me like that."

"Like what?"

She frowned, only slightly. "I have to get ready for work, and so do you."

"Right, boss."

She nodded. "Get ready. And tonight we'll have a nice evening out and talk."

"Sounds good."

And it did. He wouldn't mind getting on his motorcycle tonight with her on the back. The last time she'd been on his bike his nipple had come away a bit bruised, but it would the worth it to share the evening with her. If she wrapped her legs around his waist, he didn't care if she ripped his nipples right off.

She was also very astute. They needed to talk about it

all. They needed to talk about what happened last night, their friendship and the court date.

They needed an exit strategy, but as he watched her walk to the shower, he was wishing that they didn't need to have this talk.

For the first time in a long time, he didn't want an exit strategy. It scared him a little, but he pushed the fear away. He was pretty sure this strange sense of comfort was a blip, a fleeting thing and completely based on endorphins.

It couldn't be anything else, could it?

The day without Grace was long and just as boring as Jonah had predicted. John was a nice enough guy. They just didn't have a lot in common. He prattled on and on about things, half of which Jonah couldn't even keep up with, and he had labeled himself a player. That was definitely not Jonah's ideal.

Remaining single was one thing, but maintaining bachelorhood to sleep around was another, and that was not what he wanted at all.

At least they weren't stuck in a rig together. Today was the day that John and Jonah remained at the station house, sort of on call and dealing with dispatch. Jonah usually preferred to be out in an ambulance, but without Grace it wasn't the same, so he was more than okay to putter around at the station.

Grace came back to the station house after a long day and looked absolutely exhausted. Once their shift was over, they headed back to their condo and got changed for a bike ride through the desert.

She had put on her denim jeans, a ripped T-shirt and Docker boots. She looked like she was ready to kick some ass at all-night rave.

"Is this okay?" she asked, spinning around so he could look at her.

He grinned slowly. "Just missing a leather jacket."

"Well, I don't have one of those."

"Honestly, I wouldn't mind seeing you in a bit more leather, if I'm honest."

She quirked an eyebrow. "Oh? Do tell."

"That'll wait. Come on—before we lose the light." He handed her the pink helmet he'd bought her, and they went down to his bike.

She climbed on behind him, her arms going around his torso. The heat from her body, her breasts pressed against the back of him, just made him hunger for more and an image of parking somewhere off the highway and bending her over the seat of the motorcycle flashed through his mind and made him hard with need.

Something that wouldn't make this bike ride any easier.

Well, you did promise her a ride...you just didn't specify.

They drove off to the Red Rock Canyon, northwest of Las Vegas. It was a gorgeous night. There were no winds rushing down off the mountain, the heat of the day was dissipating, and as they approached the canyon the red seemed to be even more vibrant, like just after a rain. They drove around the canyon area on the highway.

Although they couldn't talk, Grace was completely relaxed. Her grip on him wasn't as tight as before, and it was almost natural to have her on the back of his bike. He could do this forever.

Just north of the red rocks there was a little diner. It wasn't the fifties diner that was on the highway to California—that was in the opposite direction—but it looked like a fun little place and there were other bikes parked outside, in a mix of family cars.

The music was loud, and there was a lot of neon.

It looked like it would have fit in on the old Route 66. *Kitschy* was the word. It was the perfect place to have a nice dinner and talk.

He was somewhat dreading the conversation, but they needed to discuss what had happened between them last night and where they went from here.

In a couple of weeks Grace's sister was getting married, and then a couple days after that, they had their court date and their marriage would be over. They had to come up with a contingency plan for the eventual demise.

There were too many people involved now, and he really didn't want to see her family get hurt.

The waitress at the diner took them to a corner booth, and they slipped in across the vinyl seats. The retro music was loud, but it wasn't overpowering, and their little corner booth had a window that overlooked the desert and the setting sun.

The waitress left them with two menus and said she would be back in a bit.

"How did you find this place?" Grace asked.

"Just now."

"You didn't know about it before?"

"No."

"You drove to it."

He chuckled. "That's the fun of just going for a drive. Especially on a bike."

"I can see the appeal." She glanced down at her menu. "So how was the workshop today?"

Grace groaned. "Tedious. Victor was acting all weird. He was super nice to me. He just usually blows me off. I think Travis had been telling him how well you got along with my father."

Jonah grinned. "Well, he's my father-in-law. I want to make a good impression."

"Well, Victor was always a bit possessive. My dad liked him, but I suspect he likes you more."

His heart sank. "For now."

She sighed sadly. "Right."

"I'm nervous about all of this. What're we going to do?"

"I guess we take it one day at a time."

He nodded. "No promises."

Grace worried her bottom lip. "Right. That's what we agreed."

The waitress came back with waters and then took their order before disappearing again. "Why doesn't your family know about what Victor did to you?"

He was hoping this time she'd tell him the truth, open up to him, that she'd be vulnerable with him. Always, Grace was trying to be so strong. Maybe he wasn't the only one perpetuating a facade. It worried him.

The question stung, like a slap to the face, but she couldn't blame Jonah for asking her again, because she really didn't know the answer herself. Now she could see all the red flags when it came to Victor. How come she hadn't seen that before? Why had she been so swept away by him in the past? The only thing she could think of was that she was a people pleaser.

She had fallen in love with the idea of having the most perfect relationship, one that would make her family happy and make them proud of her. Victor had been too good to be true, and she saw that now. She hadn't really been happy for a long time, because she'd been striving so hard to please everyone else around her.

She was never out to please herself.

The only thing that made her truly happy in life was her work.

And Jonah, a little voice piped up.

He made her happy in a way that she hadn't known was possible.

In a way she wasn't sure that she truly deserved it, but she wanted to hold on to it, she just wasn't sure how.

"I guess because I didn't want to seem like a failure to them again. And it's silly now in retrospect, because when this ends, when they learn the truth about us, it's going to let them down. It's going to disappoint them."

Jonah nodded. "I get that. I clung to my ex-wife because I foolishly thought that we had a strong bond, but when I married her, it was for all the wrong reasons. Fresh out of school, she was the high school sweetheart and I seemed like the life of the party."

"You mean you're not?" she chided.

"Not the way she wanted."

"And what about you?"

"I didn't want that life. Being the popular guy was lonely. I know now it was all an act."

"You're social with me," she said. "Well, now, but not at first."

"I trust you. You bring it out of me."

The idea that he trusted her made her flush with happiness. It was so flattering to have that effect on him, to know that he cared for her.

You don't know that for sure.

She nodded slowly, trying to push away those doubts. "What you said before was right—we just have to take this day by day. And we already know that we're going to stay friends and that we can work together."

"And the lie?"

Grace took a deep breath. "I'm going to tell my family before the court date."

"We both will." Then he reached out and took her hand,

giving it a squeeze to comfort her. It was reassuring. It was like they were in this together, more than just work partners.

"So tell me all about your day with John."

Jonah groaned and rolled his eyes. "It was the usual. If you know John."

"Oh, I know John."

"What, did you have a secret marriage with him too?" he teased.

Grace kicked him playfully under the table. "Cracks like that, Mr. Cute Paramedic, are going to get you relegated back to the couch."

Jonah cocked an eyebrow. "Oh, you're letting me share your bed again tonight?"

There was a husky promise in the way he asked that question. It made her insides turn to jelly and her body tremble in anticipation.

"You said friends with benefits. And why else would I agree so easily to a bike ride tonight?"

There was a devious but hungry glint to his eye as he smiled. "I kind of like this bad-girl, rebellious side to you. I mean, I was seriously attracted to the scotch-drinking badass that I knew every day, but I like this side too."

"Well, we're living a lie as husband and wife. We might as well have a little fun with it, right?"

"Oh, yes. Do you think it would be okay if I canceled our food and asked for the check now?"

Grace laughed. "I'm hungry. Eat first, and then we'll take the bike back home."

He nodded. "Sounds like a plan."

She was relieved that he was on the same page as her, that this wasn't going to be as complicated as her anxiety had been telling her. Maybe, just maybe it would be easy with Jonah.

And there was a small glimmer of hope that maybe they

might not need that court date after all. She wasn't going to fully invest in the dream just yet, but as they both agreed, they were going to just take this one day at a time and see where it led them.

She knew where it was going to lead them tonight after dinner, and that was enough to get by on now. Like she had said to him before, she didn't need promises of forever right now. She just needed to live in this moment.

She just needed tonight.

CHAPTER TEN

Two weeks later

IT HAD BEEN a magical two weeks since they'd first spent the night together and talked about their expectations going forward. There was still no promise of forever. Everything was as it was supposed to be, and their arrangement wasn't affecting their work.

The court date that would mark the end of their marriage was still in the back of her mind, but that was where she was keeping it. She didn't want to dwell on it.

Right now, she was doing something she hadn't done in a long time, and that was enjoying herself and not worrying about expectations from others. There was no need to people-please with Jonah, which was a relief. They had decided to take it one day at a time and that's exactly what she was doing. Every day was a new opportunity.

It was easy and fun.

She never thought she'd like a friends-with-benefits arrangement, but she was kind of enjoying it. In the rig, they just continued to work seamlessly together and there was no awkwardness or unprofessional behavior. There was just lots of teasing when they weren't treating patients.

And any kind of little tease played out later in the privacy of their home.

It still rattled her a bit to think of her condo as *their*

home. She only ever really thought of it as a place to come and sleep, eat, rest after work. She'd never conceptualized it as a home until Jonah moved in.

Then she began to look forward to her time off. To days off on the couch and movies, to dinner and chores. To laughter.

And the idea it would eventually end made her sad.

Maybe it doesn't have to end?

But she ignored that little spark of hope. She wouldn't let it in.

She couldn't.

Everything was going smoothly, and she wanted to keep it that way. There was a part of her that was holding her breath until the other shoe dropped. When it came time for her sister's wedding and they were packing up her car to go to St. George, she couldn't help but wonder when disaster would strike.

"Do you think they'll separate us?" Jonah teased as they pulled their suitcases out.

"How do you mean?" she asked, distracted by her thoughts.

"Separate bedrooms."

"Why would they do that? We're married."

"Oh, good. I've kind of gotten used to sleeping next to you."

Grace flushed. "Same. I think I'm used to your snoring."

He rolled his eyes. "I don't think we'll be able to do our usual bedtime routine."

"Our…" She trailed off as she thought about it. "Right, no, probably not. If they put us where I think they will, it'll be my old childhood bedroom, and yeah, that's right next to my parents' room."

"Well, you could be a rebel and make out in your room." He waggled his eyebrows, and she smacked him playfully.

"You need to behave."

"Yes, boss."

She liked this more open version of Jonah. He was still a bit of an introvert, but with her things were easy and all awkwardness was gone. As they walked up to her parents' house, his back stiffened, and she knew he was struggling with the idea of all the extra people. If she could leave with him right now, she would.

She opened the door, and her mother was rushing around in a tizzy. Melanie looked a bit on edge too. Aidan walked by and rolled his eyes; he was headed to the basement to get away from the chaos, no doubt. It was taking all Grace's willpower not to turn around, go home and just drive in for the wedding the next day. Or at the very least find a hotel so she and Jonah could relax.

"Hi, Mom. Sorry we're late, but..." Grace started to say.

"It's good you're here. You can take your bags to your room and then come back down." Her mother rushed off again.

Jonah was smirking. "She's a pretty good drill sergeant."

It was a cute joke, but she could see his trepidation under the surface. He was like her, a bit of a sponge who sucked in emotions of others around them. It was easy to shut it off at work, so why was it so hard here?

Because you care about your family.

And her heart skipped a beat, wondering if Jonah cared about *her*. He was so good at keeping his guard up, pretending around her family, but here now she saw a glimmer of him.

The real him.

Was that why it was hard for him to keep his guard up? Because he cared for her?

"Yes. It seems so. Come on and follow me."

They carried their bags upstairs and then down to almost the end of the hall. Her bedroom door still had her old childhood name plate on the white-paneled door.

"Will you still have posters up of your teenage crushes?"

Grace rolled her eyes. "No."

"No boy bands?"

Now that they were away from the chaos downstairs he was relaxing more, because it was just the two of them. This was the Jonah she knew intimately.

The Jonah she was starting to fall for.

A knot tightened in her stomach, and she took a step away from him. The realization scared her. She couldn't fall for a man when there was a quantifiable end date in sight.

"What is with you tonight?" Grace asked as she opened the door to her bedroom and flicked on the light.

Jonah was visibly disappointed as he walked in. "Rats. I was hoping to see some version of your past self in here."

"Oh? And what was your room like as a kid, old man?"

"Basic. Sports and that kind of stuff. I listened to a lot of heavy metal."

Grace quirked an eyebrow. "What?"

"Why is that surprising to you?"

"I don't know. You just don't—Wait a minute, I take that back. You ride a motorcycle and you wear leather. You're right. I shouldn't be shocked."

Jonah laughed. "I like metal music. I like banging my head, yes. But I never had my hair long."

She snickered. "I'm trying to picture you with long hair, and I can't. Every time I get a vision of you with long hair I see you with a flowing shirt on the cover one of those old romance novels, hair blowing in the breeze on a pirate ship."

"Is that a fantasy of yours?" he asked in a sultry tone.

"No."

He took a step closer and put his arms around her, pulling her body tight against him. Just that simple act made her ache with need. She liked the sensation of his hard body pressed against hers. He leaned down and kissed her slowly, teasing her.

"Are you sure?"

"No," she replied breathlessly.

He grinned that wicked grin that drove her wild. She forgot all about being at her parents' place and the fact that her family was waiting on her…until her mother rapped on the door and opened it.

"Grace!"

Grace and Jonah broke apart like they'd been caught doing something they shouldn't and were being scolded.

"What, Mom? Jeez," Grace said.

"I asked you to drop your bags and come downstairs. I need you both. This's no time for canoodling."

Grace groaned. "*Canoodling*, Mom? Seriously?"

Her mother frowned. "It's *all hands on deck* for this wedding. Get downstairs. Oh, Jonah, would you be a love and drive Aunt Gert back to her house? It's getting late, and Gert doesn't do well in the dark."

Jonah nodded. "Sure thing, Leslie. I wonder if something is obscuring her vision."

Grace stifled her chuckle.

"Maybe. I appreciate it all the same." Her mother shut the door, and Grace doubled over in laughter.

"You're so bad," she said.

"Sorry. I really couldn't resist. Every time I see that woman I want to squeegee her eyelashes." He sighed heavily, and she knew this evening would be torture for him. "We'd better go fulfill our duties. Right?"

"I suppose."

They headed downstairs reluctantly, but she could not

stop thinking about that moment she'd spent kissing him—or, as her mother had called it, canoodling him. It had left her wanting more. So much more.

What she had to remember was to keep it light, easy and fun. That way she wouldn't get attached, and if she didn't get attached, she wouldn't be hurt when it was over. That was the promise they had made to each other—not to complicate stuff.

So instead she focused on how she was going to make out with him this evening without anyone else hearing. It was kind of titillating to play the rebel child for once, instead of the one who never took risks so they wouldn't ever be a burden again.

It was hard to keep their hands off each other that night, but they did, because she really didn't want her parents to overhear their boisterous lovemaking. And they would have, because she was loud with Jonah. It was freeing to let loose like that.

Life isn't just about sex.

That niggling thought kept playing in the back of her mind.

And as she watched her sister get into her wedding dress, their mother fawning over her, Grace felt a bit sad that she'd never gotten to have this moment.

Or even wanted it, until now.

It hit her that she'd never had those kind of dreams, not real tangible ones, about Victor and her when they were dating.

She'd always expected if they didn't break up, they'd get married; when that hadn't happened she'd given up and had thought she was fine with it. She didn't need a fairy-tale ending.

But now, with Jonah…

She'd been enjoying herself, but there was a part of her that wanted more, and she wanted that something more with him.

She didn't want that court date, and she hated that it was coming up fast.

She didn't want this marriage to end, but she really didn't know how to get the words out, to tell him that she was falling for him and that she kind of wanted something deeper. Forever.

Jonah didn't want any of this. He'd had it before and made it pretty clear he wouldn't do the whole wedding thing again.

This, these feelings of rejection, of hurt, were exactly what she'd been afraid of for so long.

Her sister was beaming, glowing, and Grace was so happy for her.

"Well?" Melanie asked. "You're really quiet."

"You look beautiful, Melanie," Grace remarked, giving her sister a quick hug so as not to wrinkle her wedding dress.

"Thanks! You know, you and Jonah could just do a vow renewal," Melanie hinted.

"Why?" Grace asked.

"So you can wear the dress. You seem so far away, and I just figured you were sad about missing out," Melanie remarked. "Or is something else wrong?"

It was the way her sister said that, as if she was expecting Grace to steal this moment away. Something Grace tried so hard never to do. Her sister, even after all these years later, still struggled with what had happened when they were kids.

It annoyed her, but she swallowed that frustration down. Now was not the time and place to dredge it all up.

"Nothing else is wrong," she lied. "You're right. That's

it. I wanted to wear the dress. Kind of hard to do when you're that drunk."

Melanie laughed, and then the photographer had them pose to take a sister photograph. Grace plastered on her best smile. Only she didn't feel like smiling at all.

"It's time," the wedding coordinator said, peeking into the bridal room. "Everything is set up outside."

Their mom was tearing up as she futzed with Melanie's veil. Their dad came in, and Grace watched as he kissed Melanie on the cheek. Grace had thought she never wanted any of this, especially after Victor had shattered her trust, but now she was envious of it and felt bad for being so selfish, for wanting her own happily-ever-after.

"Let's go," Rick said, and then he smiled and winked at her.

Grace took a deep breath and headed up the stairs to meet the groomsman she was walking with. Thankfully, she hadn't been paired up with Victor. The maid of honor had that pleasure. As she passed through the country club and then out onto the small green clearing where the seats were set up, she kept telling herself to smile and keep smiling so that no one would know what was going on.

She walked down the aisle, seeing where she was supposed to line up for the ceremony, and saw Travis standing there, patiently waiting for Melanie.

It was then, as she walked toward the front that she saw Jonah in the front row next to her little brother, Aidan. He looked so handsome in his suit. Their gazes locked, and this time the fake smile he used around her family and strangers turned real. Her heart melted. She anchored herself to him in that moment.

Yes. She wanted this with him.

They were already married, thanks to too much scotch and bad karaoke, and that was fine. What she wanted was for nothing to change, to end. She wanted their *one day at a time* to go on forever. And that was a scary thought indeed, because she didn't see how it could be possible.

Jonah liked that he had been able to sleep next to Grace last night, but what he hated was that *sleeping* had been all they did. When he'd gotten back from taking Aunt Gert and her fifteen pounds of mascara home, Grace had been busy until late at night with wedding stuff.

And it had been mentally exhausting playing nice with everyone, without any down time. He had tried to help where he could, but it had been clear he wasn't much use. So by the time Grace had come to bed, she'd just curled beside him and he'd held her. It had been nice, and he'd relaxed. It had felt right.

The past two weeks had been so magical. There were no expectations. He just loved spending time with her. He couldn't remember the last time he'd felt this at peace.

And that had just firmly solidified his resolve: He was falling in love with her. He didn't really want to admit that, even to himself, but as much as he tried to fight it, it was a losing battle. He was falling for her.

And now here she was, walking down the aisle in that strapless teal bridesmaid gown that clashed a bit with her pink hair. She was the most breathtaking woman in the bridal party He lost his breath for one moment and had a flare of possessive jealousy at the groomsman who got to usher her down the aisle.

It made him a bit sad that they hadn't gotten that.

He'd seen what they did get on that terrible, lopsided, blurry video at the wedding chapel. It had been nothing like this. And Grace deserved a moment like this. She deserved it all. He just wasn't sure he could give it to her.

When their gazes locked, it was like time had no meaning and all he could see was her. Eventually, she moved to the front and stood next to the other bridesmaids. Melanie came out on her father's arm, but Jonah didn't see her. She was Travis's. All he saw was Grace, this woman that he was falling in love with.

His partner, who was becoming his best friend.

What sobered him up was—what if he lost all that?

They'd talked about this. Forever wasn't part of the plan. Honestly, Jonah really had a hard time believing that if he made any move in that direction, all this goodness, this love wouldn't be snatched away from him. He'd thought that he and Mona were going to last forever when they were first married, and that had ended. Then he'd thought that he and Justin would be best friends forever, until Justin had died. In his own weird little way, he'd thought he would have his parents forever too, but now they were gone. He hadn't been ready for them to leave him so soon, even if logically, their ages made it a foregone conclusion.

Forever wasn't sustainable. It wasn't reality, and it hurt to lose and lose and be alone. He'd gotten so used to only relying on himself. It had been easier this way, but as he watched Grace up at the altar, standing outside on a beautiful summer twilight, the red rocks of the cliffs in St. George gleaming brightly against the green of the golf course, he didn't want to be alone any longer.

He just wanted forever with her, and it terrified him because he didn't know how to reach out and take it. He wasn't sure if she wanted him back.

Melanie and Travis were married. It was beautiful. Everyone was happy and cheered. It was apparent to Jonah that they were in love. After the wedding ceremony came the pictures. As Jonah walked away, he was accosted by Aunt Gert to be a part of the family photo.

His stomach sank to his feet as he was dragged out onto the green to where Grace's family was standing.

"Found him," Aunt Gert announced.

"I thought your eyesight was bad," Jonah teased her half-heartedly. He couldn't let himself get so lost in his thoughts. He couldn't let Grace's family see this side of him. He had to put on a brave face.

Aunt Gert shrugged and blinked a couple of times. "You're easy to spot, Mr. Cute Paramedic."

Grace choked back a laugh and came over. "Thanks, Aunt Gert."

Aunt Gert waved and meandered off to get in a photo with the bride.

"I don't think I should be here," Jonah whispered under his breath.

"Yes, you should."

"Grace, but this..."

"I know, but it would look weird if you weren't. It'll be okay. I'm going to take the blame for this whole thing when it ends. I'll tell them that I coerced you." She dragged him by the arm over to where the photos were being taken, but all he could think about was what she said, how she would take the blame when this whole thing ended.

Which meant that she was planning for the end.

Here he was thinking about their future, but she was already looking ahead to the end. It saddened him, but what had he expected? And as he stood and listened to the photographer pose them for the photographs, he couldn't help but feel like he shouldn't be in the pictures. He really didn't belong here. He didn't belong anywhere.

He was alone after all.

You don't have to be. Tell her. Convince her.

Only he couldn't. His heart was breaking and it was all his fault, but as he looked down at Grace, he was still glad he'd taken the risk. Even though he'd never planned on falling in love again, he had.

He was so in love with her.

It was going to be hard when the end came, but he knew one thing: If their marriage ended and they just went back to being the way they'd been before, that wouldn't be enough for him. He would always want more when it came to Grace.

He couldn't exist where she was around and not love her, not have her in his life. Friendship wasn't enough.

So when their marriage ended, he would accept defeat and move on to another place. He would have to leave Las Vegas, because try as he might to hold it back, his heart was most definitely on the line. It belonged to her.

But he wasn't sure if her heart belonged to him, and he was terrified to find out the answer.

CHAPTER ELEVEN

SOMETHING HAD CHANGED. Jonah had been acting a bit aloof after her sister's marriage ceremony. Grace thought everything had been okay. The way he had been so flirty with her the night before and then the way he'd looked at her when she walked down the aisle gave her the impression of a man in love, but the moment that Aunt Gert had brought him over for family photos, everything had changed.

He'd become closed off, quiet.

She sensed something had shifted between them, but she wasn't sure what. Now he was sitting with her family during the wedding reception and seemed to be enjoying himself enough. She was stuck at the head table and wishing she was sitting with him so they could talk, joke, laugh.

When she was with him, she was always having a good time, and there was no one at the head table she particularly wanted to make small talk with. When she'd first started to really get to know Jonah that had been something they both had in common: They loathed idle chitchat. He was just so much better at faking it than she was.

Jonah wore a mask in order to be social. She'd thought the rapport between them had been real, but now she wasn't so sure.

After the dinner the emcee announced Melanie and Travis for the first time as man and wife. Travis took his bride out on the ballroom floor as they slow danced to their first song. Grace's heart longed to share that moment with Jonah.

When the first dance was over, her father got up to the podium to make a speech.

"Welcome, everyone. If you don't know me, I'm Rick Landon, father of the bride, and the amazing and generous man buying your dinner tonight."

There was a faint titter of laughter.

"Leslie and I are so glad to have Travis as part of the family. I thought I was only gaining one son-in-law this year, but I've been blessed with two."

Grace's stomach turned as her dad mentioned her at Melanie's wedding. Jonah smiled tightly and looked at her. She knew he was struggling with the marriage charade again. Honestly, she was too, and she wanted to tell her parents the truth. But now was not the time and place. Her father finished his speech with a lot of funny jokes about Travis and Melanie, about golf.

Once the speeches by the parents were over, the dance floor opened up to everyone. Finally Grace was able to get up and away from the head table, from her duties as a bridesmaid and spend some time with Jonah and find out what was wrong.

"Hey," she greeted him, coming up behind his chair. He was sitting alone, as the rest of the family was either out dancing or mingling.

"Hi," he responded quietly.

"Dinner okay?" She leaned forward. "Aunt Gert freaking you out?"

Jonah chuckled softly. "It's fine."

"Fine? That's all you have to say?"

"I'm…" He trailed off and laughed. "I was going to say *fine* again, but I didn't think you'd accept that."

"Probably not. Why don't we dance?" Logically she knew they needed to talk, but this wasn't the place to do that. All she wanted was to be with him.

Jonah nodded and took her hand, leading her out onto the dance floor. He pulled her in close, but not as tight as he did last night in her room. He was holding back, and it was worrying Grace.

Again she had to ask herself what had changed.

His behavior reminded her of Victor. He'd started acting this way right before she'd found out he'd cheated on her. Back then she had sensed something was wrong, but she'd pushed it all aside, telling herself back then that they were happy. She'd gone out of her way to please him. It turned out they hadn't been happy, or at least he hadn't been, and everyone had known that he'd been having the affair with Nancy. And she'd felt so small after.

This time, she didn't want to ignore the obvious signs that something was wrong.

If things were going to end, she wanted to be the first to know and go into it with her head held high.

Things are going to end though, she reminded herself. *That's the plan.*

She was getting too carried away by all these wedding emotions. That had to be it.

"You seem distracted. And don't say you're fine, because I can tell you're not."

Jonah sighed. "Okay, you caught me. I'm not."

"What's up?"

"It was the photos. I shouldn't have been in them."

"Why?" And it was a silly question, really. She knew why, but there was also a part of her that believed he did belong in those photographs with her family.

With her.

"You said so yourself, in a way. You said that you'll

take the blame when this ends. Are you already planning for the end?"

It was a blunt question and to the point. Grace swallowed the lump in her throat as they slowly danced. "We have a court date. I was just stating a fact."

"Enough about the court date," he snapped. "You don't have to shoulder this whole thing yourself. We're both to blame. My problem is I don't know how much longer this can go on."

It was the truth, although it stung.

Time really was ticking away.

"You're right. We'll tell them tomorrow."

Jonah's spine stiffened. "Okay."

"You still don't seem like you *are* okay though."

"No. I'm not. I thought…" He cursed under his breath and then nervously expelled air. "I wish your dad hadn't included me in his speech."

"I didn't know he was going to do that," she said softly.

And it was still eating away at her that her father had done that, had centered her for a second at Melanie's wedding.

Jonah relaxed and held her a little tighter, almost like he didn't want to let her go. "I really like them."

Only them? her little insecure voice asked, but she didn't ask that out loud.

"They like you too."

He nodded. "I just thought…"

"Thought what?" Her heart was beating so fast, it felt like it was going to sprout wings and leave her body. Maybe he wanted more too.

Maybe he did want her.

She was going to tell him she didn't want this to end. Yes, they had to tell her parents the truth about their fake marriage, but she wanted to make this relationship real.

She wanted to make this work. Being married to her partner and best friend would be a dream.

Because yeah, he was becoming her best friend. It had been a long time since she'd let someone come into her life and take up that role.

"When it ends, I think I need to leave Vegas," Jonah said.

Grace blinked a couple of times. "Leave Vegas?"

He nodded, not looking at her. "It's for the best."

"Is it?"

"Don't you think?" he questioned.

First, she felt a bit dumbstruck, then angry at herself for thinking this could be more. Why had she thought it could be different, that things would change?

When really they couldn't.

She should've known better.

She opened her mouth to say more when his phone began to buzz.

He pulled it out of his pocket and frowned. "It's work."

"What?" she asked, because she didn't have her phone on her. She glanced back at the table where her little bag was; her sister was motioning that her phone was vibrating too. "What do they say?"

"We're being called back to the station house. Right away. They're forecasting extreme flash flooding tomorrow. Apparently, a huge storm is bringing in monsoon rain from the southeast. All emergency services are being called in. We're officially on active duty."

She was still reeling over the fact he was going to leave Las Vegas, that he was running away.

"We'd better go."

She wanted to stay here and talk with Jonah. She wanted to solve this uncertainty tonight, but there was no time. They both put their jobs first, and right now her priorities lay with work. First, she had to tell her family she had to leave.

She moved toward the table where Melanie sat, then turned to look back at Jonah with longing. He looked a little defeated.

Grace's stomach sank into an anxious little knot. Something indeed had changed and not for the better, but after this emergency was over she was going to make it right. She was going to protect her heart and let him go.

The rain had been coming down steadily since they'd arrived back at the station house to report and change into their uniforms. They'd just left the wedding with what they'd had on them, because they could get their suitcases later. Grace had put on her flashing light that she carried in her car so that local state troopers and highway patrol would know that they were emergency services and on their way to active duty.

As they'd left the country club, the emergency warnings had started pinging on their phones; St. George had been put on a flash-flood warning too. The storm was not seasonal and highly unusual. The desert did see its fair share of flash floods and mudslides, but this was excessive.

Jonah was worried about how Grace was doing. He knew how she felt about water.

Not much had been said on the long car ride down, and he'd been fine with that. At least he'd gotten a chance to tell her that he was going to leave. She hadn't really reacted, which just reaffirmed that he'd made the right decision.

Except it didn't feel that way.

It frustrated him.

He'd wanted a reaction from her. He'd wanted her to fight for him to stay, wanted a chance to fight for her too.

Maybe he was just tired of locking everything he was

feeling away. It had been easier for him to do that in the past to cope with everything, to protect himself, but it was exhausting.

It was tiring trying to hide how he felt about her.

Now was not the time to have all these big feelings. He worked hard to lock them all down. He had to focus on the task at hand.

He had never seen rain like this. Almost as soon as the storm hit, they'd started getting calls for the emergency services. There had been no time to evacuate the low-lying areas.

The fire department, who they shared a station with, was just as busy as they were. He and Grace were running on a lot of strong coffee and adrenaline. The station had the local news playing in the background as they covered the storm and tried to give updates the best they could. There were power fluctuations as the wind brought down power lines.

"It's like a hurricane," John mumbled under his breath. He'd just gotten back in from a call and needed to change as his uniform was soaked.

Grace tilted her head, half listening.

"Is it?" Jonah asked. "I've never been in a hurricane before."

"This is like it. Same pressure changes, the wind. It's all similar. I'm from Louisiana originally. There will be flooding. Be prepared for that," John stated morosely. "Drownings. It'll be awful."

Grace sat up straight, and Jonah knew that she was worrying about that. All he wanted to do was go over and comfort her, but he held back, because they'd never shown an unrestrained amount of affection at work and that was what they both wanted. She most likely would push him away.

"Hey, Crandall and Landon. Call out on the highway

heading to Henderson. Flooding. People trapped and the road is washed out. We need an extra rig down there."

Grace nodded, but he could tell by her tight expression she was worried. "Come on, Crandall."

Jonah mirrored her nod, and they made their way to their rig.

"You going to be okay?"

"Fine," Grace remarked. Only he wasn't too sure about that.

Everything was loaded with what they needed. They pulled on their rain gear, and the ambulance bay door opened. The moment it opened, the wind drove the rain in driving pellets against the rig, and as they pulled out onto the road he could barely hear the siren over the roaring of the wind.

The wind was gusting so strong, the rig was shaking.

Grace's jaw was set with determination, her knuckles white from gripping the steering wheel as she headed out into the storm.

"Hey," Jonah said.

She barely glanced at him. "I know. This will be okay."

"We've got this, partner."

She looked at him quickly, her shoulders easing slightly. "Let's go save lives, yes?"

He grinned. "Yes."

What was usually a short drive dragged on as they dodged traffic and detours. There were many roads that were already overflowing. Reservoirs used to divert flooding were streaming fast with muddy water, and yet the rain was still coming.

There were flashes of light mixed with low rumbles of thunder, but the loudest was the howling wind. People had been caught unawares; no one expected part of the highway to wash away, especially not in the desert.

Grace pulled up where there were already a cluster of flashing lights from the fire department, police and rescue. She parked the rig, and Jonah had to fight the wind to open the door and head out into the driving rain.

It pelted at his skin, and it was cold.

It stung like a thousand knives.

He glanced over at her. Her expression was unreadable, but he knew she was feeling stressed. She was facing her biggest fear.

As they got out of the ambulance the police chief came over. "Thank goodness. We're having a hell of a time. There's people trapped in cars. We have a rope, but no one is small enough to get in through that sunroof. We get there and we sink it further as we try to make the hole larger."

"I can fit," Grace said with determination.

Jonah's eyes widened. He wanted to protest, but the police chief just nodded. "Yeah, it looks like you might. Let's get you tied up."

Grace nodded nervously.

Jonah couldn't let her do this. What if she froze and got hurt? Or worse…

It was the "worse" that he couldn't even begin to fathom. It terrified him to his core.

Echoes of blasts and scents of the tunnel from his time overseas washed over him.

Only this time it was Grace broken in his arms, not Justin. And picturing that made his stomach turn. It made him want to cry out, a silent scream that welled up deep inside of him.

There was no way he could let her take the risk. To lose her would kill him. "Let me."

Grace turned toward him. She was clearly frustrated. "I can do this."

"Can you? That's fast water. It'll be deep."

"I can do my job," she replied firmly. "Don't speak for me or presume."

Jonah wanted to stop her, hold her back, but he knew that he couldn't. What right did he have? She wasn't his.

Isn't she?

"You're not going to die."

"No, I'm not. Why would you think that?"

She turned to leave, but he grabbed her, too frantic to stop himself. It was happening all over again. The panic, the idea of losing someone he loved. It felt like he was spiraling out of control. Getting close to her had not been good for him.

"No, I won't let you."

"It's my job," she shouted. "A partner wouldn't stop me."

"I'm your husband!"

Her eyes widened. "Are you really my husband? Really?"

The truth was he wasn't. She'd made it clear the end of their relationship was coming, and he'd told her he would be leaving Vegas. Seeing her here amid all this danger should've just strengthened his resolve to move on, yet he couldn't.

He didn't want to.

And it was too scary to be vulnerable to her, to stay in spite of it all and fight for what he really wanted.

Always he'd taken the easy way out, the path of least resistance. It was simpler to do it that way instead of expressing himself.

Is it really easy though?

There was a part of him, buried down so deep and locked away, that wanted to tell her why he couldn't let her risk her life like that. That he wouldn't be able to bear it if he lost her, like he'd lost Justin.

Only he couldn't find the words. It was too hard to say

what he wanted to say. That he loved her. That he'd fallen in love with her and wanted more and needed her to know that, even if she didn't want the same.

She'd already made it clear at her sister's wedding that she was done, that she was ready to move on.

Telling her how he felt—that he wasn't ready to move on, never would be—would just drive her further away, destroy what was left of their friendship and take Jonah with it.

He could feel the anxiety rising in him. All he wanted to do was run, run from the possible pain of losing her. His heart was breaking in two.

This was too much.

This was too hard.

Coward.

"Well?" she asked.

He didn't say anymore. There was nothing he could say. She wasn't his, and he had to let her go.

She pulled away from him, slipped out of his fingers and went with the rescue crews to get a harness on.

There were people being pulled out of the water, and he had no time to watch her, he had no time to entertain his terror of her going out there and putting her life on the line or the real possibility he'd lose her.

Instead, he took the patients as they were brought to them and got them safe, dry and was assessing them for their medical needs as more ambulance sirens were being pulled into the site from all the different directions.

Only once did he glance back to see her with the emergency-rescue team. She was standing at the edge of the water receiving instructions, and then she was going, wading out into the flood and making her way to that semi-submerged car.

In that moment, he knew what he wanted, and he was done being scared or worried about it all.

Grace was facing her biggest fear to save a life. She wasn't taking the easy way out or making an excuse not to try something she was afraid of. Neither should he. Even if she didn't feel the same about him, he wanted her to know what he truly thought of her, how much she deserved happiness.

She was worthy of love. She was brave and kind and good.

She was everything, and he had to let her know. He had to take the chance and stop running from his emotions. It was time to be brave just like her.

He didn't want to lose her like he'd lost Justin. But he didn't want to push her away like he had Mona either. For so long he'd spent so much time trying to bury the horrors of that last mission, of losing Justin, that he really was spending his time pushing everyone away to regain control of his life. It had been safer that way, but what kind of life had it been?

Since he had married Grace and agreed to fake their relationship, his life had finally become worth living again and it was just hitting him now. All this time, for so many years he had just been existing.

And it hadn't been much of that.

Now, watching her on the precipice of something dangerous, something that he knew would absolutely push her to the limits, there were so many things he wanted to say to her. Suddenly it was all just rushing to come out of him. It wasn't the time. They had their work to do. Lives depended on them.

He was proud of her as she took this chance.

He just hoped that he hadn't missed *his* chance and that the woman he loved wouldn't be swept away by the currents before he had a chance to make things right, to tell her how much she meant to him. How incredible she was, how she deserved to be happy.

Even if that happiness wouldn't be with him.

CHAPTER TWELVE

Breathe. Just breathe.

Usually when Grace attended near drownings the person had already been pulled to safety, or at the very least they were in a pool that didn't have currents, other than the usual jets that circulated water. Once she had had to go into the Bellagio fountains, but the display had been turned off while they handled that emergency.

This was a first for her.

She was scared, but she'd been attached to a guide rope and had a life jacket on. The water was rushing like a torrent, and it was rising as the rain continued to come down. Before she stepped out into the water, she looked back to see Jonah helping those they had pulled out of the water.

Their gazes briefly locked in that moment, and she knew he was scared for her. She'd been frustrated when he tried to stop her, like what she was doing was foolish or selfish.

This was her job.

A terrifying part of it, but this was what she'd signed up for when she became a paramedic.

When he'd said he was her husband, for one moment she'd felt some hope, but he hadn't said anything else and she knew he was just saying whatever he could to keep her safe.

She knew Jonah had been thinking about Justin then.

She could see it in his eyes that he was comparing her to his long-dead best friend.

It should have been touching, but instead the reminder stung. That was what he thought of her. A friend.

Nothing more.

He'd confirmed it. He didn't love her enough to claim the title of *husband.*

It hurt. Just like when he told her he was leaving. As if being married to her had become a burden. So much so that he had to leave Vegas entirely, and she doubted there was anything she could do to make him stay.

And did she really want him to stay because of an obligation?

No.

She didn't want that. It hurt even more to force her heart to accept that.

"You ready?" The rescue chief shouted over the wind, interrupting her morose thoughts.

Grace nodded and gave a thumbs-up. She stepped out into the water. The current was strong, and she wasn't sure what debris would be under her feet. With each step she took she was trying to picture the freeway underneath her, but there were cars and other things being pushed and rocked and washed over the roadway.

You've got this. You're safe.

The car that was her target was about three hundred feet away. She could see the top of the woman's head and an arm as she tried to pull herself up and out of the sunroof. It was a small opening, and the car was already leaning heavily as the water rushed against it.

Another set of emergency workers were on the far side; they were closer to the car, but they had more obstacles between them and it. They were sending someone out too to help her. Grace knew without a doubt the woman trapped inside most likely was hypothermic, had probably swallowed a lot of dirty water and might have injuries that were unknown. She would die if they didn't get there soon.

She was smaller than the other EMTs on the scene and hopefully could traverse the precarious car to get the woman out. On her back she had the Jaws of Life—a hydraulic ram and cutter, so that she could make the opening wider if she needed to.

As she stepped closer, her ankle rolled on a rock or something and she slipped. The line tightened and there was shouting, but she wasn't sure if that was the shouting she was hearing from the shoreline or the screaming in her head.

Lock it all away. Focus. I can do this.

She steadied her steps and kept going. The water was getting higher than her waist, and it felt like she might be swept away. Her pulse was racing, filling her ears with the thundering beats, but she kept her eyes locked on that car. There was an EMT standing there, but every time he tried to get close, the car would shift under his weight.

Eyes still locked on the top of the woman's head and that one pale arm that was clinging on for dear life, Grace made it to the car.

"Glad you're here. She's fading," the rescue worker stated. "Every time I put any weight on it, the car gives and shifts. I can hold it, and you can climb up there. Her seat belt has lashed her down."

Grace nodded as the rescue worker braced the car with a pole he had. The two EMTs who were coming from the other side had a backboard. If they got the woman out, the four of them could get that backboard through the obstacles and to the far side. Although she wasn't sure how far her guide rope would let her go. She would probably have to back track.

She slowly climbed onto the car. It was rocking and swaying, but it wasn't tilting under her weight, not with the other rescue worker using a ram to hold it steady. Water began to bubble and froth as the intensity increased.

"My name is Grace. I'm here to help," Grace shouted at the woman.

"Janice," she woman slurred. "I'm stuck and so tired."

"I know. Just hold on, okay." Grace did a quick assessment of the woman. There was definite laceration, and it looked like her shoulder was dislocated. Grace pulled out the Jaws of Life.

They were small and portable, but they were gas powered and could still exert enough pounds of pressure to widen the sunroof and allow her to cut the seat belt that was holding the patient captive. As Grace quickly took in the situation, she was pretty sure that the seat belt was the only reason why the woman hadn't been washed away. Before she released that, she would have to have the woman hooked on to the harness she carried, or she would be carried away with the current.

Grace worked fast to get the harness around the woman's torso and had it secured to her.

"Janice, I need you to hold on tight like you have been. Nod once if you understand."

Janice nodded weakly. "Hurry. I can't feel my legs."

Grace used the cutter and the ram, spreading open the sunroof enough to allow her to slip her hand down and grab hold of the seat belt.

"Hold tight, Janice," Grace shouted as she cut the seat belt. There was a whoosh, and water came spilling out the opened broken window.

"Got her?" The EMT bracing the car asked. "The car is moving."

"Got her," Grace yelled. She used her strength, bracing

against the metal as she pulled the woman up and out of the sunroof. Grace was only five foot eight; Janice was at least five foot ten and a complete dead weight. Her other arm was at an angle, so there were definitely broken bones.

The other two EMTs had arrived and helped stabilize the car as they got Janice down and strapped onto the backboard. Grace repacked the Jaws of Life and clambered down off the wreckage. She helped get Janice clear and then got out of the way as Janice's car was pushed completely over.

"Christ! We need to get out of here," the first EMT shouted. The other two had started off toward safety on their side, carrying Janice on the backboard between them.

"Yes, I agree. Have we got everyone from the cars?" Grace asked.

"She was the last."

They both started making the walk back to their side. She could see the other two rescue workers had managed to get Janice through their obstacles and she would get the help she needed, which was a relief.

Now she had to get back and help Jonah with the patients on their side.

The water continued to rise, but she kept her eyes locked on her rig, because she knew that was where Jonah was. They might not have had a real relationship, but it was grounding to know he was there. He was her friend, after all.

In her heart, though, she knew that wasn't enough. Not really. She wanted more, so much more that it felt like she was going to break into a million pieces when she thought about him leaving. She swallowed the lump in her throat and fought back the tears as she focused on getting back safely. The rain became harder, and it was getting even more difficult to see. The wind picked up, and she was being thrashed around.

Every step was like she was walking through thick cement. It was exhausting.

"Almost there!" the EMT ahead of her screamed over the roar of water and thunder.

Grace nodded, not that he saw it, but she was getting cold and tired too.

Something hit her then, causing white-hot burning pain to shoot down her side. It dug into her skin, causing her suit to tear, and her life jacket was ripped away. She screamed in agony, and her arm went limp.

"Grace!" someone shouted from the shoreline.

She was jolted again, this time losing her footing.

Oh, God.

All she could do was grab the rope and hold on as the water came tumbling over her head and she was swept underneath.

Jonah had come back around to the front of the rig after treating a patient and getting them loaded up in another rig that had come to collect them. He couldn't drive anywhere until Grace got back, because she might have that last victim with her.

He saw that Grace and the other rescue worker were coming back from the water. On the far side of the flow, he saw the patient she had saved from the wreckage was being taken care of. He let out a breath of relief that he hadn't even known he'd been holding. He watched as Grace followed the guide rope back toward solid ground.

Then he saw the surge, the rubble that was coming directly for them.

Internally, he screamed and then shouted out, hoping that he'd been heard, but it was hard over the rush of water.

The largest piece of deadwood, from what looked like an old cattle fence, hit Grace in the side. She cried out and winced; it knocked her backward.

He ran for the water but was held back by John, who had just arrived on scene.

“You can’t,” John said firmly. “The surge is too high.”

“She’ll drown!” Jonah was wracked with worry, with grief. There was nothing he could do in this moment but watch. He was powerless with Justin, and he was powerless here too. And he’d wasted his chance to tell her how he felt, that he loved her. His fear had held him back, and he’d blown it. In that moment he dropped to his knees, taking John down with him. It was all too much, too gut-wrenchingly horrifying.

There was another surge, and the rescue worker ahead of Grace was pulled to shore. He was cut and battered.

John let go of Jonah and rushed to help him.

It was then that Grace disappeared under the torrent of water.

“Pull harder!” the police chief shouted out.

The winch was winding hard, but it appeared she was snagged on something,

“Harness me up. I’m going out!” Jonah screamed. There was no way he could let her die. He wasn’t going to lose her this way.

He was harnessed up then and attached to a winch. She wasn’t far out, and he followed her rope, which was taught. The water was gurgling and bubbling where he’d last seen her. He didn’t have much time to get to her, but he wasn’t going to let her drown again.

Not on his watch.

He made it and then reached down into the water, trying to keep his own head above the swell, and found her. He used a knife and cut the straps of the Jaws of Life, which had gotten entangled on something, pinning her down. Once she was free, he brought her head above water and lashed her to his harness.

"I've got you, Grace. I'm here. Don't you damn well die on me."

She was unconscious still, and he had to not think about the worst-possible outcome as he picked up her lifeless body in his arms and carried her to shore. She was bleeding profusely from a large laceration to her arm.

Once he was there, he laid her on the ground and started CPR, pumping on her chest and blowing into her mouth, trying to bring her back. Out of the corner of his eyes he saw an AED had been brought out.

"Breathe, Grace. Breathe!"

He blew into her mouth again, and this time there was a sputter and she spewed out the dark dirty water, gasping and coughing.

Thank God.

"Grace," he murmured.

"Again. Seriously?" she asked weakly.

He smiled at her. "We've got to get you to the hospital and get antibiotics into you. That water is dirty."

Grace nodded. "I'm so cold."

"I know." He touched her face gently and stood back as he let the other paramedics work to get her up on a gurney so they could take her to the hospital.

"Jonah," she called out.

He came to her side. "I'm here."

"I'm sorry. I won't be a burden." She passed out again, only for a moment, groaning.

"You need to go with her," John said. "We'll take care of the rig. Go with your wife."

"She wasn't supposed to be my wife."

John laughed. "I know—I was there that night. But she's your wife now. Go with her."

Jonah nodded and followed the paramedics from another station into the back of the ambulance. They were hooking up a fluid line, and Grace had an oxygen mask on. Her O2 stats were still low, and she probably still had fluid in her lungs.

She was barely conscious as another paramedic wrapped up her arm.

Jonah took a seat next to her.

She blinked a few times and looked at him. "What're you doing?"

"Going with you."

"You don't need to. I can take care of myself."

"I'm here."

"For now." She winced. "I don't need you here. I won't be a burden to you. Don't worry about me."

"Do you want him to leave?" asked Jose, the paramedic attending her, slightly confused.

Grace didn't answer as she drifted off into unconsciousness again.

Jose looked at him. "Thought you two were married?"

"We are, but waiting for a divorce." Saying it out loud gave it a finality that he really didn't like.

"Then maybe you should go," Jose suggested.

"No. I'll make sure she gets there."

She might not have wanted him—not like that—but he cared for her and she was alive.

That was all that mattered.

He sent a silent prayer to whatever deity was listening to him. Just a thanks to the universe and karma, whatever, that she was still here.

She was still here even if she wasn't his. He had a second chance to tell her how he felt. He hadn't lost her like he'd lost Justin.

Close call, doofus.

Jonah couldn't hold back an exhausted grin. That was what Justin would have said if he were here now—Jonah could almost hear his voice in his head.

Only you would this happen to. Only you would get drunk and marry someone in Vegas and then fall in love with them.

Justin would always tease Jonah about like that. Call him a wiener or a doofus. All those good-natured ribbings that would then turn into roughhousing. It was the first time in a long time that he'd thought of Justin and it hadn't been tainted with guilt and sorrow, just golden memories of joy and fun.

Usually, Jonah would lock all those memories away because he wanted to be able to control his emotions and not let his past affect his work. Right now, he basked in them. It was as though Justin was there, in that moment, reaffirming that there was no need to be afraid.

The ambulance was closed up, and he strapped himself in for the ride to the hospital. Once they got there and he was sure that Grace was stabilized and well taken care of, he had a few phone calls to make.

He had to let her parents know what had happened. Then he was going to tell Grace how he felt, even if she didn't feel the same. She had the right to know. She deserved to know. All of it. Every detail.

And once that was all taken care of, he'd say goodbye to Vegas and to his heart.

But what if you don't have to?

CHAPTER THIRTEEN

GRACE WAS IN and out of consciousness, but she was aware of one thing: She hadn't been put on life support. She had a nasal cannula, but that didn't bother her. What bothered her was the fact that she was being put on antibiotics for a while and then she would have to go in to have surgery. When the log or wood hit her arm, it had sliced into her nerves, causing damage, which meant she would be off work for some time.

At least, that was what she thought was happening.

The antibiotics and the painkillers were making her woozy, and she was having a hard time keeping it all straight. She also swore she saw Victor in the room at one point.

She woke up again and glanced over at the small recliner chair, hoping she'd see Jonah but didn't. She didn't know why she'd expected to. He made it clear that their partnership was over; he was leaving. She couldn't blame him. Not really.

She'd almost drowned again, and now her arm was useless. Once again she'd ignored advice and put her life on the line. She should've listened to Jonah.

She was a burden, and that was the last thing she ever wanted.

A tear slipped out of the corner of her eye. Why couldn't

she have just told him she loved him? Why did she have to be such a coward? It was too late, and now he was gone.

There was a knock at the door, and her heart skipped a beat.

It was her parents.

When Grace saw her mother's face, she just broke down in tears because she'd seen that haggard look before and she hated that she'd put her mother through that all again.

"Grace," her mother said, choking back a sob and rushing to her. "Oh, God, Grace."

"I know," Grace said, her voice shaking. "I did it again."

"Honey, when Jonah called us…" Her dad trailed off, and even though he wasn't the kind of man to show emotions, she knew he was fighting back tears. "I'm so glad you're still here."

"I won't be golfing for some time," Grace said, sniffling.

"I don't care about that," her dad said, brushing her hair back. "You're here."

Grace suddenly realized what her dad had said. "Wait, did you say Jonah called you?" she asked, confused.

"Why wouldn't he?" her mother asked.

"I guess…" Grace trailed off, not sure of what to say. She was surprised he was still there. He'd said he was going to leave.

"You guess what? Of course Jonah called us. He's your husband."

Guilt rolled in the pit of Grace's stomach. After everything else, she'd almost forgotten to dread this conversation. "Mom, Dad… There's something I have to tell you."

"Oh?" her mother asked, taking a seat. "Should we be worried?"

"No, I need to apologize. I lied about my marriage to him."

"You faked that video?" her dad asked, confused.

"No, we really did get married, but we were drunk and it wasn't supposed to happen. We weren't dating. It was a one-night bad choice." Heat flushed her cheeks with embarrassment.

"Oh," her mother said, confused, and yet there was already a hint of disappointment in her voice. "Then why did you lie to me that day? The day I came over?"

Grace swallowed the lump in her throat, a tight knot of emotions threatening to come out of her. All those feelings that she'd kept locked away since she was a child. Everything she had been shouldering for so long. "I couldn't bear to let you down."

Her mother raised her eyebrows. "Let me down?"

"I know I didn't listen to you all those years ago. It was the reason I almost died that day as a child. I know the hospital bills were large, that sacrifices were made because of my mistake. I hid so much from you over the years, because I couldn't face disappointing you that way again."

"You mean like Victor cheating on you?" her dad said tightly, his brow furrowed and his lips thin with what looked like barely controlled anger.

"You knew about that?" Grace asked, stunned.

"Victor came clean when you came into the emergency department unconscious," her dad stated. "I'm only sorry we pushed that relationship on you. He wasn't the right man for you. You deserve more."

"You deserve what you had with Jonah," her mom stated.

"Well, that was all fake."

"Really?" her father questioned. "Didn't seem to be."

"He really seems to care for you," her mother said softly.

"How? I mean… I'm a burden."

"Far from it," her dad interjected.

"Grace, you're not a burden to us. Never." Her mother kissed her on the top of the head.

"You're a people pleaser, and you need to stop smoothing things over with everyone and live your own life," her dad said.

"That's why we're disappointed. Not because you're a burden, but because you can't see how amazing you are," her mom said.

"So you're disappointed now? That the marriage wasn't real?"

"Only because we like Jonah so much." Her mother smiled. "Thank you for telling us the truth. I guess I'm sad because the two of you seem so right for each other. You both seemed so in love."

Her parents were right. She'd lived to long trying to make everyone else happy because she felt so guilty. Her parents, Melanie, Travis, even Victor. Everyone was happy. Everyone got what they wanted, except her.

She wanted to stay married to Jonah. He was part of her life. He'd woven himself in there, and she didn't want that all unraveled. She didn't want to let him go. And in that moment she saw every shared smile, the way he'd looked at her at Melanie's wedding, the touches, the kisses, him showing her how to swim. All their jokes, the laughter and curling up on the couch at night picking terrible movies.

Jonah never wanted her to change or be someone else. With him she could be herself.

Fully and completely.

He was more than a friend and her partner.

He was her everything, and she wasn't going to lose that.

She was going to take a chance on happiness for herself for once.

Once she was discharged, she was going to find him and tell him how she felt. Even if he didn't feel the same way, at least then she would know the truth—and that for once she'd been brave and done everything she could.

She was deserving of a happily-ever-after too, and maybe she could have that fairy tale with Jonah.

There was a knock at the door, and Jonah stuck his head in. There were dark circles under his eyes. A sob caught in her throat, and relief washed though her. All the emotions she'd been holding back came rushing to the surface like a flood.

He was here. He hadn't left.

Her mother kissed Grace's head again and then took her dad's hand, dragging him out of the room. "Let's give these two some privacy."

They slipped out of the room, and it was just the two of them left.

Grace and Jonah.

Alone.

Her heart was racing.

"You're awake," Jonah remarked, coming into the room.

"You've been here the whole time?" she asked, her voice shaking.

He nodded. "In and out."

"You told me you were leaving."

He sighed. "I know. The thing is… I wanted to run, but then, I can't live without you. Watching you face your fears made me realize that. And then seeing you in the water, you almost dying… That killed me."

"I'm sorry."

"I was scared. The thought of you not being there anymore…it was too much." His voice broke, then he took a breath and continued. "The fact is I'm never not going to be scared of losing you, but I'm willing to fight that fear to have you. Grace, I love you."

Grace almost couldn't believe the words she was hearing. Her heart was pounding so hard it had to be spiking the monitor. "I'm scared too," she managed. "The thing is… The thing is I love you as well, Jonah. I was scared to tell you in case you didn't feel the same. I didn't want to make you uncomfortable, but I do love you. I wanted you to know. I have for some time."

He smiled, his eyes twinkling as he lifted her other hand to his lips, placing a kiss against her knuckles. "I love you too, and I don't want our marriage to end. I want to give it a chance. The right way. I want you to be my wife for real."

A tear slid out of the corner of her eyes, relief washing through her. "I want that too."

"Still, it terrified me seeing you go under the water…" He trailed off and then took her hand, squeezing it gently before laughing softly. "Sorry—just had to touch you to convince myself you're still here and you're okay."

"I'm here," she whispered, squeezing his hand back.

"I know. It was the worst moment of my life. I thought I lost you."

"You saved me though," she said gently.

"I was proud of you for overcoming your fear like that."

"It was scary, but I thought back to what you taught me about grounding myself in the water and how I got into all of this to be like the paramedic who saved me, and that's kind of a hard thing to emulate when you're afraid of water. I couldn't let Janice die like that."

"And you didn't. She's going to be fine. She's in this hospital too. Her family is very thankful, but they can come by later. We have to get you ready for surgery. They want to make sure all that dirt and mulch you swallowed under water is out and that your lungs are strong enough to withstand the surgery to repair the nerves."

Grace sighed. "You're going to be without me as a partner for a while."

He nodded. "I can take a few weeks' leave to take care

of you, but yeah, until you're back on the job, I'm working with John."

"John? Oh, boy."

Jonah shrugged. "He's not so bad. He was our wedding videographer, after all."

Grace laughed and held her belly. She felt a bit woozy. "I told my parents, apologized for lying."

"You don't have to shoulder all of the blame. Shall I get them so *we* can apologize and tell them we're staying together?"

"You better."

Jonah leaned over her and kissed her softly on the lips. "You know, I'm not sure how our marriage will work."

"What do you mean?"

"It took a near-death experience for both of us to see sense."

She laughed weakly. "I think it will work. I love you, and I'm willing to work on it if you are. No running away."

He smiled, his eyes twinkling with unshed tears. "Deal. I'm not going anywhere."

He stepped out to get her parents.

Her mom was wringing her hands together as she came in the room. "So?"

"We're staying together," Grace stated as Jonah took her good hand.

"I fell in love with your daughter, and she loves me. We're going to stay married and make this work," Jonah reiterated.

Grace watched her parents' expression soften from confusion to happiness.

"Well, thank goodness! I knew you two would see sense," her mom said.

"I'm sorry I lied to you both. But I truly do love your daughter," Jonah said.

"So, have you lied to me about anything else, Jonah?" her dad asked in a teasing yet stern voice.

"I hate golf. So much," Jonah replied.

They all laughed, and the door opened as a doctor snuck in.

"Hello, everyone. I'm Dr. Page. Grace the hero, I'm glad to see you more alert. The last couple of times I've been by you've been pretty out of it. I want to do an examination on you and then go over some stuff we found from your blood work."

"Do we need to leave?" Grace's dad asked.

"No, it's fine." Dr. Page turned to Jonah. "You're her husband?"

Jonah grinned and then squeezed her hand. "I am."

"Good. I'm glad you're all here. So, we have to do some surgery to repair the damage to the nerve on your arm. You've been on a course of tetracycline to help manage the onset of infection from the containments in the water, but we're going to stop that now."

"Oh?" Grace asked. "Are my lungs clear? They feel kind of heavy still."

"That we don't know. We're going to have to get an MRI rather than an X-ray now. Just checking with your insurance now."

"Why can't she have an X-ray?" Jonah asked.

"Because of the baby. I wish that had been disclosed when she arrived and before we started the tetracycline," Dr. Page remarked, shooting Jonah a pointed glare. "This is why we always check blood work. Husbands don't always know."

"Baby?" Grace asked, dumbfounded. "I'm pregnant?"

"Six weeks. You didn't know, I take it?" Dr. Page asked, shocked.

"No." Grace glanced over at Jonah. "I was on the pill and… Pregnant?"

"Yes. So we're going to have to change our approach. We need to get the surgery done, but there are still risks involved," Dr. Page continued.

"Okay." She was still processing it all.

A baby had never been part of her plan. She wasn't opposed to the idea; it was just she had never thought it would happen, because she didn't expect to ever have a husband.

Dr. Page stopped one of the intravenous meds. "I'll be back with a change in script, and the surgeon will come by to talk about the surgery. I've also set up a consult with OB-GYN."

"Thank you, Dr. Page," Jonah said. He sounded a bit dumbfounded.

Dr. Page nodded and left the room, and Grace just let it all sink in. She was going to be a mother.

"I'm so happy!" her mother exclaimed. "It was a bit weird at first, with the whole fake marriage, but I'm so thrilled I'm going to be a grandma. Finally!"

"Come on, let's give these two some time to let it sink in," her dad said, pulling her mom away.

When they were alone, Jonah sat down on the edge of the bed.

"What do you think?" she asked with trepidation.

This was not how Jonah had thought today was going to turn out. He'd sat at Grace's bedside for the last twenty-four hours. Ever since he'd realized he couldn't live without her, couldn't leave without letting her know how he felt, he'd been so frightened.

It was scary to love someone so much, to know how much it would hurt if she didn't feel the same.

But saying it had felt good, and hearing her admit that she loved him too had made him ecstatic. And when Dr. Page had announced that Grace was pregnant, Jonah just had to shake his head in disbelief. A long time ago he'd wanted a family, but it had been so off his radar for a long time, something he'd never thought would happen.

Then again, he'd never thought that he would find love and get married again. Here he was, doing everything he'd thought was impossible. He'd been an idiot for even contemplating running away from this.

He deserved happiness too.

"Jonah, you're not saying much," Grace's voice trembled with trepidation.

"I'm at a loss for words."

"Same." She made a face, one that meant *eek*. "I was on the pill."

"Yeah, but six weeks—that's our wedding night." He ran his hand through his hair. "A honeymoon baby."

"We never really got a honeymoon."

"You get yourself feeling better, and we'll go on a babymoon."

"I'd like to go to California, see where you grew up."

He touched her face, running his fingers across her soft skin, knowing she was still here and his. "Done."

"Not on the back of the bike though."

"Yeah, probably not. How are you feeling about all of this?"

"Scared out of mind, but I'm happy. Are you?"

"Very. Almost losing you—it was too much. I never did think I'd find love again, and honestly after losing Justin like that, I didn't think I deserved to find it. I pushed a lot of people away, and I think, on some level, I was trying to do the same to you."

"I understand that. I was trying to do the same. I didn't want to be a burden. I just wanted everyone happy, except me, because I didn't think I deserved it either."

"I think we're both dunderheads."

Grace laughed and then coughed. "What?"

"We were both being stubborn and couldn't see what was right in front of us."

"Kind of like Aunt Gert," she teased. "Thick blinders on."

He winced, smiling. "That is true. I'm in love with you, Grace, and though I really wasn't expecting a baby, I'm glad it's with you. I'm glad I'm going to be a family with you. My only regret is my parents aren't here to see it and to know you." He brushed away a tear.

"I wish I'd met them too. You can tell our baby all about them and Justin."

He leaned over and kissed her. "I love you, Mrs. Cute Paramedic."

"I love you too, Mr. Cute Paramedic."

Then he reached down and touched her belly. "And I love Cute Paramedic Junior too."

Grace groaned. "Oh, no, we're not calling them that."

"I hope not."

She worried her bottom lip. "I do have one more request from you."

"Oh?"

"We need to renew our vows. I want to have that experience with you. It can be small, but I don't want our wedding photos and video to be some blurry, drunken thing. I want something real to look back on and for our kids to see."

Jonah chuckled. "*Kids* now?"

"Yes. I want more than one. No more people pleasing. I'm telling you I want three."

"Three?" he laughed. "Maybe I will run."

"I'm not letting you go."

They kissed sweetly. "I'm not letting you go ever. I keep my promises."

"I know."

He kissed her one more time, wanting to hold on to her forever, but she had to rest. There would be time for that when she healed. And it was time that he was looking forward to.

EPILOGUE

*B*REATHE. *J*UST BREATHE. *And don't kick me so much.*

It was probably never really any woman's dream to get married while four months pregnant, but this was way better than Grace's previous wedding. No one was drunk or singing offbeat songs, and the videographer was a hired professional, which had made John a little sad, until Jonah had asked him to stand next to him and Travis at the altar.

It wasn't a real wedding, because she and Jonah had decided to cancel their court date and keep that first marriage legal, but she meant what she'd said when she was in the hospital. She wanted to do it right.

She wanted the dress.

She wanted the small reception, and she wanted that first dance with her husband.

Jonah was agreeable too, as his first wedding had been an elopement.

They did keep it small, even though her mother had wanted to do something big. And Grace had agreed to have it at her parents' country club, just like her sister, Melanie.

Right now, as she stood in the bride's room, she was trying to calm both her nerves and the baby, who was doing backflips in her stomach.

Even though there had been some worry about her surgery to repair the damage done to her arm, she and the baby had come through it all just fine. She did miss work though, and she couldn't wait to get the all-clear.

She'd be on dispatch duty for a while, because she was pregnant, but at least she'd be doing something other than sitting at home.

The baby did another flip, and she reached down to touch her stomach.

"You okay, honey?" her dad asked.

"Just the baby. Kicking me."

"I can't believe you got pregnant before me and married before me too," Melanie chided.

"You're pregnant now too. Besides, I'm the oldest." Grace winked.

Once she was discharged from the hospital and Melanie was back from her honeymoon, Grace went to visit her and have a heart-to-heart. They both agreed it was time for a new beginning.

They both loved each other—they were family, but they wanted a deeper relationship. Now Grace was excited about the future and their new sisterly relationship.

"The question is when are you going to move to St. George so our kids can grow up together?" Melanie asked.

"Time will tell." Grace smiled secretively, because it was something she and Jonah had been talking about. They both wanted the baby to be close to family, and they were both working on getting transferred in the next year from Nevada to Utah, but she'd miss Vegas.

Vegas was home and had been for some time. Las Vegas had been where she'd had her fairy-tale realization.

"You ready?" her dad asked.

"Yes. Definitely."

"He's a good man," her dad said. "And I'm glad this time we can be here for it."

"Me too."

Melanie went ahead, and then their dad escorted Grace out to the main room where the family was waiting.

When she saw Jonah at the end of the aisle, all that nervousness floated away.

She hadn't seen him since they'd arrived yesterday. Her mother had been insistent that it was bad luck for him to stay at their place for the night, so he'd gone to stay with Melanie and Travis.

She'd missed him, so seeing him standing there in his tux made her heart flip with anticipation. As soon as the family dinner was over, they were getting into her car and driving to California to spend a couple of weeks traveling around to all Jonah's old haunts, to visit his parents' resting place and Justin's name carved into the war memorial in his hometown.

Her dad walked her over to Jonah.

"Take care of her, son. Not sure I can fully trust a man who hates golf though." Her dad winked, and Jonah laughed.

"Sorry about that, sir," Jonah quipped.

Her dad winked and then took a spot next to her mom. Jonah took her hands, and the officiant stepped up.

"As this is a vow renewal, Jonah and Grace have opted to say their own vows. Grace?"

Grace nodded and pulled out a little piece of paper. "Jonah, when I first met you, I thought you were just this blond surfer from California, but you ended up being so much more. You were more than just my partner...you became my best friend. You gave me the legs to stand on, and I'm glad we ended up getting to know one another. I love you, and I'm proud to be your wife."

"Jonah?" The officiant gestured.

Jonah nodded. "Grace, when I first met you, you yelled

at me about loading up the rig wrong and you refused to let me drive for weeks."

There was some laughter.

"I knew right then you were not the woman to mess with, but you were an amazing partner. The best to work with. Sorry, John," Jonah said over his shoulder.

"Not offended," John said, grinning.

"I love you, Grace. You reminded me that there is more to life. I was just existing and not living. You were very unexpected, but I'm glad that you're my wife and will continue to put up with me. I love you with my whole heart."

"I love you too," she whispered.

"You may both kiss and seal this vow renewal," the officiant said.

Grace stepped forward, and Jonah touched her face. "I love you."

"I love you too."

He kissed her gently, and she melted for him, just like she always did. There was clapping and they broke off the kiss, but she knew she wanted more of that later.

"I now pronounce you, again, Mr. and Mrs. Cute Paramedic."

Grace laughed, and Jonah just rolled his eyes as he took her arm and walked her down the aisle. Their family showered them with rose petals. She had her happily-ever-after months ago, but she was glad she was able to share this with her family.

And that Jonah was a part of her life. They were family. No longer alone.

Now and forever.

* * * * *

If you enjoyed this story,
check out these other great reads
from Amy Ruttan

Rebel Doctor's Boston Reunion
Tempted by the Single Dad Next Door
Reunited with Her Off-Limits Surgeon
Nurse's Pregnancy Surprise

All available now!

HAWAIIAN KISS WITH THE BROODING DOC
Scarlet Wilson

'You can sometimes be a little grumpy at work.'

For a moment, Jamie looked tense, but then Piper noticed his shoulders relax as he sank back further into the chair. 'And you think you'll win me around by telling me this?'

There was a hint of amusement in his voice. She kept things light. 'Well, I figured you already knew anyway.'

He let that hang for a few moments. 'Maybe. I just don't like to get too friendly with people at work.'

Wow. How to sting. She tilted her head and contemplated him for a few minutes. 'You spend more than eight hours a day at work. Sometimes you can be there for more than twenty-four hours. Why would you want to have no friends?'

'It's complicated.'

He didn't expand. But she wasn't going to let it go.

'You're not grumpy all the time. At least not around me.'

She met his blue gaze straight on. It was a challenge. They were out of work now. And she had to know if the flirtations, glances, and that touch the other day, was all just a figment of her imagination. This—whatever it was between them—seemed like a two-way thing to her. If she was wrong, she wanted to know. Before she became the talk of the hospital again. And before she started to get her hopes up.

Continue reading

HAWAIIAN KISS WITH THE BROODING DOC
Scarlet Wilson

afterglow BOOKS

DESTINATION WEDDINGS and Other Disasters
Two enemies. One wedding. What could go wrong?
M.C. VAUGHAN

The Friends to Lovers Project
She has a plan. But he wasn't part of it...
PAULA OTTONI

- ✈ International
- 🔥 Enemies to lovers
- 〜 Forced proximity

- 👥 Friends to lovers
- ✈ International
- △ Love triangle

OUT NOW

Two stories published every month. Discover more at:
Afterglowbooks.co.uk

OUT NOW!

A DARK ROMANCE SERIES

Veil of Deception

CLARE CONNELLY   FAYE AVALON   JENNIE LUCAS

Available at
millsandboon.co.uk

MILLS & BOON